cover design https://www.moorbooksdesign.com/
Join my mailing list https://reggi.club/bbb
or text BOURBON to (855) 976-9071

I dedicate this book to the freaks, geeks, and outsiders. Especially those of us who despite the cool exterior never felt as though we fit in.

I see you.

I appreciate you.

Welcome to Hoodoo, Texas

WELCOME TO HOODOO, Texas—Mayberry with magic, midlife, and a dash of murder.

I expected my forties to be filled with imbalanced hormones and an ex-husband or two. Instead, I died for the second time, was gifted a Thor hand, then sent a summons to my hometown of Hoodoo, Texas.

The one place I swore never to return after being accused of murder.

Now the plan is to get in, accept the mysterious inheritance, then get the heck out of Dodge. The good part is that the windfall comes with a lot of zeros. Unfortunately, it is also accompanied by a dilapidated haunted mansion and one heck of a stipulation.

If I refuse the money or Azure House, the fortune will go to a stranger.

Now I'm stuck wrangling unruly relatives, ghostly servants, grumpy vampires, and a vindictive ex who is a werewolf as well as the sheriff. Add a sexy and perhaps not quite human mogul, and I have a recipe for disaster.

And if that's not bad enough, witches are dropping dead in Hoodoo. Guess who's at the top of the suspect list?

Return to Hoodoo is a paranormal women's fiction novel set in a world best described as *True Blood* meets *Queen Sugar*.

Chapter 1

WELCOME TO HOODOO, Texas. The town overflowing with vampires, witches, shifters, root workers, and for the next twelve hours... me. One of those doesn't belong, and that thing would be yours truly—Gwendolyn Carter. Black, tatted, and bisexual—the trifecta of outsiders.

Or one would suspect. But nope. In Hoodoo, no one cared about your complexion, your bed partners, or even your species.

Yup, Hoodoo, Texas, a regular Shan-gra-fucking-la. And lucky me, I spent half a lifetime as the oddball in a town loaded with peculiar creatures—both human and non. Which team did I play on? Well, until I died for the second time, I'd say team human.

Now? Not so much. I was the proud recipient of a transfer to team non-human. If only I knew *what* I was.

The Ancestors, the bar I sat watching like a jilted lover, has belonged to my family since Texas was wild, free, and part of Mexico. Even then, The Ancestors thrived thanks to the vaqueros, vampires, and los lobos. And I wasn't talking about the wolves that pranced on all fours twenty-four seven, but the other kind.

The ringing laughter of women—Black, white, and in between, rocking big hair, glittering belt buckles, and jeans so tight, they probably had to lie down to button them up—faded as they walked through the bar's double doors.

Twenty feet in front of me, a cowboy sauntered past the headlights of a pickup so high, I'd need a forklift to reach the passenger seat. The halogen beams highlighted a faded dip can ring. And yee-haw, that circle was damned near as perfectly defined as his ass.

I snickered and shook my head. Nothing like a nice butt to spice up a yucky mood. What did it reveal about me that a pair of Wranglers and a sun-bleached dip circle finally made me smile?

A solid knock at my window made me squeak.

"You going to spend some of that fancy money in my bar?" Purnell stood grinning outside the closed window of my van. My cousin looked more bouncer than businessman, with his generous shoulders and bald reddish-brown head gleaming under the security light's yellowish glow.

With Purnell, it was always indiscernible whether he was laughing at or with you. Here, it was most definitely at, judging by the raised eyebrow and snicker when he glanced at my death grip on the steering wheel.

One by one, I uncurled my fingers, then slapped my hands against my thighs. "No family discount?" I asked, batting my non-mascaraed lashes.

His enormous eyes widened, a feat I didn't believe possible. "Are you shitting me? I'd make no money if I gave you jackasses a discount."

Which was true, since he was related to a quarter of the town by blood, and another quarter by marriage and... other things.

Purnell jerked the door open and stepped aside. "Get your ass out here and give me a hug."

I hopped out of the van and into my cousin's arms, which were safe, warm, and smelled suspiciously of blood and bourbon.

The knot that settled in my chest when I received the summons from the family lawyer two weeks ago loosened. Although, I doubted it would untangle any time soon. But hey, it was a start.

I pulled away and poked his substantial tummy. "Since when did you become food?"

Like most families, mine defined complicated. The Carter family tree went sideways with the first girls born in Hoodoo. Three women, three divergent paths. Daisy, the youngest, not only made her home in Hoodoo, but somehow also remained both uncursed and human.

My aunt Rose, the woman who raised me after my mother died, took a walk on the undead side almost one hundred and fifty years ago. Then there was my direct ancestor...

Honestly, thinking about her made my heart hurt. Her grave lay unmarked and untended in an overgrown corner of the cemetery, her name never whispered. The curse, the one that began with her had allegedly been broken—by yours truly.

I leaned back, shoved all the family bullshit back in the mental closet where it belonged, and grinned up at my stout cousin.

"Hey." Purnell shrugged. "I like women, even the ones with fangs…" he wiggled his eyebrows, "… if they're hot enough." Purnell tugged the keys from my hand, engaged the alarm, then jerked his head toward the front door. "Come on. If I don't get back in there, Mary Cat's going to try to drag my ass back inside."

"Try?" I gave Purnell the side eye and chuckled. Even as kids, Mary Cat kept her big brother and everyone else in line.

Purnell snorted, wrapped his beefy arm around my shoulder, then led me through one of the massive wooden doors of The Ancestors, and straight into the slaughter. Okay, that was an exaggeration. What he led me to wasn't the lion's den, but an improved entry, complete with a small gift shop selling postcards, baseball caps, and t-shirts, both plain and bedazzled.

I glanced down at my loose white V-neck tee, artfully ripped and insanely expensive jeans, and my well-loved cowboy boots that were my version of a comfort animal. If I were a woman who gave a damn about the opinion of others, I would have changed clothes. Armor comes in many forms: cosmetics, a sharp power suit, or an even sharper tongue. Mine was simple. If you didn't do one of the three f's, your opinion was moot. Even if you were feeding, fucking, or financing me, that only gave you a bit more leeway.

The Ancestors wasn't the only change. On my drive through town, old-fashioned imitation gas lampposts illuminated the well-paved streets, and wine barrels overflowed with flowers and greenery. Funny, but once upon a time, the folks from Oakridge, Conroe, and The Woodlands didn't cross the tracks. Now, Hoodoo appeared gentrified.

Unless they looked too closely at some of the eternally youthful citizens.

"You could have called a brother." Purnell paused, some of the joviality evaporating with his next words. "You crashing out at the Double R?"

The Double R, the place this orphan once called home. The place I learned to laugh and love again after my mother's death. And the seat of the local vampires' power.

I shook my head. "No."

My family could keep their almost Hatfield and McCoy level feud to themselves. I wanted none of it.

Although one thing that brought the clans together before I left was the mutual dissatisfaction with me—and my silence. As much as it sucked for all involved, I took promises seriously, especially ones given as my friend inhaled his last breath. That pitiful eighteen-year-old version of me embraced the knowledge that my friends and family knew wholeheartedly what kind of person I was. That they'd believe I wasn't a murderer.

I was wrong.

Purnell squeezed my shoulder so hard, I swear I heard bones creak. "Put all that shit where it belongs—behind you."

"Well, it's not me that's the problem now, is it?" I exhaled, then managed to unclench my teeth. "I'm meeting Phillip in the morning. Figured I'd stop by for a drink and to say hello." I jerked my thumb toward the front wall. "I'll crash in my van tonight, sign the papers tomorrow, then bounce."

"What papers?" Purnell frowned, apparently flummoxed that something happened in Hoodoo without his knowledge.

I deflated and immediately reached for the loc brushing against my neck, twirling it around my finger. Some people chewed their nails. I was a hair twister. "I was... uh... secretly hoping you'd know." *And would tell me that it had nothing to do with the accusations that chased me out of town.*

"Well..." Purnell puffed up a little. "Maybe while you're having that drink, I'll see what I can dig up."

"Thanks." This time, when my lips curved upward, my heart was lighter. Some surprises I could do without. My gut was hollering this summons to Hoodoo would be a doozy.

Purnell tilted his head slightly to the right, as if listening to an invisible voice, then gently pulled me away from the door milliseconds before a rowdy group of roughnecks bowled through, laughing and cursing. Even cleaned up without a speck of oil beneath their nails, you could always tell a person fresh off the rigs with money to waste.

Money I was`` sure Purnell planned to shift from their pockets to his bank account.

A brawny, sheepish man wearing his best Stetson and a dusting of freckles across his nose jerked his chin up at Purnell and nodded at me.

"Sorry, ma'am." A cute flush turned his brown skin a lovely shade of burgundy.

"No problem." Despite not being remotely interested in this man, my tummy warmed at the purity of our exchange. The smile tugging at my lips was as genuine and unbidden as his blush. Because to this man, I wasn't the tattooed freak who kept everyone at arm's distance. I wasn't the weirdo who spoke with the dead.

No, to this man, I was merely a middle-aged woman with a big rack and a semi-tight body.

Those brown eyes of his discreetly checked out said body, without fleeing when they reached my baby Buddha belly. Dude was adorable. Hopefully, he'd meet someone with less baggage tonight.

Especially since having sex with me came with consequences—like the coroner. But that was a whole 'nother story. One I didn't want to think about tonight.

Luckily, Mr. Sweet Cheeks (and I wasn't talking about his buttocks. At least not yet) interrupted my trip down accused-of-multiple-murder lane. "Some people don't have home training." He tilted his head toward his friends as they walked through the interior set of double doors.

I chuckled as he backed away, a shy smile on his full lips. "Maybe I can buy you a drink?"

"Perhaps." I hooked my thumbs in my belt loops and rocked back on my heels.

"What the hell, man?" Purnell sounded gruff, but the smirk ruined the effect. "What if she's with me?"

The mellow roughneck shook his head. "Nah, man, she'd have better taste. And if she didn't, I'd have to convince her of the errors of her ways." He gave me a wink then followed his friends into the bar.

Oh yeah, the second set of cheeks was just as nice as his first.

Say what you want, but some things about Texas, I absolutely missed—like manners. I tapped my fingernail against my watch, pivoted, and followed the roughneck's path to the doors leading to booze. I called over my shoulder to Purnell, "Get moving. It's half past bourbon time."

But he wasn't grinning. His face held a solemnity that didn't fit the occasion.

The smile that had finally found its way to my face faded into something less fun.

Before I could ask what was wrong, what happened, Purnell spoke. "Bring your ass home. Settle down. Be with people you don't have to front around." When I didn't answer, he kept talking. "Sometimes you gotta stop chasing happiness and let it find you."

I blinked. Purnell, the eternal life of the party, had become enlightened.

"Maybe. But what I'm looking for ain't in Hoodoo." For the first time in decades, the thought saddened me. Not that I wanted to return to Hoodoo. Folk's opinions should have no bearing on my actions. But keeping it real, since I wasn't as human as I'd once believed, being on the receiving end of hate could become my personal kryptonite.

Then again, perhaps my past was just that—behind me.

Yeah, right. I'd been gone... what? Over twenty-five years? For some, forever wouldn't be long enough.

And I couldn't blame them.

Purnell pulled the second door open, his smile softening when I hesitated as if my thoughts were visible on my face. "Go on, it'll be alright. You're a Carter—handle your business."

I didn't want to handle business tonight. I planned to sit on a stool, listen to music, and suck up the best bourbon on the shelf. Was that too much to ask?

I spun around, put my fists on my hips, then gave Purnell my best I-don't-want-no-bullshit scowl.

Of course, he just laughed in response.

"Whatever." I shook my head and froze. Which was a really, really, bad idea.

Because the first rule of ghost club was pretending they didn't exist. To look through corporeal pests. Too bad for me, my gaze locked on the man who'd walked through the main door. Like, right through the wood because a: the door was closed; and b: he was dead.

My breathing quickened as my left hand tingled. The sensation reminded me of blood hurriedly returning to an extremity. I shoved my hand in my loose jeans pocket, whispering a small prayer to whomever would listen, that the electricity aching to find its way free didn't create another hole in my pants.

This was soooo not happening. Not here, not tonight.

The skin across my face tightened as I struggled to keep my shit together. To refrain from screaming at the young man that only I could see. The young man who'd been one of my closest friends and confidants.

Duncan, the young man half of Hoodoo believed I'd murdered with black magic.

Chapter 2

DUNCAN'S PALE GREEN eyes had taken on an otherworldly glow, filled not only with death, but something I didn't give a shit about—guilt. If ever there was an instance of too little too late, this was it.

That naïve and trusting young woman who chose friendship and loyalty over caution, promises over duty was as dead as his jeans-and-flannel-wearing ass. Nope, wasn't going there. Not again.

Screw Duncan and the hell hound he rode in on.

Purnell jabbed my arm with his elbow, then opened the door. "What are you waiting for? A red carpet?"

Nah, it wasn't a rug I wanted, but freedom. From the dead, the curse that killed the last few women in my branch of the family far too young, and the loneliness I struggled to ignore. But most of all, I wanted to shed the shackles of Duncan's death. Ironically, the town council, those in charge of meting out justice in Hoodoo, had proclaimed me innocent.

Unfortunately, the court of public opinion didn't care about truth, just punishment. Which would have been fine had they not looked to make me their piñata.

Whatever.

I didn't return to this quaint hellhole for a pity party, but to sign a few documents. However, I wouldn't do shit until Phillip, Aunt Rose's human servant and attorney, gave up some facts. Like which ancestor gifted me an electric hand, and how to make it go away. One supernatural disability was enough—at least for me.

"Nope," I finally answered as I walked through the second set of doors. Nostalgia tightened my throat and lightened my step. I grinned because The Ancestors had always been a happy place. "Time to get my drink on."

Hopefully, he-who-wouldn't-walk-into-the-freaking-light would forget I existed. Trust me, I'd already forgotten about his dead ass.

Be it Dublin, Shanghai, or Hoodoo, Texas, the best local bars had that same friendly come-on-in-and-take-a-load-off vibe.

Music blared from the old-school jukebox tucked beneath a neon Tito's Vodka sign. Booze-fueled conversation and frantic laughter of those temporarily freed from the prison of their soul-sucking jobs filled the bar.

Wow. Nine o'clock on a Wednesday night, and The Ancestors was well on its way to being packed. Didn't these people have homes to tend and children to feed?

In the dim light, I wove through yuppies and ranchers, then scooted around a couple of cowboys before spotting a woman wearing a belt buckle as large as my head sliding off a barstool.

The Ancestors wasn't fancy but had always been a good time. Rita, my former bestie and partner in crime, would talk Purnell's dad Ajay into letting us bus tables and occasionally sling drinks in the summer.

It was all kinds of illegal for fifteen-year-olds to serve alcohol, but he didn't care. Especially since the local inspector not only worked for the state of Texas, but was a longtime family friend and member of the pack.

"Woo!" Mary Catherine, also known as Mary Cat, whooped, shoved her tray full of drinks at a confused cowboy, then ran across the bar. "Is that who I think it is?"

Before I knew it, I was wrapped once again in the soft arms of family.

Only this time, Mary Cat rocked us back and forth before putting me at arm's length, probably cataloguing my every line and wrinkle, then started all over again. "Girl, I missed your ugly ass," she said, giving me one last heavy-handed pat on the back that would have dislodged an airway obstruction.

Ouch.

"Surprisingly enough, I missed you too." I tried to glare, but my lip-twitch messed up the pissed-off-Black-woman vibe. Oh well. I surrendered and let the smile loose as the knot in my chest unfurled.

We were both older, allegedly wiser, and a whole lot softer, but age and life had been kind to my cousin. She wore a red head wrap that matched her tight Ancestors t-shirt. Yes, she was heavier, but in my eyes, she'd never been more beautiful. Mary Cat was a couple of years older than me, so she'd become my de facto big sister when I moved to Hoodoo.

Whether she'd wanted to be or not.

With as much trouble as I started, most days were on the *or not* side of the equation.

I placed my hands, one over the other, high on my chest. Whether it was to keep me from saying something stupid like I wanted to move home, or to remind myself that whether I loved these people or not, the only person I could depend on was me.

Whether that was truth, delusion, or somewhere in between, I had no idea. But I'd enjoy tonight and let tomorrow unfold as it may. And right now, I was staring into the eyes of a woman, one that I loved.

One I might never see again once I left this town and its secrets in my wake tomorrow. I grabbed both of her immaculately manicured hands, giving them a squeeze. "You look amazing. Then again, you always did."

"Girl, stop lying." Her words said stop, but that grin... was worth the trip home. Mary Cat gave my hands one last squeeze, then pulled a fancy electronic device from her pocket. "Take a load off. What do you want to drink?"

"Make sure she pays for that shit," Purnell's deep voice boomed over the noisy crowd. "We ain't running a charity."

"Shut your pie hole." Mary Cat winked at me, then headed for the bar.

"Hey, what do you want me to do with this?" The confused cowboy, still holding the tray of tequila shots, followed behind Mary Cat, seemingly hypnotized by the long line of her neck.

Interesting.

Mary Cat tapped the heel of her hand against her forehead, then spun around. "Bless your heart. Most of these jackasses would have left me with nothing but a bunch of empty glasses," she said while relieving him of the tray.

"That wouldn't be right," he said in an aw-shucks voice, which made Mary Cat reconsider the dark-skinned man with soft eyes.

"Who are your people?" Mary Cat asked, her predatory gleam on full display as she walked away, the man following her seemingly entranced.

I snagged the empty stool at the bar and scoped out the upgrades.

This was...nice.

The interior of The Ancestors had been as spruced up as the outside. Crimson pendant lights hung above the bar. Pictures of friends, families, and neighbors decorated the walls between fluorescent Shiner Bock signs, decorated mirrors, and hooks for hats and coats.

The peanut shells on the floor were long gone, but the ambiance remained the same—fun, friendly, welcoming, and most of all, neutral ground. Violence wasn't the do-not-pass-go offense in The Ancestors. But use of magic, especially on humans, won the offender a lifetime ban.

And when you're the only game in town…

"The first one's on me." Purnell leaned his beefy arms on the bar. "What do you want?"

I looked past him to the upgraded bar and the backlit liquor options. "World peace?"

He shook his head. "Can't help you with that one."

"Fine…" I shrugged. "Since it's free, I'll take a glass of your best bourbon—neat. Make it a double."

"Why am I not surprised Miss Fancy Ass won't settle for a Lone Star?" He rapped his knuckles against the gleaming wood bar before ambling off, pausing to yell a greeting to a man as wide as he was tall.

If ever there was a person born and bred to be a barkeep, it was Purnell. The man's personality was as large as his bubble eyes. That, and he wasn't about that waking-up-early life.

My stomach tightened as he disappeared. And once again, I was alone.

These people had known me since I was a knock-kneed kid with multicolored beads decorating the ends of my braids. But that girl, the one filled with wonder, grief, and rage, was long gone. I knew my family loved me, because hey, how could they not? But there remained a part of me that never belonged. Not in Hoodoo, and keeping it real, not anywhere. Not because of the ghosts, or even the annoying new Thor hand.

It was like I'd been dropped into the wrong timeline. But there was something else, a feeling that along with my memories of the accident, something else that had been stolen. That something often scratched and banged against the edge of my consciousness… yet remained just beyond reach.

And I sensed it was evil.

To the world, I was a confident, tattooed bad-ass. Unafraid to move through every echelon of society holding my head high while owning the skin I was in. Because in a world filled with predators—both magical and non—I preferred a position near the top of the food chain.

So if I had to tap into my chaotic evil, so be it.

I exhaled through pursed lips and rotated my shoulders, grimacing at the soft snaps, crackles, and pops. Gee, wasn't getting older fun? Wait, actually...yeah. This was the big age where not giving a shit became hella fun because you could say anything and have it chalked up to menopause or raging hormones. Besides, reaching middle age still bitching and kicking was better than taking the big dirt nap.

The haunting twang of a guitar filled the bar. By the time the chorus began, three couples two-stepped clockwise around the outer edge, while two women slow-danced in the center. I leaned back, elbows resting against the bar, watching an older Hispanic couple execute a fancy spin followed by intricate footwork.

There was a calm joy about the two, making me believe they moved through life as smoothly. Not that the years were always easy, but they had each other.

Of course, they could have just met five minutes ago, but damn it, let a sister have her fantasies. At the three o'clock position on the other side was a Black couple smiling at each other with a promise that the night would end with a happy ending or two. The mountain of a brother shouldn't look so graceful guiding the much smaller woman across the floor looking like a two-stepping Fred and Ginger.

My pocket buzzed, so I slid my phone out of my jeans and smiled. Ash Modeus—a complication I hadn't seen coming. He was rich as sin and sexier than a man had a right to be. Oh, and he confounded and terrified me. Luckily, he was on the other side of the world.

Before I could open the text, a pair of sweet pointed-toe boots stopped in my line of sight.

"You have some nerve coming back here." A short, round redhead that I didn't know from Adam sneered at me like I'd left a steaming pile of poop on her front lawn—in broad daylight. On a hot summer afternoon.

"And... you are?" I glanced from a face that would be cute if it weren't scrunched up, to her relaxed hand, and back. Was this a middle-aged girl gang initiation where she picked on the newbie then ran off to Trader Joe's to stock up on Two Buck Chuck?

Three women walked up behind her—including Rita.

Alrighty then...

I slipped into ninja-level bitch face, nothing resting about this one. Rita, the woman who'd once been my best friend, watched me with flat, expressionless blue eyes. Once upon a time, we'd created our dream lives centered around Hoodoo and our pretend children. We'd even selected imaginary husbands.

But that was a lifetime ago. Before suspicion clouded the hazel eyes that, depending on her mood, could lean to either green or brown. Before the faint wrinkles painted the corners of her mottled pale skin.

Before her twin Duncan made me vow to keep his dark secret.

"Hey, Rita," I said, ignoring the little heifer standing in front of me.

"Hey," she answered, her Texas twang as strong as ever.

Was that what I'd sounded like when I went off to University of Texas, Austin? Probably. But hearing it from Rita's lips wounded me in a place I believed long healed. Okay, her reception wasn't too bad. Maybe the years had dulled the pain while sharpening her deductive skills. She had to know that I'd never kill anyone.

No, that wasn't the truth. I would kill. If it came down to choosing between my life and someone else's? They could bet their sweet ass I'd do my best to arrange an invitation with their maker. But I would never deliberately harm someone I considered family.

My lips curled in a toothless smile before I exhaled and went for it. "When you have a minute tonight, let's talk." I studied my former friend, the sister of my heart, waiting for a twitch, a smile, or even an angry fuck off.

Anything.

Nope. Rita dished out a whole lot of nothing. The way she looked through me, it was if I didn't exist.

I shrugged and exhaled through the jagged ache of old scars reopening.

Before I could say anything else, Duncan materialized beside his younger sister, watching her with two lifetimes worth of love. He reached out, his ghostly fingers passing through the fall of blonde hair with a healthy dose of gray grazing her shoulder.

In front of me, Carrot Top raised her shrill voice. "About what? Whose family are you planning to destroy now?"

The ghostly Duncan flinched, before his gaze darted in my direction.

"Ilona," Rita said, her voice infused with power, "enough."

Well, well, wasn't that interesting. Like me, Rita had wanted nothing to do with the coven, or magic. Looked like I wasn't the only one who'd changed.

"Why? She should go back to L.A. where she belongs." Ilona narrowed her eyes at me, looking like were we anywhere else, even the ladies' room, she'd whip out a quick curse. "Nobody wants you here."

"Speak for yourself," called out a man somewhere on my right.

A few people chuckled.

I'm glad someone found this shit funny. I didn't come into The Ancestors to be the entertainment. But if this wench wanted to put on a show, then that was exactly what the fuck I'd give her. I was too old, too cute, and too tired for bar fights. But this little witch—I wanted to use the b-word, but I was trying to clean up my language—had crossed the line.

I smiled, and it wasn't friendly. Hell, it wasn't even a bless-your-heart smile. It was the one that usually preceded the removal of earrings and slathering my face with Vaseline. In other words, it was my butt-kicking face.

Creeping anger thrummed through my body, caressing and coaxing my anger to life, before flowing down my arm awaiting the tiniest of sparks to convince me to burn it all down.

I stretched my fingers to alleviate the searing burn in my left hand. *Shit. Shit. Shit.* Why Lord, why couldn't this heifer have just hung out with her witchy friends and talked about me behind my back like a normal person?

And worse, why did I have to be a freak?

What I needed was for little Miss Ilona to leave me alone before things got bad. Which wasn't a threat, but a fact, because I had no idea what was going on with my body. Apparently, death came with side effects.

I exhaled, relaxed my shoulders, and tilted my head to the side. I might not be able to control my hand and what felt like electricity flowing beneath my skin, but my emotions? Those were all mine. Allowing her to provoke me into anger meant little Ilona won.

Not going to happen.

"Look, Raggedy Ann." I wiggled my fingers, which now felt like a hand rather than a portable generator. "I'm not the one. No amount of magic will keep you safe if you keep fucking with me. Check yourself." I returned my behind to the stool.

Since the verbal altercation had ended, Ilona had a choice to make. Old-fashioned fisticuffs, which would end with her embarrassed and me in jail thanks to Krav Maga, or my new, unpredictable magic.

I crossed my arms and gave her the once over again. She glared at me long enough that I knew this wouldn't be the last time Raggedy Ann and I would face each other. I suspected next time, we wouldn't have an audience. As the kids say, or rather, used to say, it would be on and popping.

"Here you go, cuz." Purnell thumped his fist on the bar.

The tinkle of ice cubes hitting a glass made me swivel on my stool. The bourbon deserved my full focus. "Took you long enough," I mumbled as I nodded at the accompanying glass of ice water.

But apparently, Ilona was not only a pain in the behind, but not finished with her humiliation. "Are you threatening me?" she all but shrieked.

I sighed, then took a sip of my bourbon. "Are you still here?" Reluctantly, I sat my glass on the little napkin, giving Ilona my full attention. Whatever she saw on my face made her retreat half a step before she caught herself.

"Play stupid games, win stupid prizes." I cleared my throat, and when my next words fell from my lips, my voice was deeper and raspier than usual. As a matter of fact, my voice didn't seem to be coming from my larynx at all, but somewhere deeper, somewhere darker. "I need you to hear me. The next time you disrespect me will be your last."

The music stopped, as did the conversation. The only thing missing was an official proclaiming, *so it is written* or some shit, followed by a gong.

After hearing the next voice, I so would have preferred the metallic sound resonating through the room.

"Gwendolyn," interrupted a rumbly male voice, "not a good idea to make threats in front of witnesses. Maybe I should arrest you now and save myself a lot of trouble."

And my night had just gone from bad to freaking awful.

Chapter 3

THE WITCHES MOVED ON to the next hapless victim; well, all but Rita. Unlike the other people in the bar, she didn't bother pretending not to watch me and Carlos. Regret hit me like a boot to the stomach.

Then again, maybe I needed to shed that hair shirt. Because it wasn't me who chose to run, not walk, away from a relationship that was supposed to be forever. Had the tables been turned, I would have listened, trusted, believed. Had teenaged Carlos murdered someone, I would have helped him hide the body. But when he found me kneeling on the floor wearing only a bra because my shirt was pressed against Duncan's neck to staunch the flow of blood, Carlos didn't call an ambulance—but the sheriff.

So, in the end, what Carlos and I had hadn't been love or that fated mate fairytale bullshit, but infatuation and an overabundance of hormones.

"What do you want, Carlos?" I grabbed my glass to distract from looking into those soulful brown eyes. I once thought brown eyes boring, and even wished mine were a different color until I met him. Even as rambunctious kids tearing through the woods, fishing, or building forts, I'd sneak looks at him.

I knew, even at eight years old, that I wanted to marry Carlos Hernandez.

His nostrils flared slightly, as if waiting for the emotional response he'd never receive. "I see you haven't changed."

Oh, but he had. That young man that I'd fallen head over heels in love with had filled out and grown up. Carlos' eyes, while still brown, were far from soft. And those lips... Gah. Even pressed together in anger, they were still full and kissable.

Nope, wasn't going there. I swirled the disappearing ice cubes in my glass to keep my mind from wandering too close to the gutter. Not wise to even get a little aroused around a werewolf. Especially this one.

I also wasn't going to admire the chest beneath the slim-cut and untucked forest green shirt. And ignoring the muscular thighs beneath those jeans? A necessity.

I cut my eyes at Carlos, switched my water for something stronger, then raised my still half-filled glass of Black Saddle Bourbon closer to my lips, and shrugged. "Wrong—again," I said, my voice sing-songy.

He looked me up and down, and from his expression, found me lacking. Carlos' gaze paused at my arms, taking his time on my tattoos. My left was a full sleeve of Japanese-inspired art that I designed to incorporate my birthmark; a discoloration shaped like a trio of jagged lightning bolts. My right half-sleeve was American traditional, which I'd also designed. It included a Black pinup girl sitting on the state of Texas, and one particular tat that Carlos could never see.

All my tattoos were done with my family's blessed ink. Which meant, that even on darker skin, the colors were unusually bright and vivid. Had we chosen to patent and sell the ink, we'd be a whole lot wealthier. But Conjure Ink delivered more than color.

Blessings and protection were imbued with some of the pigment. So, if an artist from the shop or family worked on you, it was a big deal. The rumors of continuous good fortune sent customers flocking to our chairs. And if someone with a tainted soul or ill intentions came to any of us for tattoos?

We either sent them on their way or used the unblessed ink.

"You staying?" Carlos asked when he finished his inspection of my arms.

Right about now, I regretted my choice of outfits. Ripped jeans, cowboy boots, and a plain white short-sleeved t-shirt wasn't exactly a make-him-regret-dumping-you outfit.

At least he hadn't sneered at my ink. I'd take it, and my leave of him. "Not that it's any of your business, but no. I'll be out of your hair in the morning."

"Everything in this town is my business. We haven't had any trouble, and I plan to keep it that way. Comprende?"

"What part of I don't want to remain in Hoodoo do you not understand? Should I speak slower?" Okay, now I was just being a bitch, but he deserved it.

I shook my head in both disappointment and disgust. With him or myself, I wasn't sure. But if I had to guess, that was Carlos' intention. To get me off my game, upset and hurt about something that happened when we were kids. "What next, you going to order me out of town tonight?"

"If I could, I'd happily take you to the county line myself." Carlos' hard stare was as cutting as his next words. "I don't want a murderer in my town."

Heat rushed through my body, but I bit back the rage and disguised the rush of sadness by rolling my eyes. Carlos could stay here with his small attitude and even smaller life in this stinking town.

The love I felt for him and Hoodoo was long gone. It left when they all tossed me out like garbage.

"How about this?" I leaned close enough for him to taste the oaky bourbon on my breath. "You stay out of my way for the next twelve hours, and I'll do the same." I couldn't take one more second of that handsome face without either kissing or punching him, so I spun around and leaned my trembling arms on the bar.

"Need another?" the grinning Purnell asked.

"Leave the bottle." Black Saddle was my friend tonight. "You're being awfully generous."

"That's what you think." Purnell sat my liquid ambrosia on the bar, shook his head, then winked. "High-class artists with shit in fancy-ass magazines can afford to pay full price."

There was no getting a swollen ego in this family. Deflating high and mighty attitudes were a family pastime.

"Well, since you put it like that..." I raised my glass, swirling the liquid that reminded me too much of Carlos' wolf's eyes. I shoved those bittersweet memories away and focused on my cousin.

Purnell grabbed a rack of dirty glasses and moved to the cleaning station behind the bar. "So... where are you off to next?"

"I'm not sure, but I'm overdue for a vacation. One that doesn't involve a hospital bed."

"Heard about that." He sat the glasses in the rack and grabbed the towel draped across his shoulder, drying his hands. When Purnell spoke again, he lowered his voice. "How you holding up?" He looked into my eyes as if reading my every secret. Maybe it was a bartender thing, but Purnell was waiting not just for an answer, but the truth.

"Mostly good." And freaked out about the fact that I'd been shot in the back a mere three weeks ago, yet all that remained were two faint scars. Other than that, and the occasional glowing hand, I was fine and damned dandy.

"Tell me they caught the asshole." He scowled. The expression was one that stopped fights in The Ancestors before they started, especially since the winner would deal with Purnell when it was over.

And he didn't fight clean.

Regardless of how sweet Purnell could be to family, protective of women in the bar, generous with friends, and even the occasional adversary—including domesticated cats—he had the look of a man who'd beat your ass then laugh about it.

I shook my head.

What was I supposed to say? That I'd passed my expiration date years ago and had been living on borrowed time? That whoever had killed the rest of the women in my branch of the family almost got me too?

None of that mattered. I was still here. Anything else was extra.

"I doubt it. I was in Morocco and in the middle of nowhere."

"I know you're annoying, but I can't see nobody hating you enough to want to kill your narrow ass."

I chuckled; how could I not? Only in Texas would these hips be classified as narrow. But hey, I'd take it.

"Yo, Purnell. Can we get another round down here?" a beefy cowboy hollered jovially from the other end of the bar.

"Be right there." Purnell jerked his chin and knocked twice on the immaculate bar next to my glass before he left.

What I knew, or rather thought I knew about the world when I moved to Hoodoo as an eight-year-old orphan would've fit into a thimble. Before then, my mom and I traveled around the country with a church one cup of Kool-Aid short of a cult.

They preached the evils of magic and the one-way ticket to the lake of fire for those who used it, which sucked for a kid whose only friend was a ghost. From that extreme to moving to a town where fairy tales might as well be true — I was a prime candidate for therapy.

A wave of coldness like ice crystals covering a wintry window swept up my arm.

Really, universe?

Can't a woman have a single night without a conversation with someone from the other side of the grave?

"Gwennie...I—"

"Shut it." I closed my eyes and exhaled through pursed lips, as if that would block the deep voice of my dead former friend. "Haven't you done enough? You've ruined my life once; I'll be damned if I give you another chance."

I tossed back the rest of my bourbon, then slapped a hundred-dollar bill on the bar before hopping off the stool.

"You'll never know how sorry I am for my choices back then," Duncan said, his voice holding sorrow so thick, it slid across my skin. "I was an asshole, yes. But I'm not the only person who lied to you."

It didn't matter. Hoodoo, and the people who didn't want me here were going to get their wish. I was leaving—again. Only this time, I'd never return.

Chapter 4

WHEN I WOKE UP IN PURNELL'S guest room above the bar, I checked my messages. Phillip had changed our meeting from his office to Azure House, which was odd, but whatever.

Unlike yesterday, I dressed for the occasion. Oh, I wasn't opposed to getting dolled up; as a matter of fact, my fashion choices were eclectic. I collected vintage clothing, with my preferred era being the 1940s and 50s. But I also scoured the earth to find old concert t-shirts. And we won't even talk about my therapy-level boot collection. But today, I was dressed sedately in high-waisted, wide-legged jeans and a fitted lightweight crimson cashmere sweater.

Now, standing in front of the gothic Victorian mansion, I regretted not declining the change in venue. Never have I seen a house more suited for a horror flick. The only thing missing was a mask-wearing, chainsaw-wielding serial killer.

Everything was so... fifty shades of brown. From the landscaping that had been dead since I was a kid, to the tobacco-colored tiles that looked like a sturdy wind would send them flying.

I couldn't imagine my mother, who was a bubbly woman, growing up in a house that looked like a funeral home.

And if that wasn't bad enough, Hoodoo's infamous haunted house was perched atop a hill with a spectacular view of the cemetery. I wrapped my arms around my waist and stared down the grassy slope through the swirling black wrought-iron fence. As far as cemeteries went, this one was beautiful, with lush rolling hills, regal oaks, maples, and even pecan trees.

I won't mention the award-winning pies made with nuts gathered from Shady Glen. St. Marks had its own small cemetery, but since a chunk of town had been refused plots on their hallowed grounds, many chose interment next door.

Duncan appeared, sunlight shining through his still transparent body. The dead, whether newly or the long departed, could appear to me in various forms. Some were mere glimpses of light, their soul energy swirling, creating a kaleidoscope of brilliant colors. Others, those who were more powerful or filled with purpose—not all of them good—appeared solid.

Then there were those like Duncan. He was, for lack of a better word...fading. Like the Gods of old, human souls, without active remembrance and celebration, they were simply forgotten, diminished.

In these parts, it was primarily the root workers and those of Mexican and Hispanic descent who venerated or paid homage to the dead. While those who practiced Hoodoo honored the ancestors on a regular basis, the others primarily did it on Día de los Muertos, or Day of the Dead.

While I wasn't welcome at Duncan's funeral, Mrs. Evans let me go in the back of the funeral home to say my goodbyes. So I know good and damned well that Duncan wasn't laid to rest rocking a plaid shirt, cowboy boots, and Levi's.

But unlike the rest of us, Duncan hadn't aged, except for his eyes. They held a weariness that said he'd seen some things.

I shivered, then rubbed my left forearm. The afterlife was one thing I could wait to learn more about—much later.

"Gwennie..." Duncan licked his thin ghostly lips.

Another wave of trembling rocked my body, but these were from pent-up anger. I had almost three decades of frustration to let loose.

"What, Duncan? What could you possibly have to say after all these years? It would have been helpful if you'd have popped your ass up..." I waved my hand. "I don't know, maybe when the town blamed me for your fucking death?"

He flinched.

Three plump pheasants shot out of the thick bushes, undoubtably startled by my raised voice.

"Would they have listened? Would they have even believed you?" Duncan stepped closer, reaching out a hand.

I shook my head and retreated. "Go away."

"Did you hear what I said at the bar? Or are you still too pig-headed to listen to something you don't want to hear? Thought you'd have grown out of sticking your head in the sand."

"You're right. I've learned I can't trust anyone. Thanks for that." My nod was jerky, and far from friendly.

Of course, he didn't listen, didn't leave me the hell alone. Instead, his pale green eyes glowed with... irritation? Anger? I had no idea, but judging from the flattened lips, Duncan was about as happy with me as I was with him.

Good.

"I wasn't the only liar in your life back then. Ignorance isn't bliss, Gwennie. Don't you want to know what they—"

"No, Duncan. I don't want to hear shit you have to say. The time to talk to me was twenty-seven years ago. Before you ripped my life and the town apart."

"Why do you think I stayed?" Anger and that unearthly glow faded as he slipped his hands in his pockets, looking every bit the boy from back in the day.

Duncan understood feeling like an outsider. For him, it started at birth, when his twin sister, Rita, was gifted with the magic. She was always the special one, the golden child. And him?

Like me, Duncan watched power with his nose pressed against the glass. I was tired of this shit. And him.

"Duncan, I swear on all that's holy, if you bother me again, I will search the earth for a psychopomp, be it Gabriel, Agwé, or Lucifer himself, and I will find someone to take your ass to hell, and away from me."

Duncan opened his mouth but was interrupted by a raised silver F-150 turning off the road.

The truck growled up the wide circular gravel driveway, stopping behind Stella, my badass stealth camper van. As the engine quieted to a purr, the gumbo of anxiety, hope, and fear residing in my gut roared back to life.

Mr. Zhu, the best (and only) lawyer in town and my aunt Rose's human servant, hopped out of the super-sized truck. It's all jokes about us Texans and raised vehicles until a flash flood made that cute little hybrid a canoe.

"Gwendolyn." He took in my outfit, then nodded in something that could be approval—or constipation.

"Hey, Mr. Z." He'd remained a tall, lean, long-haired, thirty-five-year-old-looking man with a face meant for magazines. That human servant gig was working for him. And so were those jeans.

When I first moved to Hoodoo, in my eight-year-old mind, he was a Chinese prince who turned into a dragon to swoop in and rescue the beautiful princess. That lasted all of a second. Because I quickly discovered he was as dour as he was handsome. Which was a shame.

"Please, call me Phillip." He put his hands on his jeans-clad hips and stared up at the house that had seen better days—about a hundred years ago. "Stay at the ranch. It would please your aunt," he said in a tone this side of an order.

I avoided looking at the wreckage of a house, choosing instead to study Phillip's damned near perfect profile. "Nope," I said, putting a little something, something on the p, making it pop. "Not just no, but hell no. I'm not staying at all."

Okay, it was weird having a full-on adult conversation, curse words included, with someone so much older than me. "The overdue and tearful reunion straight out of *The Color Purple* sounds great in theory. In reality? Not so much."

He shook his head and his lips quirked ever so slightly upward, as if he'd remembered how to smile.

"May I sign the papers so I can leave?" I turned away before the usual disapproval tightened his lips. Maybe one of my cousins would buy Azure House, rehab this mess. Or better yet, tear that bitch down and start over with something a little less frightening.

"That's not how this works."

"Excuse me? Then why did you to drag me out here to this…" I waved my hands at the shutters that looked like they were held up by rust and spiderwebs. "…monstrosity."

"That monstrosity," Phillip snapped, "will be your home for the next six months if you want your inheritance."

I clenched my teeth to keep from saying something disrespectful. Phillip and I might have looked the same age, but he was over a hundred years old, so dude was absolutely my elder. Plus, I had promised my mother after I died in Morocco that I would return to Hoodoo—for answers.

"You expect me to live in that?" I shivered. "Phillip, I'm not exactly poor." I looked back up at the lopsided chimney.

Aw, hell to the no. I might occasionally look like a Haight-Ashbury reject straight out of the sixties, but the truth of the matter was not only was I a celebrity tattoo artist, but I also sold original paintings as well as textiles.

Depending on the day and the stock market, I was worth a healthy seven figures.

I shook my head. "Give it to someone else in the family. I don't need money that bad."

"We're talking life-changing money." Phillip's voice grew softer and more serious. "You'd be the second richest person in town, after your uncle Raul."

I blinked so fast, it was surprising I didn't take flight.

Well, damn.

The Double R, Uncle Raul's ranch, was one of the oldest in Texas. Hell, it had been in his family when the United States was a grand experiment. To say he was loaded was an understatement. When you're a vampire, compound interest takes on new meaning.

"Finally, I have your attention. Gwendolyn, you're it. The last of your bloodline."

I shook my head. "That's not true. I have a buttload of cousins."

"Not from your direct matriarchal line." His usually stern brunch-daddy face softened, giving me the distinct impression that this was the beginning of the bad tidings. "After Rose married Raul and moved to the Double R, Your great-grandmother Hyacinth was willed Azure House because the third sister Daisy…" Mr. Z shrugged. "…wanted nothing to do with the house or her siblings."

"Why are we taking this trip down memory lane now?" I shook my head as I waggled my right index finger. A bitter laugh crawled through my tight throat. "I don't give a shit how much money it is, I'm not for sale. Tell your master that it's a no for me."

Put a fork in me because I was *done*.

I headed for my van, stopping, then turned around to yell at Phillip, expecting him to be ten feet behind me. Of course, being a human servant came with gifts other than eternal youth and vigor. The man was as stealthy as his mistress, so I nearly crashed into him.

"Since I'm not planning to have children, looks like the house and the money will both sit unbothered."

"Not really." When I turned around, Phillip shrugged, his handsome face unchanged, but his annoyance flickered through his dark eyes. "Fine, if you don't care that a descendant of the family who once owned yours will profit from your ancestor's labor, it's not my place to judge."

My feet were suddenly rooted to the packed gravel driveway, but I flinched as if I'd been rocked with a jab. I cleared my throat. "You're a liar. First of all, both of my ancestors, when they moved to Texas, back when it was Mexico, were free."

When I arrived in Hoodoo last night, I may not have known what I was. But until two seconds ago, I was certain about the who. I was Gwendolyn Carter, descendant of a free Black man who'd been given a land grant from the Mexican government and one of the founding families of Hoodoo. I was born of people who, along with the local shifters and the vampires, risked it all as part of the Underground Railroad to help enslaved people travel deeper into Mexico—and freedom—once Hoodoo became part of the Republic of Texas.

Now I was supposed to believe something else? I pushed my palms toward Phillip as if that would block the bad news.

"About that." Phillip licked his lips as he rocked back on his heels. "That's not exactly the truth."

"You have got to be kidding me." While I may have been able to keep it together enough to not yell, tingling began in my left arm, marching toward my hand as if the phantom pain was a formation of Texas-sized fire ants.

I exhaled loudly, then filled my lungs and repeated the process. This wasn't Phillip's fault; he was merely a convenient target.

"I wish I were." The usually unflappable Phillip pinched the bridge of his nose. "Everything else you've been told is true: the land grant, the founding of the town, the helping people. All of it. You're the same woman you were a couple minutes ago. We're not sure how she did it, but when Cosette made it to Texas, she was barely alive. Job found her and never left her side while she recuperated. It's because of her strength and their love that you're here."

While their story was sweet, I wanted a man who'd scorch and salt the earth to save me. And slaughter anyone who merely considered doing me harm. Whoa... Where the hell did that come from? Had a psychopath taken up residence inside my brain, or had I always been that ruthless?

I curled my fingers under, rubbing them against my jean-covered thighs as I stared at patches of dead grass long enough to shake off the shame of how callously I spoke of death. With each passing day, the struggle to remain sort of good seemed impossible.

"So, what now?" I finally asked when I gathered myself.

"Either accept the inheritance as well as your legacy, or...not. Toss it out like rubbish." He walked past me, stopping two feet from his truck, then moved backwards. "The house. The money. The library. The history. Everything."

"Library?" I snorted and swung my left arm wide toward the house. "I doubt there's a page left unchewed. Let me get this straight. Azure House and the money has always been mine? At any time between eight and eighteen when I left, Aunt Rose could have told me." It was Phillip's turn to flinch, but I kept talking. "Was she hoping I'd die so she could somehow keep it?"

Phillip remained silent.

"Why does she hate me?"

This time, Phillip answered, his voice soft and filled with something odd—empathy. "Rose loves you. You're the child she never had."

"That's not love, Phillip," I whispered, not bothering to conceal the unhealed pain.

"Rose may not have loved you how you needed, but she does the best she can." He seemed to struggle, then sighed.

"Sure."

We looked at each other for a few terrible seconds, each waiting for the other to bend. To come to their senses. Too bad for them I was feral enough to chew my arm off to get free.

"Well, let's go sign away your legacy." Phillip walked to his truck and withdrew a soft leather briefcase.

What a mess.

Chapter 5

CONGRATULATIONS. I was the new owner of an old money pit. Yay me.

I watched Phillip drive down the hill, waiting for the film crew to spring out from behind the dilapidated house to tell me I was being punked.

None came.

When push came to shove, no fucking way could I walk away.

Maybe it was a GenX thing, but I didn't whine. When you came from a family with "life isn't fair, so either get over it or kill it" painted on the family crest, you handled your business in silence.

Well, I wasn't about to kill anyone. But I was a petty bitch, and I'd be damned if some slaver's descendant would get one cent from my family. They'd have to pry the deed out of my cold, dead, middle-aged hands.

Now, all I had to do was rehab it enough to live in and remain in Hoodoo for six months, then the house and the money was mine to do with as I pleased. And I was sure it would please me to have one of the other relatives live in Azure House.

I turned and walked back up the driveway to a small rise overlooking the cemetery.

Two ghosts, a man and a woman, stood beneath a tree gazing at the sky. The dark-skinned woman wore yellowish-green kitten heels and a matching A-line dress that swayed gently with the breeze, and her partner, a few shades lighter, wore a dark, well-tailored suit. The clothing looked straight out of the 1950s, but their affection was forever.

Feeling like a peeping Tom, I turned and marched to my immediate future.

I placed my foot on the bottom stair, wishing I'd worked a little harder to lose those last twenty pounds.

A snort so unladylike slipped out, I bet they heard it downtown.

It was *thirty-five* pounds, but I wore them well. I was big-boned. That's my story and I'm sticking to it.

I placed both feet on the bottom step, shocked that the rotted wood didn't disintegrate. Looking skyward, I whispered, "Thanks for helping a sister out. Now, if you could keep the rest of the house from collapsing, I'd appreciate it."

Hmm. I tapped the short nail of my index finger against my front tooth. I liked old things. Exhibit A: Uncle Raul and Aunt Rose and the rest of the vampires in the local congregation.

Instead of seeing the house as a burden, I should flip the script and enjoy the project. Living in Hoodoo forever was *so* not going to happen. But I could make Azure House something special. Maybe even a bed and breakfast if I could find a partner to run it.

Beneath the cracked and chipped paint, wear and tear, and the don't-mess-with-me aura, Azure House was beautiful, if you looked close enough. The deep wraparound porch begged for new rocking chairs, massive urns filled with flowers, and ceiling fans overhead to keep mosquitos at bay during the sticky Texas summers.

Gingerly, I moved to the second step. Just when I was about to hop off the ancient stair to save my ankles and my pride, not only did the wood cease groaning and squeaking, but it... straightened?

What. The. Fuck?

Something, be it magic, or premonition, or plain old-fashioned terror washed over me, coating my skin.

No no no no no.

Streaks of bluish light flowed and danced beneath my skin. The glow circled my wrist before traveling down the delicate bones along the back of my hand until even the beds of my fingernails joined in on the light show.

In an instant, the skies that were bright just a second ago dimmed. Even the soft breeze that had tickled my cheek ceased.

I pressed my lips together, balled my hands into fists, and shook my head. Hell to the no. This was job for the big guns. Time to call the cousins to come cleanse this bitch.

Without thinking twice, I jogged to my van and grabbed the phone from the passenger seat.

Shoot off a text to Kyle, my best friend and lawyer? Done.

Text to my cousin Loretta, the most powerful and knowledgeable root worker in Hoodoo as well as the Houston metropolitan area? Handled.

Now, all I wanted was a flashlight and some bourbon to calm my damned nerves. I didn't plan to do the horror movie white girl thing and enter the abandoned house alone and disappear. But opening the door to peek inside wouldn't hurt, would it?

I spun around, tapping the flashlight against my thigh. "Okay, house, if you're taking requests, I'd appreciate if you didn't have any rodents in residence. I can't handle rats, squirrels, raccoons, and especially possums."

I marched up the walkway fighting back a shiver. I was sure possums were nice and all, and I appreciated that they were tick and bug Hoovers, but... ew, just no.

I'd faced down death—on two occasions—moved to small-town Texas, and into a house filled with vampires. I'd even gotten my first Brazilian wax a few years ago. In comparison, checking out a long abandoned house was piece of cake.

Still nervous about falling through the aged wood, I hurried onto the porch then reached for the doorknob, my hand hovering above the tarnished brass.

Life was filled with momentous crossroads. Today, this moment, was one of mine. And I'm not even gonna lie, I was terrified. Not of the house per se, and not even of what I'd find inside.

But what I might learn about myself. This was one of those be careful what you ask for moments. Would the universe allow me to exchange a fortune for a pony?

I snatched my hand away and whispered, "Why are you so afraid?"

"Maybe because it looks like the last inhabitants were the kids before Hansel and Gretel—"

I yelped and spun around, which was about all I could do, seeing that my heart had moved to the vicinity of my esophagus.

"You know, the ones who didn't get away."

Apparently, the laser beams shooting from my eyes were ineffective, judging by my cousin Maria's grin. "You shouldn't sneak up on people like that." I gladly left the porch and walked closer.

"You got soft in your old age," Maria said.

"Heifer, who you calling old?"

Even in blue scrub pants with a coordinating top complete with pastel bunnies, Maria looked like a bad-ass. Big hips, big eyes, and a big heart. Okay, her heart might have been more wicked than mine, but from what I remembered, my cousin loved hard. And I would so steal that shoulder-length wig if I could figure out how to get my locs under it.

I crossed my arms, doubling down on the glare. "I'm only a year older than you."

"Like I said, ancient you are."

"Sweetheart. You're no Yoda." I couldn't help but grin. You know how they say cousins were your first friends? Well, they're also your first frenemies. Exhibit A stood beside a pearly white Escalade. "Maria, what are you doing here?"

"What do you think?" She tossed her keys on the driver's seat and closed the door. "I want to see the inside of this house. You know how many times I tried to break in?"

"No, because that's what most people call a felony." I grimaced, handed her my flashlight, and snagged another one from Stella. "If you tell anyone, I'll deny it, but I'm glad you're here."

She snorted. "Whatever. You know you missed me." She raised her shirt, sliding a silver-plated 9mm from her bellyband holster. "Now I'm ready."

I stood on the uneven gravel, blinking.

"What?" Maria looked at me as if I was the one who pulled a bazooka out of my pants. Which, come to think of it, might not have been a bad idea.

"Nothing." I shook my head.

Maria tapped her gun against her thigh. "You need something? I have more."

"No, and I'm surprised I hadn't considered anything bigger than a flashlight." Mostly because bullets couldn't kill the things waiting behind the door.

But I'll keep that part to myself. "Welp, let's do this. You ready?"

Maria nodded, closed her SUV door, then looked from me to Azure House. Her brows drew together in a confused frown. "You know, it doesn't look as beat down as I remember."

"Not exactly my thoughts when I drove up, but I'll take it." As we returned to the front door, I whispered a silent prayer that the house wasn't a secret portal to hell—or worse.

"Hurry up." Maria nudged me with her hip.

"Hold your horses; this is an important moment here." The keys were labeled and color-coded. So I used the one marked "front door" and willingly entered my new home.

And it was...

Just a house. No band of roving armadillos waiting to attack. No scary creatures from the bowels of hell. Honestly, there wasn't even very much dust. Were we in the right house?

Open concept wasn't always a thing. Older homes tended to have plenty of doors to contain the heat. This house was no different. The foyer was wide and open, with the beginnings of a grand staircase visible just past the open parlor tucked away off to the right.

Having watched one too many horror movies where some stupid person wandered into the house and the door slammed shut, I turned to Maria and jabbed a finger at her. "Wait there."

"Not a problem." As soon as I hustled off, Maria shifted, assuming my place as protector of the escape route.

I stopped in the small parlor and looked around at the formal room and sheet-covered furniture, imagining women in long dresses and fancy updos greeting guests and sipping tea. A room that wasn't as decrepit as it should have been. Aunt Rose might not have touched the exterior, but luckily, she ensured the interior was less scary.

A short bench sat under the bay window, so I grabbed it, sheet and all, dragging it to the front door.

Now that Maria and I wouldn't become haunted house captives, we both entered, and from Maria's wide eyes, she was equally amazed. I might have felt a certain way about being all but blackmailed into staying in Hoodoo, but a part of me anticipated the exploration of Azure House.

While Maria moved around the room ripping sheets off furniture, I did what I should have done when I stepped on the grounds this morning. I opened that part of me that sensed not only the dead, but other supernatural creatures.

Of course, I'm not certain how accurate my creature sensor was these days, but in addition to ghosts, I sensed the big three—vampires, fae, and shifters.

"This doesn't look too bad." Maria pulled the sheet off a sofa and gasped.

I spun around, flashlight at the ready, only to see my grinning cousin.

"Girl, this stuff is nice." She rolled the sheet and sat it on the spotless dark wood coffee table with inlaid marble. "You want to tell me how not nary a cobweb or creature has moved in here?"

"If I had to guess, I'd say Aunt Rose had something to do with it. If not..." I scratched the back of my neck. "...I'd rather not know."

Maria snorted. "How are you so scary?"

I crossed my arms and looked down at the 9mm she'd replaced in her in holster. "Dirty Harriet, I know you ain't talking. I'm not the one packing heat, ready to kill Casper."

She shrugged, as if saying, *Ain't-no-shame-in-my-game.* "Speaking of Casper, you still seeing dead folks?"

"Yup." I snatched a sheet off a mahogany side-boy topped with an untarnished silver tea service, tossing the crisp white cloth on the coffee table with the others. "And they're as pushy as ever."

"Could be worse, I guess."

"How?" I asked as she joined me, and we exposed the remaining larger pieces together.

"At least you'll know if your house is haunted."

"Let's go over there." I pointed across the hall at a closed pocket door. Okay, I really did want to explore. What I didn't want to do was share that we were not alone. Weirdly enough, the vibe I got from our otherworldly guest was giddiness.

Between the happy ghosts and the beauty that was this house, perhaps returning to Hoodoo wasn't a mistake.

Maria and I continued exploring the downstairs rooms, opening doors, uncovering furniture, and appreciating what looked to be original art. I was happy as a hog in slop to find cushions free from vermin. As a matter of fact, the entire interior appeared untouched by the decades.

Eventually, we grew tired of exposing furniture. It was time to wander, and we did, traipsing through the rooms downstairs. Azure House was larger than she appeared and felt like a giant maze. The quick trip through most of the downstairs, especially the large old-school kitchen featuring an antique but massive and working range, combined with Maria's banter, brightened the day and my mood.

Too bad for Azure House, I'd only be here long enough to make sure that it, as well as the money, remained in the hands of family—the ones of my choosing.

"Hey, I'm going to the second floor. You're taking too long." Maria all but ran to the stairs, not bothering to hide that she wanted to be the first to step foot in the upper chambers. Hell, she was probably even going to claim a room for when she visited.

"You're not afraid of the ghosts anymore?" I grinned when she stopped moving as if someone had disconnected her power cord.

Maria grabbed the railing with both hands and stared down at me with eyes almost as big as Purnell's. "What the hell are you talking about?"

"Who's the scaredy cat now?" I asked in a sing-songy voice. When she glared at me, I waved my hand. "Go on, I'm just teasing."

"Alright..." She backed up the stairs, looking not too certain.

I raised my right hand and held up three fingers. "Scout's honor." Because the happy ghost wasn't upstairs. She'd gone out back right before we'd entered the kitchen.

"You were kicked out of both the Girl and Boy Scouts, remember?"

"Yeah, I do. It was your fault."

Maria gave me the double middle finger salute before jogging up the stairs, her lovely alto laughter trailing behind her.

I slid my hand along the dusty wood to a closed and, unlike the others, locked door. I glanced at the keys dangling on the large silver ring looped over my wrist, then repeatedly tried to unlock the mysterious entrance.

"You're going to make me work for this, aren't you? I thought we were friends." I placed my palms against the sides of the delicately carved frame surrounding the door. Warm pulsating energy thrummed through my hand before reverberating through my body.

The rational part of my brain demanded that I prepare for an attack, and be on guard. But my gut said something else. This new sensation wasn't frightening. I shook my head slightly. No, this felt like...

A soft smile raised my lips and softened the lines between my brows as I acknowledged my truth. This room had rolled out a low-voltage welcome mat.

Was it too late for freaking out and fleeing? Hell yeah, I was a Carter woman; we didn't run from trouble, we started it.

The lock gave with a soft click before it opened unaided by these human hands. Mostly because I'd slapped mine over my mouth. I whispered against my fingers, "Oh my God."

Chapter 6

I'D EXPECTED A STOREROOM, a closet, or maybe even an old-school sex dungeon. But this was waaaay better.

I pressed my hands to my chest and stared open-mouthed at the treasure trove. I, Gwendolyn Carter, was having my very own Belle moment—minus the Beast. A trio of massive stained-glass windows filled the opposite wall, the bright sunlight converting the space to a giant crimson, lemon-yellow, and cobalt-blue kaleidoscope.

After taking two steps deeper into the room, the wonder faded into something else. A shiver of unease crept up my spine and grabbed hold of the muscles in my neck. Uh, this was no freaking fairytale, and if it was, it wasn't the homogenized, colonized, and safe-for-all-ages version.

Every kid in Hoodoo, including myself, had come to Azure House on a dare, throwing rocks and breaking windows, only to return the next day to find her in the same state of disarray, yet not one pane shattered. And in every visit to this mausoleum, not once did I spot this triptych of stained-glass windows—anywhere.

Well, trippy glass aside, my ancestors obviously adored books and created a setting worthy of the leather-bound tomes. Unlike the other rooms, the furniture was uncovered. The other thing missing? Dust.

The rest of the house wasn't bad, with token sprinkles of dust here and there, but the library was... pristine.

I shook my head and drifted to the mantel as I squinted at the two odd iron spikes. Interesting. Must be candle holders. But where was the bottom piece to catch the wax? No, that didn't make sense, because between the two weird spikes stood an elaborate silver candelabrum filled with five long, tapered cream candles.

As I twisted the ends of one of my locs, I studied the mantel. From the door, the wood looked like any other, with outdated swirling patterns and curlicues, which would be consistent with the Victorian styling of the house. But close up, those swirls looked more like hieroglyphics. This mantel told a story, beginning on the continent of Africa, across the middle passage, with one line going to Louisiana, and the other first to France, then Mexico, before merging in Texas.

Okay, that made sense. While I didn't know much about all things magic or supernatural about the family, both the patriarch and matriarch were human. Or at least that was what I was told. When you grow up in Hoodoo, you learn not only Texas history, but that of the town.

During the period that Spain controlled Texas, they gave generous land grants to its citizens. That was when Uncle Raul inherited what is now the Double R Ranch. My ancestor, on the other hand, was granted his land for his gallantry fighting on the side of Mexico during their war of independence from Spain.

According to the story, he built this home for his bride a free Black woman. Now that I've had some time to reflect, it wasn't shame that threw me earlier, but the lie. Because, hell, what she had to endure making her way to freedom was damned impressive.

I trailed my fingers along the top edge of the pattern, tracing the tree with roots spreading wide and deep. Wait. The story didn't end in Texas or even Azure House. I leaned closer and sucked in a breath. What in the seven hells?

The tale went along and over the lip of the mantel, going along the top before disappearing beneath the spike. Okay... this was like the windows and everything else in Azure House—not exactly what it appeared.

This was probably another bad choice in a litany of bad decisions, but perhaps the spike simply appeared to be embedded in the wood. I tugged, and nope. That bad boy was lodged tight.

"Oh well." I shrugged but kept hold of the cold iron. "Didn't hurt to try."

Suddenly, I heard a scream. *Maria!*

I sucked in a breath and spun, facing the door. Before I could call out or run to the rescue, pain sliced through my right palm. "Shit."

Well, at least there wasn't man wearing a hockey mask standing and waiting at the door.

The stinging increased, and my palm burned as it throbbed in rhythm with my heartbeat. This was not going to be good. Like at all. I curled my hand into a fist, holding it over the mantel.

Well, the good news was Maria hadn't screamed again. Wait, that could also mean that she was dead. I groaned. This was way too damned complicated. I dared a look at my hand and was happy I'd decided to keep my keep it over the wood because a: the curiously dust-free rug was too cute to bleed to death on, and b: my palm was doing its best stuck-pig imitation.

Maria rushed into the office, her eyes widening as she stared. "Whoa, are you okay?"

"Not even." I shook my head, emitting an unamused sound somewhere between a grunt and a chuckle. "I think the house is trying to kill me."

"You seem to have that effect on people."

"Gee, thanks. That's some bedside manner you got there, Nurse Ratchet."

Maria smirked. "I aim to please." Stopping in front of me, she reached up and unwrapped the scarf holding up most of my locs.

"What are you doing?" I wanted to back up, but the thought of this beautiful room looking like a crime scene kept me rooted in place.

"What's it look like?" she asked as she folded the large silk square that matched my sweater perfectly. "Here, let me see."

I shook my head, because that bandage was looking more like a tourniquet. Yes, despite the tats, I was a giant wimp. There was no shame in my game. "No, I'm fine." Which, come to think of it, my hand no longer throbbed. Blood pooled on the glossy wood, but not as much as a few seconds ago.

This house and everything connected to it was stressing me out.

"Stop being a wimp." Maria grabbed my wrist and efficiently tied the soft fabric around my hand.

"Wow, I think it's safe to say that I'll live." I wiggled my fingers. "Hey, why'd you scream? You scared the hell out of me."

"Girl, I thought I saw something move."

"Like... a mouse?" Okay, *that* sent a shiver down my spine.

"I wish." Maria shook her head. "Let's just say whatever it was hadn't been alive in a while." A sly smile tugged at her full lips, exposing the dimples I'd always coveted. "Were you worried?"

"Not even." I glared at my cousin, ignoring her wide grin. "Let's go outside. Stella has a proper first aid kit."

"Who the hell is Stella?"

"My van."

"Still weird." Maria shook her head and walked away laughing.

A frisson of electricity rolled through me.

Only this wasn't warm and welcoming like the energy when I entered the office. No, this was something else. It wasn't scary exactly, but different, and not in a good way. The buzz began at my feet, meandering through my trembling body. My mouth may have gone bone dry, but my brain was fully functional.

I got the hell out of Dodge.

By the time Maria grabbed the first aid kit from Stella's garage, the space beneath my platform bed, I was sitting on the top porch step. Did I mention that Maria was a nurse? If I hadn't known beforehand, I would have at her show of appreciation of the contents of my kit.

Maria unscrewed the bottle of hydrogen peroxide and grabbed a couple of Steristrips, opening one of the packs.

"Maria, what do you know about this house and the people who lived here?" I blurted to distract myself. That whole peroxide not stinging was a lie. Yes, it was better than alcohol, but only marginally.

"Not much. Everybody 'round here acts like it's top secret and I don't have a clearance." She unwrapped my hand and poked around at my palm.

"Hey." I tugged at my hand, but she held tight.

"Stop being a baby. Considering all that blood you left on the mantel, it's not as bad as I thought." She poured the dreaded liquid on my palm, and we watched it bubble.

Hm, no pain. I could get down with that.

We sat in silence as Maria wielded her medical magic. While I may not have returned to Hoodoo in years, Loretta kept me up to date on the goings on. If gossip was an Olympic sport, then Loretta held multiple gold medals. She'd told me that Maria did private care nursing in the neighboring township. The Woodlands was one of those upscale planned communities, complete with mini mansions, the mall, and an outdoor music arena.

In other words, there was money there, and Maria took every dollar she could.

She deftly dried my hand with gauze and applied the small fabric wound closure. After one last swipe of her finger and the addition of a bandage, she nodded and gently squeezed my hand. "All done. What I do know is that no one has been inside since your mama left."

"No one? I'm sure Aunt Rose sent one of her minions to—"

"No one. Zip. Nada."

"But that was..." I looked up at Maria, stunned.

No.

Freaking.

Way.

Maria nodded and replaced the top on the peroxide bottle. Then she gave me a look that simultaneously said both nothing and everything. "Exactly."

We sat in silence a good thirty seconds as I looked out over the yard and down one of the rarer hills in East Texas and studied the cemetery. Not going to lie, as far as neighbors, I could have done worse. If the dead stayed off my property and out of my business, then we'd be cool.

I jerked as my words replayed. My property. No, I shook my head. I didn't want any of it. Not the house, not the town, and not the lingering animosity. But handing it over to a stranger?

Over my dead body.

"Better?" Maria nudged my shoulder.

"Yeah, much. Thanks." I looked at the quickly healing scar. A scar that in less than five minutes had stopped hurting. Nope, not even going to think about. Not today. Not tomorrow or—ever.

Yes, bourbon and avoidance were my best friends.

I stood, smoothing the front of my jeans. Enough fuckery for the day. "No more exploring. How about an early lunch?"

"You buying?"

"Of course. That's the least I could do after your medical expertise." I walked toward the van. "I'm starving. Hell, I can't remember the last time I..." I said to the empty space to my right.

When I spun around, it was to find Maria standing on the porch steps where I left her, looking baffled.

"What's up?" I asked.

"I left my phone in the library."

"I'll get it. Come to think of it, I should lock up the house. I know this is Hoodoo, but..."

"Girl, this ain't southwest Houston. The worst thing that's happened in this town since your drama was a drunk driving accident that took out the front of Miss Gloria's Clips and Claws."

"Whatever." I rolled my eyes then jogged past her. "Hang on, I'll grab it. God forbid you go an hour or two without your digital pacifier."

"Like you're so different." Maria followed me inside. "Don't want you getting killed before I get my free meal." She tossed the words over her shoulder while walking past me, headed straight for the library.

Maybe this time she could share some body fluids for the cause. I shouldn't be so mean, but damn if I couldn't hide the grin.

"Nothing says I love you like..." Maria paused; no, not paused, but stopped so suddenly, her Dansko clogs damn near squeaked at the threshold of the office.

What now?

When I stopped beside her, my vocal cords went on strike. If I wasn't wearing mascara and didn't want to look like a raccoon's taller, curvier sister, I would have rubbed my eyes, but at this point, all I could do was blink.

And blink again.

"Please tell me that was there before we left," Maria whispered, her voice filled with something that sounded like fear mixed with awe.

I stared at the mantel, the one devoid of blood, and in a different position. "Unless I lost more blood than I remember, that black hole into the unknown wasn't there."

Was it weird that I was both psyched and more than a little nervous about owning a house with a door leading to a hidden lair?

"Look, your phone's on the mantel," I whispered. Because cool or not, Maria was armed with more than her wits.

Maria, being the bad-ass Black woman she was, shoved me into the room.

I'd like to say that I marched to the mantel, grabbed the phone, and used the flashlight to get my Dora the Explora on. But...that would be a big fat lie. Because something was down there and waiting—for me.

What I did do was snag Maria's phone from the now blood-free mantel and sprinted the hell out of this damned fifty shades of spooky house. It was never too late to back out of this ridiculous bargain that felt too much like blackmail.

But should I?

Chapter 7

MARIA AND I STOOD IN the entrance area of the Crossroads Café, home of the best breakfast in East Texas. The cholesterol-hiking scent of cottage fries loaded with onions and peppers, bacon, and chicken fried steak welcomed us to the restaurant with open arms.

The Crossroads Café looked like a cliche straight off a Hollywood lot. Except here, the food was full of fat and laden with calories. In other words, perfect. In all the years I'd visited the café, regardless of how busy it was, the black-and-white floor always sparkled. I wondered if they'd replaced the large tiles or the floor had been bespelled, because they looked the same.

Either Maria was a Hollywood-caliber actress, or the discovery of a secret portal was no big deal. "Why are you not freaked out?" I asked.

She shook her head and made a noise somewhere between a groan and a laugh. "Your house. Your ghosts. Your mess to deal with." Maria crossed her arms.

"Soooo you're not coming back?" I couldn't tell whether it was relief or worry making my stomach do a tumbling routine.

"Girl, please. I need to make sure you don't slip through a portal or some weird shit. So don't you worry. I'll go back in that house with your scary ass." Maria grabbed two menus off the holder next to the register and strutted into the diner like she owned the joint.

Eleven am, that beautiful lull between lunch and breakfast, which meant finding a table wouldn't be a problem this Wednesday morning. But on weekends, the restaurant was hopping until it closed at three.

"Gwendolyn Diane Carter, is that you?" The owner, a buxom Black woman who would never allow a bland-ass hairnet to touch her hair, walked around the corner rocking a festive red print scarf in a complicated wrap that matched her apron. No one could ever accuse Miss Sadie of being boring.

"Hey, Miss Sadie." I smiled.

After the craziness of this morning, seeing her non-magical and oh so familiar face was a joy. Not that Miss Sadie didn't have power. Honey, those pies of hers *had* to be laced with crack. Because one bite, hell, one slice was never enough. Good thing men in this town appreciated thick women. And the way it smelled in here, I was about add a little more junk to my trunk. I wiggled my fingers. "It's good to see you."

Miss Sadie wrapped me in a hug that smelled of coffee, cinnamon, and comfort. "Girl, it sure is good to see you," she said as she pulled back, holding on to my arms. "Larry," she bellowed, "look who's in town!"

Had I mentioned her mouth was as big as her heart? If I'd forgotten, my ringing ears were a potent reminder.

"What about me?" Maria interrupted, wading in to the rescue with a wink and a grin.

"What about you? Girl, you're in here damn near every day. You don't give me a chance to miss you." Miss Sadie nudged Maria's arm before giving her a quick hug. "Go on and find yourself a table and I'll bring you out some coffee. Gwen, you want some too?"

"Yes, ma'am," I said.

"Unlike that one," Miss Sadie nodded at Maria, "you always were sweet."

Larry yelled through the open pass-through that led to the kitchen. "Sadie, you leave my next wife alone. Maria, don't you listen to her. Sadie just mad I didn't give her none last night."

Miss Sadie flicked her fingers at her husband of half a million years. "You old fool, that girl don't want you."

Laughter along with a couple of not-quite-bawdy comments filled the small café. Yeah, Hoodoo had its faults, but it was home. At least for a little while more.

"Hey, Gwen." Larry waved with one hand while working the grill with the other. The big man looked like a ginger Viking with a Marine Corp haircut. But dude was a giant teddy bear.

"Hey yourself." I tilted my head to the side and somehow my grin got even bigger. You're looking as handsome as ever." And he really was. Had Larry and Miss Sadie been in another small Texas town back in the day, would they have had the courage to pursue their relationship?

I hoped so. Talk about opposites. They were both gregarious, but Larry had a more serious side, and the man was protective of his wife and children. To look at him, one would categorize the tall, broad, and white former Marine as a good old boy. And he was to some extent, until folks started talking out of the side of their necks.

He shut bigots and jerks down with a quickness. And if words didn't work, Larry wasn't against using those hands.

"Don't be letting Sadie hear you; she's likely to get jealous." Larry winked, then disappeared into his kitchen kingdom.

"Ignore his old behind. I do," Miss Sadie stage-whispered as the chime over the door jingled and she called out greetings to the next patrons.

Maria and I found our way to a booth next to the window. "I'd honestly forgotten this part. You people are strange." I laughed and tapped my menu against the table.

"Well, you better get used to it." Maria flipped her plastic menu open, hiding her face, but not before I spotted her crooked smile.

"After that little surprise, I'm not sure I want to stay—consequences be damned." I stared out the window at the half wine barrels exploding with tulips and lush ferns, gleaming storefront windows, and the tidy trash-free gutters. Hoodoo, Texas—Mayberry with melanin and magic.

And folks all up in your business. Only here, Andy and Barney were not only smoking hot, but occasionally sported fangs and fur.

"Why not stay? This is your home."

I sighed, then pursed my lips. "Next subject." I traced the sparkle of the Formica table and watched the happy people walking down the sidewalk.

For a shining few moments when I stepped into the library, I'd been entranced enough to believe that maybe, just maybe staying wasn't such a bad idea. Was I was ready to deal with the witches' vitriol and the shifters' suspicion? I could deal with their bullshit. But did I want to? Life was too short to intentionally be miserable.

However, discomfort may be a small price to pay to keep Azure House in the family.

"How 'bout we talk about you getting shot." Maria crossed her arms and leaned back against the red pleather. "And while you're at it, what kind of miracle drugs they have in Morocco that you're running around like new in three weeks?"

"Here you go, ladies." The waitress put two white mugs filled with chicory coffee and a carafe on the table. "What can I get you this morning?"

While watching the waitress's high pony swish back and forth as she walked away, I realized that I'd fallen so deep in my thoughts, I had ordered, yet still had no memory of what she looked like other than white, young, and attractive. Not only was that rude, but sloppy.

Were I anywhere but Hoodoo, I'd say my lack of attention could also be downright dangerous. But hell, there were few places I was safer. I bet everyone, including the three old women across the way, was strapped. A robber would be screwed if they walked in this joint.

As amusing as I found all that, I couldn't afford to be careless. For one, I couldn't be sure I was curse-free, and two—I had to decide whether I truly wanted to be the keeper of my family's legacy.

After the whole hidden stairway debacle, all signs were pointing to no.

Like a pile of blocks, I reassembled my vertebrae until I sat up straight. In my world, fortification wasn't complete without caffeine. I gulped a few scorching mouthfuls before returning the half-empty cup to the table.

Maria studied me as she filled her white mug with enough cream and sugar to qualify her beverage as a dessert.

In addition to good food and mostly good people, I finally had the freedom to discuss all things magic. For so long, I'd been forced to keep everything—my feelings, my family, and most of all, my secrets—so bottled up, sharing felt...odd.

But I was going to do it anyway. I looked around the café as people went on with their lives unconcerned about my drama. Right here, right now, I had support from someone who *knew*. Leaning my arms on the pristine white table, I let loose. "You know about the curse, right?"

Maria shook her head. "No. The old folks around here refuse to talk about it. You going to put me out of my misery?"

"That's just the thing." I drummed my short nails against the side of my mug. "The only thing I know for sure is that the women from my branch of the family tree are cursed to die early." I raised both my hands, palms facing her. "And before you ask, I don't know the whys or what fors, only that if I lived past my forty-fifth birthday, that, allegedly, I was safe."

"Holy shit," Maria whispered and leaned closer. "Do you believe it? I mean, the part about you being safe."

"I don't know." I sighed, and my shoulders sank. So much for that earlier pep talk. "I sure as hell hope so. I let my guard down too early before, and it almost got me dead."

"Is that why you came back to Hoodoo?"

"Yes. And no."

The waitress returned.

Harriet, said an open cursive font on her white name tag. She was cute. Blonde in a way that didn't come from a bottle, but women spent a mint trying to get. She had the wholesome white girl look down so pat, she could earn serious dollars making commercials. But that name was unfortunate, and about fifty years too old for the young woman who was twenty tops.

"Here you go, two short stacks with bacon." After she set the plates down, Harriet looked at me as if she wanted to say something, then shook her head, smiled, and took off.

Maria must have noticed my look of confusion and laughed. "Get used to it. You're a celebrity in this town."

"That was... weird."

"Yup, kind of like you. Enough about life on the Z list; tell me about the curse and getting shot."

"The short version? I was finishing up a job in Dublin when I was found." I took a sip of coffee and rolled my eyes. "That's a conversation for something stronger than coffee. Let's just say it was a night filled with assassins, trains, planes, and automobiles. With help, I made it to Morocco and what I believed to be safety, but..." I shrugged, then concentrated on my pancakes.

"But what? You can't just leave a sister hanging." Maria cut into pancakes so fluffy, I was surprised they didn't float away.

"A...um...new friend took me to an oasis for a picnic and—"

"Hold up." Maria waved her fork. "How you going to just throw that out there like it's nothing."

"What?" I bit into my own pancakes and moaned. Yup, the food was as good as I remembered.

"Oh, so I like went on a picnic in the desert with a hot guy." Maria did an awful imitation that made me sound like a Valley girl. "Spill, bitch."

I laughed. Damn, these people were rude.

"I didn't say he was handsome."

"You didn't have to; you had that look."

I smiled, and despite myself, relaxed, thinking about Ash. He was...well, a lot of things. In many ways, he reminded me of Uncle Raul, except Ash wasn't a vampire. As a matter of fact, he was all human, but powerful in a way I couldn't understand. I liked it, and him. A lot. But hell, we hadn't even kissed before I was shot.

And after, he was so... freaking sweet.

Maria waved her fork at me. "See, there you go again. Dish."

"Honestly, there's not much to tell. We met, he took me to his kick-ass compound, then flew me for a day trip, where I was shot." I shrugged. Like anything about Ash was simple—or uncomplicated. "But he's... a lot."

"Handsome and rich?" Maria asked, her voice filled with something like awe.

"To answer your question, yes and yes."

Oh boy, was he handsome. And dangerous. Not necessarily to me, but also like Uncle Raul, Ash seemed to be a man one didn't cross without dire consequences. I pulled out my phone and a picture of the two of us smiling and laughing just before we took off to the desert.

"Holy shit. Does he have a brother?" Maria finally tore her gaze from the screen.

"Not that I know of. And yeah, like I said, he's a lot." I trailed my finger through the condensation on my water glass. Leaving Morocco and Ash was far more difficult than it should have been. Which was why I needed to be a continent away. It wasn't far enough.

"Are you going to see him again?" Maria looked almost hopeful. Like I was her last chance to watch a fairytale unfold.

"I doubt it. Our last date didn't go so well."

"He ditched you after you got shot?" Her voice darkened.

"Oh no. Not at all. He was incredible. Like if I had to pick a man to be at my side during recovery, I couldn't have selected better." I looked out the window. Did I want to see Ash again? Yes. But did I want him involved in the craziness that was my life? Absolutely not.

"It's not Ash, it's me," I added before Maria went off on a tangent, threatening to shoot the man—or worse. Since I was laying it out, might as well put all my trash on the table. "I have another cloud over my life. Except for one man, every person I've been intimate with has met sudden and gruesome deaths."

"Holy shit. You're like a regular black widow."

"Gee thanks, Maria. You sure know how to make a woman feel good." I shook my head and chuckled. Hell, it was either that or cry.

"What can I say. It's a gift." She shrugged, then leaned her elbows on the table. "Well, I know at least one man, or should I say wolf still breathing."

The jangle of the bells above the door interrupted the interrogation.

Both Maria and I glanced at the door, our reactions immediate. I groaned, then clenched my teeth, while my least favorite cousin as of two seconds ago guffawed.

"Speak of the devil." Maria rapped her knuckles twice against the table before sitting back as if preparing to watch the show.

As if the thought conjured him into existence, Carlos sauntered into the café. Whether it was the cop in Carlos or the wolf, he looked around the room. Of course, his gaze landed on me like a ton of judgmental bricks.

"May I take those plates for you ladies?" Harriet stopped by the table, breaking my stare-down with the good sheriff.

"That would be great." I looked up at the waitress, who still had that youthful glow. The one announcing that life hadn't beat her down yet.

And I hoped it never did.

"Now that you're back in town, is there a chance you'll do one of those reality shows out of Conjure Ink? Something exciting needs to happen in Hoodoo." Harriet couldn't hide the hopefulness in her green eyes.

"Yeah," a woman said from another table.

"That would bring a lot of business to town," a man wearing denim overalls added.

"It's not like anyone here is hurting for money," I said, kind of chuckling.

Because, unlike most small towns, Hoodoo was flush with cash and provided its citizens a universal income. The other difference was that young people were fully supported, graduating college without debt thanks to a fund set up by the supernaturals in town. And if those graduates returned, low-interest small business loans were available.

"I don't know about you fancy Hollywood types, but one can never have enough money," an old woman with blue hair called out. "Right, Sheriff?"

"Gwendolyn doesn't care about the goings-on in Hoodoo. She's leaving."

"Oh no." Miss Sadie put her fists against her ample hips. "I was hoping you'd stick around so I could finally get that tattoo."

"I'm sure one of the other folks at the shop can help you. Miss High and Mighty has better things to do." Carlos stared as if expecting me to cower .

"Don't answer for me." I pressed my palms against the table to keep from beaning him with my empty coffee mug.

"Why? *I know you*." His deep voice was somewhere between a purr and a growl. And all the way sexy.

The prick.

"No. You *knew* me." And abandoned me. Something that I would have never done to him. That's what people did. They left. They disappointed. They died. In the end, like always, I found myself alone. The slow upward curving of my lips were more of a threat than a smile.

And damn, it felt good.

We stared at each other for a few tense seconds before I spoke, my words fired as rapidly as bullets. "That girl is gone. You helped knock the shine off her years ago." I spread my arms. "So maybe I should express gratitude rather than what I really want to say."

The café had gone quiet, people looking back and forth between Carlos and me like spectators at Wimbledon.

"And what would that be?" His eyes flashed amber.

Carlos may not be the big 'A' alpha, but he was a high-ranking pack member. Challenging any shifter after their animal peeked through probably wasn't the best of ideas.

Ask me if I cared.

I looked down at my neat nails, then let out a bored sigh before glancing back at the annoyed sheriff. "One guess. Two words. Seven letters. To keep you from taxing that little brain of yours, I'll even give you a hint. The first word starts with an f, and the second an o."

"Daaaammmmmn," Maria whispered with something like awe, or it could have been fear, filling her voice.

"Still reckless and self-centered." Carlos looked at me, his fiery gaze pausing at my lips before moseying down my torso like a caress. When it returned to my face, his beautiful brown eyes were filled with...disgust. "Finish your food and leave. This time, try not to kill anyone."

Someone gasped. Another someone, I think Miss Sadie, admonished Carlos for being rude.

But I couldn't hear past the blood pounding in my ears and the electricity pressing against my fingertips demanding an exit. "Well, it's a good thing you're the sheriff and not a fortune teller. I'm staying."

Chapter 8

THE ANCESTORS WASN'T the only thing that had changed. I closed Stella's door, hit the alarm, then against my will, grinned up at Dhesi's, the local supermarket. The former neon sign was long gone and replaced with the store's name scrawled across the windows in a thick retro font. Downtown Hoodoo had never been raggedy, but it was now refreshed and updated with new paint, flower boxes, and reproduction antique streetlamps.

After the run-in with Carlos at the Crossroads Café yesterday, Maria and I finished chit-chatting about the house, the future, and my temper. Of course, I blamed my bitchiness on hormones and hunger rather than nostalgia and regret.

Yesterday, I made a trip to The Woodlands, checked into the Marriott Hotel on the waterway, and treated myself to a massage, room service, and every bit of pampering available. Because tonight was about picking up supplies and motivating myself to get to freaking work.

Tomorrow, I planned to clean Azure House and get her fit for habitation. Which wouldn't be too bad since the interior was remarkably free of both rodents and ruination.

And I was thankful for it.

I strolled into the store, and it took all of ten minutes to regret not shopping at the H.E.B. on Market Street, rather than returning to town. But noooo, I wanted to support a local business, forgetting that I'd also give fodder to the gossips. After a few minutes, I blocked out the gawkers rolling by in their squeaky overloaded baskets, and focused on the task at hand.

So, I, Betty Badass, seer of ghosts and tattoo artist extraordinaire, managed to turn a simple shopping trip into a marathon session of gathering groceries. Everyone knew stress eating wasn't your friend. But judging by the items in my cart, stress shopping was also a no-no.

As I reached for another bag of Oreos, I froze as a ghost who looked like he was on his way to the O.K. Corral tipped his hat at me before walking through the shelves loaded with chips of every flavor then straight into the freezer section.

Note to self, fresh veggies only. I did not want frozen peas covered with ghost cooties.

"Shit." I forgot to buy art supplies. There should be something in the van, but just in case, I'd grab a notebook and some pencils to take home and draw.

Home...

That hunk of an almost beautiful house was mine. Unless brain-eating zombies or soul-sucking demons lived in the basement, I'd make up for all the love Azure House hadn't received—at least until I left in six months.

Unable to help myself, I chuckled. I was like a woman dating someone for the potential rather than the reality. The exterior of Azure House was a hot mess. Hell, I wouldn't be surprised if she didn't start falling apart on purpose. But that's okay, I was up to the challenge.

While Carlos and maybe even Rita would believe my change of plans were out of spite, that wasn't it. Well, not all of it. I wanted—no, needed—answers. And I would get them, whether from Azure House, Aunt Rose, the rest of the family, or a combination of the three. And I had another ace up my sleeve should I decide to accept his assistance—Duncan.

I shook my head and grunted.

Yeah, that wasn't going to work. How could I trust the person who forced me into a blood vow to keep the secret of his mystery partner? Then, as if that wasn't bad enough, Duncan's death looked more like a murder than a suicide.

Especially to Carlos.

But, for now, broken hearts and shattered friendships would have to be tabled. My immediate issue was the origin of the family curse. Why did most of the women in my twisted branch of the family tree die early? Why not Rose or the descendants of Daisy, the second sister? Was the curse good and truly broken?

And the most important question: would my future lovers meet similar fates as the last few?

Because you best believe that the last thing I needed in Hoodoo was anyone connected to me mysteriously or magically dropping dead.

But for the moment, my life was reduced to arguing with myself, while debating the merits of double-stuffed Oreos, when obviously, the cookie was the true hero.

Without looking, I placed my snacks in the cart as gingerly as I would have handled a carton of organic farm-raised eggs laid by blessed chickens. The fine hairs on my arms stood on end, each hair frosting until a white halo hovered above my tattoos.

"Whoever you are, leave me the heck alone," I all but growled, not bothering to check out my new company.

If big hair placed you closer to God, then the woman staring at me as she pushed her processed-food-laden cart must be a damned saint. She could have at least attempted to avoid staring at me like I had a one-way ticket over the cuckoo's nest.

Then again, only one of us conversated with ghosts in public. I pointed to my ear, wagging my finger at an imaginary wireless earbud, then nodded.

She gave me a half-assed smile before scurrying away.

Don't worry, lady, I'm not contagious.

I looked over my shoulder, and of course, she was already whispering with another stretch pants and Crocs-wearing woman.

When they looked in my direction, I may have snapped a little. "If you want to know something, ask. Don't just make shit up."

Their eyes widened, then like roaches exposed to light, they split.

"Cowards."

I smiled at the next person that came down the aisle and then headed back to the meat department. Thank goodness Hoodoo wasn't about that vegetarian life. Back in the day, Dhesi's sourced their meat, poultry, and as much of the produce as possible locally. It was cheaper to buy veggies at the store than the Saturday morning farmer's market. Those prices were jacked up for the bougie folks venturing across the tracks to what they considered the "low-rent" district.

They had no freaking idea.

I reached the beef section and smiled. "Now that's what I'm talking about." I trailed a finger across a package holding a marbleized T-bone so pretty, the damned thing was probably nibbling grass yesterday. After snagging two, my lust moved to a package of baby backs.

"Finally, something you and I can agree on," said the second to the last man on the planet I wanted to hear from—Carlos.

"You have got to be kidding me." The words slipped out like steam from a pressure cooker. To keep from exploding, I counted to ten—in English, followed by Spanish, French, then my dusty Latin.

It still wasn't enough.

"Gwennie..." Unlike the last time, Carlos' tone lacked disdain.

My heart lurched at the childhood nickname. Call me shallow, but hating Carlos would be easier if he didn't look like a muscular snack. He wore his usual jeans, but rather than the khaki work shirt with the city patches on the sleeves, the sexy sheriff wore an unbuttoned black sports coat over an indigo blue shirt.

I was feeling all warm and gushy until I recalled him being a big tool yesterday at the Crossroads Café. I shook my head, then blindly grabbed not only the T-bones, but both beef and pork ribs. Looked like I planned to take stress eating to a whole new level.

"Goodnight, Sheriff," I said, placing my food in the cart, then gripped the handles. Without even half a backward glance, I pushed the cart forward.

"Wait." Carlos wrapped his warm, slightly calloused fingers around my bicep. "We need to talk."

I looked from his tanned fingers covering the vivid tattoos inked on my dark skin up to the hard line of his lips. There was a time when that mouth would curve upwards whenever I stepped into a room. A time when neither the man nor his wolf hated me.

I hardened both my heart and my tone. "What you need to do is get your damn hand off of me."

He stepped closer—without releasing my arm—lowering both his chin and his voice. "It's not like that. I—"

"Don't give a damn what it's like," rumbled a male voice with a slight upper-crust British accent. "Remove your hand from Gwendolyn's arm should you wish to keep it."

Only one man pronounced my name as if it were a prayer, rather than something that went out of vogue three decades ago.

I spun around.

"Ash." I'm not even going to lie; the man was illegally hot. Dude looked like he could have been a pharaoh. Then again, wearing that uninterrupted black outfit, including an insanely sweet pair of pointed leather shoes, he looked more like an assassin or a business mogul.

My smile reached straight down to my toes, stopping off at a few other places below the belt. "What are you doing here?"

Carlos growled and his fingers tightened, his nails biting into the tender flesh of my inner bicep.

I looked back at the man who should have never put his hands on me. I didn't play that pulling me around bullshit. Well, outside of sexy times. But this wasn't that kind of party.

"What the hell is wrong with you?" I asked, lowering my voice.

In response, Carlos' eyes flashed, lightening from their usual chocolate brown to something closer to copper. This was going to get bad — like with a quickness. I relaxed my body by lowering my chin as I stopped tugging against his hold. In other words, I'd become as submissive as I could while wearing clothes. "Carlos...."

"Shit." He looked down at my bicep and his eyes flashed again. While he hadn't set me free, his grip loosened as he stroked his thumb across the small wolf print tattoo hidden within my Japanese-inspired half-sleeve. "I guess I left a mark after all." His voice had gone all growly again, but for a different reason.

I shivered as his hand fell away, his fingertips caressing the skin from my bicep to my wrist, pausing with his thumb on my thudding pulse.

"I have no idea what you're talking about," I managed to say around the heart that had skipped straight to my throat.

"If you say so." Carlos tapped his index finger against the side of his nose. *Jerk.*

Carlos was alpha enough to smell a lie. And yours truly had just told a big fat one. Oops. I rolled my shoulders, backed up a step, then turned and grinned at Ash.

This would have been a good time for Carlos to remove himself from the vicinity, but no...

This was my life we were talking about. Instead, Carlos walked around me, pausing with his arms hanging loose and his legs spread wide. After looking Ash up and down, Carlos let out a huff of disapproval. "Who the hell are you?"

Rather than become offended, Ash relaxed and smiled down at me. "Is this the usual Texas greeting? Fisticuffs alongside the porterhouses?" When Ash looked back at Carlos, his expression grew deadly, but his voice remained as casual as if the two were speaking about the weather. "Who or what I am is none of your concern."

Carlos pushed his jacket back, exposing the badge and gun riding on his hip.

Ash stepped closer to Carlos. "And that's supposed to impress me... how?" he asked, voice filled with equal parts boredom and humor.

"Ash, please," I whispered.

There must have been an announcement for a blue light special on ribs. Because at least seven people—mostly women—stood watching.

Not that I'd blame anyone for checking out either man. Ash was... a lot. We'd met in Dublin on the eve of my forty-fifth birthday. Apparently, he'd been low-key stalking me for a tattoo. I turned him down flat—even with the hefty paycheck. Dude was hot and all, but I didn't trust him then.

Yet, with one early morning phone call, Ash had unwittingly ensured I'd escaped Ireland and the monsters determined to end my life.

Ash's eyes narrowed for a nanosecond before he nodded at Carlos, then retreated the few steps to return to my side.

"Ash Modeus, this is Hoodoo's sheriff, Carlos Hernandez." I rested my hands on the cart handle. Anything to keep from touching Ash. I'm not sure what it was about him, but when I woke up after getting shot, all I wanted to do was wrap myself around the man and bury my face against his neck. Oh, and I wouldn't have minded him burying other things in select places.

But the intense attraction felt abnormal—at least for me.

I tilted my head and looked at the pissed-off Carlos. "Was there anything else?"

"Have you seen Ilona?" Carlos all but barked.

"Who?" I frowned, which for some reason, made the lines in Carlos' forehead ease.

"The redhead from the bar." He looked over at our audience, then lowered his voice. "The one you threatened."

Chapter 9

I STOOD BETWEEN THE radishes and cucumbers trying to wrap my head around what had just happened. The whole tattoo fiasco was...pathetic. I preferred to blame the tiny wolf paw prints on the rapper Eve and tequila. Which would be a big fat lie.

The truth was that I'd been lonely and the only cup I'd fallen into was that of self-pity.

After Carlos asked me about that rude heifer, I walked away, leaving him and Ash talking about lawyers and improper questioning or some mess. I wasn't a clueless schoolgirl who didn't recognize when a man wanted her. Well, mostly. But that absolutely, positively was not the case with Carlos.

So why did he flash on Ash like that?

With a soft hiss, a mist of water shot out of the small nozzles above the array of colorful veggies. I wrapped my fingers around a large, firm cucumber, which sent my mind on a dangerous detour. It had to do with a certain unexpected visitor and whipped cream and—

"Don't worry." Ash's warm breath caressed my ear, and yay me, I managed to not moan in the produce section. "The sheriff lives," he said.

"Not my problem."

Between the refrigerated coolness at my front and Ash's heat against my back, my body sprang into overdrive. I glanced over my shoulder at Ash's grin and sucked in a breath. Was it possible he'd even gotten more handsome?

"So, let's say your acquaintance should disappear. You'd not miss him?" Ash chuckled behind me, the vibration stretching the limits of my self-control.

I spun around, putting a little space between us before something dirty happened. Talk about being the subject of town gossip. Some of the things I could do with and to this man were still illegal in some states. "Hey," I managed to croak.

In my mind, I was sexy and sophisticated. In reality, I probably looked like a giant grinning dork. The best part? I didn't give a crap. At this big age, being anyone other than myself was energy and time I didn't have.

Either accept me as is—or kick rocks.

Ash and I were neither lovers nor friends. He was about to become the former when I was shot. And since he was here, I suspected we'd at least become the latter.

I extended my hand. "I'm not sure why you came to my small and unexciting corner of the world, but I'm glad to see you."

"And I you." He pressed a soft kiss on my forehead.

Before I knew it, I'd slid my arms around his waist, sinking into his warmth, and holding tight. Damn, he smelled good. Like sex, sand, and sunshine, but with an undernote of ruthlessness. What did it say about my character, or lack thereof, that dangerous men did it for me? I'm sure my therapist would say it's a result of my father figure being a centuries-old vampire.

Ash pulled away, cupping my face. "Now that was worth crossing an ocean for."

"You tell the prettiest lies." We both chuckled, slipping back into the pal zone. Love I didn't do, but a woman could never have enough friends.

When I looked back up at Ash, it was to find him studying me. "Why are you here?" I blurted. No one could ever accuse me of being a flatterer.

"You owe me, and I've come to collect."

"Fine, since you're so determined to be a pest." I gave him my best fake glower then grabbed a bunch of radishes. "So, how long do I have you for?" I asked as I pushed the cart down the aisle, grabbing bib lettuce, avocados, and tomatoes.

"How long would you need?" He looked up and down my body, smiling when he reached my boots.

"Would it be fair to assume you planned to participate in... ranch work?" Ash's lips tightened as if he were holding back a laugh.

"As a matter of fact, yes. Well, not ranch work, but I inherited a house." I left out the haunted part. "It needs a little TLC and elbow grease." *And perhaps an exorcist.* I leaned my forearms against the cart, resting my foot on the bar across the bottom.

"I excel at manual labor. I'd be happy to help for as long as you need."

I glanced at his perfectly trimmed and buffed nails and let out a disbelieving snort. "Really?"

"Don't let the smooth taste fool you." He spread his bent arms and shrugged. The action was so incongruous with his polished, urbane, and deadly exterior, I couldn't help but laugh.

"Okay, but trust me, you may live to regret it when you see Azure House." I continued throwing things in the cart, happy that I wouldn't spend my first few nights in the house alone. I wasn't afraid, because I loved my own company. But Maria had been right. Solitude was a choice, and tonight, I was choosing differently. "Have you eaten?" I lowered my voice and leaned closer. "Lie if you must. I'm starving."

Ash dipped his chin, black eyes alit with laughter. "It would be my honor to dine with you."

"You're so fancy." I enjoyed making Ash laugh. He struck me as a man who didn't do it as much as he should. Maybe that was something we could change during his visit.

Ash and I spent the next few minutes shopping, laughing, catching up, and talking about nothing of importance.

And it was perfect.

I'd been so wrapped up in his delight and disgust of the highly processed and chemical-laden foods on American shelves, I hadn't noticed the two elderly women until they passed us the third time. The way they checked out Ash's butt, they hadn't returned for canned tuna.

"The citizens of Hoodoo are quite curious." Ash chuckled.

"You can say that again." I turned and had to bite back a laugh when the older Hispanic woman gave me two approving thumbs up. "You're new in town. They can't handle all that hotness."

"You don't seem to be having any difficulties."

I shrugged. "Takes more than a pretty smile and a nice butt to impress me."

He stepped closer and lowered his voice. "How about a big, thick…"

My heart shifted into a rumba cadence.

"…bank account." Ash grinned.

I snorted, then burst out laughing. "Woo, Mr. Fancy Pants got jokes." I wiped at my eyes. Whether it was stress surrounding Azure House or Carlos' weird response to Ash, the laughter loosened the lasso binding my stomach tight. Tonight, I would ignore the sibilant warning that danger still haunted me.

Tonight, I would have fun.

Ash dipped his chin, giving me *that* look. The one promising to wreck me in the best of ways. "You'd be surprised—and pleased—with what else I got."

His use of improper grammar sent me into another fit of giggles. But they dried up at the sight of a different set of women at the other end of the aisle. "Great," I muttered.

His gaze followed mine. "Problem?"

"That would be one way of putting it." I pressed my lips together to keep from yelling something foolish and looking like an immature ass in front of Ash.

He shifted, blocking my view of the five witches. Which was...nice. But nothing Ash could do would protect me from the wounds left by cruel words and false accusations.

"Oh, conflict of the female variety, I assume." When I neither confirmed nor denied the statement, Ash shook his head. "Should you wish, I can ensure those witches never bother you again."

For a few sputtering heartbeats, I froze. No blinking, no breathing, no nothing. Hell, even the frigid breeze from the ceiling air conditioning vent paused.

"Gwendolyn?" Ash squeezed my shoulders. "Are you unwell?"

I shook myself out of what felt like a dream, or a premonition or something. Because there was no way in hell Ash could see or sense their magic. Or could he? I stared into his inky and damned near ageless eyes before catching the small set of wrinkles between his thick dark brows.

Once again, I tried to unlock the door that led to that part of me which sensed the others, the supernatural, the non-human. And...nothing.

"You speak like a man lost in time." I smiled. It wasn't large or toothy; I didn't believe I could manage that big of a lie. Not today. Plus, if by chance the sexy Mr. Ash Modeus was playing human, he'd know.

"Is that a problem?" He ran his thumb across the wolf print tattoo as Carlos had done earlier.

My lady parts did a happy dance. "Not at all," I whispered. Remaining unaffected with Ash looking at me with enough heat to start a forest fire, it was a miracle I could string syllables together.

He slid an arm around my waist, pressing his palm against the small of my back, leading my body until it pressed against his. Ash paused, as if asking for permission.

If I were a deer, he would be the headlights speeding down the dark road. I couldn't move, nor did I want to.

"Just so we're clear, this isn't about the women watching us, the good sheriff prowling around the store, the tattoo you owe me, or the guilt that haunts me because you were harmed while under my protection."

Comparing Ash and me to an unavoidable collision wasn't an apt description. Oh no, he was a dark and deadly spider, and I'd allowed myself to become ensnared in his web. The only problem was that I wasn't sure I wanted to escape.

My vocal cords finally came to life. "Then what is this about?"

"You. I want you, Gwendolyn, ugly boots and all," he whispered right before pressing his smiling lips against mine.

Chapter 10

YEE-FUCKING-HAW.

Kissing Ash was an experience. One so damned good, I knew that another press of his body and lips against mine, and I'd be hooked. Terror and hunger warred in my body. For now, this moment, I surrendered to lust. I needed this, needed him, to feel desired rather than hated or tolerated. The yearning, both mine and Ash's, caught fire, scorching me to my very soul.

At some point, Ash's hand had left my cheek, and had slid around the back of my neck and his fingers now rested between my locs as he pressed my body against the shelves.

"Get a room," a man said, his voice ringing with judgment.

"They could use mine." This time it was a woman, and from what I heard over the blood rushing to my head, she was Team Do Ash.

Thank goodness, he ended the kiss, since I lacked the strength. Ash pressed his forehead against mine, then stroked his thumb along my cheekbone. "Now *that* is an appropriate greeting."

I opened my mouth to speak, but I couldn't quite manage. So I cleared my throat and tried again. "Well, I didn't think our first kiss would be next to the creamed corn, but okay."

Ash swiped his tongue across his bottom lip. "But you've been thinking about a first kiss."

"Nope, not at all." I chuckled at the blatant lie. My smile as well as my heart saddened at the harsh reality. So I slipped deep into resting bitch face and shrugged. "As lovely as that was—"

"Lovely?" His eyebrows became acquainted with his hairline.

"Ego need stroking much?" I kept talking before he decided to convince me otherwise. "It was stupendous. Happy now?" I stepped right, giving me room to breathe without getting drugged by his super pheromones. "It won't be happening again—like ever."

"If you insist." He kissed the tip of my nose then snagged the cart as if domestication were the most ordinary thing in the world for a billionaire.

I stood watching Ash as he walked away. Maybe we could be friends—even without the benefits.

Finally, he noticed I wasn't at his side and looked over his shoulder. "Come." He jerked his head toward the other end of the aisle. "Let us finish gathering your groceries."

"I have everything I need," I said, still not moving.

"No, Gwendolyn." His dark gaze captured mine, conveying a plethora of sensual promises. "You do not."

Nope, I wasn't going to take the bait.

"However, I'll be here when you're ready." Despite being a good three feet away, his words were like a caress, a whisper, a vow. Ash gave me the tiniest of nods, before walking away with the cart and the last of my will.

By the time I shook off my stupor, the items were rung up and the cashier was taking Ash's black American Express card.

"What are you doing?" I pulled my wallet out of my back pocket.

Ash looked down at the cashier's name tag. "Tammy, would you please place the purchases on my card?"

Tammy, a big beautiful Black woman with joy literally shining out of her eyes, laughed. It was a sound that made me forget why I was annoyed in the first place. "Honey, trust me when I tell you this. Accept the gift. He's a rare one."

"Obviously, he doesn't know her well," said a witch I'd not seen before. This one had thick box braids, and the kind of dark perfect skin I'd always envied.

"Perhaps not. But of the two of you, it isn't she who's classless." Ash slid his arm around my shoulder.

One of the witches, a white brunette wearing ripped jeans, her cheeks red with embarrassment, mouthed an apology before the automatic doors slid open with a soft whoosh, and she slipped outside.

That was... unexpected.

Tammy made a disapproving sound. "Here you are, sir. If you'd sign right here." She handed Ash a pen with a giant orange Gerbera daisy on the end.

"Not your crowd, I take it?" I returned my wallet to my pocket.

"'Bout as much as yours," Tammy answered before sliding the credit card slip in the cash register and closing the drawer. Apparently, Dhesi's hadn't upgraded everything.

I shrugged. Hell, if Ash remained in Hoodoo more than five minutes, he'd learn my entire sordid history. Then again, he didn't seem like a man who'd allow a small thing like murder to dissuade him.

"Well, I think they need to mind their business." Tammy slipped the pen in her black apron pocket. "Something about those girls ain't right. Did you two just move to town?"

"No, I lived here a lifetime ago. How about you?" I asked as I placed another paper bag in the cart.

"Yup." Tammy smiled and nodded. "Only been here a few months."

"You like it?" I asked.

"It's good enough. The rent is cheap, and the job pays better than most. But you know how it is trying to make friends as an adult, especially being a single and childfree woman in a small town."

"It'll get better." I handed her my business card. "Give me a call. Maybe we can do lunch."

"Thanks." Tammy dipped her chin and gave me *the look*. "Don't act like you don't know who I am when I call."

"I won't." I raised three fingers in a scout salute. "I'm looking forward to it. I could use a friend in town who I'm not related to."

"I'll put these things in the boot of the car. Take your time." Ash winked, then strolled off with the cart. For the first time since I'd met him, Ash's smile and demeanor didn't hit right. His eyes held humor and the remnants of heat from earlier. But something about his lips...

They looked hard—and dangerous. And not in the I'm-going-to-seduce-you-out-them-panties way.

I watched him leave, and not just his butt this time, and he glared at the group of witches standing between a raised blue truck and what looked like a gray Toyota. One by one, the women stopped chatting and looked at Ash.

They may have been bitches, but damn if they didn't have good taste.

"No offense, but I'd have to lock his ass up and make him my sex slave," Tammy said, with her hands pressed against her hips.

"None taken." I ripped my attention from the luscious man outside then muttered, "Trust me, I've considered it."

Tammy burst into peals of joyful laughter. Oh yeah, she'd fit right in with the nuts in my family.

The doors hissed open and a woman wearing an oversized orange Aggie hoodie entered the store, grabbed a hand basket, then stopped in front of me.

"Looks like you have a customer. Text me your number, Tammy."

"Will do." She gave me a little finger wave, then leaned to the side. "May I help you, miss?"

The woman in orange shook her head.

I stepped to the side, and she moved with me, finally exposing her face. Great. The chick with the box braids. My left hand tingled.

Shit. I inhaled, shoving my annoyance aside before it finally morphed into something uglier. Something I couldn't yet control. It wasn't working. "What? Don't you have some spells to cast or toads to boil?"

"Please," she said in a rushed whisper. "I just need thirty seconds." She walked over by the rack of free real estate magazines and the *Green Sheet*, that little flyer filled with job postings.

My curiosity got the better of me, so I joined her. "I'm listening." The witch was pretty now that she wasn't being a shrew. Which was the real woman, this one or the earlier version? The way I saw it, it didn't matter, since she didn't have the eggs to stand up to her little crew.

"If you still care about Rita, you need to warn her," she said before her gaze darted first to the back of the store, then over her shoulder.

"I'm not sure what version of the past you heard, but the last time I tried to help someone in Rita's family, I got the short end of the stick. I lost not only the trust of people I loved, but people I believed loved me."

A flash of movement in my peripheral vision caught my attention. I sighed as my gaze slammed into Carlos'. He stood on the other side of the registers watching, waiting, and unfortunately—listening.

In those few seconds, years of mistrust, harsh accusations, and maybe even the mourning of youthful love hung between us. But it didn't matter, none of it did, because in the end, Carlos would never choose me.

I looked back at the witch, not seeing her face, but Rita's filled with scorn, then shook my head, tossing in a one shoulder shrug for good measure. "If

Rita is in danger, that sounds like a her problem." I walked past Aggie chick, managing two steps before her freakishly strong fingers gripped my wrist. What was wrong with people in this town?

Hello... boundaries, heard of them?

"You need to leave Hoodoo—tonight." She coughed.

"Um...no." I twisted my wrist and jerked free. Homegirl could keep her advice and her cooties to herself.

"Is an inheritance worth your life?" She cleared her throat again, and I expected a real frog to fall out.

I ignored the question about the inheritance, filing it away to examine later. "You should get something for that cough."

Terror flared in the witch's eyes as her mouth opened and she thumped her fist against her chest.

I looked over at Tammy, who was ringing up Joaquin, a coyote shifter who worked at Conjure Ink. The way they watched each other, the store could've burned down, and they wouldn't notice. Perhaps Tammy would have a local friend sooner than later.

When I looked back at the little witch, her already dark skin was edging toward purple. Since she had air enough to cough, the Heimlich Maneuver was useless. But I pulled my phone from my back pocket, prepping to call 911.

See? *I wasn't a complete bitch.*

"Gwendolyn," Carlos called out.

I pinched the bridge of my nose. "Seriously?" What in the seven hells... Just kill me and get it over with.

"We're not done," he said as he walked through Tammy's aisle, nudging Joaquin to pass behind him.

"Wrong, Carlos. We were done a long time ago. A few spots of ink changes nothing."

"We need to talk about that male," he said.

I rolled my eyes and glanced back at the chick, who looked about to cough up a lung. "Sorry about that. You were about to give me the 'get out of town or else' speech."

Of course Duncan chose that moment to pop his ghostly ass into the picture. "Gwen..."

"Go away," I snapped, forgetting that I wasn't alone.

Carlos put his fists on his hips. "How about no? We're going to talk, and it's going to happen now."

And it probably would have, if the witch hadn't chosen that moment to open her mouth. Unfortunately, she didn't drop pearls of wisdom. No, of course not. Obviously, she needed to turn my evening into a true nightmare. Something fell from her mouth, alright.

Then skittered across the floor.

Aw hell to the no.

I gagged and retreated until my back slammed into something solid and warm, and too beefy to be Ash. But right now, there was another shit show to focus on. Giant Texas-sized cockroaches were all but swan diving from that woman's mouth. A lot of them.

"What the fuck?" Carlos put his hands on my hips, shifting me before stepping slightly in front of me to my right.

"They're going to —" she managed to get out between coughs and bugs.

This bitch had my full attention. Even if it was all I could do to keep my lunch down, I moved around Carlos.

"Who is they, and what's the plan?" Carlos might not have been the alpha of the local pack, but his voice was filled with goosebump-raising power that made me happy it wasn't aimed at me.

"M-m-m kill —" In the annals of famous last words, this witch's would go down in history. Not because of what she said, but the fact that her head exploded.

Chapter 11

I SAT IN THE INTERROGATION room of the Hoodoo Sheriff's Department. Judging by the stack of boxes in the corner, it doubled as a storage area. I'd tucked my fingers between my thighs to a: keep my hands from shaking, and b: to hide the glow that I hadn't been able to control.

Forget never letting them see you sweat. I'd passed that point forty minutes and a partial panic attack ago. What I needed involved a shower, then a tub, and a scrub brush. Oh, and some and bourbon.

The table as well as the chair I sat huddled in were bolted to the floor. On the other side sat Carlos, studying me so hard, you'd think he could read my mind rather than scent my emotions—which were all over the freaking place.

To the world, I was a friendly but aloof bad-ass, capable of handling and doing anything. Since I hadn't expected to live past thirty, I tended to be a balls-to-the-wall kind of gal. No adventure was too scary when you didn't give a shit. Yes, I'd allowed the myth of my invincibility to morph into a daredevil legend. Those who knew the real Gwendolyn, the one who could bungee jump into a canyon lined with jagged rocks, but was terrified of a field mouse, chuckled at the hype. They saw the walking, talking hot mess, beneath the tats and locs.

And as of tonight, everyone in that supermarket knew.

Gwendolyn Carter, celebrity tattoo artist, was a big-ass chicken. Because, baby, after that bitch's head exploded, and once my lungs regrouped, the scream that came out of my mouth was ripped straight from my soul.

Yes, I saw ghosts. Yes, I grew up a human raised by vampires. But damn it, never have I ever had a person explode all over me.

Ew.

Carlos and his deputy stared at me as if I'd buckle beneath their glares. They'd better get the heck outta here with that shit. Finally, I leaned back against the chair and crossed my arms. "What? Are you waiting for me to thank you for the jail jumpsuit? I have to tell you, grey and white stripes aren't my jam."

"Why don't we start with you telling me what happened?" Carlos mirrored my position, leaning back against his chair.

Why was he doing this? Both Carlos and that jackass of a deputy, who I didn't know, but already hated, were shifters. While I may have resting bitch face down to an art, frankly, after watching a woman's head explode, that I wasn't a big pile of goo on the floor was damned near award-worthy. But regardless of my expression, there was no hiding emotions.

The deputy looked vaguely familiar. I studied the dark brown face that would've been handsome if not for the drawn brows and tight lips. I exhaled on a sigh. Shit. He was in The Ancestors with one of the witches.

So much for innocent until proven guilty.

At least Carlos could smell the truth of my words, a truth he'd asked repeatedly, and which I'd refused to answer until I was allowed to change my clothes. They could smell my fear and revulsion, and it was clear neither Carlos nor his deputy cared.

Thank goodness they wanted my answers rather than my suffering, so they gave me this scratchy jumpsuit.

"You first. Why wasn't I allowed to go home and wash the bits of brain matter from my hair? Then, for an encore, why am I here?"

Of course, he didn't answer. Probably some cop trick. But I wasn't a suspect. I sighed, which unfortunately released too much of my indignation. Once upon a time, Carlos would have rushed to my rescue, been my defender against the world, whether the fight was hopeless or not.

A frisson of power, however weak, brushed against my arm. I didn't want to look. Souls, like scents, fingerprints, and auras, were unique.

Duncan sat on the cold metal chair beside me. "You ready to listen yet?" Duncan's East Texas twang hadn't faded in the afterlife, and judging by the undercurrent of laughter, neither had his twisted sense of humor.

I glared at Duncan. "Are you shitting me?"

"You think this is a joke?" The deputy left his spot in the corner, lumbering closer. He looked like a man who probably played college ball back in the day, maybe even a couple years in the pros. He had one of those bodies that could go from burly to fat with a few Whataburgers, but he'd obviously worked hard to stay fit. "What kind of black magic bullshit was that?" He slammed a massive fist against the table. "Tonight wouldn't be the first time you left a corpse behind. But I promise you it'll be the last."

I flinched and sucked in a breath. Holy shit. Asking how he knew about Duncan's death was one thing, but only the Tribunal, Hoodoo's version of a grand jury made up of all the groups in town, including humans, knew the truth.

Which was why I'd been exonerated.

But I didn't have the time or energy for that shit tonight, especially with the good deputy looking at me like he'd like to catch me alone on a dark country road. Dude had issues that went beyond a dead witch. His face, a couple shades lighter brown than my own, was twisted with a hate that I hadn't earned. Not from him.

Duncan sucked in a breath. "This is bad, Gwennie."

I gave Duncan the no-shit-Sherlock side-eye then looked up at Deputy Johnson.

What, did that yahoo think he could coerce me into confessing to exploding a woman's head? Now, I'd be a better suspect if a bullet were involved, but magic? Some things changed, but that wasn't one of them. I shook my head. "I'm done here."

Deputy Johnson lowered his voice, which was scarier than the yelling. "You're done when we say you are."

Had I had a different upbringing, one that didn't involve teenaged and young adult years surrounded by creatures who could rip a man's head off and use it for bowling ball—I would be terrified.

Too bad for him, the only thing I could drum up was annoyance. He and the caterpillar of a mustache needed to take a hike. "I'm not saying anything else without an attorney present." I raised my chin, then slipped my hands between my clasped thighs. At least I wasn't handcuffed to the table—yet.

"Marcus, give me a minute?"

"It's not safe to leave you in here with her."

"If I was going to be turning folks into cockroaches, it wouldn't be Carlos." When Carlos snickered, I glared at him. "Don't be too flattered. At this point, I'd make you something far worse."

Marcus's bass voice filled the room as much as his massive body. "Did you threaten —"

"Enough." Carlos' voice was soft, but a low growl rumbled through the word. "Both of you."

Deputy Marcus Johnson stood straight. Then, with his giant hand on the doorknob, looked back at me. "Where is Ilona?"

"Why do you guys keep asking me about that heifer? I have no idea—"

"For once in your miserable life, tell the truth." Where Carlos' anger was soft but powerful, Johnson's was like the braying of a foghorn.

Let's just say I never wanted to find myself alone with that man.

If Ilona was in a relationship with this dude, I could see why she was avoiding him. "I haven't seen her since that night, and if our paths never cross again on this side of the grave, I wouldn't lose a bit of sleep."

He and Carlos exchanged a look, then the good deputy shook his head and left the small room, the door closing behind him with a soft snick.

Carlos and I stared at each other. More than the smooth metal table separated us. Time, mistrust, misdeeds, and his need for vengeance would do the both of us in.

He leaned his muscular forearms on the table, pulling out the I'm-your-friend-you-can-confide-in-me face. "I have always had your back. True?"

In the end? No. Because rather than believing in me, Carlos dumped me over a corpse.

"Who was that male?" he asked.

"What? Don't tell me I'm here because of some personal shit." I stared up at the ceiling, at the little dome that probably held cameras.

Who was on the other side watching?

I returned my full attention to the man in front of me. "I have nothing to say until my attorney arrives. Am I under arrest?"

"I can hold you as a material witness for up to thirty-six hours." He drummed his fingers against the table. "Just tell me what I need to know so you can be on your way. A shower probably sounds good right about now."

Prick. "I want my phone call." I leaned closer. "And my boots."

"Who are you planning to reach out and touch?"

"That, Sheriff, is none of your concern."

"Again, true." Carlos drummed his knuckles against the table. "You know there'll be strings if you call the Double R."

"Not your problem. I'd suggest this might be a good time to handle your own business. A woman exploded in Dhesi's. Don't you have work to do?"

He nodded, looking like he wanted to say something else, to act like my friend. But instead of pushing his luck, he sighed and stood. "I hope you know what you're doing."

Probably not, but I wasn't in a sharing kind of mood. Who would I call? Carlos might have been an asshole, but he was right about Aunt Rose. She'd send Phillip, her human servant, but then what?

A soft knock came at the door before Deputy Johnson poked his massive head through a crack. "There's a man out here claiming to be her lawyer."

"Well, is he?" Carlos asked, looking at me.

"If that's what he says." Wow, had Aunt Rose committed a random act of kindness without the extraction of a pound of flesh?

Duncan left his chair, walking around the table to stand next to Carlos. He looked down at his friend with the same mournful expression as he had Rita that first night at The Ancestors. Duncan placed a ghostly hand on Carlos' shoulder before turning to me. "You and I need to talk."

I shook my head.

"Please. I'm sorry I screwed up your life by asking you to keep secrets."

I crossed my arms, because that wasn't all that fucker did; it was because of the lies written in his journal that I was taken into custody. It was because of his needing to prove that he was worthy of belonging to the coven that led to his death.

So no, I wasn't too interested in hearing more of his bullshit.

Duncan shoved his fingers through his strawberry-blonde hair. "Look, just hear me out. Allow me into Azure House so we can have privacy. Once we're done, if you never want to see me again—I'll leave you alone. But the evil has returned—and it's near my mother and Rita. Hate me all you want but help me protect them."

Vampires, and sometimes shifters say that they can taste the truth. I couldn't, but the pain in Duncan's green eyes was hard to fake. He could be a stupid-ass, but he loved his family, which could explain why he was still in Hoodoo.

Before I could answer, a soft whoosh of cool air drew my attention to the opening door.

Slowly, it opened wider, and in walked Ash.

Alrighty now. If he looked like a million dollars back in the grocery store, that version was a pauper compared to the prince now commanding the room.

Gone were the jeans and fitted Henley. This version of Ash was clad in black custom-tailored armor. From the set of his jaw and the heat all but radiating off his lithe body, it was fair to say I was glad he was on my side.

"Sheriff, so we meet again." Ash tossed his briefcase on the table, then walked straight to me, wrapping his strong hand around the side of my neck. "Gwendolyn, are you okay?"

"Of course she is." Carlos puffed up, ready for a fight. "You're no damn lawyer."

"And you know this how?" Ash's tone was as smooth as his suit.

Deputy Johnson, who looked downright sheepish, cleared his throat. "I checked his credentials. They're legit."

"Lawyer, that's a good occupation for your kind." Carlos' voice held so much disdain, I expected him to spit on the floor.

"Carlos!" I snapped. "How could you say something so, so..." I pressed my hand against the top of my chest wondering if I'd ever been so disappointed in a person. And that was saying a lot since I often dated men. "That was... vile," I whispered as I shook my head.

Carlos' voice had deepened, and his eyes slid from human to oh fuck. "He's not who you think he is."

"Seems to be a lot of that going around." I stood. "Ash, let's go home. I need a shower." And to get him away from Carlos before he shifted. It was bad enough I had to explain the exploding head. But the sheriff morphing into a giant wolf?

That was above my pay-grade.

"You don't need a ride from him."

"Actually, Carlos, I do. You brought me here, remember?"

Carlos bared his teeth. "I will take you."

"I wouldn't let you take me to hell."

Carlos' gaze shifted to Ash. "Your new friend might be able to help you with that. Take her home, but, Ash, unless you do me the honor of getting the fuck out of my town, you and I are having a conversation."

Ash's grin scared me way more than Carlos' growl.

Feminine frailty and calling on it in an emergency wasn't my gig, but desperate times and all that. I placed trembling hand on Ash's arm and whispered, "Please."

Ash nodded with a single jerk of his head to me, then looked back at Carlos. "Sheriff, until that meeting, I'll be at Gwendolyn's side, and in her bed."

Excuse me?

Ash continued speaking, his voice shifting from taunting to I-want-to-see-your-innards. "I'll be going nowhere. But you, Sheriff, I will make space in my schedule for. Name the time and place."

Hold up, had they scheduled an interview or a freaking duel?

"Done." Carlos stretched his fingers, leaned back in his chair, then dropped the mother of all bombs. "I should just sit back and watch it happen, but your client has a habit of leaving dead bodies in her wake."

I gasped.

"Right, Gwennie? Duncan was merely your first."

Chapter 12

I STORMED PAST THE front desk and the sneering deputy with his caterpillar of a mustache. As tempted as I was to pull a Lara Croft and kick the doors open, with my luck, my foot would go through the glass. Then my behind would be arrested for real this time.

Thanks, but no thanks.

Instead, I left the sheriff's office and Carlos behind me, following Ash into the humid night air.

"Well, don't you look like a candidate for the chain gang." Kyle, my best friend, lawyer, and former college roommate, leaned against the passenger side of a gunmetal gray Mercedes SUV.

While my face didn't lose the scowl, my heart smiled at the sight of my friend. He was everything Ash wasn't—short, Black, and androgynous with his wickedly handsome face.

"Kyle, what are you doing here?" I walked closer so he could get a good look. Maybe tomorrow, we'd laugh about it, but tonight was awful in the worst kind of way.

He popped one of those Swedish Fish candies in his mouth and shook his head as he took in my itchy jumpsuit complete with wide gray and white stripes and the equally horrible slip-on jail-issued sneakers, which were not only too big, but lacked arch support. Obviously, fashion and comfort weren't a concern for the department.

Just wait 'til they get my Yelp review.

Leaving my clothes in Carlos' custody as evidence was no skin off my nose, because honestly, I was never wearing them again. But my boots were another story. They were old, ugly, scuffed, broken in, and my favorite to kick around and work in.

And I wanted them back.

Kyle shrugged and pushed off the SUV. "Doing what I always do—keeping you out of trouble."

"Well, you're too late." When I invited, okay, begged him to come to town in that text, I hadn't expected this for a reunion.

"Obviously."

Compared to his nicely tailored blue slacks and slim fit shirt he wore tonight, I looked like warmed-over crap. But with his compact body, even in jeans and a tee, Kyle managed to look dressed up.

"I'm lacking the functioning brain cells for a witty comeback. So... bite me." I glanced at Ash, who'd walked past me and was staring at the jail, his arms crossed, and looking ready to tear it down brick by brick.

Call me sick, but it was kind of cute.

"Gwendolyn, are you sure you're well?" Ash asked, finally tearing his gaze from the building.

I nodded. "Yes, considering the circumstances." Like watching a woman's head explode and Carlos believing that even if I had the ability, I would do something so...foul. "Thanks for running to my rescue. Again."

I wish I could've sounded more grateful, but I prided myself in self-sufficiency in all areas of my life. Without it, who was I? The answer was simple—the very thing I'd always despised—weak and needy. Not good traits, especially in a woman.

"You are most welcome." Ash placed his palm against his chest. "I'll ensure Sheriff Hernandez never again bothers you."

Kyle gasped.

I clapped my hands, punctuating my words. "Time to go." Especially since it sounded a whole lot like Ash planned to hide Carlos' body in multiple remote deep holes. My stomach soured, so I swallowed to keep from barfing all over Ash's expensive shoes. Bits of our conversation from the supermarket floated through my fragmented mind especially the off-handed comment about getting rid of the witches.

Then, shortly after, one of them died.

Needing to stay on point, I tucked Ash's threats away to unpack later. Death seemed to follow both of us. All that time I spent running, could Ash have been the pursuer? Was I the fly to his spider?

I shook my head. No, that made no sense. If Ash wanted me dead, I have no doubt I'd still be that way. But if he possessed the ability to retrieve souls...

The door to the jail opened and out stepped the false arrest twins. Carlos and Deputy Dickhead stood at the top of the three stairs flooding the small parking lot with testosterone and ill will.

Time to bounce.

I stepped closer, placing my second hand against Ash's chest. "Please," I said softly, my eyes pleading. "No more bloodshed. Not tonight."

Carlos laughed, but even from twenty feet away, there was no missing the rumbling growl.

This was beyond not good.

Ash and Kyle needed to leave Hoodoo. There were too many secrets. Plus, badge or no badge, Carlos was dangerous. The kind of dangerous that wouldn't think twice about killing for duty. Ending Ash's life would be a bonus.

I had one mission. And no one, not Carlos, Kyle, or even Ash, would deter me. Since I was forced to stay in this wretched town for six months, I needed to uncover the origin of my family curse, and ensure it ended with me.

"Carlos, don't you have other innocent people to harass?" I all but hissed. The night sky decided to match my mood as the humid air pressed against my skin. Thunder rumbled as clouds rolled in, blocking the stars.

"Is that *the* Carlos?" Kyle whispered, but not low enough that Carlos' wolfy-ass ears wouldn't hear it.

Judging by Carlos' cocky grin—he had.

I was done.

Pressure built inside me. My skin felt like a chrysalis harboring a tornado of rage. Later, I might wonder why my heartbeat sounded like a giant kettle drum, or why each exhale singed along my upper lip. But now, beneath the quickening skies, I bathed in and relished that anger. Like a deadly oil, it soaked into my skin, filling my veins and coating my bones. If it were possible, the emotion ripping through my body felt almost...sentient.

And both the anger and I wanted to turn the slick bubbling rage into something mortally painful—for Carlos.

Lightning flashed, sizzled, and danced between the clouds, ricocheting like a pinball machine. The wind, which began as a whisper, expanded, straining to reach a crescendo. It circled me, pushing against my skin, my hair, and my clothes, before moving on to chase another.

"Gwennie," Carlos yelled over the growing storm.

A massive boom shook the ground, responding in my stead.

Before I could turn and share with my former lover what a cruel, petty tyrant he'd become, Ash's hand whipped out with a speed exceeding any I'd seen from him, capturing my arm with a firm, but not cruel, grip.

I looked down, not at the tanned fingers circling my wrist, but at the light show beneath my skin. When I glanced up at Ash, his focus remained on my face and that disgust he'd worn earlier had been replaced with concern.

"Let's get you home," Ash said, his smooth voice a contrast to the turbulence rumbling through both my body and the night.

"I'd like that," I whispered as he led me to the passenger side of the SUV. I also appreciated his thumb caressing the sensitive skin of my inner wrist. "Seems like you're always coming to my rescue. FYI, I'm not a good damsel in distress."

Ash chuckled, squeezed my hand, then opened the front passenger door as he whispered against my ear, "I noticed."

We drove away, slipping into the comforting darkness.

Ash had made an enemy, a powerful one. And unless he'd changed dramatically, in Carlos' mind, everything and everyone was either good or bad. Black or white. And if Ash and Kyle remained on my side, that made them the opposite of good.

Honestly, I had no idea whether Ash was the hero of this story either. But if he was a villain, I'd rather he be my personal monster. I almost chuckled. It was either that or cry, because driving down the dark road putting distance between Carlos and me, my thoughts about the witches—all of them—weren't exactly kind.

Rather than focus on my dearth of empathy, I stared into the now clear night skies. Hoodoo's sheriff's office used to be on Main Street. But according to Loretta, the pack decided to build the new station on pack land since, by the town's charter, shifters oversaw policing.

Which made sense. How did one lie to a creature who can taste the falsehood before it left your lips? Very carefully.

"Do you know how to get to my house?" I tugged the jailbird jumpsuit's sleeve down to cover my flickering left hand, then wrapped both arms around my waist. Each time I thought something couldn't go wrong, shit got worse. Looked like I was going to fall back on my good friend pessimism.

Ash nodded.

"Talk to me, Gwen," Kyle asked from the back seat. "What the hell happened in that store?"

"A woman who I don't know and doesn't like me was allegedly trying to deliver a warning." Should I explain the coughing, the blood, and... I gagged at the memory. But I had to say something. So I shared the truth that Ash and Kyle would find believable. "She was there one minute, and gone the next."

"Tammy, the lovely cashier, said to call when you're feeling up to it." Ash stopped at the stop sign and hit his blinker. "She's looking forward to hanging out with you."

I shook my head. "I'm not so sure about that. It's not safe to be near me."

Ash's eyebrows drew closer, but he remained silent. No argument, no nothing. He gave me a single nod, then turned right, which was off pack lands and toward Azure House.

I shivered. Closing my eyes would make the memories sharper, the blood redder, and the bugs crunchier. A small whimpering sound escaped as I dug my fingernails into my palms and exhaled slowly.

Once I got myself together enough that I wouldn't flee from a moving car, I glanced at Ash. Shadows fell across his angular face, exposing the angry line of his mouth. "I'm surprised you let me in the car without covering the seats," I said, trying to inject levity into the moment.

"It's a rental." Ash's voice was flat, but his lips twitched.

I made a chuffing noise, not a laugh, not a snort, but somewhere in between.

"And even if it were not, I wouldn't care."

"Whew, a man after my own wicked heart," Kyle said. I could almost imagine him fanning himself in the backseat.

Not a subtle one, that Kyle.

I tensed. Ash might have been a worldly gazillionaire, but he was a straight man. It sucked, and I was all kinds of a jerk for the lack of confidence, but I'd learned to expect the worst. While I wasn't certain if Ash and I would become lovers, we couldn't even be friends if he was transphobic.

That, and being mean to any of my friends were non-negotiables.

Ash chuckled, looked up into the mirror, and nodded. "I am flattered."

Some of the tension in my shoulders dissipated. Okay... Rich, handsome, chivalrous, and not a bigot. And let's not forget the great kisser part. Mr. Modeus's lack of flaws was going to make it even suckier when I made him leave.

I once again focused my attention to the thick woods lining both sides of the road.

Ash squeezed my shoulder, and after a couple of shaky breaths, I covered his hand with mine. If Ash wanted to fondle a woman covered with bug juice—he could have at it.

I glanced at my watch: nine thirty-five. Well, I had no idea of the condition of the upper floors of Azure House, but if we could find habitable bedrooms, both Kyle and Ash could stay until the morning.

Before I knew it, the car stopped, pulling in behind my van, which was parked on the road, rather than the curved driveway in front of the house.

I stepped out of the car, then pinched the bridge of my nose. Ignoring Azure House wasn't going to make the monstrosity disappear. So I put my big girl panties on, exhaled,

then opened my eyes and yelled, "No fucking way!"

Chapter 13

ASH AND KYLE LEAPED in front of me, guns drawn, bodies tensed, gazes sharp.

But it wasn't them who'd captured my attention. Gone were the dead bushes and shrubs. Nary a shutter remained lopsided, and holy mother of the man upstairs, the windows were so clean, they reflected the stars.

I patted my chest and exhaled a loud breath. "Sorry, guys." I shrugged. "I... uh thought I saw a mouse." As far as lies went, that was lame. "Or a rat. A big one."

I wasn't sure how to respond to Kyle standing there ready to eliminate the threat. He was far from soft. Au contraire, homie was fierce when it came to negotiating contracts and going to court. And if his words couldn't get him out of a jam, Kyle would beat your ass with a quickness. It was just that I'd never seen *this* man.

So... deadly.

And I never wanted to see it again. Crying wasn't something I did, like ever. But tonight, watching my dearest friend prepared to kill did something to me.

Something I didn't like.

And I knew that if Ash and Kyle stayed, the next time they reached for a gun, it might be their last. Besides, those weapons were useless against magic. My conscience, what was left of it, couldn't bear another scar.

Ash lowered his sweet chrome-plated 9mm but remained tense as he scanned the property. "A rat?" He finally stared down at me as if waiting for further information.

"Hey, it was Texas-size," I said, trying to look sheepish. I turned to Kyle and frowned, watching him expertly tuck his .380 into his waistband holster. "When did you start carrying a gun?"

"With women getting assassinated in the Hoggly Woggly, I should be asking why you aren't. But we can talk about this wild west of a town later. Let's get to the important part." Kyle motioned to the house. "Honey, that is... charming." His voice went from excited to suspicious, with a hint of hurt. "I could have sworn you called this an..." He pulled out his phone and touched the screen, the light illuminating his handsome face. "... oversized monstrosity."

"That's how I remembered it." And how it looked yesterday morning. For the mere price of a pint of blood, you too can have a magical makeover complete with a portal to the unknown.

Ash closed the driver's side door, rapping his knuckles twice on the roof. "Perhaps we could save the house hunters conversation for later."

Kyle nodded to Ash. "You're right," he said before looking at me, taking me in from the pulled up locs, past the hideous gray and white chain gang outfit, to the oversized shoes. "Let's get you into something a little more appealing—like a bathtub."

"As much as I'd like to argue, you get a free pass on being a butthole. You'd better mark this day on your calendar." I rolled my left shoulder, trying to ease the knot in my back. Which was a big fail. How surprising. *Not.* "Hey, guys, thanks for bringing Stella home while I was in the pokey."

Ash stopped beside me, dangling my keys. "I would have taken the groceries inside, but the front door wouldn't cooperate."

"The house—" I cleared my throat. "—I mean, the locks are old and tricky."

Ash placed the ring of keys on my palm, closing my fingers over them. In the darkness, standing in the shadow of my new house while covered with brains, blood, and guilt, he watched me with a combination of gentleness and something I was too tired to begin to decipher.

The first time I met Ash in Dublin, it was followed by getting chased by a vampire, dodging Paul Bunyan's Irish kin, and evading assassins on a train. Come to think about it, perhaps all this danger and death wasn't about me—but him.

"Go. Grab your things." Ash placed his hands on my shoulders and turned me to face Stella. "Open the house. Kyle and I will care for the rest."

I hit the alarm twice, unlocking the van. Then, like a zombie, I opened the back door, exposing the garage area beneath the platform bed. The space that should have held my suitcases, ammunition, and art supplies, but was now empty of everything but Duncan.

His grinning ghostly behind was perched on the bed, transparent legs swinging gently. "We need to talk. Or rather, I need to talk, and you should listen. My moth—"

"Stop. In case you haven't noticed, the coven, and especially your family, hates me," I whispered, not bothering to disguise the sadness lacing my voice.

"My mother never hated you. Believe that if nothing else." Duncan raised his hands, palms out, rushing his next words. "Before you banish me to parts unknown, there's something else you need to know."

"What?" I crossed my arms, waiting for another load of bullshit.

Duncan looked past me while shaking his head. "No. Invite me into Azure House."

"Who are you talking to back there?" Kyle walked around the side of the van, hands filled with bags of groceries.

"No one," I grumbled as I slammed the doors on Duncan and his nonsense.

With each step closer to Azure House, it became more difficult to ignore my former friend's warnings. Unlike me, Duncan had remained in Hoodoo, whether it be by choice, chance, or penance, I had no idea.

And honestly, I didn't care. But something horrific happened tonight. That poor witch had attempted to do the right thing, tried to warn me, but no... I was all up in my feelings. Had I taken sixty seconds to listen rather than paint her with the same stained brush as the rest of the coven, perhaps I wouldn't be in this current conundrum.

As much as I hated Duncan for his part in my exile from Hoodoo, right now, he allegedly held the clues to unlock secrets pertaining to me. Regardless of my feelings for Rita, her mother didn't deserve to bury her last child.

Maybe I could call Miss Eleanor later. And tell her what? That Duncan says she's in danger? Hmph. He was a liar in life, so I couldn't and shouldn't expect him to change after death.

I looked over my shoulder at Duncan, now standing on the road, and shook my head.

My gaze shifted from the disappointed young man to the sparkling lights on both sides of the doors and the large ceramic pots now filled with flowers as I trudged up the porch stairs.

Okay, my house was magical. Keeping it real, I should have figured that out earlier. But noooo, I chose ignorance. Too bad for me, the house chose violence. Not in a physical way, but Azure House wasn't having it. There was no sticking my head in the sand or another equally dark place. I had to either face my new enchanted reality or freak the fuck out.

The shining brass knocker on the oversized door gave me a gleaming welcome home, so exhaustion and pragmatism won. I placed my palm on the dark wood. "Okay, house, please be nice to my friends. I'm tired, I'm dirty, and I'm hungry. I don't have the time for crap right now."

I aimed the key for the lock, but the door glided open. Great, who needed an alarm system when you had your very own hexed house? "Thank you," I whispered as I crossed the threshold.

"Who you talking to now?" Kyle asked, still loaded down with my canvas grocery bags.

I wasn't kidding when I said I was exhausted. All I had was the truth. "The house."

"When did you become superstitious?"

"I've reevaluated my position..." What choice did I have? Between the Thor hand and the house, I had to accept that, with my death, life had irrevocably changed. On one hand, I'd accepted and even loved magical and supernatural beings. On the other, I'd refused to accept it in myself. Self-hate was a pervasive and ugly thing. However, self-acceptance would be easier if I knew *what* I was.

Whoa.

Devoid of not only dust, but the white canvas covers Maria and I left piled on the floor, Azure House was impressive. The crystal candle holders, Tiffany-inspired floor lamps strategically placed in corners, and the ornate medallion above the chandelier in the wide-open entry way made me feel as though I'd stepped back in time.

I pointed past the parlor to a hallway. "The kitchen is through there." At least I hoped it hadn't moved.

"Um, Gwen…" Kyle stared not at my face, but my head. "Be sure to wash your hair." He leaned closer, opened his mouth, then closed it again before straightening with a grimace. "You probably don't want to know."

I nodded and headed to the stairs. "You're right. I don't." I didn't want to think about Ash, Kyle, exploding heads, witches, shifters, or anything else. All I wanted was to wash away the craziness of this day.

But, still, I paused on the stairs. How could I not? Because, holy shit. Kyle was right. This house was freaking amazing. And once I had the pieces of insects off me, I planned to slip into full-on Dora the Explorer mode.

On the wall going up the stairs were newly hung pictures; they were pretty, yes, but it was the pristine wallpaper that held my attention. From what I'd seen, most houses built in the 1800s, the walls were either painted or humiliated with over-the-top ornate wallpaper. But this…I trailed my fingers across the dainty rose pattern, so delicate and beautiful against the cream paper, was wallpaper I could live with.

I reached the top of the stairs, looking both ways down the wide hallway. To my left were four closed doors, two on each side. Straight ahead, past the four bedrooms, was an open door, exposing a second set of stairs that appeared to lead to the third floor.

To my right stood one door, which I had to assume would be the master bedroom, and therefore mine. I dragged ass there, pausing to appreciate not only the gleaming dark wood, but the beautiful, polished brass handle and, further down, the thick oriental carpet.

As far as haunted houses went, this one wasn't so bad.

I exhaled a soul-weary breath then slipped into the room romantically lit by hurricane lamps filled with fat white candles. There was obviously electricity in the house, but candles felt somehow more fitting. And far more welcoming.

But… who lit them?

I glanced around the room again and squeaked. Because standing right in front of me was a smiling, not quite corporeal Black woman wearing a crisp maid's uniform straight out of the late 1800s.

Walking into a house that had a one-day magical makeover?

I could deal.

Not having to bust my butt pulling weeds and chopping down stuff? Even better.

But entering my bedroom to find a semi-ghostly ladies' maid might just push me over the edge. "No offense, but you and this damned house are going to make me have a nervous breakdown."

The woman curtsied. "Oh, ma'am, this house isn't damned, and neither are you. We're glad you've returned home."

"We?" I pinched the bridge of my nose and counted. I'd almost reached twenty when she spoke again. I guess the fact that I hadn't leapt from the window gave her hope.

"Oh yes, but don't you worry about that none. Come on in, we'll take good care of you."

"Could you tell your ghostly buddies to just chill for a minute. Having you here is enough." The woman's glorious smile fell. Great, now I was Gwendolyn Carter the crusher of ghosts, splitter of heads, first of her name. I grabbed the end of a loc and twirled it around my finger as I exhaled. "Sorry, it's just been a long day."

"Yes, ma'am." She looked at my jumpsuit and muttered, "I can tell."

Great. I finally get a servant, but not only is she dead, but a smart-ass.

I unzipped my chain gang outfit, dropping it to the floor, then stepped out of it and the ill-fitting and uncomfortable sneakers.

"Would you please throw those in the garbage, burn them, or whatever?"

Her face brightened, as if I'd given her the keys to the kingdom. "Yes, ma'am." She pointed toward a door across the room with a full-sized mirror in a dark wood frame stationed on one side, and a massive chest of drawers topped with a lit hurricane lamp on the other. "Your bathroom is through there, and hot water is waiting for you."

"How..." I raise my hand shook my head. "Never mind, we can talk details later. After the breakdown."

"Yes, ma'am." She curtsied.

The walk to the bathroom was like dragging my feet through wet sand. Halfway there, I paused and turned around. "Excuse me, what's your name?"

"Lucille, ma'am." She curtsied again, bowing her head to hide her grin.

"Lucille, can you do me a favor? No curtsying. I'm not royalty."

She frowned, nodded, then gathered up my clothes. The whole curtsying and ma'am thing had to go, but having somebody to pick up my crap? Very nice. "Lucille?" I called out. "Thank you. I appreciate your help."

"No, ma'am. Thank *you*. You've made us all incredibly happy." She headed for the door.

"Excuse me," I called out. "Will I be the only person able to see you guys?"

"Yes, unless you don't want to see us." I could tell that she tried to keep her smile, but it wilted a little.

"I'm a woman of a certain age, so know what it is to feel invisible—and I hate it. So, please, let me see you. I just worry about my friends; I wouldn't want them having a heart attack." Thinking about Kyle having a case of the vapors made me snicker.

"Whatever we touch becomes as invisible as we are. So don't you worry, your guests won't be able to see us."

"Thanks, that's good to know. Maybe later, you could give me the grand tour."

"I'd like that a lot. You enjoy your bath now."

"I'm sure I will." But whether I'd enjoy this house was another story altogether.

Chapter 14

AS FAR AS BATHS WENT, this one had to be in my top two. The oversized clawfoot tub was not only comfortable, but as enchanted as the rest of the house. How did I know? The water, despite having been in the tub long enough for me to look like a raisin, had never cooled.

Now that was magic I could get down with.

My ancestor, bless her heart, must have been quite the pampered princess with impeccable tastes. Of course, some of the improvements could have come from later generations, but they merely polished a nearly flawless gem.

I raised the bar of handmade soap and inhaled lavender and heaven. Talk about questions. Did my friendly ghosts just stroll into town to buy supplies? Did they make them by hand or just poof everything into existence?

Those questions as well as the rest of the world could just go away, at least for tonight. I sighed and rolled my neck, which thanks to hot water and silence, was a little looser.

All I wanted to do was slip into my pajamas, snuggle beneath the thick quilts, then sleep until next week. Ash and Kyle could tour the house on their own. A soft knock interrupted my peaceful fantasy. So much for Calgon taking me away. If my guests were still here, unfortunately, the rest of the world wasn't going anywhere either.

The intruder knocked again.

"Go away," I grumbled then scooted lower, hiding most of my body beneath the bubbles. When you owned a house with servants capable of walking through walls, was privacy a realistic expectation?

The door opened. "Bitch, you been keeping secrets."

Okay, *not* the maid.

Kyle closed the door behind him, tossed a candy fish in his mouth, then took a seat on the small vanity bench before looking around the bright bathroom with appreciation.

I glared at my best friend. "Hello, I'm naked."

"First, I used to have breasts, remember? Secondly, I've already seen all your goodies. Speaking of," he leaned closer, looking over the edge of the tub, "didn't your girls used to be a bit higher?"

I flicked a handful of suds at him. "Jerk."

"Twat." He grinned. After I returned it, he asked, "Feeling better?"

I shook my head, groaned, then slid the rest of my body beneath the steaming water.

Seeing that I couldn't hold my breath forever, I eventually resurfaced. As soon as my head cleared the bubbles, Kyle started in. "I'm your best friend. Okay, your *only* friend. I need to know—everything. First, honey, I see why you lost your young mind about Carlos and gave up the cookie, but he took you to jail. He is not on your side."

"I know. He's going to be a problem."

"I'm thinking we should let Ash take care of him. And speaking of Mr. Ash Modeus..." Kyle bit down on his lower lip. "Have I mentioned how hot he is?"

"The panting and drooling on the ride here made it clear enough." And no, I didn't want to discuss Ash. I also didn't want to examine my insane attraction to him.

The way I desired Ash felt... overwhelming and downright unnatural.

"Was there a reason you interrupted my Zen time? How about making yourself useful and handing me a towel?" After he placed the thick blue piece of Turkish heaven in my hand, I went ahead and wrapped it around my heavy locs.

Note to self, I needed to make an appointment to have them retwisted.

"Oh, with all that talking about your nonexistent love life, I forgot. Your people—I'm assuming they belong to you—are downstairs."

I covered my face with my hands, making a noise reminiscent of a small, wounded animal.

"Why didn't you tell me these folks were the Hoodoo Hillbillies. The only person missing is Mr. Drysdale."

"Tell them I'm not here." I really wasn't in the mood for this level of calamity.

Of course, Kyle ignored me and continued his torture. "Loretta, who is adorable, by the way, ordered me to tell you. And these are her words, not mine. That if you're not downstairs in fifteen minutes, she'd come and snatch your narrow tail out of the tub."

I grimaced.

"Family or not, they came bearing food, a variety of herbs and candles, and more than one of them are carrying firearms. And Loretta is watching Ash like she's not sure if she'd rather strip him of his skin or clothes." From Kyle's expression, it was clear which he'd prefer.

"Please tell me they didn't threaten you."

"Not too much. I managed to escape with my hide intact. But I'm not sure if that'll be the case if I don't return with you."

BY THE TIME KYLE AND I got downstairs, there was a full-on party happening. Luckily, there were only three twigs from my twisted family tree in attendance, but one didn't need more than that for chaos.

"Hey, guys," I said as Kyle and I paused on the landing.

Ash, a man who looked as though he could single-handedly face down Attila the Hun's ravaging horde, appeared intimidated by an elderly Black woman wearing overalls and black Chuck Taylor sneakers. Not only was the man Croesus-rich, sexy, and well-mannered, he recognized a threat.

"Get on over here." Loretta put her fist on her hips. "I know you hungry and ain't have time to cook after the incident at the market."

"Does the whole town know?" I crossed the living room, giving Loretta a quick hug and peck on the cheek. Had things been different, and my mother managed to get both of us to Hoodoo alive, I imagine that she and Loretta would have raised all kinds of hell. And this big, beautiful house would have been my home.

To play in, to laugh in, and to love in. Instead, both Azure House and I had lived our lives alone.

"We heard," Maria yelled out from across the room. "Hey, cuz." She widened her eyes in silent communication. If I wasn't mistaken, they asked what the hell was going on with the house.

I shrugged in response, then added, "I bet my butt had barely touched the chair at the sheriff's station before the entire town knew every sordid detail."

"Yup." Maria, who'd exchanged her scrubs from earlier for pair of blue jeggings and a light oversized scarlet sweater, gave me a quick hug and an infectious grin. "You know how folks around here are. What they don't know, they invent. We also heard about Mr. Sweet Cheeks and the kiss in the supermarket. You go, girl."

"Come on in here and eat." Loretta looked from me to Kyle then Ash, and back. "Looks like you brought more to Hoodoo than a fancy van and those goofy boots."

"Let me get this right, the woman who marched in here with a rack of ribs and a shotgun? Is critiquing my accessories?" And speaking of said boots, I needed them back. Immediately.

"Food and bullets are like a little black dress; they go with everything." Loretta said with a shrug and a wicked twinkle in her eyes.

"Did you actually introduce yourself," I said before she got too out of control, "or just terrorize my friends?"

"Well, if they scare that easily, you need an upgrade," Loretta answered, her East Texas accent thick as hell.

"Maybe I should download new relatives too." I looked skyward for assistance or protection; I'd prefer both.

"Well, I disagree." Ash moved to my side, extending a hand. When Loretta returned the gesture, rather than shake, Ash pulled a smooth move, placing a kiss against her dark wrinkled knuckles as if she were a duchess. "I'm pleased to meet you. I see Gwendolyn's beauty is hereditary."

Color, somewhere between purple and burnt sienna, shot up Loretta's cheeks and didn't stop until it reached her short salt and pepper afro. "Girl, you better watch out for this one," she said before giggling like a teenager.

Dear Lord. Loretta was now watching Ash less like a suspect and more like a candidate for the next ex-husband position. Gradually, her attention shifted from the man to the room. I could almost see memories, both happy and poignant, move through her eyes as her face first softened, then wrinkles appeared in her dark forehead.

I slipped my arm through hers, and we slowly walked from the parlor to the formal dining room. "Has it changed much?"

"No, baby. Unlike these old bones, Azure House hasn't aged." She looked at me and smiled. This time, some of that impishness that always reminded me of a wood sprite returned. "Your mama and I used to have a good old time running around this house."

"Really?" I don't know what Ash heard in my voice, but he moved closer. The man was protective. What was he going to do, eliminate a seventy-year-old woman for making me sad? The thought made me chuckle, especially since I'd bet a non-vital organ that she was carrying concealed.

I looked up at Ash, compelled to share something of myself with this strange and wonderful man. Then Carlos' words echoed through my mind.

But I wasn't offering Ash my body, just a sliver of my past. That much I could give. "For a long time, I was just so..." I shrugged. "...angry, I didn't want to hear about my mother."

"Angry about what?" Ash asked, his voice swirling around us like a sexy cone of silence.

I ignored Kyle's wide eyes.

I knew what he was thinking. So much of my life I'd been spent closed off from everyone but Kyle. Yet even he didn't know all my secrets. Then again, I knew less than nothing about his family and past. Since Kyle never poked and prodded at my skeletons, I let his graveyard of secrets remain buried.

"Everything." Like losing my mother, the center of my small universe. Being forced to live in a house with vampires. For getting stuck with an aunt who expected an eight-year-old to just get over her mother dying on a deserted highway.

Maybe it would have been if not easier, but quicker to learn to live with the pain, but regardless of what I did, or what kind of therapies I tried, that night remained a giant black hole.

I recalled us passing the exit for FM 2920, and singing along with the radio as we sped up Highway 45. I remember Mom's infectious laughter and soft hands, and the golden lights reflecting off her glasses. Then her eyes widening, followed by...nothing.

The smile I gave Ash was sad, but not as painful as it had always been. Whether it was a hallucination, a dream, or actuality, but after I was shot in Morocco, I'd spent a precious few moments with my mother in heaven. Seeing my ancestors waiting for me on the other side was a sizable bandage on my wounded heart. Because when I finally did leave this meat-suit behind, I wouldn't be alone.

Ash intertwined his fingers with mine, giving them a squeeze.

A tiny shiver raced up my back. The warmth of Ash's flesh against mine was nice, but it was the emotional support I appreciated most.

But could I trust it?

I squeezed Ash's hand in gratitude, then refocused my attention on Loretta, who intently watched not only Ash but our silent interaction. "Maybe after dinner, you could give me a tour?" I asked. Mostly because I wondered if she knew about the passage in the library, and the other secrets the house held tight. Like the ghostly staff.

"I could." Loretta nodded, then walked toward the kitchen. "But this house is a lot like sex; half of the fun is in the discovery. And baby, every door is a kiss that will unlock a secret. What you do with them is up to you."

"Sorry, Gwendolyn." Ash placed a hand on my stomach and moved between me and Loretta, who'd reached the large open kitchen and took her bony hand in his. "Will you marry me?"

Everyone burst out laughing.

"I don't know what y'all finding so funny. Thank you, baby," Loretta said, patting Ash's hand, "but I don't think you can handle all this."

I snorted again, which set off another round of giggles and guffaws.

Maria and I glanced at each other. Thankfully, I wasn't the only person struggling to keep it together.

Maria pursed her lips.

I snickered.

Then mere giggles became pure, unbothered laughter. Suddenly, the inheritance with its attached titanium strings, and even the incident, didn't matter.

Right now, I was filled with gratitude to be surrounded by people who, if not loved me, were concerned about my well-being. And that had to be enough for now.

"Heifers." Loretta raised her chin and flounced off to the butler's pantry.

I crossed my arms and shook my head. "Ash, she's going to be unbearable now."

Maria snorted. "Going to be? She was born that way."

"I heard that," Loretta yelled from the small adjacent room.

"Cheese?" Looked like my night of surprises was far from over.

"Hey, girl." My cousin Frederick, who we all called Cheese, paused from peeling aluminum foil from a large bowl. "Looks like life has been good to you."

"Cheese?" Kyle said as he stopped beside me.

I shrugged. "I'm sure there's a story behind it. I just don't know it," I said to Kyle, who, like Ash, blended right in with the madness that was my family. But then again, that was Kyle's gift, along with having what seemed to be an endless supply of Swedish Fish candies. "You're not looking so bad yourself. When did you get back?"

"Yesterday. I had to, you know, say hello to the ladies." He wiggled his eyebrows and stepped away from way too much potato salad for six people, then opened his beefy arms for a hug.

It was oddly comforting how affectionate these people were. I remember the prickly kid who was forced to live in this odd town with these weird people. Strangers hugging you because you're genetically related. They had no concept of personal boundaries but gave me space for a few months before deciding enough of that nonsense.

While I would never admit it, no one gave hugs like the folks in Hoodoo. Maybe that was what was missing in the world. If people hugged more, they wouldn't be filled with so much hate.

When Cheese released me, I smiled up at him. "So, are you finally retired from the Marines?"

"Yup, thirty years." The gold open-faced crown he'd went out and put on his front tooth (against his mother's wishes, I must add) was long gone. Like most Black families, ours had a variety of complexions. From the bluest of blacks to light, bright, and damned near white. He was on the lighter end of the scale.

And as charming as he was handsome.

"You've been around the world and you're moving back here?" I asked.

Cheese returned to his project, sticking a wooden serving spoon in the bowl of potato salad, handing it to me, before doing the same with a bowl of collards. "One of these days, you going to learn that home may be the last place you want, but the one thing you need. Put this on the table."

I glanced down at the .45 in Cheese's shoulder holster and the one on his side. "Why are you loaded for bear?"

"Did you or did you not find yourself in the middle of some shit tonight?"

I glared at Cheese then cut my eyes at Kyle and back. "No more talk of death and destruction. I'm hungry." And would like my friends to keep believing I was mostly human.

Chapter 15

DINNER WAS AN EVENT. The ribs tender, the smoked brisket juicy, the banter witty, and the conversation non-stop. And Ash? He fit right in. Say what you want about Texans—especially the citizens of Hoodoo. If they don't like you, you're going to know it. With a quickness. Not saying people wouldn't be polite, but there was none of that fake niceness so many embrace.

The more time I spent around Ash, the more I liked him. Not in a sexual way, which was a given. But watching him give as good as he got earned him the family's admiration—and more of mine.

For the Carters, the many hands make light work adage was damned near gospel. So it took almost no time to clean the kitchen, return the table to its former glory, then plop our behinds on the prissy couches in the smaller of the parlors.

Loretta looked around the room and that soft smile from earlier returned. "I almost feel guilty sitting in here with a beer. We couldn't even walk through the house carrying a glass of water." Yet it didn't stop her from taking a pull from that Lone Star.

"Welp, since it's mine now, Azure House has new rules." I raised my glass of bourbon.

It was my turn to look around. I imagined a room filled with women of all hues, sitting around in beautiful long dresses sipping tea or coffee laced with a little something-something, gossiping about the goings on around town. How often had my ancestors sat in this very chair? Would they find me lacking?

I glanced down at my tattoos and wide-legged linen pants and almost said yes. But I was more than my ink. Like most people, I occasionally fell short. But honesty, loyalty, kindness, and intelligence were traits I had in abundance. If that didn't satisfy the ancestors, that was a them problem.

A soft vibration began at my feet, radiating up the chair. Since the conversation around me droned on, and the liquid in not one glass—even mine—sloshed around, I had to assume this wasn't an earthquake. The vibration turned into something warmer and gentler, surrounding me with something close to an energy-filled embrace.

It felt like acceptance. It felt like pride. It felt a whole like lot love. And it wasn't the love of strangers; no, it had the essence of something comfortable and familiar. If the energy could speak, I imagined it would whisper, *"Baby, you are not alone. You never were."*

An unfamiliar pressure built behind my eyes as my heart squeezed tight. Before I could catch myself, I whispered, "Thank you."

"What was that?" Ash, sitting next to me in a matching brocade armchair, asked.

I fanned myself and tried to smile to cover my embarrassment. Nothing like getting caught talking to yourself. "Just thinking out loud. I came here once to see where my mother grew up."

He tilted his head to the side, waiting, watching, reminding me of a predator looking for the right moment to strike.

"I figured there had to be something horrible about this house. Mom left, never looking back, and without sharing much of Azure House or the town of Hoodoo. When she did try to return... well, we all know how that story ended." I wiggled my eyebrows at Ash to lighten the mood. "The kids in town called it the devil house."

"Really. And why is that?" Ash leaned back in his chair and stretched his long legs, crossing his feet at the ankles. The man wasn't tall, per se; just a smidge over six feet. But it always seemed there was almost too much power and energy shoved into a body too small to contain it.

Maria leaned forward, placing her elbows on her knees. It looked like she held the same joy in sharing the tale with Ash as she had with me so long ago. "The way I heard it, if you come by on a moonless night, ole Lucifer himself comes to mourn his lost love Hyacinth. Who happens to be Gwen's great-great-grandmother."

"Wouldn't she be yours too?"

Maria shook her head. "Nope, she would be my great-great-aunt, sister to my ancestor."

Kyle's eyes grew to the size of small saucers. "Gwen, that makes you Lucifer's heir and a literal princess from hell." He then fell into an unseemly fit of giggles.

I swirled my bourbon then took a fortifying sip. "Yes, if you believe in that sort of thing. I don't." Even as the words formed in my brain, it sounded ridiculous.

Denial was a lovely thing.

Besides, if that legend held truth, and Lucifer was an actual tangible being, that worsened my situation. Either good ole Lucifer, lord of demons and fallen angel, murdered the women in my line or failed to prevent it.

That thought then the one that quickly followed made bile rise in my throat.

What if the unbelievable tale was as real as the vampires who raised me, and the werewolves who'd once accepted me as family? If I was the descendent of the Lord of Darkness, what did that make me?

Loretta, Cheese, and Maria shot amused glances at each other.

Ash shifted in his armchair, scrutinizing me for a what felt like ten minutes, but was probably about four seconds, before he spoke. "What is love if not magic? What is childbirth?"

"Romantic love is a type of psychosis caused by out-of-control hormones. As far as childbirth…" I shifted in my chair, twisting my torso toward Ash. Whatever he wanted from me, I didn't have to give. Not even a night of pleasure. He needed to find another woman, someone available. Someone human. "Childbirth, as beautiful as it may be, is a physiological miracle. Not magic."

"That's unfortunate that you feel that way."

I shrugged and lowered my voice. "It is what it is. Besides, you should thank whatever god you worship that I swore off love a while ago. Because, Ash, the people I love die."

Loretta clapped her hands, then sprang out of the armchair. "Look, it's late, but I brought some things to cleanse this old house. Did you buy a broom?"

I nodded. "That's not really nec—"

"The hell it ain't." Loretta put her hands on her bony hips.

Kyle snickered.

I flipped him off without removing my gaze from my cousin. I exhaled, hoping my next words wouldn't come out rude or disrespectful. "I'm not sure I can deal with the smell of turpentine tonight."

Loretta opened her mouth to argue.

"No. Not sprinkled abound the house, not used to mop the floors, and absolutely not placed on my person." I crossed my arms and leaned back in my armchair, probably looking more like a sullen teenager than a middle-ager.

Kyle cleared his throat. "Sorry, but that doesn't sound like an enticing perfume."

"It's not." I looked back at Loretta and smiled. "I do appreciate the offer, but I'm tired." Besides, I had no idea if the root work would affect the current ghostly residents. This was their home, and had been for centuries, no way would I displace them.

At least not yet.

Loretta made a harrumphing sound, then grinned. "Well, at least you ain't forgot everything. But I'm not leaving here without sweeping."

There's a method and madness when it comes to sweeping for folks who practice Hoodoo. Side to side moving of dirt was a no-no. While it may clean your porch or sidewalk of leaves, you'll also stir up trouble. The proper way to sweep was from the back of the house to the front. When you cleaned the outside, long strokes away from your front door were mandatory. And don't do it immediately after a guest leaves unless you'd prefer them not to return.

Unable to contain myself, I hugged Loretta. "I'll get the back."

When I finally let go, Loretta cupped my cheeks. "Baby, I'm glad you home, but I gotta feeling your troubles are just starting." She looked over at Ash, studying him for a few seconds before looking back at me, grazing her right thumb along my cheekbone. "I think you brought some of it with you."

Chapter 16

PORCHES WERE SWEPT, laughs were had, hugs were given, and the Hoodoo Hillbillies, as Kyle had so lovingly nicknamed the crew, were on their way to wreak havoc elsewhere. Now, Kyle and Ash, with their suitcases in tow, followed me up the stairs.

It took an amount of self-control that I'm surprised I possessed not to put a little extra swing in my hips. Of course, that would've send Kyle into spasms of laughter, and we'd have a play slap fight, embarrassing ourselves in front of company.

So, I kept it classy. When we reached the top of the stairs and the long hallway, I paused, staring at the closed doors daring me to open them.

"What's up?" Kyle asked.

"This is the part where I'd show you to your rooms if I knew where they were. I mean, obviously, most of the guest rooms are on this floor. I just haven't seen them."

"Are you shitting me?" Kyle sat his massive suitcase down and put his hands on his hips. "What in the haunted house hell?"

"Something came up yesterday morning and I had to leave." Like a secret passageway requiring a blood key.

But other than that, it was an ordinary day.

Not.

Kyle dipped his chin and gave me that bossy look.

The only thing I had to give in return was a half-assed smile. Especially with Loretta's warning about bringing Ash and trouble echoing through my wired mind.

Before I could formulate a witty response, Kyle took two steps, then wrapped my hands a comforting squeeze.

I was such an idiot. Kyle was the one person I knew would always have my back. Doubting him after all we'd been through was an insult not only to our friendship, but him. While I couldn't tell him about the town, I could share my secrets.

And I would—eventually.

"Sweetie..." Kyle's usually teasing voice softened and filled with something I sure hoped wasn't pity. "Why don't I sleep with you?"

"That won't be necessary." Ash glared at our clasped hands.

I looked at the firm set of Ash's lips and onyx eyes, and all I could do was blink.

Kyle, however, snickered.

"He's right." I slid my hands from Kyle's and crossed my arms. "And, boy, get your mind out of the gutter."

"Why? It's fun down here." Kyle winked as he executed a graceful about face, reclaiming his suitcase.

Whatever.

I looked at Ash and rolled my eyes. *Men.* While I appreciated his protectiveness, going all caveman wasn't it. "Buddy, you and I need to have a conversation."

"Rut roh, somebody's in trouble," Kyle said, doing his best Scooby Doo impression as he scurried down the hall and out of the blast zone. He paused at the first door. "You kids keep the noise down. Wouldn't want to wake the neighbors."

"The cemetery is next door. They're dead."

"Exactly." Kyle opened a door, turning on a light before slapping his hands against his chest. "I don't know how you managed to get rooms ready while in the pokey, but you're a regular Martha Stewart."

I sprinted down the hall, reaching the door before it closed.

Holy guacamole. While not quite as large as mine, the bedroom was roomy and decorated primarily in navy and cream, with hints of gold.

On the nightstand sat a carafe of hot water along with tea bags and a lovely cup, saucer, and silver spoon. The dresser, made of the same dark wood, was decorated with a cream-colored porcelain bud vase with a single blue-black rose.

Wow, Lucille, or one of the mysterious *we* floating around the house, deserved a raise.

"How many bedrooms are in this mausoleum?"

"From what I was told, including the master bedroom, seven." I leaned against one of the four posters. "And now I've seen all of two of them."

"And you're going to live in here all by your lonesome?" Kyle pulled the navy brocade drape aside and peered into the darkness.

"That's the plan. But I have enough family around, when they visit and get hammered, I'll have plenty of room for them to crash. Plus, I can finally create my dream art studio." I pushed off the bed, crossing to the window, and Kyle. "Go to bed. I have a feeling tomorrow will be just as interesting. Goodnight, honey." Like we always did, I gave Kyle a quick kiss on the mouth.

He hugged me and whispered in my ear, "Are you trying to get me murdered?"

"He's hot, but Ash ain't the boss of me."

"He seems to think so." Kyle chuckled, spun me around, then nudged me toward the door. "Good night, sweetie. Things will look better tomorrow."

"I doubt it," I said, closing the door behind Ash and me.

"I'll escort you to your room," Ash said, his voice a lazy rumble.

I stopped walking, or rather, tried to, but Ash placed a too warm hand on my lower back. He'd be the perfect sleeping bag companion in cold weather camping. Damn, I wished I wouldn't have gone there.

Especially this close to available beds.

"We should find you someplace to sleep." My words escaped in a frustrated rush.

"Your family is amusing," he said, ignoring my suggestion.

"Don't change the subject."

"I'm not. I'm giving you time to get to yes."

I placed my hand on the doorknob to my sanctuary for the time being, then turned around and looked into his obsidian eyes. "Look, I'm not trying to be rude, but—"

Ash placed a finger against my lips. There was a time when I'd have shanked a person for shushing me like that. Okay, not really, but I would think about it — like really hard. But he looked so serious.

"You're not dense, so obviously, I haven't made myself clear enough. Gwendolyn, I am interested in you, and as more than a friend."

The ho side of me wanted to suck his finger into my mouth and swirl my tongue around the tip, then drag him into my bedroom and end the drought by riding this man like a pony. But the practical, and dare I say kind, part of me didn't want this man to die.

I already had Carlos breathing down my neck. Doing the whole death by sex thing — not a great idea.

"I'm flattered. But..." My words kinda died because there was not a bit of moisture left in my mouth. Ash was staring at me like he wanted to eat me up. Not that I would complain.

My tummy did a triple somersault. And we won't even talk about the rest of me. Lawd. How much willpower was I supposed to have?

"I'm going to kiss you. If you don't want that to happen, you should probably leave — now."

I stood frozen for a few seconds, until Ash's face lowered to mine. Then common sense kicked in, and I dashed into my room as if the hounds of hell were on my heels.

"Chicken," Ash said before his chuckles grew distant.

The man must have been a ventriloquist, because his rich voice seemed to be in the room, in my ear, and in my brain. Finally, I pried my back from the door and was headed for the window when Lucille, my personal ghost-in-the-box, sprang through the freaking floor.

My stomach did more acrobatics, but these weren't pleasant. As a matter of fact, they were so unpleasant, my dinner threatened to make a reappearance. I hopped back.

"Oh, ma'am, I'm so sorry."

"Are you trying to scare me to death?"

Lucille's full lower lip quivered slightly, but her posture remained impeccable.

I exhaled a slow breath, then another as I lowered my hands as well as my shoulders. Finally, my heartbeat returned to the normal range. "It's okay, Lucille. I just wasn't expecting you."

This was going to take some getting used to.

"Do you need anything before you retire? I've turned your bed down."

What I needed was the house free of testosterone and dead people. But saying that would be downright mean.

Judging by Lucille's polite nod, my lack of an answer meant no, so she walked toward the exit rather than doing her popping through the rug bit. With one leg through the door, she looked back at me with a watery smile. "Goodnight. I hope your sleep is restful."

While I may have just met Lucille, it was clear that she was a proud woman. Hell, I doubted she'd accept an apology. A mere two seconds ago, all I wanted was solitude, but I needed something else—an ally and answers. So I asked, "Do you have a couple minutes?"

Lucille nodded.

"I'd love to ask you a few questions. "

"Of course. Anything you want to know. "

We walked—well, I walked, and Lucille pretty much floated to a pair of damask armchairs tucked in the alcove created by the trio of massive bay windows.

"It's nice to finally have a blood heir under the roof again."

"Mr. Z used that phrase earlier." I kicked off my flats, bending my legs to curl up on one of the chairs while motioning to the other. "Please."

"Thank you." Lucille sat on the chair with the grace of a ballerina, with her back straight and legs crossed at the ankles, giving me a lovely view of her little lace-up old-fashioned boots. "Well, yes. While the law can dictate inheritance, the house has two requirements for true possession of everything. First, one must be the legal owner. And second, it can only be controlled by one of the blood. Which would be you, a direct female descendent of Lily, the original owner."

"So if I were to sell or give it to someone in the family, they'd have access to everything?"

Lucille hesitated, and eventually nodded. But she sure as hell didn't look happy about it.

It was a struggle, but I managed to remain still, rather than do a happy wiggle in my chair. It sucked for Lucille and Azure House, but eventually getting a relative in here would be a win/win as far as I was concerned.

Rather than gloat, I asked, "Did the curse begin with...Lily?" It felt strange, bordering on disrespectful to call my ancestor by her name rather than an honorific.

"No, that came later, with her daughter Hyacinth, who would be your great-great grandmother." Where once Lucille's voice was matter of fact, it had grown thick and heavy with loss at the mention of Hyacinth.

I so didn't want to see this sweet ghost burst into tears. How did one comfort the dead? I had no freaking idea. But what I could do was steer the subject to happier waters.

"Soooo, what was she like, Hyacinth?" Other than the vampires who seemed to want to forget the past, I finally had an opportunity to see history through the eyes of one who lived it, while remaining cognizant that the old days weren't so good for everyone.

The longer Lucille sat speaking to me, the more solid and corporeal she became. Honestly, I wasn't sure if it was the sparkle in her dark eyes or the crazy deep dimples in her round cheeks that made her look impish, almost fey, but Lucille was absolutely adorable. I sure hoped she could drop the whole ma'am thing.

"Oh, she was something else. Just like the rest of y'all." Lucille shook her head and got a far-off look.

Oh crap. Maybe that wasn't the diversion she needed. I opened my mouth to claim fatigue and give the ghost an out but paused at Lucille's secretive and wistful but happy smile.

She looked back at me, examining me for a couple heartbeats before she spoke, the joy still lighting her eyes. "The women in the family kept diaries. Have you continued the tradition?"

That was a random conversational detour, but okay. I nodded, thinking about how I'd debated keeping a digital accounting of my life, but was obsessively drawn to paper. "Actually, yes."

Lucille clapped her hands. "Good, we can add them to the library. But only when you're ready."

Which wouldn't be anytime soon. The last thing I needed to expose were my past failures and struggles while alive and vulnerable to judgment.

"What about your mother?" Lucille asked, halting my slide into the ocean of what if's.

I shook my head, sadness about the lost knowledge and possibilities making my nose sting.

"Not surprised." Lucille pursed her lips and made that tsking sound made famous by southern women of all flavors. "That one wanted nothing to do with her inheritance."

"She didn't care about money," I said, the words shooting out as my back straightened. From what I could tell, Lucille was cool and all, but ghostly nanny or not, I wasn't about to let her talk shit about my mama.

"Money?" Lucille waved a slim, perfect hand and stood. "That's unimportant. I'm speaking of her gifts. The ones she hopefully passed on to you." She stood, smoothing the front of her dress. "I'll see you in the morning, and when you're ready, I'll introduce you to the rest of the staff. Oh, and don't go nosing around the kitchen house. Cook is kind of cranky." Lucille nodded, then walked through the wall.

Chapter 17

AN ENTIRE SIXTY MINUTES crawled by and here I was, still awake. Every second, every shared word, and each tangled emotion I'd experienced since returning to this damn town played on an unrelenting loop. Especially that young woman's death. Had that curse been meant for me? Fear's icy claws narrowed my throat to the size of a straw.

Without turning on the lamp, I sat up in bed, pressing my back against the mountain of down pillows, wrapping my arms around my bent legs. My breaths became shallower and more frequent as they echoed through the silent room.

Not good.

To avoid getting dizzy, I filled my lungs with lavender scented air, then held my breath captive to fight off the oncoming panic attack.

Remaining in Hoodoo for money I didn't need had been an error. Let's just hope it wasn't as fatal for me as it had been for the poor woman in the supermarket. A flash of...I'm not sure what it was—light, movement, or the sensation of being watched—made the skin across my entire body pebble.

I slid hand under the pile of pillows to my left until the cold handle of my 9mm filled my palm. Funny how quickly the mind ran though scenarios. Not so funny when they all sucked. I debated rolling off the bed like they did in the movies. But I had to use a step stool to get up here, and it would suck to break my neck the first night in Azure House. So my choices were few.

If this situation was a nail, then me and my 9mm were the hammer. With my left hand, I jerked the dainty chain on the lamp and with the other swept the room.

And... nothing other than the tall chest of drawers topped with a vase overflowing with tulips, daffodils, and grape hyacinths. A few feet away stood the ornate framed mirror.

Air and spent adrenaline leached from my body. The anxiety keeping my shoulders up around my ears? Still there. Mostly because of Duncan—and his words.

I was no naïve little bunny fresh from the woods. Life had dulled that shine years ago. By nature, I was an observer, finding joy in the smallest of things: a drop of dew perched precariously on blade of grass, a child's unbridled laughter, and even the sweet scent of puppy breath.

Like most people, I was many things. None of them included gullible.

As I crept to the windows, apprehension tightened my shoulders and spread down my back, each knot building upon the last. Duncan, the little butt wipe, might have answers that Loretta didn't, and Aunt Rose wouldn't divulge. However trusting Duncan's ass damned near got me imprisoned—or worse.

Pulling the curtains apart, I spotted the object of my derision sitting on Stella's roof. Yes, I was goofy naming my van, but she was a bad-ass. My version of a trusty steed. The weight of not only Duncan's gaze, but his guilt seeped straight through my pores, landing somewhere in the vicinity of my bubbling stomach.

"Well, are you going to stare all night or invite me the hell in?" Duncan yelled as his dangling legs swung back and forth, disappearing through Stella's side panels, before reappearing just as quickly.

Unsure if ghostly ears could hear through glass, I unlocked it, then raised the heavy but well-oiled windows before leaning my hands on the ledge. "You can come in," I shout-whispered. When Duncan's face lit up like an expectant teenaged boy who'd been invited to lover's lane, I raised an index finger and shook my head. "Hol' up. You aren't staying."

This house already had enough ghosts.

He nodded. "I can handle that."

"But can you say the same about telling the truth? The way I remember, honesty wasn't one of your strengths."

Duncan flinched, then bit down on his transparent lip. "I deserve that. And more." He disappeared, then reappeared in my bedroom, looking far more solid than he had earlier. "I owe you and..."

My heart demanded I comfort the friend who'd been cheated out of experiencing life's trials, triumphs, and yes, even tragedies. Too bad for Duncan, my head ran this damned show. I ignored his distress.

While he stared at the plastered ceiling, I studied Duncan's unchanged face. What would he have looked like as a forty-something man? Would he have a paunch, or inhabit a similarly buff body?

He'd always had that Marlboro man vibe, even as a kid. And the four-wheeler accident that left the scar on his chin only added to the attraction. Girls, and a couple of boys, pursued Duncan relentlessly. Thankfully, I wasn't one of the horde. But we'd been close—or so I thought. Until he'd pulled a wicked-looking knife on me, jabbering about some compulsion and killing yours truly.

"You're not going to make this easy, are you?"

"Uh no," I answered, voice filled with plenty of *duh*. "Let's do this. You and I aren't going to rekindle our friendship because, obviously, we didn't have one."

His already pale face blanched. "Gwennie, I—"

"Oh no. You'll get your chance. First, you're going to stand your dead ass there and listen."

Duncan's Adam's apple bobbed, then he nodded, wisely keeping his trap shut.

If I were a dragon, fire would have accompanied my words. I'd carried two decades of betrayal, and I needed to unpack those bags and lay them where they belonged. On Duncan. "You ruined my life and my relationship not only with the town, but my family."

"Like Rita." Duncan's voice was a mournful whisper.

"No shit, Sherlock." I really wished I could punch him. Either that or knee Duncan in his favorite body part.

"I've always been your friend, Gwennie." He exhaled, swiped his hand down his face, then licked his lips. "That's how I... why I... I died."

"Oh, so now it's my fault?"

He shook his head vigorously. "No. No, that's not what I'm saying." He raised his palms toward me, the gesture somewhere between a surrender and a defensive posture. "You and I lived surrounded by powerful creatures. But everyone, even you, was more gifted than me."

Wow.

My mouth fell open, amazed at the gall of this asshole. Death had given Duncan neither perspective nor wisdom. It just made him more of a self-centered jerk. "Seriously?"

"I was damn near a null!" Duncan shouted, color rushing to his translucent face. Oddly enough, the longer we spoke, the more he solidified. The spray of tiny freckles on his right cheek were more visible. When he spoke again, Duncan's voice held skin-ruffling anger.

Well, well, well. Maybe little Duncan gained something in death after all.

"If anyone in this shithole town could empathize with me, I thought it would be you. But I was wrong—again." He scratched the back of his neck as if considering blaming me for his failures.

Not today, motherfucker. "When did your insecure bullshit become my fault?" I patted my hand against my upper chest. "Because, baby, I didn't see you running to my rescue when the Tribunal was about to execute my ass for using black magic. Where were you then, Duncan?"

He opened his mouth to speak, but I rolled right over him.

"And where the fuck were you tonight when I was wearing that poor woman's brains all over my shirt?" I raised my hand to stop him from speaking. "Don't bother. I already know the answer. Like always, everything is about you. What you want. What you need. And what you don't have. You're a narcissist, Duncan. You used me and I have no idea how many others. And like clockwork, you roll up wanting to do the same again."

I put my fists on my hips and leaned closer. "Guess what? I'm not playing. Just say whatever secret you supposedly possess, then get the hell out."

Duncan's shoulders sagged before he opened and closed his mouth. Finally, he fully deflated and fell languidly into an armchair, leaning over to place his muscular forearms on his thighs just above his knees. When he spoke again, gone was the belligerence; all he sounded was tired. "You may want to take a load off for this next part."

My stomach tightened at the anguish in Duncan's eyes as I eased into the seat across from him, mustering up as much dignity as a woman wearing flannel pajama pants decorated with suitcase-toting cows could.

"Speak, but let's do the abbreviated version." I tilted my head then snapped my fingers in front of Duncan's face. "Hello? My eyes are up here.

Don't stare at my boobs." Especially since the girls were thirty-eight longs beneath my white tank top.

"Sorry." He shrugged, not looking the least bit apologetic. "It's been awhile."

"Let's skip the ghost sex conversation." I leaned my elbow against the arm of the chair.

"Speaking of sex..." He looked over at the empty bed. "You married? Divorced?"

I snorted. "That would be a no and a no. Mostly, because any lover I managed to get close to died—and violently—before we made it to the love part."

He watched me for a few minutes, unblinking, face unreadable. Finally, Duncan sighed, and something akin to anger filled his pale green eyes. "Damn, Gwennie."

I tilted my head and smirked. "Hey, let's bump uglies. Maybe you'll do me the favor of dying all the way."

"Ouch."

I shrugged, then chuckled, the sound like dried twigs snapping beneath a boot. "You know what the cops call you when you have a string of dead ex-lovers?" When Duncan didn't answer, I filled in the blank. "Suspect."

"I know you don't want to hear it—"

"I don't."

Being the jackass that he was, Duncan spoke anyway. "I'm sorry."

"I doubt you travelled across the globe to screw up my love life." I flicked the free hand resting on my thigh. "At least that part's not on you."

This time when I laughed, it didn't sound as if it would shatter into a thousand angry pieces. Yay me. I glanced at the ceiling, and the subtle white on white fleur de lis pattern stamped into the plaster.

"Enough about me, Duncan. What was ..." The energy rolling off him was suffocating, coating my skin like humidity on a July afternoon.

I swallowed. Hard.

"Those dead lovers were a curse, but they have nothing to do with your family."

I licked my lips.

"It wasn't me who wished you harm." Duncan sat up straight, his shoulders back and chin high. "Until you destroy the Adze, she won't stop until you and everyone we both love are dead."

Chapter 18

MY HANDS TREMBLED AS I poured water from the delicate glass pitcher etched with vines. Damn it, I should have never returned. And staying didn't seem to be the right answer either. Except, if Duncan was being truthful, that could be a death sentence for my family.

As I stared out the window, one question ate at me. Who would the creature kill next? Death came for us all. And honestly, leaving this hell hole we called Earth wasn't as frightening as remaining and trudging through this thing we called life.

But what if the...the...whatever it was offered me the choice of my life for my family's?

I bit down on my lower lip. At my core, I was a brawler. I had to be. Some people believed because I lived in the largest house in town that I was a pampered princess. They didn't have a clue. I didn't want a bodyguard twenty-four seven, so I had to learn how to defend myself. Having a heartbeat, being a walking, talking blood donor made me a liability for Rose and Raul. Not that I was inherently unsafe in their home or with their congregation, but there was one rule: outside of the family, trust no one.

So if they wanted a fight, I was down. I may be older and my body a little softer, but if that monster wanted to fuck around, they'd sure as hell find out.

"Gwennie, are you okay?" Duncan asked from behind me.

Was I okay?

Was I fucking okay? That he'd bothered to ask was proof that not only was Duncan dead, but out of his ever-loving-mind.

"I'm just dandy," I snapped, still clutching the glass older than most people in this town. I exhaled slowly. "Give me a sec. The last few hours have been..."

"A lot," Duncan finished.

When I finally turned around, Duncan was close enough to reach out and touch—with my fist. Whoever said violence was never the answer had never lost everything, then created a newer almost beautiful life, only to have it too destroyed with lies, betrayal, and once again...death.

"Sorry, boo." I walked over to the round lace-covered table and placed the empty glass on it before reclaiming my seat. "If you expect me to trust that your motives are pure, that you won't benefit from finding the..." I struggled to remember the word.

"Adze," he completed as he took the opposite chair.

I flicked my fingers. "Adze, zazee, whatever the hell it is. I'm not going to help you."

"I thought you loved my family. Rita was your best friend."

"A friend who, like a third of the town, believed that I murdered you." I leaned back and crossed my right leg over my left. "Hey, since they hate me, they should be safe."

"They don't—"

"Yes. They do. The shittiest part is that I can't blame them. You set me up, Duncan, and you did it good. What I don't understand is why?" This motherfucker was going to tell me everything, or he could get out and I'd find and kill the Adze myself. Of course he remained silent, so I pushed on. "And while you're at it, did the exploding witch have anything to do with whatever messed-up deal you have going?"

Duncan covered his mouth with his hand and stared down at the oriental rug. When his gaze returned to mine, those green eyes were hard, determined, and held a fury so molten that translucent waves vibrated around him.

"You're right. I would get something out of eliminating the Adze—safety. For you, my family, and the coven. But most of all, I'd finally have my revenge." Duncan sprang out of the chair, marching to the almost floor-to-ceiling window overlooking the cemetery where he'd been interred.

I smiled, and even to me it felt malicious, malevolent, and gloriously mad. "Revenge. Now that's something I understand."

Duncan whirled around, his eyes widening at whatever he saw on my face.

"Start from the beginning. Tell me how you allowed jealousy to ruin everyone's life." I bounced my crossed leg.

"I *was* jealous," he said, voice as flat as his expression. After staring through me for what felt like an eternity, Duncan returned to the armchair, then sank into it and the story. "When we were kids, while y'all were out having grand adventures in the woods, I researched rituals to reclaim my gifts that Rita absorbed in the womb. I tried everything, from arcane magic to wishing on stars."

The wall around my heart crumbled ever so slightly, standing witness to his torment. While not identical, I did relate to his struggle. Growing up human in a house filled with vampires wasn't a walk in the park either—especially once I'd been nicknamed Blood-bag.

"Weren't you a little young for working spells?" I asked, the words falling into the silence like a stone through a pond's surface.

Duncan dipped his chin. "When did you see your first ghost?"

I frowned and shook my head. "That's completely different."

"No, Gwen. It is not." His voice deepened from his boyish tenor to a dark, determined baritone. "I thought you wanted to get this done."

I mimed zipping my lips shut, uncrossed my legs, scooted back, and settled in.

"Considering my age and lack of magical abilities, my efforts were less than effective." Duncan paused, his gaze distant as he traced his pinky along the edge of his lower lip. "I wish I could say nothing came of those stolen nights. What I believed to be an amusing and extra curious firefly turned out to be far more dangerous."

I pressed my thumbnail against my thigh to keep my condemnation in check. Because honestly, any of us kids could have made the same mistake. For as much as the children of Hoodoo lived surrounded by the supernatural, we lived an uncomplicated, simple, and relatively safe life compared to most American children.

"Did it...hurt you?" I asked, my voice barely a whisper.

"No, not really. But that beautiful hypnotizing light offered a place to belong. To be my..." He looked off in the distance as if the pain hovered just beyond the promise of pleasure. "...someone."

Crash. There went another piece of my armor. "I could have done that. Been your person."

"Thanks, but your dance card was full. Even when we were eight years old, the way you looked at Carlos was..." It was Duncan's turn to smile, and it was heart crushingly lonely. "...one more thing to be jealous of."

We sat in silence for a couple of minutes. All I could do was replay our childhood on fast forward. What else could I have done? Like he'd said, I did have my own shit, but all of it wasn't Carlos. There was no way I could have repaired what was broken with Duncan.

Hell, I couldn't even fix myself.

"With each year watching the coven hover around my twin, excited about her magic. The magic she only had because she'd absorbed mine. Well." He shrugged, as if to say no big.

But we both knew it to be a lie.

"With the Adze's constant whispers, I grew more and more resentful, which eventually grew into something far more dangerous—rage."

"Oh, Duncan."

"Yeah." He nodded, the movement so slight, I would have missed it had I not been studying his pale face. "The toxic emotions exposed me to unfiltered evil. For the small price of sharing my body could have anything I ever desired."

I covered my mouth with my hand. Oh, I was still angry with Duncan, and nowhere near close to forgiving him, but damn, I ached for the young man who used to be my friend.

"Like every bad fairytale, I failed to read the fine print. The other cost of my power was your life."

Chapter 19

FORGET DENIAL, I WENT into full avoidance mode after Duncan dropped the mother of all bombs in my lap. What he wanted to do was discuss and unwrap the motive, but what I needed was space.

Thankfully, he poofed away to parts unknown.

Too bad for me, not even a good thirty minutes later, Duncan's semitransparent head popped up through my gleaming wood floors. "You asleep?" he whispered.

"Does it look like it?" I scowled, not from my bed, but the sweet rose-colored fainting couch tucked beneath one of the massive floor-to-ceiling windows.

"I have just the thing to cheer you up. Come with me." He extended a hand.

"We're not friends, I still hate you. You know that, right?"

His smile wilted. "Hate hate, or finding a way to forgiving me?"

"Have I given you any indication that I want a relationship with you, especially friendship?" I rolled my eyes, then my body away from him, staring out the windows at the errant cloud floating across the moon.

Had I committed some grave offense in a past life? Because I didn't understand why payment was due in this one. Little did we know that that space between a rock and a hard place wasn't the choice, but fear and loneliness. And I alone would be forced to walk the path that I chose.

Would it sound to wussy to say that I didn't want to be strong? That right now I wanted someone to come and make it better, make the choice for me. What was that saying about a wish in one hand and shit in the other?

"I guess you know about the cool-ass basement?"

I sat up then turned to face him. This ghost was getting on my nerves. I could see a banishing in his future. "This is Texas; we don't do basements."

I already knew that for a lie since that passageway behind the fireplace led somewhere. Perhaps I should be pleased about the lack of an elevator to hell.

Then again, maybe it wouldn't have been a bad thing if it shuttled Duncan away.

"You're in for a treat." Once again, Duncan extended a ghostly hand. "Come on, Gwennie, let's have an adventure."

"Don't call me that."

He nodded, watching me expectantly, eyes filled with too much hope, too much longing, and way too much sorrow.

"Fine," I snapped as I stood. Did he expect me to intertwine my solid and very live fingers with his? That was not how this worked. Duncan had been dead long enough to know better. "This changes nothing."

I refused to get sucked into another Duncan drama. The last one didn't work out well for either of us. What I wanted to do was hurt him in the only way I knew. The thing most ghosts wanted most wasn't life, but to feel again. Time to remind him that he was dead—and would forever remain that way.

So I smiled and extended my left hand, the one with the lightning bolts. My Thor hand.

Duncan's eyes widened.

Whether in suspicion or surprise, I had no idea. Were he smart, he'd choose the former. My hand hovered over his pale palm and we stared at each other, our gazes holding in the fading night. As my palm passed through his, everything happened at once.

My hand tingled as if I'd jammed a fork in an electrical outlet. Light flared, running first up my arm, then through Duncan's hand. Only it didn't stop there for him. The current, power, or whatever the hell it was that filled me since I did my version of Lazarus rising from the dead ricocheted through his body. Everywhere my power flowed became solid, whole, real.

I gasped, and for the first time since Duncan appeared, his chest rose and fell. This time, his eyes were filled with something greater than guilt and headier than sorrow—wonder.

"Please, don't let me go. I feel so... so..." Duncan's fingers gently circled my wrist as he exhaled through his pursed lips. "...alive. Something that obviously I hadn't experienced in a while."

I stood transfixed by his radiant smile.

A too solid thumb traced the delicate skin of my inner wrist. Did I mention that Duncan was a bit of a letch? Not even death can cure some things.

"Don't even think about it." I tugged at my hand, which by the way, he had no intention of releasing. He opened his mouth to play innocent, but I gave him the look.

"Fine." He paused his newly working lungs, and one by one, peeled his fingers from my wrist.

We both waited, me barely breathing and him not at all, for him to return to his translucent ghosthood.

When he remained solid, I moved to the next subject. "What did you want to show me?" Despite being all kinds of pissed off and confused, I chuckled when Duncan wiggled his eyebrows. "Boy, focus. Some of us need sleep."

"Maybe a short walk through your secret passageways will wear you out."

"Sounds good." I took a step toward the bedroom door.

He grabbed hold of my hand this time, sighing as his still cool fingers interlaced with mine. "Nope, this way. You and I are taking a trip into your closet."

"Thanks, but no thanks. Who I sleep with—"

"Now whose mind is in the gutter? I'm talking about a door that leads into the bowels of your home."

"Well, since you put it that way."

Hand in hand, Duncan and I strolled to the deep closet, which had probably gone through a few iterations in its life. Honestly, I was more surprised that the entrance wasn't some kind of stupid blood door like on the fireplace.

Many older homes were notoriously short on closets, since for tax purposes, it was considered an additional room. But Azure House, along with Uncle Raul's home out at the Double R, and a couple other houses predated tax rolls, since they were built when Texas belonged to Mexico.

We took three steps inside before I was surrounded by inky darkness and the comforting smell of cedar. "Wait, I need a flashlight." I stopped.

"You have got to be shitting me. Are you afraid?"

Yes. "No, but hello..." I jabbed a finger at myself while whispering furiously, "Human, remember?"

Although I couldn't see Duncan's face, I suspected it held an if-you-say-so expression. His next words proved me right. "You're something alright, but human ain't it. At least not anymore."

I stomped out of the closet, dragging Duncan's ghostly ass with me. Only after snagging my phone from the nightstand and making sure it was on silent did we resume our expedition.

Could I trust Duncan to not betray me? Hell no. But he needed vengeance more than he wanted to harm me.

Too bad secret passages only came with the flashing "enter here" signs on cartoons. But after some fiddling around, we found the latch, despite completing the task with our hands joined. I whispered a small prayer to the ancestors asking for not only a rodent-free corridor, but lubricated hinges. Well, maybe, just maybe my prayers had been answered. When the door opened, it was without a squeak from either the metal or furry invaders.

Yeah, but that didn't mean I was ready to surge forward when the rush of stale lilac-scented air pushed my locs over my shoulder.

I swallowed, shaking my head as Duncan passed through the entryway, tugging me behind him with a strength that shouldn't have been possible.

"Come on." He turned around, capturing my right hand as he walked backward. "There's the stairwell leading to the first floor. Let's go to the basement."

"How about we not," I shout-whispered.

Without releasing my hands, Duncan flapped his bent arms before pressing his lips against my ear and whispering, "Chicken."

I rolled my eyes.

"Then let's go see your boyfriend."

"No, that's rude."

"Well, I wasn't the one who put the man, if you want to call him that, in a room with not one, but two peepholes." This time, he put some oomph behind the tug, giving me little choice but to follow or make a scene.

Seeing that I didn't want Ash to hear me cussing out someone he couldn't see and think me nuts as well as a peeping Tom, I grudgingly surrendered to Duncan's ridiculous scheme.

"Wait. What do you mean if I want to call him that?" I whispered as the wide blue beam from my phone illuminated the dust-free floor. The narrow corridor was wide enough for two people to walk side by side, and long enough that my dim light didn't reach the end. "Please tell me there aren't viewing ports in all the bedrooms."

"From what I could tell, yes. All but yours."

I had a buttload more questions, but the murmur of Ash's deep-accented voice filled the claustrophobic silence.

The angel on my shoulder preached the merits of privacy, but my feet had other ideas. I turned the flashlight function off and drifted to the pinhole of pale golden light coming through the wall.

Like so much of this night, spying on a guest was a mistake, mostly because I couldn't understand a word he said. Just as I parted my lips to inform Duncan that I was done, Ash switched from what sounded like Arabic to English.

"No, I haven't had time. This night has been..." I could almost imagine Ash swiping his hand down his face. "Difficult."

I peered through the wall, barely biting back a moan. Damn, why did he have to be so fine? Gone was the crisply tailored suit, replaced by a pair of silky pajama pants. Screw sweatpants; this was a level of sexy that should be on Only Fans.

"No, I haven't told her. Have you not listened to a word I said?" Ash grunted. "The fucking sheriff is a wolf, and who knows what the hell else is going on in this town."

This time, he did swipe his hand down his face, but it barely registered, because his words slammed into me first.

Ash nodded, then spun in my direction.

Had I made noise? Breathed too hard? I squeezed my eyes closed, then held my breath. Oh, Ash... Why? Why didn't you talk to me? Probably for the same reasons I hadn't come out of the magical closet to him—he couldn't.

At least I hoped it was the reason. Because otherwise, it was one betrayal too many. I opened my eyes to find Ash facing me, his tattoo-covered chest exposed. I wanted to trail my fingers across the Arabic lettering inked on his stomach before I left my own work upon the pristine flesh of his back.

Eventually, I dragged my gaze up his body to his face, and the eyes that felt as though he stared through the wall and straight through to my soul.

"My intention has never been to lie to Gwendolyn. Not then and sure as hell not now."

He paused as if listening to the person on the other end. "Last night was…" Ash closed his eyes and pinched the bridge of his nose. "It was bad."

Yes, Ash, it was. But having you there made it better. I was safe, at least for a little while. I mouthed a silent thank you.

This time when Ash opened his eyes, they were red.

Not red as in he'd had a sudden allergy attack or wept from loneliness because I wasn't beside him. No, that would almost be normal. I'm talking the pupils that were so dark I once thought them bottomless, along with the rest of his eyes, moved like lava, with glimpses of gold and black flowing through the sea of crimson.

I wanted to move. I wanted to run. I even considered screaming, but his next words held me hostage. "I will destroy this town and everyone in it to protect Gwendolyn. Do you understand me? I don't care about treaties, vows, or any of that shit."

A low buzz filled my ears, growing louder until I couldn't think. What in the Sam Houston was going on? Was there anyone in my life I could trust?

Duncan squeezed my hand. But I couldn't look at him, didn't need to see pity in his dead eyes.

"Look, it's remarkable that with everything she's been through to remain unbroken. Gwendolyn has flourished despite the odds, ignoring the sword of Damocles dangling above her head."

Okay, that was nice. But it still didn't forgive the whole glowing eyes thing.

"I don't give a damn," Ash said after a short pause. "Their lies aren't my problem. The clock is ticking. They have forty-eight hours to make it right. Or I will. Because I'm done."

So am I Ash, so am I.

Chapter 20

I PADDED ACROSS MY bedroom rocking Birkin-sized bags under my eyes, a slouchy gray lounger set that matched my mood, and thick fuzzy socks. After a day filled with exploding heads, a trip to the pokey, the ghost of teenaged past, and drumroll, please...the hot guy betrayal, I couldn't sleep.

If I was going to be this damned tired, it should be because of a night of multiple orgasms. And if non-self-induced pleasure wasn't on the table, bourbon would've been nice.

Since I was awake, I'd concocted the perfect plan: march into the kitchen, then I'd lay it all out. Not the ghost and supernatural family tree part. Or that I knew for sure that not only was Ash a lying rat bastard but playing for team non-human. Rather, I'd merely explain that I needed to relax, recover, and reacclimate to small town life. Which, at least in my exhausted mind, sounded reasonable.

Until a few hours ago, all I'd felt for the Ash was a healthy dose of lust, flavored by a blossoming friendship. Now, not so much. That belief had morphed into something else—disappointment with myself for once again believing in a man, and anger that Ash was one of many liars surrounding me.

And I held the fuck on to that simmering burn, until I reached the doorway of the kitchen and my brain cells scrambled.

It wasn't Kyle and Maria huddled at the table like judges at a tighty-whitey contest. It wasn't even the platter holding what looked to be a whole damned hog of crisp bacon and still steaming sausage. And it wasn't the stack of pancakes, so fluffy, they could float away.

No. My full, hormone-addled attention was on the unobstructed view of rippling muscles across Ash's back.

"Good morning, sleeping beauty." Kyle, dressed in a fitted navy-blue sweatshirt and matching bottoms, raised his mug in a toast.

"Hey." I waved at Kyle.

Yes, I'd spied on the shirtless Ash a few hours ago, but the sight of him half-naked *and* cooking was... a lot. If my ovaries still functioned, I'm sure the remaining half dozen eggs just released, hoping for a last hurrah.

Dream on, bitches.

Maria handed me her mug. "You want to fill this while you get yours?"

"Who said I was having coffee?" I snatched Maria's cup then marched my ass over to the machine, ignoring her snickers. I grabbed the lone mug filled with warm water, before glancing up at Ash. "Morning. You know you didn't have to cook, right?"

"Well, we need sustenance, and those two didn't seem interested." Ash winked, then flipped three pancakes with the efficiency of a short order cook.

"Maybe they'd be a little less distracted if you wore clothes." Was that heartburn or jealousy stomping around in my chest?

Ash slid the spatula under a pancake, adding it to the pile. He did all this while gluing me to the spot with those taunting dark eyes. "Am I a distraction, Gwendolyn?" His voice got sexier and his British-tinted accent more prominent.

Kyle stage-whispered from the table, "Ooh, this is getting interesting."

I gave Kyle my best death glare. "I hate to disappoint you two, but this," I swirled my finger like a magic wand, pointing around the large bright kitchen, "isn't some tawdry reality show."

"Tawdry?" Maria frowned. "I know you old, but damn, you sound like my grandmama."

"We're a year apart. If I'm old, what does that make you?" I emptied the water warming my mug in the sink before refilling Maria's with coffee and cream, minus the arsenic.

"A cougar. Rawr." She clawed the air in Ash's direction.

I rolled my eyes at the peanut gallery and focused on Ash. "I made a decision—"

"Oh, I know that face. This should be good." Kyle nudged Maria with his elbow.

"Thank you for the support last night, but the three of you enjoy your breakfast—then leave."

"Sure, no problem," called Maria from the table. "Would you dump more cream in there?"

Seriously? "Now I remember why I moved," I muttered as I grabbed the old-fashioned tiny white pitcher and took it and Maria's coffee to the table. Yay me. I even managed not to dump it on her new wig, this one curly.

"Don't be blaming me." Maria leaned back in her chair and crossed her arms over her peach scrub top. "You moved because of your prissy Aunt Rose. Oh, and that other thing."

"Would that other thing be the good sheriff? I got quite the eyeful last night." Kyle fanned himself. "You're gonna have to fill me in. Because Ms. Gwendolyn left out the juicy parts."

"Hello...? I'm standing right here." I accidentally on purpose nudged Maria's arm with my hip as she poured and proceeded to spill the cream.

"Heifer." Maria grinned.

"Tramp." I scowled at her, but my lips curled up at the corners.

"What is the story with you and the sheriff?" Ash asked, his voice grumbly, reminding me of that early morning in Dublin when I called asking for help in escaping supernatural hitmen.

"That story happened so long ago, it no longer matters." I crossed the room to my coffee because, Lord knows, I needed the caffeine to deal with this crowd.

Ash dipped his chin, watching me before he spoke. "Perhaps not to you." He flipped two more perfect pancakes.

How many people was he planning to feed? There were only four pulse-owning folks in the room.

I leaned against the counter next to Ash, wrapping one arm around my waist and pressing the warm mug against my chest as I sought the right combination of words to kick him out of my home without outing him to the humans. "I appreciate last night, as well as Morocco. But this, I'm handling on my own."

Ash looked at me for one second, then another before turning the fire off beneath the griddle. Then, with grace and efficiency, he placed the last silver-dollar pancakes on the heaping platter.

"Hello? Did you hear me?" I wanted to rap my knuckles against his thick skull.

"Yes, Gwendolyn." Ash removed the mug from my hand, setting it gingerly aside before he pressed his hands on the counter, trapping me between his tattoo-covered arms. "I heard you. Now it's time for you to listen."

"Is this what I've been missing not hanging out with her?" Maria asked.

"Oh, honey, you have no idea," Kyle whispered.

Right about now, I regretted not locking myself in my bedroom.

"Be honest, this isn't about your capabilities, is it? Give me forty-eight hours and you can have that truth." His voice was just above a whisper. The message was for an audience of one.

My lips tightened as I studied his angular handsome face. Well, at least we'd moved past pretending. I curled my fingers to keep from caressing the short well-groomed hair now covering his jaw. Finally, I asked, "And what do you want in return?"

An almost wistful air filled his onyx eyes and tugged at the right corner of his mouth. "No more than you're willing to give."

"How about the truth?" I swallowed and waited.

And waited until my mouth grew so dry, I imagined tumbleweeds rolling around in there. Although I couldn't say the same for anatomy south of the border.

Ash exhaled, giving me...was that hope blooming in my chest, or dread? Which would I be happy with?

"Yes. If that is what you wish, but you should have come to me last night." The *rather than spying* part remained just beneath the surface.

The shape of Ash's eyes remained the same, but rather than last night's lava-lamp light show, inky black spread across his eyeball, replacing every speck of white. Then his iris, now a glowing red, spotlighted the elongated, almost reptilian black pupil.

Perhaps the raging hormones had fried my brain cells, but rather than be horrified, or terrified, I smiled, utterly mesmerized. Yup, something was wrong with me.

"Another war is coming to Hoodoo," Ash said, his lips barely moving.

That may be so, but it would never rival the one raging between my heart and mind. If I had a lick of sense, I'd walk him out of Azure House with a gun at the small of his back. Wait, did lead or even silver work?

For that matter, what was he?

Rather than await my reply, Ash's molten gaze drifted to my lips, studying them as if he waged his own battle. Finally, he surrendered and kissed me — hard. His tongue, unforked and still human, traced the seam of my lips.

When I refused him entrance, Ash pulled away, licking the taste of me from his lips, which almost sent me into a lust-induced heart attack.

"Trust me, Gwendolyn, it's coming. And I'll be damned if I leave you and your human family to battle alone."

"Now who's being dramatic? Nothing's coming to —"

I was interrupted, not by a demanding kiss or comments from the peanut gallery, but the doorbell.

"You three go ahead and eat; that should be for me." Ash kissed my forehead and left the kitchen, followed by three pairs of eyes.

Before I could catch myself, I called out, "You need to chill with the bossy shit. This ain't the bedroom."

Ash stopped walking. If he was a car, he would have skidded to a halt, sound effects and all. He looked over his shoulder, and the tiny grin on his lips almost did me in.

"Please tell me I didn't say that last part out loud," I whispered as I prayed that my haunted house had a trap door. Beneath my feet.

And it would open—like now.

"You sure did." Maria grinned and fanned her face. "Woo. That was too much for my delicate constitution."

"I don't want to interrupt your viewing pleasure, but you may have some squatters in that little building out back." Kyle took another sip of his coffee.

"What little building?" I frowned, because as far as I knew, the closest structure was a family crypt. Which was in the cemetery.

Maria returned to the table with a healthy serving of both pancakes and bacon. "He's probably talking about the kitchen house. But ain't nobody out there, trust me."

Kyle's freshly threaded brows drew together and he shook his head. "I... don't know what a kitchen house is, but I saw lights last night and smoke this morning."

Yikes. Looked like I needed to meet Cook, sooner than later.

Luckily, Maria used her big mouth for good. "Some people called them summer houses, but they're a separate kitchen that usually enslaved women cooked in. They not only kept the main house cooler and allegedly cut down on fires, but keeping it real, it just kept the help out of sight."

"Okay..." Kyle gave me some wicked side-eye.

I shook my head. "Before you ask, no. The ancestors who built this house didn't own people, which would be..." I shivered. Then again, with each passing moment, I was learning that I didn't know squat about either myself or my family.

I stuffed a fork filled with pancakes in my mouth to keep from saying something stupid as Ash returned to the kitchen. *Whoa,* these were amazing. Ash absolutely, positively had to leave. No male's food should be as yummy as his other...assets.

"It was nice of you and Kyle to visit." I shoved more food in my mouth and maybe even moaned. Oops. "Don't worry about me when you guys leave today. I'll be safe thanks to my family, and my good friends Smith, Wesson, and their pal Ruger."

Not to mention my ghostly alarm system.

Chapter 21

I STOOD IN THE LIBRARY, which, other than my bedroom, I'd designated as my happy place in Azure House. Well, at least until I left.

But then what...?

Ash's confirmation regarding his inhumanity made it easier to toss him in front of a bus. Unless he tossed me in front of it first. Should I give him the time he asked for? I don't know, a lot could happen in two days. If my death was something Ash wanted, I'd already be pushing up daisies.

Damn, why did life—and death—have to be so complicated?

I wandered across the room, inexplicably drawn to the trio of stained-glass windows, stopping at the center panel. The intricate and impressive leaded glass portrayed the expulsion of Lucifer and his crew from heaven. It was vibrant, colorful, and like the rest of the house, unblemished by age.

A soft knock at the door interrupted my inspection. "Come in," I said, both hoping and dreading that Ash would walk through the doors.

Kyle popped a Swedish Fish in his mouth as he strolled in, as if the gleaming mahogany floors were a catwalk.

Watching the wonder on his dark, expressive face made me smile. I tried to see the two-story room through his eyes. The walls of books, the spiral metal staircase with its gleaming brass railings leading to the upper landing, not to mention the pristine furnishings.

Yeah, I totally got where Kyle was coming from.

"Wow... This is beyond magnificent. What kind of magic kept people from breaking in?" He meandered across the thick rug, pausing briefly to check out the pattern, then focused on the bookshelf.

Kyle looked from a book to me and back again before carefully slipping a leather-bound tome with gold lettering along the spine from the shelf, flipping it open. He gasped. "Woman, this is a first edition," he said, voice filled with something like reverence.

I was impressed, but not surprised by his discovery.

The respectful wonder in his eyes made me smile and forget my troubles. The man was all about learning and the written word. But there was something else about my friend that I'd yet to unravel. He was a man who seemed to love having it both ways. Kyle loved, almost worshipped everything old, but also craved new and exciting. The way he cradled *Great Expectations* to his chest like a beloved infant, Kyle was having a moment with the old.

I leaned to the side, peering through the door, hoping to see his oversized suitcase. No such luck. Oddly enough, I wasn't sure how that made me feel. Along with the pancakes, my tummy was a bubbling mixture of hope and fear. Hope that my friend remained as ride and die as he always had, and fear that should he stay and he be injured, or worse...

Pressure built behind my eyes. If Kyle so much as broke a fingernail, I'm not sure how I'd forgive myself.

"Did you come to say goodbye?" I finally asked.

"Yes."

My eyes widened.

Kyle smirked, returned the book to the shelf, then looked back at me, his full lips tight and eyes filled with... something. "Just for the afternoon. Sweetheart, you're out of your ever-loving mind if you think I'm leaving after what happened last night."

I sighed. "That's about what I figured." While my flat tone and rigid body shouted that wasn't a good thing, I'm pretty sure my grin ruined the effect.

He walked over to me and opened his arms for a hug, which I wholeheartedly accepted. Kyle was my person, the one I shared my hopes, my fears, and most of my secrets with. Yet I'd withheld my most important parts.

Or had I?

When it came down to it, we were all complicated creatures. The sum of my hurts, losses, and fears, forged both the woman I'd become and the younger, more damaged girl that he'd met in college. Honestly, I'd only allowed Kyle, my dearest friend, access to the palatable and mundane pieces of me.

Why? Because I was scared that he'd walk away.

The ending of a friendship hit different than romantic loss. Sure, the rational part of my brain knew people were in your life for a reason, a season, or lifetime. But the heart wanted what it wanted.

And for me, that was for Kyle to never leave, to remain the person who'd never betray me.

"Trouble is coming to this town." *And I'll do what I must to protect you. Even kill.* But I kept that to myself, plausible deniability and all that.

"Then leave. This house is nice and all, but you're more important."

I smiled, and it wasn't a happy one. "If only it were that easy."

Kyle slipped his fingers into mine and led me to the couch.

I stood there like a gargoyle watching his graceful descent. Calling it sitting would be an insult. How was it that, even rocking a suit as expensive as one of Ash's, Kyle limbs flowed as if he wore a leotard?

"Come on." Kyle patted the empty cushion beside him. "Talk to papa."

"You're such an ass." I plopped down and stretched out my legs. "You look nice. Where're you off to?"

"No changing the subject, sweet cheeks. What's keeping you from walking away from this house and this town? I get why you don't want to ditch the Hoodoo Hillbillies. Those folks had me hollering."

I smiled again; this time, it was real. "They're touched, but I love em." And for some reason, they loved me. But what if the danger dogging me spilled over onto them? That tugged not only at the corners of my mouth, but my heart went into a downward spiral. I looked at my friend and confidant. "Someone in this town wants me gone. Last night was personal."

It was time I got real about who. As far as I knew, there were only two people magically powerful enough to lay that kind of spell, but only one of them was motivated by something akin to hatred.

Rita.

Giving life to the accusation gave me the chills. I looked down at the pebbled skin on my arms and sighed. My body also knew the score. If this were the movie *Ghost*, I would have been Molly.

"Any idea who?" Kyle's face, usually so happy and playful, grew hard. In that moment, I knew I wasn't the only person in the room capable of murder.

So I lied. "No."

A single sharp nod was Kyle's response, but his eyes were filled with doubt. "If the mysterious someone wanted you gone, why didn't they shoot you rather than that unfortunate young woman?"

Crap. This was it. The moment that could break our relationship. I exhaled then cracked the door to my life. "That woman last night... she wasn't shot."

Kyle's head jerked back. "Excuse me? What, did the dentist fill her cavity with plastic explosives?"

"That would have been kinder." I sank into myself, recalling the terror on that woman's face as she tried to warn me. As she attempted to tell me from where the danger came. "She was killed by magic."

"Magic?" he asked, sounding not like he planned to have me committed, but merely seeking confirmation.

I nodded, then looked at him, expecting censure, disbelief, or anything except what I saw in his bottomless brown eyes—understanding.

"Then I'm not going any-fucking-where." He popped another Swedish Fish into his mouth. "Something else you want to share?"

"Yes." I pushed off the small couch, grabbing the sheath of papers from the desk. Once I found the document with the sum of money I stood to inherit, I slipped it from the pile. "This is one of the reasons I'm staying. If I walk away from the house and the money, it leaves the family."

"Then who would get it, the state of Texas?" Kyle grabbed the paper and his eyes widened. "Holy shit. I'd kill your ass for this kind of money too."

I leaned my hip against the desk and crossed my arms. "I'm not sure last night had to do with the inheritance."

"Don't kid yourself, sweetheart. Who stands to hit the jackpot should you take the big dirt nap?"

A taste more bitter than bile, yet sweeter than honey filled me. Whoever said revenge was pointless had never possessed the ability to deny a person an inheritance built on the backs of trafficked humans. And I'd be damned if they got one hot cent of this money.

I raised my chin and answered, "A descendant of the family that once owned my great-great-whatever grandmother."

"Oh, hell naw." Kyle stood, tugged his cuffs, and returned the document to my desk. "I wouldn't care if it was one dollar, but damned near a hundred million? Nah, I'll make sure it stays in your family—with you."

Oh snap, Kyle had on his fighting face. The one he slipped into when some bozo started shit but didn't have the sense to walk away before it hit the fan. Just because Kyle was slender didn't mean he couldn't throw hands.

"Look," Kyle smoothed the front of his dark slacks, "I have to wrap up one last case, then I'm here for the long run."

The butterflies nesting in the center of my chest broke loose. "I don't expect you to rearrange your week to run to my rescue."

"Week? Bitch, naw, I'm here for the long haul." He closed the folder. "I need a vacation anyway. May as well be here in your little Mayberry with melanin and magic."

I looked from Kyle to the floor, and back again. His dark handsome face and loving eyes remained unchanged. A relieved breath burst out of my mouth, riding the back of a small laugh.

"That's it?" I slid my fingers beneath my locs, scratching the back of my head. "No third degree, no questions?"

Kyle winked. "Oh, darlin', I have a ton. But, judging by those larger-than-usual bags under your eyes—"

I poked him in the side. "Bitch."

"Right back at ya." He wrapped his strong arms around me, holding me tight. After four silent breaths, he spoke again, voice gentle. "You've had enough sharing for the morning. I'll be right where I'm supposed to be—at your back—helping you grind your enemies' bones into dust."

"I love you so much," I whispered before kissing the underside of his chin.

"I know. You can't help yourself. If I weren't strictly dickly, I'd distract you and help you get some sleep." Kyle kissed my temple, gave me a little squeeze, then let me go. The grin told me I wasn't out of the woods yet.

And I was so right.

Kyle opened the library door and looked back at me. "But I'm sure Ash could help you out with that," he said with a grin before flouncing off to parts unknown.

Hm, after what I overheard last night, I should do Ash. If he was as powerful as I suspected—he'd be a'ight.

And if he died? Oh well, not my problem.

Chapter 22

AFTER CONVINCING MYSELF not to hate-fuck Ash, I stood transfixed in front of the library's stained-glass triptych windows. Why was I so fascinated with this depiction of Lucifer's fall? It's not like I hadn't seen some of the most impressive stained glass in the world. Hell, one of my favorite back pieces was inspired by the windows of the Chartres Cathedral in France.

This image of not only Lucifer, but his winged buddies was... so sexy, it felt sacrilegious.

I leaned closer, my gaze traveling across cadmium yellows and Chinese reds along with a rainbow of vivid colors. Something wasn't clicking; everything felt so...disconnected. Like life, sometimes art required stepping back to see the entire canvas rather than individual pieces.

"Holy shit." From four feet away, everything changed. This version of hell on glass skipped the cliched lake of fire and tortured souls. Lucifer and his crew weren't sent to underground caverns of pain and punishment, but the torturous place in between. Earth.

Whether or not it was the artist's intention, I agreed. For many, hell was here, on Earth, suffered by the living.

The doorbell rang, making me damn near shoot out of my cowboy boots.

I pressed a hand against my chest, thankful that I'd changed into something halfway decent. Well, calling artfully ripped loose jeans and a tight black Million Dollar Cowboy Bar tee dressy might be a stretch. But hey, at least I was wearing a bra.

"World, can't you leave me alone for half an hour? Is that too much to ask?" As I stomped to the door, I recalled that not only did I live in a house with a ghostly staff, but Ash also lurked somewhere beneath my roof. In other words, alone time wasn't something I'd have in my near future.

Come to think of it, I needed to meet the rest of the ghosts staffing my country-ass Downton Abbey. Was there a bell to ring when I needed Lucille or did I just whistle?

I jerked the door open and blinked. Then blinked again. Nope, still there. On my porch stood a pinched-faced and silent... Rita?

Standing there dressed similarly to me in a jeans, boots, and a "The Ancestors" tee was the last person I expected to find on my doorstep. My heart didn't see the angry woman, but rather the odd and accepting little white girl, bouncing with glee that another human her age would be at the Double R Ranch.

I missed that girl. I missed the us that we could have been.

Yeah, but that wasn't the woman before me.

The longer I watched her tight lips and rage-filled eyes, the quicker my breaths came. That tender ache of sorrow dissipated, blooming into the sweet heat of anger. How the fuck was Rita mad at me? She wasn't the one forced from the only true home she'd known.

Fuck her. As far as I was concerned, I'd shed enough tears. I pressed my fists against my fleshy hips. "Look, if you've come to accuse me of—"

"Murdering my brother?" Rita dipped her chin. Let's just say that if looks could kill, I'd be a smoking pile of ash.

Fuck that. I opened my mouth to let loose, to lay Duncan's secrets and sins on the table, but a soft throat-clearing veered me off track.

Damn, two feet to Rita's right stood a vaguely familiar woman wearing Doc Martens and a flowered flowy dress, and looking like she should a Black backup singer for Fleetwood Mac. If that part of me that saw auras and sensed supernatural creatures hadn't gone on the fritz, I'd be able to see past the large seemingly friendly eyes and skin a similar brown with golden undertones as my own.

"Merri, I can't deal with her." Rita handed an aged brown leather book to her companion.

I gave Rita the *I-know-the-fuck-you-didn't* head tilt and went in. "Then why did you come rolling up to my door?"

Rita's eyes narrowed. "This is coven business, which has nothing to do with me."

I jabbed my index finger at the woman formerly known as my best friend. "You know what, I could stand here and feel guilty for some shit y'all believe I did. But guess what? I too am done." The magical gag order expired ten years ago.

Of course, Duncan chose that moment to appear between me and his sister. Unlike last night, he wore an unbuttoned blue, white, and black plaid shirt over a tight white tee, jeans, and square-toed cowboy boots.

"Don't." He looked at Merri, tilting his head and squinting a little. "And not in front of an audience."

Whatever. I was tired of carrying the weight of Duncan's death and planned to unload that shit at the soonest opportunity. Like, we were having this shit out now.

I shifted slightly to my right to get an unimpeded view of my former friend. Rather than returning Rita's energy, I smiled. The expression wasn't friendly, but it fell short of an I-want-to-rip-your-face off that I felt down in my soul.

The fingers on my left hand tingled. *Shit.*

Duncan flashed next to me. "Gwen…" he whispered, his ghostly plea brushing against my anger. "Unless you want them to know you're about as human as I am—"

"Fine," I snapped, the words not only for Rita and Duncan, but myself.

There were many things I needed to embrace before the past and its lies swallowed me. The biggest of those being the truth. The reality that while I may know the who, I had no idea what I was.

But that was a Gordian knot to unravel in private.

With a bottle of bourbon.

I stretched my fingers and exhaled. "Since it's clear the only place we want to bury the hatchet is in each other, get off my property."

Rita jerked as if I'd slapped her.

Good, 'cause I wasn't the only one who needed to be uncomfortable.

"But—" Rita began to argue.

"What's the problem? You just said how you couldn't do this. So I'll make it easy for you. Go. You are not welcome on my land or in my home."

She nodded first at me, then Merri, then silently raised her chin and sauntered off my porch.

Since I wasn't one to leave well enough alone, I called out, "And when you finally learn the truth, I hope you're as free with your apologies as you were with the blame."

"What was I supposed to do?" she asked, her voice soft, East Texas twang on full display. For the first time since I'd returned to town, I saw something in her eyes other than loathing.

Uncertainty.

"Believe in *me*." My voice thickened. "Trust *me*."

Duncan did his ghostly teleporting thing, reappearing at the bottom of the porch next to Rita, tracing the streak of gray in her honey blonde hair. When he looked back at me, his heartbreak was as heavy as my anger. "Would you tell her how much I love her?"

"Not in this lifetime," I mumbled.

Merri stepped forward, probably to derail this emotional train wreck, but I stopped her with a shake of my head and a raised palm.

"Are you staying?" The words were for Merri, but the anger and sorrow? That was all for Rita and her brother. They were quite the pair; he broke my life and the future I'd dreamed of, and she rendered my heart useless.

Funny, lovers came and went, but real friends were supposed to be in your life forever. And when that unraveled...

Merri nodded. "Yes, this is urgent."

The three of us, four if you counted Duncan, stood outside in an emotional OK Corral. "Not trying to be rude, but share the message and be on your way."

Merri lowered her voice. "This is best done in private." She turned her face toward the cemetery and a large solitary Black man leaning against a six-foot-tall cement angel with tucked wings.

I didn't need supernatural vision or a keen sense of smell to recognize that dickhead deputy from last night. "Fine. Come on in." I pushed the door open and stepped inside, followed closely by Merri.

"I don't mean to overstep..." She moved up beside me, placing her warm fingers against my forearm.

"Then I suggest you don't," I said as I closed the door.

Standing in the foyer of my haunted mansion, my heart broke in increments. A pain I believed long healed held me captive, the wound reopening one wretched stitch at a time.

Soft footsteps descended the stairs, and a familiar tug, one tethered to both my heart and sacral chakra. My subconscious wanted love, affection, and protection. My brain wanted to expeditiously fix the riddle of my life and resolve the inheritance. And my body? Well, a good dicking would be a welcome stress reliever.

Merri gasped.

Yeah, sis, I knew the feeling. Ash was the epitome of BDE. Homeboy could bottle some of that big schlong energy and get even richer.

Unlike Kyle earlier, Ash wasn't dressed to the nines; quite the contrary. From the wide landing in the stairs, he watched me like a barefoot and feral guardian angel wearing the same loose-fitting jeans from earlier. At least he'd added a t-shirt to the mix. Unfortunately, it was tight.

Damn it. The ovaries with one foot in the grave and the other on a banana peel did a happy dance as I appreciated every inch between his narrow waist, pausing at his nipples, then moving on to the lickable tats on his neck.

Life, at least mine, was so freaking unfair.

At this moment, with Ash standing there looking like a whole ass snack, I wanted to toss common sense aside, and Merri out the door, followed by discovering if Ash's big D energy was just that.

He grinned, and it was so hot, my locs damned near caught on fire.

"My god," Merri whispered reverently.

"No. Merely a male ensuring that his woman is well." Ash descended the last few steps, prowling closer, his smooth rhythmic movement somewhere between a dancer and a warrior.

And I was his prey. I should be flattered that someone like him—rich, handsome, and deadly—had set his sights on me. But what were his motives? We all had secrets—hell, I had a whole wardrobe full of skeletons—most of them not mine.

However, none of my lies affected him.

Didn't the man have an empire to run or lives other than mine to destroy? I stepped back before I was trapped in Ash's seductive web. "I asked you to leave."

"And I said no. If there's going to be a fight," he turned to Merri, then back to me, "I'll be in it with you. Whether you want me here or not."

Before I could stop him, Ash slipped two fingers in my empty belt loop, tugging me closer, wasting no time touching his lips to mine then trailing his tongue along my lower lip.

And if that wasn't bad enough, his hand slid around my waist, settling at the base of my back, pressing our bodies close enough that not even a dirty thought separated us.

Against my will, my body relaxed.

How could a man who was so hard everywhere have such soft lips? I may have moaned a little, but I couldn't hear shit over the thudding of my heart. Let's just say that it was a good thing that Ash didn't have a shifter's olfactory talents. Because dude would know without a doubt that this nonverbal communication skills made me a very happy woman.

Oh snap. Maybe he did know.

I closed my eyes and groaned. And it wasn't the let's-get-naked-now variety.

A feminine sound of wonder, jealousy, or want came from beside me, but I couldn't move, couldn't stop sipping from the cup of Ash.

His fingers flexed, pressing against the top of my ass before he sighed and ended the kiss.

Thank goodness, because I was all out of willpower for the afternoon. Especially since I suspected that I'd need my wits for whatever Merri planned to share.

Chapter 23

I WATCHED ASH'S DELECTABLE derriere until he disappeared up the stairs. If I had a lick of sense, I'd get Uncle Raul to toss Ash out of my house and life. But I had a feeling it would end in bloodshed. Whose? I wasn't sure. However, what I did know was that if Merri wasn't present as the bearer of what I suspected was bad news, Ash and I would've been deep into christening the foyer of Azure House.

Merri grinned. "With such a..." she licked her lower lip, "...charming houseguest, I'm surprised you answered the door. How long have the two of you been together?"

"We aren't." I crossed my arms, hoping my hard nipples weren't visible. It's not like I could blame them on the air conditioning.

"So, if I wanted to shoot my shot..." Merri wiggled her eyebrows, then bit her lip as her gaze slithered down my body, pausing at the sliver of skin exposed by my white tee.

"Neither Ash nor I are on the menu." Ironically, it was the casual invitation in her stare that made the energy build in my hand. The thought of any woman's hands on Ash made me want to commit an act of violence.

And I let the thought dance across my expressive face.

"Pity." Merri shrugged, not looking the least bit upset.

"This way." I walked toward the library as I attempted to get my heart rate under control. Whether it was Ash, jealousy, or the aged dark leather tome tucked against Merri's chest that made me more nervous, I couldn't decide.

I motioned for Merri to enter, and my anxiety ratcheted up three levels.

"This is magnificent." Merri stood at the wall of books, stopping at the ladder, caressing the thin wrought-iron handle that ran along its length. She looked over her shoulder, expression neutral, almost pleasant, as if she were attempting to bury her real feelings.

That witch could lie to herself, but I wasn't the one. Any person, alive or dead, human or non, who lived in Hoodoo, Texas, was curious about Azure House for one of two reasons. Either they wanted to reenter and relive memories, or get inside and snoop in the local haunted house.

"I've always wanted to explore your home, but she wouldn't let me in."

"Really?" I answered, feeling happier than I should. Azure House had more loyalty than most lovers. Plus, she'd never die.

Merri dipped her chin and smirked. "Like that's a surprise."

When I merely shrugged, she laughed, the sound deep and melodious like one of those Tibetan singing bowls. It was seductive and disturbingly captivating.

She leaned against the ladder, resting one of her Doc Marten-clad feet on the bottom rung. "One of these days, I'd love a tour—if that's okay."

A harumph escaped unbidden from my chest. This chick was getting a little too comfortable. Not only with me, but my home.

I froze when a not unpleasant tightness settled in my chest. The phrase "time stood still" took on new meaning.

When did Azure House cross the emotional threshold from house to home?

I shoved the errant thought and unsettling emotions aside, hooked my thumbs in my belt loops, then rocked back on my heels. "What about the whole enemy of my friend gig? I thought you witches stuck together."

"We do. Rita's next in line for coven leader, but she doesn't yet participate in the day-to-day happenings. I am Eleanor's second."

Interesting.

One thing about power, most want it and would do anything to get and keep it. How the hell was I supposed to trust a woman who wasn't honest with herself? I almost chuckled out loud. I was a fine one to talk. *'Hello pot.'*

"And... you're okay with that?" I asked.

"It is what it is." She jerked her right shoulder up and down in a half shrug. "Would I prefer to be Eleanor's successor? Yeah. Am I bitter about the rules and traditions in place generations before I came to town? No, not even."

"Then what's your agenda?"

Merri placed her booted foot on the floor and pushed off the ladder. What she didn't do was answer. Finally, the muscles in her face relaxed and an impishness that bordered on evil filled her eyes. "There's no need for us to be adversaries. You and I have much in common; perhaps we could find a way to friendship or something more."

This chick was aggressive. And were I in the market for a lover, perhaps it would be interesting to explore. But she and I had a sense of... sameness. The woman was attractive, I'd give her that; however, none of that led to even an inkling of sexual attraction.

I shook my head. "No offense, but I'm not in the market for a relationship—even a platonic one."

"Given your situation and the events of last night, I understand. But one can never have enough allies. Especially well-placed ones."

I stared at the bold witch, then nodded. It wasn't exactly agreement, but she was correct in my need for local allies. I was just not sure it should be her. "So what's this information you need to share?" I finally asked.

Merri's gaze darted to the two chairs in front of the desk, then licked her lips before returning her anxious gaze to mine. "Perhaps we should—"

"No. I prefer to face bad news on my feet."

"I respect that." Merri smiled, a tiny uplift of the corners of her luscious mouth. "How much do you recall about the accident?"

There was no need to expound upon which accident. That was only one that mattered—at least to me. In my life, there was the before and the after. On paper, the after was more than a step up. It was like a whole five stories of improvement.

And I'd return every piece of designer clothing, the horses, and even this beloved town for my mother to be alive.

I walked to the fireplace, now free of dust—and the blood I'd spilled that first day and rested my arm on it before facing Merri and her sympathetic eyes. While she wasn't as tall as me, anyone who saw us together would mistake us for, if not sisters, then cousins.

No wonder I wasn't attracted.

"Not much," I finally answered.

"There's a reason for that." Merri's long inhale whistled as if she had a deviated septum. Her words rushed out on the exhale. "Your memories were erased."

I spun around, pressing my back against the mantel for support. The air rushed from my pursed lips as I rooted around in my memories like a dog searching for a long buried bone.

And found nothing.

Memories could never be fully erased, especially something so traumatic. From what my Uncle Raul told me, it was more like a dam walling off and replacing the event. Which was how the citizens of Hoodoo were able to leave and have a life outside of town, which kept the secrets safe.

But once they came home, that lifetime of magic and memories also returned full force.

So why hadn't that happened for me?

More importantly, did I want it to?

Merri placed the book on the desk and walked slowly toward me, her hands low and palms out. "Are you sure you don't want to sit?" she asked, using a calming voice, one I'd frequently used for skittish horses.

"What I *want* is answers."

Merri licked her lips, then nodded. "Everything you need or want to know is here in Eleanor's diary. But the CliffsNotes version is that Rose was worried about the trauma and..." sympathy filled her eyes and softened her voice "...the guilt."

Boom!

I wasn't sure if the sound was my heart or my life imploding. What I wanted to do was go off, but seeing that both my brain and vocal cords had ceased functioning, all I could do was stare.

"I'm so sorry. Rose should have been the one to tell you this, but..." Merri pointed at the book resting on the corner of the desk like a landmine. "It's all in there. So you haven't had any dreams or flashes of that night?"

I shook my head.

Merri swallowed so hard, I heard it across the room. "Your ability to see ghosts wasn't your only gift. Whatever other powers you were born with were bound along with your memories."

What in the seven hells?

I pinched the bridge of my nose while studying the burgundies and navy blues nestled among the swoops and swirls of the antique rug. If ever there was a Calgon-take-me-away moment, this was it.

Ironically, it wasn't the further confirmation that I belonged to team non-human that nudged me closer to the edge, but the betrayal...

Merri crossed to the window, occupying the same loveseat that Kyle and I had lounged and shared secrets on only a couple hours earlier. "You're not surprised."

I shrugged, then walked to the intimidating dark desk, leaning against it. Merri watched me, as if waiting for the imminent breakdown.

Don't hold your breath, little witch.

The last time I'd shed a tear was when I learned that not only had my mother passed, but her funeral had been held without me. Comparing that pain to this? It was like a losing a limb on one side of the scale and a paper cut on the other.

Not even close.

"So what am I?" My voice was flat and unemotional, but something inside me cracked.

"I don't know."

When I raised my eyebrow, Merri laughed, the melodious sound caressing my bare arms like velvet.

"Fine." She sank back against the chair. "I tried to open the diary, but just like the house, you are the key."

"I appreciate your honesty." I pressed the thumb of my right hand against the fleshy mound at the base of the opposite thumb.

"Have you seen Duncan?" she asked.

"Why?"

Merri glanced at the closed door, then leaned forward, placing her forearms against her thighs. "I've been doing some asking around for years. From the little I've pieced together, it leads me to believe that Duncan was possessed."

I didn't answer, mostly because I was trying to keep my expression blank, even if my stomach was in turmoil. Duncan, that little shit, wasn't lying. Okay, I knew in my gut that he wasn't, but him and the truth weren't the closest of pals.

"I'd like to help." Merri raised her chin. "I may be second in command, and I may also be the third most powerful witch in Hoodoo, but let's keep it real. I'm an outsider."

"I know the feeling." I drummed my fingernails against the gleaming desktop.

And waited.

"I won't pretend to be altruistic. It's not that kind of party. From what I've seen, you and I are very much alike—ruthless. Although I believe you're far kinder than I."

I tilted my head and smirked. *Alrighty now...*

"What I'm proposing is a win/win." Merri stood but kept her distance.

"What will you gain by helping me? Regardless of the outcome, you'll never run the coven."

"Second place puts me next in line."

"If Rita suddenly dies, don't think I won't make sure you follow her."

"See, I told you we were alike." Merri grinned. "She doesn't deserve your loyalty."

"Maybe not, but that's my business."

"True dat." She withdrew a business card from her dress pocket. "I'll leave you to it. But I suspect whatever killed Duncan has returned." Merri pulled the massive door open before looking back, her face solemn. "Either that, or it never left."

Chapter 24

THIS DAY, HELL, THE past few months have been a motherfucker.

Naw, that was the epitome of understatements. With Merri's visit, I'd skipped over the border of fear and had moseyed deep into horrified territory.

What if I discovered the one truth I couldn't bear? The one that would untether me from all that I held dear. That despite my flaws, my propensity to push people away, and even my stubbornness, that I was a good person.

My world hung on the answer to a solitary question. *What if I was responsible for my mother's death?* Because that was the only reason I could see Aunt Rose doing such a thing.

I wished I could say that I was brave. That as soon as the door closed behind Merri, I ripped Eleanor's journal open, unveiling the secrets and lies shrouding my memories, but I didn't. Instead, I gathered some purple irises to place at my mother's grave along with the other ancestors.

While I knelt in the damp grass, surrounded by headstones, happiness, grief, and a few ghosts, I filled my pockets with grave dirt before Ash invited me for a drive.

I probably should have declined, since I rebuffed every effort at conversation on the ride to Main Street.

Ash slid his rental car into a slanted parking spot near Conjure Ink. "Things are never as bleak as they appear," he said, his voice as soothing as a hug.

I nodded and drummed my short nails against the top of the box of two dozen hot and greasy Shipley's doughnuts. "Yeah. Sometimes they're worse. Pardon the melodrama, but my life is the *Titanic*, and this town... my iceberg." I closed my eyes, lulled by the air conditioner against my cheeks and the low thrum of the engine.

"Tell me; perhaps I can be of assistance." Ash turned off the car, unfastened his seatbelt, then shifted his body in my direction. "Unload your troubles, Gwendolyn."

It was my turn to unbuckle and shift. I stared at Ash, really looked at him. Yes, he was beautiful. And he sure as shit was rich as dirt. But that wasn't what attracted me to him. It was there from the moment we met in Dublin, and rather than my desire decreasing as it usually did with partners, it intensified.

I reached into that part of me that saw auras and recognized most supernaturals. The part of me that had gone dormant after being shot. Zilch. Nothing. Nada. That door was welded shut. The only available tools were my wits and Ash's honor.

"You first. Share your secrets, Ash." I crossed my arms beneath my breasts and waited.

He chuckled, the sound so sexy, folks would sell their souls to hear it again.

Folks, or just me?

"Gwendolyn, you have but to ask."

Could it... be that easy? Had I been mulling all this crap over in my mind, creating multiple scenarios, from he was married, to an international gun smuggler trying to snare me in his web. Okay, that last one was a little wacky, but this was me we're talking about.

"Why are you here, in Hoodoo?" I finally asked.

"For you."

"For me? You came halfway around the world to get a tattoo from me?" My expression slipped into the you're-full-of-shit face, complete with pursed lips.

His lips quirked. "The tattoo is a bonus. The universe gifted you to me, us to each other. Not even death could interfere."

My skin tingled right before a flush of...adrenaline, fear, or something shot through my body. I wasn't sure if I should toss the doughnuts or my panties at the man.

I chose sarcasm. "Dude, that's one step away from wearing my skin as a suit."

Ash laughed, tiny wrinkles fanning out from the corner of his eyes, making the man even hotter. "I have a couple of ideas of what I'd like to do with your skin. Wearing it as a suit isn't one of them." His voice deepened.

And raised goosebumps on my arms. But I couldn't get distracted by Ash the walking pheromone. I cleared my throat to erase the vision of my skin pressed against his.

"I'm glad to hear it. I have another, more important question." I exhaled. "What are you?" I blurted, my face heating immediately.

I swallowed as the next dark thought flittered across my consciousness. Perhaps he was lying sack of magic, and his true purpose was to finish the job someone started generations ago.

I shook my head and flung the door open, wincing as it banged against the truck parked too close. "Never mind," I said as I slammed the door shut then pressed my back against the warm metal.

"Gwen," Ash called out as he set the car alarm and prowled toward me.

I shook my head, raising my left hand while balancing the doughnuts in my right. "No. I don't have the bandwidth for this conversation."

"It should have happened long ago." He stalked closer, unaware and uncaring of the attention of the women walking down the sidewalk.

"Are you here to kill me?"

His lips curved up in a wicked smile.

My mouth went dry, and my animal brain screamed, "*You betta run, girl.*" But I couldn't. My feet and everything else were frozen to the spot.

"No, Gwendolyn, I'm not here to kill you." He leaned closer and lowered his lips. "Unless it is the little death you speak of. That, I'd do repeatedly."

"Would you tell me if you were?" I whispered around the stranglehold this man had on me.

"Absolutely not." He kissed my forehead, then turned me around, herding me to the door of Conjure Ink.

We walked a whopping four steps before my rational mind overrode the rest of me. Hol' up.

"Don't fucking manage me." I pivoted, glaring up at the overbearing jerk, ready to give him a piece of my mind. Not that I had much left. Between out of whack hormones and the general crazy that was life, I wasn't firing on all cylinders.

I opened my mouth to let loose, but a flash of movement in the periphery caught my eye.

For the second time in less than ten minutes, I froze.

Unfortunately, it wasn't lust or a fawn response that hijacked my body. For there, standing on the sidewalk to my right was Duncan. It wasn't he who had me shook, but was his companion—Ilona, the rude red-haired witch from the first night I came to town.

Only this time, not only did her already pale skin carry the taint of death, but her lips were crudely sewn shut.

Chapter 25

I SCURRIED INSIDE CONJURE Ink, hoping like hell that Ash wasn't capable of scenting emotions. Unfortunately, Joaquin, coywolf shifter and tattoo artist extraordinaire, watched me with a frown narrowing his beautiful brown eyes. He looked from me to Ash and back again, his upper lip trembling as if he were about to growl.

Shit.

I shook my head and pressed my palms together in a silent plea while mouthing, *Please don't.* Because nothing says meet my friends like one of them turning into a giant fucking animal. Besides, there was a good chance Ash already knew what Joaquin was.

Joaquin remained silent and unmoving. That he didn't attempt to rip Ash's throat out was the most I could ask for.

More than The Ancestors, and even the Double R Ranch, Conjure Ink felt like home. The inside had been spruced up, but pretty much looked the same. It had a similar vibe as the Crossroads Café, decorated in old-school black, white, and red. But that was where the similarities ended.

Conjure Ink had a sexy cocktail party vibe, with the red leather couch, the antique frames highlighting a variety of flash tattoos, and the wall filled with images of the family, the famous, and even the infamous that we've inked over the years.

I plastered on a smile. Not too bright, because this was me we were talking about. Loretta would get suspicious if I was too perky. Of course, she'd probably think I got laid. Mostly because that was what she would have done.

When I turned to Ash, he watched me suspiciously, then looked over his shoulder out the window.

Which was my chance to do the same. And yup, Ilona and Duncan were still outside, only now, they looked at me like I was Jessica Fletcher. Baby, this wasn't *Murder She Wrote*, and I was nobody's detective. Ilona's death was a her problem. My plate was already overflowing with supernatural dilemmas.

Duncan and I were going to have a chat. I couldn't help every random ghost in Hoodoo. Homegirl was on her own.

"I was about to call the fire department to separate you two," Loretta said.

Ghost girl effectively dismissed, I needed to get in the game. This wasn't a social visit. Okay, it was, but if Loretta sensed I was freaked out even a little regarding Ash, she might try to hurt him.

And I wasn't sure I wanted him gone.

So, I exhaled, relaxed my shoulders, then stepped into my big girl panties. "Get your mind out of the gutter, Auntie. Ash and I were only talking."

Loretta harrumphed. How could one sound have so many meanings? This one was filled with you-keep-telling-yourself-that. "What I saw was a masterclass in seduction."

"And I, her hapless victim." Ash placed the box holding two dozen of the world's best doughnuts on the counter, then slapped an overly dramatic hand against his chest.

"Oh, you got jokes this morning." I scowled at the unrepentant male, but a chuckle escaped despite my best efforts.

But Ash was on a roll. He sighed like a damsel in distress. "Miss Carter, my fragile heart is sorely bruised."

"I can think of a few tender places to damage," I said, giving him my best Loretta imitation.

Ash laughed. And it wasn't one of those polite ones either. That sexy baritone sounded as if it came from the seat of his soul.

And damn if I didn't want to hear it again and again.

Woo, Ash's stunning smile was a sight. And judging by Loretta's sigh, I wasn't the only one flummoxed. As a matter of fact, the man should be locked away for the good of woman-kind.

I stretched my fingers and cleared my throat. "Everyone, this is Ash. Ash, everyone."

Pam, my cousin and Conjure Ink's manager, whose hair went gray in high school, shook Ash's hand as the two of them fell into easy conversation.

I left them to it, walking to Loretta, giving her a big hug and kiss on the cheek. "Hey, Auntie."

She looked over at Ash. "You have a good night?"

"It was... interesting. Before you get too comfy down there in the gutter, Ash spent the night in his room. Without me." I ignored the disbelief painting Loretta's dark brown face. "Whatever. Do you have a workstation I can use for the next six months?"

"After the craziness of last night. You still staying?" Loretta asked.

I hadn't shared about the money or exact terms of the inheritance, so I could see why everyone, including Loretta, assumed I'd leave.

But somewhere between Merri and Rita's visit and seeing Ilona's dead ass out on the sidewalk, I'd decided to fight and show folks that I wasn't the one. Passivity was perceived as weakness. And weakness would get me dead. Nah, son, if someone was trying to take me out, if I couldn't give them a solo express ticket to hell, then I'd make sure if I went, they'd go with me.

Just call me Kamikaze Karen.

I smiled, and it wasn't a nice one. "Especially after last night."

"What about him?" Loretta jerked her chin in Ash's direction. "I may be old, but I can appreciate the male physique. That there man has quite the body, but..." Loretta grunted. "I pray to the ancestors you don't get hurt by that one."

I stopped myself from agreeing, because Ash hadn't bound my powers. It wasn't him keeping secrets and information that could've kept me safe. And it sure as hell wasn't him who lied about my humanity. So, from where I was standing, Ash wasn't the villain.

I folded my arms and stepped closer to Loretta. "Speaking of ancestors, I need your help."

Loretta grinned, then pulled me further away from Ash and the others.

"Can you come to Azure House tonight? I have some grave dirt and want to open a line to my mom and grandmother." *And have a conversation with fewer ears.*

All that worry dissipated, replaced by a happiness that made Loretta's impish face damned near angelic. "Baby, that house wasn't the only thing waiting for you. Are you finally ready to embrace your magic?"

I nodded. "Seems to me, I don't have much of a choice."

"You don't know how happy I am to—"

The soft bing-bong of the chime drew both of our eyes to the front door, and the tight-lipped Carlos.

Not who I wanted to see today, or if I had a choice—ever.

Loretta waved. From the smile she gifted Carlos, obviously she didn't have the same reservations.

"Hi, Miss Loretta. How are you doing today?" Carlos removed his cowboy hat, tapping it against his thigh. Between the mussed and a little too long hair, the snug jeans, with his badge and gun sitting at his hip, and the fitted polo, the sheriff was a badge bunny's wet dream.

Too bad for him, it took more than a tight ass and a pair of handcuffs to rev my engine.

Loretta beamed from her toes to her salt and pepper afro. "It's getting better. First these two arrive bearing sweets, now you." She walked across the room and hugged Carlos as tight as she had me.

But if I wasn't mistaken, she held on to him a bit longer. And were her hands drifting down his back?

Just kill me now.

Carlos extracted himself, then smiled down at the elderly woman he'd known his entire life. "Hate to say it, but I'm here on business." He looked at me, any traces of kindness long gone. "Gwendolyn, we need to talk."

WHEN A MAN WITH A GUN, a badge, and a grimace wants to have a conversation, it's never a good thing. Especially when the man packing a whole lot more than a pistol was your ex.

"What's up?" I asked, keeping my expression and emotions in check as I crossed the room, stopping in front of Carlos. It was hard to believe that I once loved this jerk. "I told you everything I knew last night."

The walking inferno that was Ash moved up behind me, placing his hands on my waist. I remained silent, because hey, wasn't that what cops advised? Sheriff Carlos Hernandez sure as hell wasn't the kind young shifter I'd given my virginity and my heart to. Not anymore.

Since I was on the honesty train this afternoon, it bothered me more than I wished. If only, even now, Carlos would be open to a civil conversation or be willing to hear my truth of what happened to Duncan, maybe we could find our way to friendly strangers.

A squeezing sensation in the center of my chest made me exhale a little too loudly. Shit.

"I have no idea why you'd want them, but I brought those ugly-ass boots back." He jerked his head toward a paper Dhesi's grocery bag sitting on the couch.

Carlos stared down at me, his eyes drifting from my face to Ash's hands casually resting on my hips. "Like I said, I have a few more questions. Let's step in the break room."

"That's not going to happen." Ash shifted slightly, moving to my side. "Unless, of course, you meant the three of us."

Touché, Ash, touché.

Carlos made a sound that was a little too close to a growl. When his gaze hit mine again, those soulful brown eyes flashed copper. Eventually, he cleared his throat. And when he spoke, his voice had returned to normal. "As your friend —"

I wagged my index finger. "But there's the rub. You and I, Sheriff, are not that. Old chums don't take their friends to jail when they're covered with blood and body parts."

"Besides, Sheriff, Gwendolyn doesn't need friends." He resumed his position behind me, pressing every inch of his toasty body from his thighs to his chest, against me. And just in case that didn't get the message across, slid his hand around my body, pausing at my soft stomach before sliding it ever so slowly higher. "She has me now."

Most times, I didn't mind being the center of attention, but this wasn't one of them. So, as much as I enjoyed Ash's body as well as his freakishly high body temperature, this needed to stop. Not because Carlos gave a shit who touched me where, but I did.

I pressed my hand over Ash's just as his thumb grazed the underside of my breasts, which thanks to the industrial strength bra I rocked today, were higher than normal "Honey, you're not helping,"

Ash's posture became a little less aggressive. "Perhaps, but it's the truth, is it not?"

Carlos made that growly sound again, then leveled the full power of his almost alpha-strength glare at Ash.

I rolled my eyes, then walked over to the counter. When the going gets tough, the tough grab food. And these doughnuts were the perfect combination of carbs, sugar, and grease. I ripped off, then ungracefully shoved a hunk of plain cake perfection in my mouth as I stared out the window.

After swallowing, I sighed and relaxed. The world would be a better place if everyone grabbed a pastry when they were pissed off.

Ready to face the Carlos, I raised my chin and turned around. And you have got to be freaking kidding me.

I did a slow blink, hoping I wasn't having a daymare. Ilona the rude ghost was still outside with Duncan. Unfortunately, they'd brought along a friend. The second woman, also white and very much dead, had joined the ghostly crew.

I shoved the second half of the doughnut in my mouth, shook my head, and wrapped my trembling fingers around one of the mugs of coffee Loretta brought out.

After washing down the lump of dough, I whispered a prayer. Trust me, I wasn't asking for something as frivolous as erasing those last fifteen pounds, but rather that the universe would make both the ghosts and Carlos disappear.

Not only were the women still there, but now there was a foggy area as if they'd steamed it with their warm breath, which was impossible. Because a: they didn't have breath, and b... well, I couldn't think of a b since a pretty much covered it all.

Now, I'd dealt with enough ghosts that, by this time in the program, I'd have just flipped them off and went about my business. But the single word was a repeat of last night's message: *danger.*

Shit. Shit. Shit.

I said to no one in particular, "I need some air."

"Not now you don't."

I did the slow head turn and narrowed my eyes at Carlos. "Excuse me?"

Carlos closed the few feet between us and extended his left hand as his right hovered near his gun. "Keys."

"For what? I haven't done anything." I stepped closer to Carlos and whispered, "You know that."

The longer I studied Carlos' stoic face, the angrier I became. I wish I could say it was a menopause-induced hot flash causing the light sheen of sweat between my breasts. But judging by the concentration of...power...electricity... or whatever the hell my magical handicap was, pooling in the fingers of my left hand, it was safe to say this wasn't caused by hormones.

With each passing second, the pain increased. Now, instead of the fire blazing beneath my skin, it felt as though my hand had been shoved in lava. Freaking ouch. If I was going to be gifted with a cool superpower, invisibility, or something less painful, would have been cool.

Ash hooked two fingers in my back belt loops, pulling me away from Carlos. "You're welcome to the van, but first, we'll need that search warrant."

Carlos pulled a folded piece of paper from his back pocket, handing it to Ash. "Here you go." Then Carlos shifted his attention to me. "By the way, when's the last time you saw Ilona? "

Chapter 26

NEVER, NOT ONCE IN my forty-five years, had keeping my mouth shut gotten me in trouble. It's never gotten me out of it either, but pretty much, silence was at least gold-plated.

While I may have been able to shut down the vocal response, my body was a whole 'nother matter. Let's just say hips weren't the only body part that didn't lie. Carlos' nostrils flared while I availed myself of my fifth amendment rights.

Luckily, Ash broke the moment by guiding me out of Conjure Ink and leading the procession of vehicles to Azure House. On the drive, I shot off a text to Kyle to let him know about the warrant.

"Are you okay?" Ash asked as we turned into Azure House's circular driveway.

"Not even close," I whispered. "Tell me. I'm ready to know. Today has been filled with secrets and lies. It's time to expose that shit to sunlight. And it starts with you."

I braced myself as I awaited the answer. Judging by the ease by which Ash's eyes shifted from scary to normal, it was obvious the male was powerful. But there were too many beings in the universe for me to even begin to guess without terrifying myself. Were I a regular woman with a mundane life, I'd be freaking out, but the last thing anyone could call me was normal.

Ash stopped the car, unfastened his seatbelt, then reached across the divide to cup my cheek. "First, if you believe nothing else I say, I vow no one in this wretched town will harm you."

His words held weight, wrapping around me like chainmail, before seeping through my pores and settling into my bones. I've read that the fae could gift you with a promise, or even their sacred name with a kiss. I imagined it felt similar. Like in my darkest hour, I could call out for Ash like the genie in Aladdin's lamp and he'd arrive, prepared for battle.

I could do nothing but respond to Ash's pledge with a solemnity that matched his. "Okay."

He nodded, then his gaze darted past my shoulder. "Regarding the other issue, this is perhaps not the appropriate time."

The passenger door jerked open, followed by a blast of warm moist air and skin-rippling power.

What Carlos wanted was to dish out a healthy dose of intimidation. But that was not what the good sheriff got. I unbuckled my seatbelt and spun around. Judging by the flash of amber in Carlos' usually brown eyes, the old boy's grip on humanity was slipping.

This was where I should have lowered my gaze. But you know what? I was kind of done with his shit. Keeping my mouth closed was about as good as it was going to get.

Ash opened his door behind me. "Gwendolyn –"

"It's fine." I raised my hand, never removing my gaze from the predator in front of me. "Let's get this done."

Carlos extended his hand. "Keys."

"I'm surprised you're not breaking in. Remember that time —"

Carlos leaned down, placing his face a kiss away from mine. "Now."

Not one thing since I'd returned to Hoodoo-freaking-Texas had gone as planned. In a perfect world, I would have signed a few papers, deposited a check, and been on my way.

But noooo.

Now I was accused of I don't know what and getting judged for the girl I was rather than the woman I'd become. Screw Carlos. I raised my chin, ignored the extended hand and got out of the car, refusing to cower beneath his glare. "They're in the house."

"Johnson," Carlos yelled. "Escort Miss Carter to retrieve her keys."

"What do you think I'm going to do, slip out of a secret tunnel?"

Deputy Douchebag stopped beside Carlos and glared down at me. "If it were up to me, you'd already be in jail."

"Now," Carlos said, sounding like that knot at the end of his rope had unraveled.

I walked around the hood of the car, touching Ash's arm like a talisman.

"Don't worry, your boyfriend will still be here when you get back," Carlos said, the disdain in his voice obvious.

"Then again, maybe the two of you can be cellmates," Deputy Dickhead said low enough that I wasn't sure if he meant for me to hear.

I followed Johnson up the small rise to the porch. Movement caught my eye. The curtain covering the small window to the right of the door shifted. Crap. I blurted the first thing that came to mind. "So how long have you been in Hoodoo, Deputy Johnson?"

He didn't bother to respond. Apparently, I didn't exist for him. Which, come to think of it, was okay with me. I took the porch stairs two at a time, rushing past him to the ornate front door.

"For a woman who allegedly doesn't use magic, this sure was a quick renovation." He stood beside me, watching my hands like I'd pull a Samurai sword out of thin air.

Well, two can play the ignoring game. I pressed my lips together.

"What, no smart-ass answer?"

"Oh, was that a question?" I gave him my sweetest bless-your-heart smile, which in this instance meant a big eff you, before focusing on the task at hand, getting Carlos and his vengeful crew the hell away from me. Once I unlocked the door, I looked up at Deputy Dickhead. "I don't want you in my house." I pointed to the narrow table with a vase filled with fresh tulips and sitting beside it, a blue and white bowl that I'd started using to hold stuff. "My keys are right there. I'll go grab them and you can sally forth and harass someone else."

"Was that a question?" he asked, tossing my words back at me. "What you want doesn't matter." He swept his arm as if leading me to the dance floor.

I muttered some unkind words not quite under my breath as I walked inside. "Well, are you coming?" I was so caught up in being pissed off, I missed the confused expression on his handsome but brutish face.

The not-so-good deputy aimed his frown from the empty doorway to me. "Stop bullshitting and let me the fuck in."

It was my turn to be confused. "Um, hello... the door is open. Unless you're a day-walking vampire, why the hell are you standing out there?"

He took another step. Or at least he tried to. DD, which was his new nickname, came to a jarring halt as if he'd slammed into an invisible wall. "What the hell?" He stood there looking like a mime on steroids, moving his hands against the invisible barrier.

Holy guacamole.

Last night, Ash had mentioned being unable to open the front door to Azure House, and it hadn't clicked. I had other things on my mind, like getting bug pieces out of my hair and all. But to see my supernatural security system live and in person was...whoa.

I stood there with my mouth hanging open.

Duncan appeared beside me, luckily without his new ghostly friends. "Gwen, we need to talk."

"Not a good time," I said, doing my best ventriloquist imitation.

Carlos yelled, his voice distant, yet still powerful. "Stop fucking around, Johnson."

Johnson stopped his mime impression and turned around. "It's under control."

Lucille appeared, glaring at Duncan. "What in tarnation are you doing in this house?" She pointed at the door. "Get out of here and don't dare cross this threshold again."

"Lady, I don't know who the hell you are, but Gwennie invited me. Last I checked, she was the mistress here."

Okay, this was not good. "Lucille, I should have mentioned him this morning. Sorry about that."

She dipped her chin in a jerky nod. "Why are those shifters here?"

Thoughts swirled and coalesced into an idea. Wasn't sure if it was a good one, but it would pause the territorial fight with Duncan, show Lucille her value, and get the information I needed. Finally, something might go my way. "Lucille, can you follow someone?" I whispered.

"Yes, ma'am." She puffed up like a sergeant receiving orders from a respected general.

I grinned, hope blossoming in my chest. "Good. Follow Carlos and find out what's going on. Meet me back here tonight whether you have answers or not."

"Yes, ma'am." She grinned and nodded, seemingly happy for a covert assignment.

"Who you talking to?" Johnson yelled. Now, rather than watching me like a criminal, he looked at me like he'd decided I was one taco short of a combination plate.

"Myself. Since I seem to be the only person willing to listen." I handed Hoodoo's finest Stella's alarm and key. "Here."

Someone should start a ghostly branch of the CIA. Not only was the sweet Lucille eager to go out on a spying mission, but she'd changed her outfit. I chuckled at the sight of the woman in a Sherlock Holmes-looking hat, as well as a tweed jacket and those riding trousers with the puffy thighs.

"What's so damn funny?" DD sniffed then looked over his shoulder.

Rather than answer and risk him smelling the lie, I walked past him, stepping out on the porch, only to be rewarded with a view of Carlos and Ash glaring at each other. I sighed and walked down the five porch stairs to intervene.

"Johnson has the keys." When Carlos didn't bother looking in my direction, I cleared my throat. "Look, I know you hate me, but—"

Carlos' head whipped in my direction and the heat coming from his eyes pushed me back a step.

Yikes. Maybe I should have left this an a and b conversation and seen my way out.

Then, he drove the dagger straight into my heart. "Hate implies I ever cared."

Ouch.

Once upon a time, those cruel words would have crushed me. Now? Not so much. I wasn't that insecure girl looking for a place to belong, believing that Carlos' arms would become my home. I didn't need him; finally, after forty-five fucking years, I was good in my skin.

The only opinion that truly mattered was my own, which meant embracing my raging hormones and staying pissed the eff off. But yay me, rather than yell, I encased my tender feelings and rage in a block of ice.

I aimed my brightest and fakest smile at Carlos. "Alrighty. Well, I hope you can get out of your non-feelings long enough to be gentle with Stella."

"Who the fuck is Stella?" he asked.

"My van," I said, the duh clear in my voice. "I guess asking to remove some art supplies is out of the question?"

"That would be correct. Look, this isn't personal, it's business. I may not be on television shows or fly around the world, but I'm a professional."

"If you say so." I tilted my head and scrunched my nose like an aged Valley girl. "It's just I have yet to see it. But you do you."

"Good day, Miss Carter." Carlos stared at Ash five long seconds, then turned his head and spat on the ground.

Oh. My. God.

Ash stepped forward.

I gasped, then a horrible combination of shame and anger roiled through my belly. But before shit got out of hand, I grabbed Ash's arm and held on for dear life. "Let it go—please."

The flesh beneath my hand might as well have been marble. Ash had stopped moving, but a slow, wicked (not in a good way) smile softened his lips as he nodded. "For now, Sheriff. For now."

A familiar raised silver Ford F-150 growled up the road, driving past the sheriff's vehicles and flatbed tow truck to park behind Ash's rental car. The door opened, and I cursed. "Shit."

"Who is that?" Ash placed his hand over mine as we turned and faced our new guest.

"That, Ash, is Phillip, my aunt's lawyer." And human servant, but he didn't need to know that part. Well, wasn't this day getting better and better?

Uh, that would be a hell to the no.

"What's going on?" Phillip asked as if he didn't already know. When no one volunteered, he looked first to me and Ash then to Carlos.

Carlos tossed the keys to the approaching tow truck driver, then focused on Ash and my joined hands, shaking his head before his gaze rose to mine. I expected more of his casual cruelty, but when Carlos spoke again, he was calm, almost sad. "Don't worry, we'll take good care of your Stella."

A knot the size of Texas clogged my throat. There he was.

That was the Carlos I spent my childhood climbing trees with. The thirteen-year-old new werewolf who ran with me on all fours through the woods, tackling me and rolling around on the grass before we went skinny-dipping in the lake.

And the young man I fell head over heels in love with.

Fearful of the weight of nostalgia making my voice break, I nodded.

Carlos sighed and gave me a sad smile, that if I were to read something into it, said that he also remembered. But he simply turned and walked away.

If I'd been blessed with a super sensitive nose rather than a tingly hand and seeing dead people, would Carlos smell of sorrow for what we'd lost?

Phillip, Ash, and I stood silently as the police caravan left my property. I watched in horrified confusion as they drove down the road and right through Ilona—and two other female ghosts.

"Gwen?" Phillip gently squeezed my bicep. When I turned around, he asked, "Why was Carlos here?"

Ash answered, "A search warrant regarding the disappearance of Ilona Naughton."

Phillip tapped an envelope against his thigh as he stared at the now empty road.

"Did you even know her?" Phillip asked, sounding incredulous.

Welcome to the club, buddy.

I shook my head. "I interacted with her once, three nights ago." I frowned. Dear ancestors... How could three days feel so damned long? Now, thinking back on it, who had Ilona been trying to impress by picking a fight with me? I doubted the woman sewed up her own mouth then killed herself.

A part of me suspected Rita, espccially after our interaction yesterday. I frowned. No, that didn't make sense, Rita was no wilting flower. She'd fight her own battles—especially with me.

I looked off into the distance as a second car, a pale blue SUV of some kind, crept past the flatbed tow truck, now loaded with Stella, along with the convoy of three Hoodoo Sheriff's department vehicles. Too bad the newcomer didn't swerve and run over Carlos.

Hey, it's not like it would kill him.

Phillip moved his free hand in the universal get-on-with-it motion. "And...?"

"We argued." And now she's very dead.

The door to the SUV opened, and the witch Merri's high heels followed by a pair of long jean-clad legs exited as she hitched her large boho bag on her shoulder.

My heart did a quick rat-a-tat-tat as I stared into Merri's somber brown eyes.

Phillip cleared his throat again, and I returned my attention to him and the immediate problem.

"Are you certain Ilona's missing? She could have easily gone off to visit a friend." Phillip's face settled into a mask of serenity, which meant his mind had gone into overtime. Either that, or he was communicating with Aunt Rose.

"According to the warrant and your sheriff," Ash said, irritation on full display. "Although I wouldn't accept anything that male says when it comes to Gwendolyn."

I unclenched my jaw and exhaled a weary breath as I peeked up at Ash. "It's been one drama after another. No tattoo is worth that much trouble."

"You're correct." I inwardly flinched, but his next words rooted me to the spot. "But you, however, I would rend worlds to protect." Ash wrapped his hand around the side of my neck, sliding his fingers beneath my locs.

The warmth of his skin against mine soothed me. "Um, wow. I've never had anyone offer to end civilizations for me. Thank you?"

"Okay, talk about feeling like a third wheel." Phillip chuckled as he extended a cream-colored parchment envelope embellished with the Double R's wax seal on the back and my name written in ornate calligraphy on the front.

"What's this?" I asked as I accepted the envelope with growing dread. Rather than answer, Phillip watched as I snapped the crimson seal then slid the formal invitation from the square envelope. "You have got to be shitting me."

"Is everything okay?" Ash looked down at me, his eyes weary and brows drawn.

"No. We're being summoned to the Double R Ranch for a formal family dinner. Tomorrow night."

"I'll be on my best behavior." Ash grinned. "I'm sure your family doesn't bite."

Phillip laughed and waved as he hopped back in his truck.

"That's where you'd be wrong." I tapped the envelope against my thigh as my shoulders sagged.

Ash shrugged. "Decline."

God, I wish it were so easy. I shook my head and shrugged. "That's not an option—at least not for me."

Chapter 27

I WAS A GROWN-ASS WOMAN. So why did a formal dinner invitation jettison me back to those awkward pimply-faced, braces-wearing teenaged years? Maybe if it had just been Aunt Rose, Uncle Raul, and I, it would have been cool. But formal family meals included the coven as well as every vampire in the local congregation who wasn't away on business.

"If you must enter the lion's den, I'll be your shield." Ash's stern face was so sincere, I was torn between wanting to laugh and cry. But before I could do either, Phillip made it worse.

"By the way," Phillip, now standing next to his open truck door, called out, "your other friend, Kyle, is also invited."

"Why?" I called out, not bothering to hide my panic.

He winked, then cranked up his engine. "I am but a servant of Rose," he yelled. "Don't worry, your friends can hold their own."

It wasn't them I was concerned about, but me.

And of course, two more vehicles rolled up the driveway. One, a now dusty black Mercedes SUV that belonged to Kyle for the week, and the other, Maria's Escalade.

Maria stepped out and strolled over to Phillip, who was now leaning against the side of his truck with his chest puffed out.

What was that about? Looked like I wasn't the only woman in the town keeping secrets.

"Now that you have company, I must leave." Ash placed a hand on my lower back.

Merri hiked her purse higher on her shoulder and raised her chin. "As long as I'm here, Gwendolyn will never be alone."

Rather than get annoyed, Ash looked bored, looking Merri up and down, starting at the puff of tiny spiral curls atop her head.

"Go," I said to Ash before turning to Merri. She seemed cool and all, but hers was also not the company I wanted to keep. Not today. "Merri, I appreciate you stopping by, but we need to reschedule." I smiled to soften the words. See? I could be nice. "I'll be fine. I always am."

Ash moved in front of me, watching and waiting. For what, I had no idea. When I didn't drone on, he sighed. After stepping close, he leaned down and placed an almost chaste kiss on my forehead before stepping away. As he walked down the road, Ash greeted Loretta and Maria before pulling Kyle aside for an intense chat.

"Hey, girl, sorry it took so long for to get here." Maria pulled me in for a hug.

When she finally set me free, I asked, "Shouldn't you be at work?"

"Naw, I was finished." Maria tapped her watch. "Hello, it's damned near six o'clock."

"Wow, this day has been..." I shook my head. Gee, time flies when you're getting accused of a crime.

"Hi, Miss Loretta." Merri's smile was small and tentative.

"Hey, sweetheart." Loretta looked back and forth between Merri and me, before wrapping me in her thin but strong arms. "We came to take you out to dinner."

Despite the dreary circumstances, I smiled. "Food heals everything, I guess."

"That and sex." Loretta winked. "But according to your friend Kyle, you're not doing any of that."

My cheeks heated, and both Maria and Loretta cackled.

When she aimed her gaze back on the witch, Loretta's smile was still warm, but her eyes had narrowed. "What brings you to these parts, Merri?"

Merri glanced over at the cemetery and shook her head. "It's regarding a book I loaned to Gwen. I found the sequel in my family's library."

I looked around the property. Azure House sat up on a hill, so it was difficult but not impossible for people to hide in the oleander bushes on the side of the road. But the truth of the matter, a wolf, or hell, a bird shifter wouldn't have to be on my property to eavesdrop.

"Great, but I haven't even cracked the first one open." I tapped two fingers against my ear. "Let's go see what we can rustle up to eat in the house."

Maria nodded.

Finally, Kyle joined us as we moved the conversation to the porch. As we walked, I gave them Cliff Notes version of my altercation with the now deceased Ilona at The Ancestors that first night. If someone was listening in, this information was already widely known. Hopefully, it held the added benefit of clearing Maria and Loretta of involvement.

"Gwen..." Kyle pinched the bridge of his nose.

"What was I supposed to do, let her call me out in front of everyone?"

"I would've just punched her in the mouth," Maria said.

Everybody laughed.

"Where'd Ash go? I'm surprised he let you out of his sight." Maria opened the screen door to take the party—and conversation—inside.

I shrugged, attempting to play nonchalant, apparently failing, judging by Kyle's chin dip. "He has business to attend to."

"Just as well." Loretta spat over the side of the porch.

Holy hell? What the...?

"Why don't you like him, Loretta?" I asked once we were all in the house and the door closed behind us.

"I like him just fine. Don't trust him, though." Loretta walked into the small parlor where we chopped it up last night. "Those ain't the same things."

We all moved into the room, taking seats. All but me. I moved to the window. The parlor overlooked not only the front gardens, but the cemetery.

And the sad faces of Ilona and her two ghostly friends.

I shook my head and took the empty damask armchair. "If it makes you feel any better, I get it." I thought back to that first night I met Ash in Dublin. I was getting my flirt on with a colleague and Ash rolled into the pub, setting my hormones ablaze. It wasn't a case of fight or flight, but fuck or flee.

I chose to flee but wound up in his company anyway. Maybe it was fate.

"Do you know where the witch is?" Maria asked.

I had to smile, because Cuz was all about getting down to business. Like most families, ours was built on a graveyard of secrets, some of the bones buried so deep, they'll never be excavated.

"Gwendolyn..." Kyle cleared his throat and leaned forward. "As your attorney, this is a conversation we should have alone." He looked first at

Loretta and Maria, then over at Merri, who was still hovering beneath the curved arch between the parlor and entry hall. "No offense."

Loretta nodded. "None taken," she said as she stood, motioning to Maria.

"No, don't leave." I raised both hands, stopping Loretta's movement and Kyle's protests. "We're going to need Loretta's help." I exhaled, then slid my jaw from side to side. "I do know where Ilona is."

"You three." Kyle wiggled his finger, pointing back and forth between Maria and Loretta before jerking his chin up at Merri. "Give me a dollar each."

For once, my relatives didn't ask a zillion damned questions. They just forked over the money. Loretta must have liked Kyle a lot; she gave him the whole five dollars she dug out of her bosom. Merri removed her wallet from her purse, sliding a ten into Kyle's outstretched palm, then her butt in an empty chair.

"Okay, now that I have the titty money," Kyle waved the bills in the air like he was at a strip club, "don't leave us in suspense."

I leaned back in the surprisingly comfortable chair, interlocking my fingers over my soft tummy. I really needed to get back to the gym.

"Any day now," Maria said, sounding agitated.

I blurted, "Ilona didn't leave town."

"And you know this how?" Kyle asked, leaning forward and resting his elbows on his thighs.

"Because she and two friends are standing just inside the cemetery gates."

They jumped up and ran not to the window, but out the front door to the porch. Not everyone, though, for Merri sat unmoving, watching me as if she knew the other three would return disappointed.

And she wouldn't be wrong.

The three trooped back in the house, Kyle looking confused, Loretta worried, and Maria curious.

Maria looked at me, asking the inevitable. "Are you saying what I think you're saying?"

"Yup." I nodded once.

"Sorry, what are you saying?" Kyle plopped down on the couch, then waited for clarification.

"There's some things you don't know about me, Kyle." I blew out a breath. "My ancestors weren't the only ones cursed. I see dead people."

I swallowed—hard. All the air was sucked out of the room, or maybe it was just my lungs. I raised my chin and braced for the backlash. This was it. Any moment now, he would grab his shit and flounce out of my home and my life.

Never one to take the easy way out, it looked as though Kyle planned to make me suffer first.

He stroked his freshly shaven chin with his thumb and forefinger before he spoke, his voice flat and unemotional. "Just tell me that I'm not Bruce Willis in this scenario."

Chapter 28

KYLE, MY RIDE OR DIE, the person after my exile who cracked my shell and snuck into my heart. He'd refused to allow me to hide in my dorm room wallowing in my crap and drinking away a broken heart. Now, twenty-five years later, he stared at me as if I were a stranger.

I sucked as a friend. Maybe I deserved to be alone.

Shame, wrapped up in guilt, sizzled through my body, landing in my gut like a hot brick.

After laying bare his gender identity issues and allowing me to support and encourage him through transition—I remained silent about my stuff. I was ashamed. I hated seeing ghosts and didn't care much more for any other magic. It wasn't that I had a problem with anyone else's way of life, be it fang, fur, or whatever.

All I wanted was to be mundane, magic-free, normal.

I refused to lower my gaze and hide from Kyle's judgment. But even without looking, Maria and Loretta's pity singed my nerves.

"Do you hate me now?" I finally asked when I couldn't take another second of silence. My throat tightened as I waited for him to kick me to the curb.

Kyle's dark eyebrows pulled together as he shook his head. This expression I recognized—disgust.

"I know you didn't fix your mouth to ask me that?" Kyle frowned, then reached his hand out, palm up, his dark, handsome face in an if-you-don't-stop-being-silly expression.

My throat loosened as I placed my hand in his and held on tight. Kyle was the friend that I'd failed to be. Not just to him, but to Rita, and in many ways, myself. This is what friendship was about, calling the other person out on their shit and loving them anyway.

"Okay," I said, the single word coming out on a rush of relieved air. I held tight to Kyle's hand and looked at the others. "Where should I start?"

"How about with considering your talent as a gift. It's no different than your art, and, honey..." Loretta dipped her chin and gave me her *mom* look. "It's not going away."

I nodded.

Kyle clapped his hands twice. "Moving on. What can you tell us about Ilona? Why can't you just ask her who killed her."

"Yeah, y'all go on down to the cemetery." Maria leaned back in her chair. "I'll be waiting right here."

"Chicken." I rolled my eyes and chuckled, recalling how she had my back when we explored the house that first day. No way in hell would she miss an adventure. She would go to the cemetery, complaining all the way.

The little bit of happy that I'd found evaporated. I wasn't a Hoodoo queen, but I had a feeling my next words would make things worse in a way I didn't want to face. But I didn't have the luxury of ignorance. "That can't happen. Her mouth has been sewn shut."

Both Loretta and Maria sat up so quick, it was as if invisible strings tugged at their shoulders.

"That ain't good," Loretta said, her brown face ashen.

I shook my head. "Not at all. The dead part was bad enough, but I've never seen anything like that." I looked at Kyle. "And I've been seeing ghosts since I was a kid."

Kyle asked, "So did you see Ilona again after the altercation at The Ancestors?"

Again, I shook my head. "Not alive. And not until today on the sidewalk in front of Conjure Ink." I raised a hand to stop the barrage of questions. "She wasn't alone."

Kyle cleared his throat. "Are you saying there's a serial killer in Hoodoo?" His eyes widened before he got that aw-hell-no face. "Sweet cheeks, maybe you should reconsider that inheritance."

Maria cracked her knuckles. "Hold up. We'd know if women got kidnapped. Maybe your spook detector is broken. Because none of that has happened."

"Maybe, maybe not. But I saw what I saw." I shrugged.

"This is where I may be some help." Merri pulled a book from her bag, placing it on her lap, then set her crossed hands on top of it as if the book was sacred. "I've been doing some research." She turned to me with an apologetic grimace. "My place in the coven was tenuous at best, and I wanted to prove my worth and loyalty."

"Let me guess, by throwing me headfirst under the bus."

Merri nodded.

Well, at least she was honest, but that didn't soothe my rising annoyance.

She raised her hands and shook her head. "Hear me out. The deeper I dug, the less I believed your guilt."

"Gee, thanks."

"Wait." Kyle crossed his arms. "Guilty of what?"

"Murder." Loretta shifted in her seat and glared at Merri.

"That's not relevant," I said as a wave of fatigue washed over me. Guess you really can't outrun your past.

"The hell it ain't." Kyle mouthed *later* to me before studying Merri as if she were the star witness for the prosecution. "This is a real shit show, but go on,"

Merri cleared her throat and leaned forward. "We all know Gwen didn't kill Duncan. Well, I'm close to having solid evidence to prove it. Do you guys know what an Adze is?"

Thanks to Duncan, unfortunately, I did, but before I could answer either way, the others spoke up.

"This may sound fantastical." Merri's gaze shot to Kyle, then back to me.

"Look, just say it." Kyle pointed from me to Loretta and Maria. "We already have the ghost whisperer and the Hoodoo Hillbillies here; how much worse could it be?"

Loretta snorted.

Maria cackled.

But me, my mind raced, and I grew angry all over again. Were it not for Duncan, my life and future would have been mine to control. However, anger wouldn't solve my problems, at least not this one. It was a struggle, but my expression remained neutral as I twisted the end of one of my locs and settled in.

Merri looked around the room as if it was kindergarten story time. "Immigrants and enslaved people brought more than their bodies from their home countries. With them came beliefs, legends, gods, and even monsters."

Kyle stretched out his legs, crossed his ankles, and leaned back, but his relaxed posture and often easygoing nature had lulled many a fool into complacency.

"One of those legends is the Adze." Merri looked over at Maria. "When you were a kid, were fireflies common here in East Texas?"

"Oh yeah. It used to be thick with them."

"Hmm." Merri tapped her chin with her index finger. "Unfortunately, one or perhaps more of them were feeding off of the children in Hoodoo."

"Like mosquitos?" Loretta asked.

"No. Like vampires." Merri's words dropped like a bomb.

I half expected Kyle to burst out laughing, but from the faint lines between his Botoxed brows and the downturn of his lips, he was anything but amused. "Please, go on." His voice may have been soft, but it was deadly quiet in a way that I'd never witnessed.

Merri licked her lips. "Well, the story goes that they feed off the blood of the innocent. In other words, children or infants."

"That doesn't make sense. Duncan was eighteen. He wasn't a child, and he sure as hell wasn't innocent." And it would have been cool had the prick shared the unabridged version of his fuck-up.

"Sorcerers, and those possessing the even tiniest of magics, can make bargains. In exchange for voluntary possession, the Adze exponentially increases the host's abilities."

I swallowed. Hard.

"Hold up." Maria stood and paced the length of the room, stopping at the window before turning to stare at Merri. I wasn't the only person in the room who'd been friends with Duncan, and from Maria's scowl, she wasn't having the slander. "Apparently, you need to go back to the drawing board. Duncan didn't possess magic to bargain with. What other lies you planning to tell?"

"Don't get all worked up." Loretta moved to Maria, squeezing her hand. "It don't much matter now since Duncan ain't here to ask."

"Is that true, Gwen?" Merri asked, her voice low. "Is he here?"

"No," I blurted without pausing to explain.

Honestly, whether Merri believed me or not, I didn't give a shit. While I appreciated her help, Duncan didn't seem eager to share his existence with her yesterday. The male may have ruined my life and be a current pain in my ass, but for now, I'd respect his wishes.

Keeping it one hundred, I didn't fully trust Merri either.

Merri sighed and returned the unopened book to her purse. "You really haven't opened Eleanor's diary?"

"No, I haven't. What's up?"

"I'd like to compare some of the sections to my notes." She stood and gave me a single nod. "I know what's between those pages is personal, but it's crucial I understand what Eleanor knew."

"You could just ask." Maria moved to stand next to my chair. I really hoped she didn't plan to shoot that poor witch.

"That's an excellent question." Kyle stood, then walked nonchalantly to the mantel, "Why not chat with Eleanor?"

"I have, but regardless of what they say, hindsight isn't 20/20. It fades, it changes, it lies." Merri paused at the threshold. "Oh, the other part of that tale is that when the Adze isn't possessing a body, they have the ability to change their form—be it animal or human."

I threw my arms wide. "Then who the hell am I supposed to trust?"

Merri shrugged then simply said, "No one."

Chapter 29

AFTER DINNER AND CONVERSATION, accompanied by healthy doses of bourbon, Azure House was finally empty of everyone but Kyle and my ghostly staff. I plopped on the floor beside my bed, pressing my back against the wood, closing my eyes before proceeding to methodically bang the back of my head against the side of the mattress.

Thump, thump, thump.

I stopped moving, but the noise continued. "Ash, not now," I said, the words more of an elongated groan than a sentence.

"Lucky for me, I'm not Ash." Kyle slipped into my room like a wraith. "But he did ask me to come."

I pressed my lips together and inhaled a quick breath. Fatigue, both physical and emotional, had taken a toll today, but I patted the spot next to me.

Kyle raised a perfectly threaded brow and moved to my side. "I wasn't expecting easy."

"Then it's lucky for you that I'm all out of fight."

"Oh, sweetie." He wrapped an arm around my shoulder, but his touch was tentative, until I surrendered my weight. Then, as he'd done so many times, Kyle held me tight. No judgments, no questions; this man knew me like no other.

I whispered, "At this big age, I've some bad days, but these last few were..."

"I know, sweetie." Kyle rested his cheek against my hair.

This was nice. I bathed in the strength of our friendship, one of the few constants in my adult life. More than a few seconds drifted past before I spoke. "You heard Merri. Who can I trust?"

Kyle pulled back, gently placing a knuckle beneath my chin to raise my face until our gazes met and held. "Gwendolyn. You can trust me."

"I'm.... scared," I whispered, my voice filled with shame and so much more. Duncan's vulnerability made him the Adze's target, but if not him, the creature would have chosen someone else. So, in the end, Rita was right. I was responsible for Duncan's death.

Looked like I was the bad seed after all.

"Baby cakes," Kyle said, interrupting my pity party. "Let's toss the hair shirt. It's not a good look. Your aunt and uncle's plasma diet? I know. Rita, and her witchy family? Yup, know that too. And drumroll, please... Yes, I'm more than aware that your little sheriff's bite is far worse than his bark."

I blinked slowly. This wasn't a conversation I thought would show up on the batshit bingo card.

Before I could unpack any of that, Kyle spoke again. "Sweetheart, you're not the only one with a complicated family tree."

I cupped my hands together in the prayer position, pressing my clasped fingers against my chin. I wasn't exactly praying, but if ever there was a time for divine intervention, this was it. "How?" I asked, not sure if I genuinely wanted an answer.

"Oh, darling," Kyle placed a hand to his chest, being overly dramatic. "Because I'm not human."

I could've been disappointed that Kyle had never shared. I could've been hurt because we'd been cheated out of a deeper relationship due to Hoodoo rules as well as my fears. But that was then. How I responded at this point was my choice. Did I want to be the friend and ally to Kyle that he'd always been to me? Absolutely. Because when it came down to it, none of that bullshit mattered. I loved Kyle regardless.

"Soooo...have you... uh, ever been? Human, that is." Damn, I was sounding like Yoda.

"Darling, the only reason I'm sharing at all is because you need to know that you can *always* trust me."

I nodded.

Kyle shifted, removing his arm from my shoulder and grabbing my hand. "Alrighty. You know me better than any human. Think about it, about me. How I prefer to have things both ways. It's not a flaw, but a feature." Kyle smiled.

No, to call Kyle's expression a smile was an understatement. Yes, his mouth had moved, exposing those pearly whites, but it was something else. The change was like the subtle slide from dawn to day. He'd shifted from beautiful to brilliant. The only way my mind could categorize it was that Kyle was...glowing.

"Hold on to your wig, baby, you are in the presence of a motherfucking god. Like with a capital G. I am Erinle."

Was the lack of a reaction a response?

Sitting on the floor in my new haunted house, with new freaky-ass powers, and let's not forget the old shapeshifting enemy, I couldn't even get worked up. In the scheme of things, it could be worse, right? Kyle could've have been a fanged soul-sucking demon.

Now *that* would have been screwed up.

Finally, I did respond—with a shrug and a grin. "No wonder your ego is so big," The ridiculousness of this day was never-ending. I studied Kyle's handsome androgynous face and concluded that I wouldn't care if he was a leprechaun.

I loved him as a woman.

Then I loved him as a man.

Looked like I'd have to keep loving him as a god, even with the capital G. "Sorry, but your name's not familiar. Like what pantheon are you from?" I pursed my lips, then snorted. "I guess it's safe to say you're not one of Zeus's many offspring?"

Kyle looked at me like I'd barfed in his favorite pair of shoes. "I forget, you're a child." He winked. "*And* American. But I won't hold that against you."

"Bite me." I crossed my arms and glowered. Or rather, I tried to.

When he spoke again, Kyle's voice had become musical, painted with the rhythm of waves washing against sparkling sand, and dancing with the undernotes of the continent from which my ancestors came. "I know you're already aware of the magnificence that is me."

Despite the ridiculously dangerous path my life had taken, I laughed.

"Chuckle if you want to, bitch, but check this out." Kyle unfolded himself from the floor, moving in front of me.

Then, the handsome and wicked-smart man morphed into the young woman that I'd met in college. I almost whispered a name I hadn't uttered in years, one that died with her. But Erin wasn't dead, was she?

Dear ancestors, this gave new meaning to the pronoun they.

"Holy shit." I pressed the tips of my fingers against my thighs. The metaphorical ball was now in my court.

I stood, nowhere near as graceful as they'd been. Watching the eyes that for the first time since I'd met them in college, my friend appeared uncertain. Rather than ask questions, I pulled down the quilt then slid into bed. "This is a snuggle kinda night. Wanna stay?" I asked while patting the empty spot next to me.

They didn't answer for what felt like a few decades.

My heart sank. Had I not responded fast enough, or said something unintentionally offensive? My stomach bubbled at the thought.

Kyle's—or hell, in this form, should I call them Erinle's—eyebrow rose. "You... want me to?"

That boot on my chest lifted. "Don't be stupid. You can tell me about preferred pronouns and the God stuff tomorrow, but honey, I'm exhausted." I yawned. "Let's go to sleep."

They turned off the overhead light before joining me beneath the covers. "So... do you have a gender preference?" When I frowned, Erinle pressed their lips together. "In how you see me, in how I present around you..." they licked their lips "...and your family?"

"Nope. Kyle, Erin, Erinle — don't matter. You're still my best friend."

They kissed me on the cheek. Judging by the lack of five o'clock shadow, it was Erin I'd rest with tonight. "Ride or die, sweetie. Ride or die," they said before gathering me in warm arms.

That was awesome, but I hoped I didn't have to do the dying part anytime soon.

"Erinle," I whispered. "What is Ash?"

They exhaled and held me a little tighter. "Sweetheart, that's not my tale to tell. But like me, he wasn't born of a woman."

Chapter 30

I SPENT MY DAY THE same way I woke up after Kyle's big reveal—gloriously alone. No ghosts, no cops, and best of all, no surprises. Well, except for the extent of the secret passages traversing my home. Azure House was a kid's hide-and-seek fantasy. Hell, you could get lost forever behind these walls.

Which was why I'd avoided the attic and basement. They wouldn't be finding my dead and desiccated body down there. Nope, I wasn't that woman. You know which one I was talking about? The one who investigated scary sounds in the woods armed with a cellphone and privilege.

So now, after a day of exploring, reading, drawing, and everything I could think of to avoid reality, it was time to woman up. For at least the next six months, only death could rip me from Azure House.

When I faced the reaper, I wouldn't be leaving without a fight.

Before I turned into a giant raisin, I stepped out of the shower, wrapped myself in a bath sheet, and grabbed the lotion. Hey, just because my life was in turmoil didn't mean I skipped moisturizing.

I twisted the top off the simple brown glass bottle with a label covered with Texas Bluebonnets and a tiny drawing of Azure House. Wait? Did Lucille or Cook make this? They weren't merely ghosts, but artists. I waved the bottle beneath my nose. "Mm." The subtle lavender and the undernotes of citrus were yummy.

I marched to the dresser, grabbed my iPhone, then cranked up my Texas playlist. Yes, I had a playlist titled "Texas." We were our own brand of crazy, but regardless of how long and how far I travelled, my heart belonged to Hoodoo.

Uncultured non-Southern folks teased me for my love of country music, but even my hip-hop loving friends changed their minds when I introduced them to Breland. As he sang about tossing back whiskey, I threw my hands in the air and shook, shimmied, and bounced like a tattooed manic pixie.

Then I closed my eyes and swayed as he sang of finding that place where he belonged. Thank goodness no one was here to see my uncoordinated ass. I'd never hear the end of it.

By the end of the third song, my lips curled up at the corners. I wouldn't exactly call it a smile, but I wasn't ready to burn down the world. At least not tonight. Plopping down on the divan, I stared out the opened curtains at the fat moon hovering low over the cemetery.

I slathered cream on my legs and attempted to understand why Aunt Rose would want Ash and Kyle in her home. The woman abhorred outsiders. Did she know that Kyle was a god, and Ash was...

A soft knock against the door made me drop the lotion. "Just a minute," I called out. I jerked the door open, hoping see Lucille's dark smiling face carrying another tray of chocolate, and hopefully some snickerdoodles.

But too late, I remembered that she didn't use no stinking door. So there I stood half-naked blinking up at the grinning Ash.

"Now that's a welcome home I can get used to."

So was the five o'clock shadow covering his jaw, the heat in his inky eyes, and the gray button-down that was fitted enough to emphasize his chest, but loose enough to leave a bit to the imagination.

Unfortunately for me, that imagination involved ripping those buttons open and trailing my fingers across the Arabic lettering on his stomach before I headed...

I shook my head. Nope, not going there.

"Did you, uh... finish with your business?" I tightened the towel, struggling to not fidget. "I'm kind of busy here. Need something?"

That too dark gaze took its time making the journey from the towel covering my locs to my face, pausing at my lips before traveling down the full sleeve adorning my left arm. "As a matter of fact, I do."

I'm not sure what set me off, the smile, the arrogance, or him constantly inserting himself in my life, but I was tired of feeling like everyone's plaything. I stepped back and touched the door, intending to slam it in his smug face.

"Wait." He placed his palm on the door, his expression sliding into a mask of concern and maybe a little anger. "Tell me who I need to kill."

Nothing says "I want to do you" like offering to unalive some unlucky bastard. *It was hawt.* Dear ancestors, what the heck did that say about me that being around a man who casually threatened death—or worse—turned me into a horny teenager.

I wrapped my arms around myself, grazing my fingernails against the pebbled skin of my biceps. "Thanks for asking, but there were no more unexpected visitors or falling pianos."

"Maybe this will cheer you up." Between his raised fingers dangled a shoe bag, and somehow I'd been so busy checking dude out, I'd missed the garment bag. "May I enter?" he asked, all traces of hubris and humor gone.

"Sure." I stepped aside before scurrying to the bathroom to slip out of the towels wrapped around my hair and body and into a fluffy blue robe.

"You didn't have to change on my account," Ash said when I returned.

I rolled my eyes. "You do realize that everything isn't about you, right?"

Ash's chuckle was as alluring as the rest of him. "Touché, Miss Carter, touché. I hope you don't mind, but I wanted you to have this for tomorrow night." He motioned to the garment bag lying on the bed. "May I?"

"Knock yourself out." I poured myself a glass of water, holding it front of me like a shield. "You've purchased clothes for me—again."

"Did you bring evening wear?" He leaned over and removed the garment from the black cloth bag, gifting me an unobstructed view of his beautiful bum.

I gulped some water to quench my suddenly dry mouth.

"This was supposed to be a quick trip." Not twenty to life. "So no, but we do have malls in these here parts," I said with an exaggerated Texas twang.

"I've saved you a trip." He pulled out a blood-red dress that looked like it was held together by rhinestones and a prayer.

And I freaking loved it. I'm nobody's food, but walking my size twelve ass into a house filled with vampires, I was going to look like a motherfucking snack.

THE LIMO TURNED OFF the main road and onto the private lane leading to the Double R Ranch. According to Texas records, it was one of the oldest that has remained in the same family. Which, in my Uncle Raul's case—the same man.

A smile rose unbidden at the sight of the massive gates as we drove through. It might not have been perfect, but the Double R was home.

That whole making plans and God laughing thing? Truer than true.

Last night, the dress wasn't the only thing Ash had returned with. He'd found the one Mediterranean restaurant in The Woodlands and put together a picnic, which we had in my bedroom on the floor. Ash plied me with wine, hummus, stuffed grape leaves, lamb kebobs, and other things I didn't know the names of, but ate and loved.

And the conversation? Light and sublime. Ash tickled me with his observations of Texas in general, and Hoodoo specifically. Without being condescending or mean, he did imitations of my family members that were so on point that I laughed until my sides ached.

As we chatted and teased sitting on a blanket spread on my bedroom floor, I remembered why I liked Ash. That man, the one unguarded and laughing, who looked at me like I was the most beautiful woman on the planet despite the ripped orange plaid pajama pants and matching University of Texas tee.

Somewhere after finger foods and story time, I fell asleep, waking up not on the floor lying on the pillow facing Ash, but as always—alone.

Now, after a day of getting polished, pampered, plucked, and exfoliated (also thanks to Ash), I was dressed and ready, physically at least, to stroll into the Double R.

"How many boyfriends did you bring home in high school to meet the 'rents?" Sitting in the dimly lit limo across from Ash and me, Kyle grinned and tugged at the sleeves of his fitted dark gray suit.

Where Ash was broad and muscular, Kyle seemed dainty in comparison. But to underestimate him would be a mistake. It would be like dismissing a rapier, declaring it unintimidating and not a threat when contrasted to a battle axe. They'd both kill you, but the sword would leave a thousand tiny cuts before being plunged into your heart.

"None." I looked out the window at the night skies. The stars in Texas shone brighter after being gone so long.

"Not even Carlos?" Ash asked.

I turned to Ash, and once again, I was blindsided with the virility packaged in one man. Thank the ancestors he didn't wear a tux. I'm not sure my poor heart or my ovaries could have taken it. But the black suit, tie, and shirt made him look like a being who'd whip out a contract and bargain for your soul.

I'm not sure how many would resist.

Finally, I shook my head. "Not even Carlos."

"I'm not a boy, but I'm honored to be the first."

"Let's see if you feel the same after." I smiled, reached over, and squeezed Ash's hand. The man could have and should have declined the invitation. But beneath it all, I'm a selfish and occasionally vain creature. Having Ash as well as Kyle by my side made me hold my head a little higher. For tonight, I didn't have to face judgment alone.

Time to lighten the mood. "Well, I would have rather gone to Whataburger."

"In that dress, you'd cause a riot," Kyle said.

"You outdid yourself, Ash. Thanks again." If the dress looked good on the hanger, on... it was chef's kiss, if I don't say so myself. Honestly, what there was of it was simple, chic, and made for a woman with plentiful assets. Thank goodness for the patron saint of shapewear, convertible bras, and kinesiology tape.

The girls were lifted, and the blood-red fabric hugged what it should and camouflaged what I'd rather be hidden—like my little Buddha belly. Did I mention that my back was exposed except for a thin strip of rhinestones that ran down my spine, putting the set of wings tattooed on my back on full display?

The car stopped in front of the house. And I reverted to that insecure and awkward teenager. Were the dress, the limo, and the men too much?

As if reading my mind, Ash spoke into the darkness. "You're a formidable woman now; it's past time your family, the rest of Hoodoo, and you acknowledge that."

"While I appreciate the sentiment, perhaps I should have chosen to make a splash wearing more clothes."

Ash chuckled, and the sound was like velvet against my skin. "I want the world to see what I see. And know that you're mine."

I blinked and dipped my chin, giving Ash a you're-not-the-boss-of-me look. "Excuse me?"

The limousine's engine stopped. Without its smooth growl, the dimly lit car filled with suffocating tension and bold choices. Once again, Ash had declared that he considered me his. Okay, that was flattering and all, but did I feel the same?

No, I can't say that I did.

But when we walked through those doors and Ash caused a stir, which he would, would I feel a certain kind of way if women made advances on Ash?

Absolutely.

But that was more of a me thing. About the disrespect, the dismissal that no way would a male as smooth and urbane as Ash want a woman covered in ink. Ink that I probably would have chosen not to display tonight. Ink that was personal and beloved, at least by me.

The immaculately dressed driver opened the door closest to the house, which stopped me from saying anything embarrassing. Nothing said gauche like threatening to snatch a bitch bald for hitting on a man I hadn't claimed.

"I'll...uh...wait for you kids outside." Kyle slipped out of the limo, murmuring something to the chauffeur.

Chicken.

"Give us a moment," Ash said to the driver.

What I should have done was climbed over Ash to escape the conversation that we'd been leading up to since the day we met. What I could have done was send Ash on his way that first night he came to town, and I saw that my life was becoming increasingly complicated.

But I was weak.

So, what I did do was bask in the attention and company of a man I liked. Not for the money and the power, but because he challenged me, spoiled and pushed me, and because he was just... Ash.

Sitting in the cocoon of leather and steel, it reminded me of Morocco, where Ash spent afternoons at my bedside reading books and telling stories, just watching me sleep until I healed enough to return home.

That was the man I knew, that was the man I had learn to trust. I trusted him; it made absolutely no sense, and it was probably the stupidest –

Well... second stupidest thing I'd ever done. Something about the male called to me. Like Lucifer in the garden, every word from Ash's lips was a seduction.

He might as well be the Borg, and this woman was tired of resisting.

Kyle and the driver stood chatting a few feet from the limo. Ash and I should talk about our feelings and whatnot later. Because we needed privacy for this conversation. That, and Aunt Rose's patience wasn't endless.

Shifting and the slide of fabric against leather made me look at Ash, who sat holding what looked to be a navy velvet box too large to be a ring, and too small to be a necklace.

"If you would do me the honor of wearing this tonight, I would be humbled."

Yeah, right. I doubted anything could bring Ash Modeus down to terra firma. From the reactions of damned near everyone else, Ash may as well be Lucifer reincarnated. That was enough to swell anyone's head.

He gently placed the box in my hand, which lay palm up on my thigh. "I had hoped to give this to you in Morocco, but... things didn't go as planned." Ash's words seemed to be filled with a combination of frustration, anger, and something that sounded too close to longing.

A muscle flexed in his jaw before he shifted his gaze from me to the closed window.

"You could say that again." Before I was sucked into the vortex of memories that included my pain and death, I whispered, "Thank you. For the gift, Morocco, your friendship... and hell, everything." I leaned in to kiss his cheek, but Ash turned, pressing his lips gently against mine.

There was no tongue, no fireworks, just the tickle of his spearmint breath, our mouths barely touching, but whispering silent promises.

Luckily, Ash retreated before I jumped his bones. Once my haziness cleared and I could actually focus, I bit back a moan as Ash sucked on his lower lip.

Woo lordy. I wanted to fan myself, but that would ruin the whole sexy woman of the world thing I had going on.

"You're most welcome," Ash said, his voice rumbly.

I pressed my lips together and focused on the box before I made the ultimate of indecent proposals to this confusing, confounding male. I flipped the box open—and gasped. There, lying on a bed of blue velvet, so dark it was almost black, was a wide gold cuff, encrusted with diamonds and rubies the size of the nail on my pinky.

My mouth formed a silent O as I blinked to make sure this wasn't a hallucination. I raised the box, looking closely at something that looked like it belonged in a museum, and was flooded with skin-tightening emotion.

"Holy guacamole," I said when my mouth finally worked again. I looked up at Ash. "This is —"

"Don't you dare say too much." He tried glaring, but the twitching lips ruined the grumpy rich guy effect.

"Whoa, not even." I returned the box to my lap, removing the jewelry from its home. The cuff, if one could call it that, would be over the top outside of an Indian wedding. And I freaking loved it. With a closer look, the swirling pattern along the gold edges wasn't a pattern at all, but undecipherable lettering.

I frowned. How did I know that?

The longer I looked, the more the design shifted and swirled and mutated. I trailed my fingers along the soft metal, tracing the words, then a spike of energy zinged through my flesh. "Ouch."

"Here, allow me." Ash slid his nail along the edge, hitting an invisible latch, and the cuff snapped open.

"Whoa, talk about craftsmanship." I admired not only the diamonds and rubies, but Ash's long, deft fingers.

He closed the bracelet. "A friend of mine is a god with jewelry and metalworks." Ash traced his thumb just beneath the bracelet and over the fragile veins crisscrossing my inner wrist. "Now, wherever you are, a piece of me will be with you."

I wrapped my fingers around the oddly warm jewelry, pressing it against my chest. "I will cherish this always, thank you. When we get home..." I cleared my throat. "Back to Azure House, screw the forty-eight hours. Let's finish that conversation."

"Do you believe in destiny?"

I nodded.

"Good. You and I were meant... promised. That first night in Dublin, I should have..." Ash opened his mouth, then closed it again.

Was he having a moment of... uncertainty?

That, more than the jewelry, the clothes, even the spa, had to be the most precious gift I'd ever received.

"Promise that you'll hear me out."

Those happy tingles faded at his tight expression. "Just tell me you aren't married. Anything else, I could probably deal with."

Ash chuckled. "No. I am not." He bit down on his lower lip, and this time, the look in his obsidian eyes had nothing to do with uncertainty.

Plop. There went the last of my pitiful defenses.

"Let us go before..." Rather than finish the sentence, Ash kissed my forehead, then opened the door.

Kyle was all but vibrating waiting for us join him. He leaned around Ash and grinned. "Woman, you didn't tell me your uncle was J.R. Ewing."

The limo door closed with a solid thump. Subtext wasn't my forte, but in mixed company—half with supersonic hearing—I was forced to pretend this was a normal, everyday meet-the-parents occasion.

I chuckled, then looked back and forth at my two dates. "Gentlemen, this is your last chance to back out." Of anyone I could have strolled into the Double R Ranch with, these two men could hold their own. So perhaps I should have embraced them as the assets they were, rather than liabilities.

"What kind of man would I be if I feared your frail elderly uncle?" Ash pressed a hand against his chest.

He was so full of shit.

"You know how they say Black don't crack? Well, he may be Mexican, but it's the same premise." I accepted Ash's bent arm, looking not into those dark eyes, but at his lips, wanting to once more feel them against mine.

"Okay, lovebirds, you're gathering an audience," Kyle stage-whispered.

Ash leaned down, placing his lips against my ear, whispering, "Later."

I nodded, then looked at Kyle and winked.

At least that was the plan, but something, or should I say four somethings caught my eye. There, about ten feet past Kyle stood the dead Ilona. This time, she was accompanied by two additional ghostly friends, bringing the number of dead witches stalking me to five.

Chapter 31

AS ASH, KYLE, AND I approached the massive double doors, they swung open, liveried human butlers on both sides bowing in tandem. Dramatic much?

I wanted to roll my eyes at the ostentatiousness of it all, but the expansive entry hall, the fresh flowers, the dim lighting, and even the faint bitter smell of old blood screamed welcome home. I pressed my lips together, remembering the first time I walked through these doors, angry, alone, and heartbroken.

But even then, I was impressed. Eight-year-old me would have given everything, up to and including my life, to see my mom again, but driving up to this oddly placed Spanish-style mansion was still like a fairytale.

Ash handed one of the footmen the invitation.

The man nodded before handing off the envelope and the three of us to another unfamiliar servant. What was happening with the congregation that required the vampire equivalent of a state dinner?

Kyle stage-whispered, "I was expecting Little House on the Prairie, not..."

We stopped on the landing behind the steel-spined servant.

"Well, the Spanish brought more than disease, colonization, and Catholicism to the Americas." The nervousness about seeing Aunt Rose and the self-consciousness about my dress faded into a low hum at the sight of Uncle Raul's warm, massive grin.

Kyle looked down on the crowd. "I get to bask in my very own Cinderella moment. Ooo." Kyle fanned himself and stared at a tall Black vampire with damned near blue-black skin and a face that belonged in magazines. "And I believe I've found my next Prince Charming."

I rolled my eyes and looked up at Ash. "You're not surprised."

"I do not enter situations unprepared." He trailed his fingers across my knuckles, then shifted, removing my hand from his arm, and placing a kiss where his thumb had recently caressed. "You, however, have caught me quite unaware."

The footman's booming voice shattered the moment. "I present Miss Gwendolyn Carter, Kyle Inle, and Prince Ash Modeus."

The simultaneous gasps sucked the air out of the room.

But I couldn't even do that since my lungs had ceased working. "W-what did he just say?" I asked through what I considered my pageant smile.

Rather than answer, the bastard winked and led me down the stairs.

"I take it this was on the list of topics," I said out of the side of my mouth, uncaring who listened.

"You would be correct, but it's not the most interesting tidbit." He spoke without moving his lips.

If Ash was the ventriloquist, what did that make me?

Ash leaned down and placed a kiss on my cheek before whispering, "It's going to be fine. Just another thing to discuss before..."

I pulled away and gifted Ash with my iciest smile. "Before what?"

"Before I separate his head from his body if he doesn't unhand my niece," Uncle Raul said from behind me.

Ash performed an elegant bow. "Gwendolyn is her own woman. However, Ignacio, it would be wise to recall I am not one so easily defeated." He grinned and took half a step forward to stand at my side. "Besides, I've grown quite attached to my head over the years."

"Raul, step aside so I can greet my niece while you two nincompoops play your testosterone games," said a hidden honey-sweet alto tinted by a lifetime lived in the South.

Aunt Rose glided from behind her mate and stopped, looking at me. A flash of something like hurt shone in her dark brown eyes before she drowned the emotion beneath her lake of ice.

As to be expected, Aunt Rose still looked like the Black fairy princess eight-year-old me believed her to be when I woke in that hospital bed.

After she bound my powers.

My throat tightened, and I pushed the pain, the questions, and yes, the betrayal behind me and walked into her arms. The women in our family tended to be tall, and Aunt Rose was no exception. People commented that they could see the family resemblance in the two of us—I couldn't.

Aunt Rose was a few shades lighter brown with almost elfin features and a wide, full, mouth that was usually pinched tight. The only thing we had in common were our noses and attitude.

"I missed you," I whispered in her ear. When her arms tightened and my ribs began to scream, I wheezed two words. "Can't breathe."

Aunt Rose chuckled as she traded the embrace for my hands as she studied me. Who did Auntie see, the girl who'd failed to live up to her lofty expectations? Or a woman who'd merely failed?

"You couldn't have longed for my presence overly much." She dropped my hands. "Three days, and this is the first I see of you."

And... of course she'd go straight to complaints rather than admit affection. Or gasp...pride. Fortunately, Uncle Raul had no such objections. He moved beside his mate of over a hundred and fifty years and opened his heart and arms.

"Uncle Raul." I wrapped him in a hug and kissed him on his smooth cheek. "It's so good to see you."

"We are both pleased that you've returned to Hoodoo, and to us." Uncle Raul flicked two fingers at a waiter carrying a tray filled with champagne flutes.

I motioned to both Kyle and Ash. "I'd like to formally introduce you to my friend Kyle." After both my uncle and aunt shook hands with him, I looked up at Ash, who handed me a flute. "Thank you."

He tilted his glass to mine for a toast, which I happily gave before taking a sip. "And this is..." When I looked at not only my aunt and uncle, but the people standing next to them, they were all staring.

Not at Ash. Not at Kyle. But me. Well, not my face, but my bracelet.

Note to self, be sure to put an insurance rider on this bad boy. I extended my wrist, rotating it so they could get the full impact. "Isn't it beautiful?"

"It's... something alright," Aunt Rose muttered.

Whatever.

I wrapped the fingers of my free hand around Ash's bicep. Mostly, because I was ready to stab the dark-haired Latina vampire standing behind Aunt Rose. The heifer wore a dress short enough that the slightest movement, the entire room would know if she'd waxed.

She had.

Ash chuckled and rested his hand on my lower back where the fabric gathered, stroking his thumb across my spine.

"Ash." I smiled up at him, a silent thanks that he'd not laughed at my sudden bout of stabbiness. "You've already met Uncle Raul. This stunning woman is Rose Ignacio, his wife. Aunt Rose, this is the man who saved my life in Morocco, Ash Modeus."

That odd hush at the mention of his name happened again.

"You have our gratitude for saving one so precious to us." Uncle Raul dipped his head, in what for him could be considered a bow.

"It was both my honor and duty." Ash leaned down, placing a tender kiss on my temple. "For I, too, care deeply for our dear Gwendolyn."

A memory, one that had been buried, unearthed. I'm not sure what did it, the champagne, the candlelight, or the fact that I'd decided to mostly stop fighting the attraction to Ash, but it was there, like a splinter that had worked itself loose. "I'm not sure if I told you this, but after I..." *Not the time, Gwennie.* I cleared my throat and shook my head. "Never mind."

"Oh no, I'd like to hear this." Aunt Rose took a dainty sip of her champagne. "It would be rude to keep us in suspense."

"It's silly really. I was...um, with my mom, after I died." My mouth was suddenly as dry as the Moroccan desert as my body battled my common sense. Some primal part of me knew I shouldn't say it, to keep the memory to myself.

But it was too late for that. It was easy to accept vampires, gods roaming the earth, and other magical creatures. It was believable to accept the existence of an afterlife and ancestors waiting to welcome you. But for Ash to have power enough to retrieve me from the arms of death meant something that my mind either couldn't comprehend, or worse, wouldn't accept.

Ash and I watched each other; our gazes unflinching.

"And...?" Kyle asked.

Kyle's words were for me, but I couldn't rip my gaze from Ash's. As a matter of fact, other than our small circle, everyone ceased to exist. "You came for me." Even my hallucinatory version of Ash was overbearing and rude. Especially since at that moment, standing on the shores of the afterlife, I wanted to remain dead.

"What exactly did he say?" Aunt Rose asked, her voice pleasant, but with an icy undertone.

Once again, I spoke to Ash, still caught in his spell. "You chastised my mother for failing to protect me. *Which was rude.* Good thing it was a dream, or I would have punched you in the nose."

Ash's lips twitched. "What else did I say?" His velvety baritone was an intimate caress.

I swallowed.

Hard.

Occasionally, I forgot the presence that was Ash. This man was bold, arrogant, and held a version of a power that rivaled the vampires. Everyone standing in the entry hall watched and waited for the conclusion of my tale. I inhaled, stared into Ash's bottomless eyes, and whispered, "You said that I belonged to you."

Aunt Rose hissed.

Uncle Raul growled.

And Ash? He grinned as if I'd given him the keys to a vault filled with gold. "It pleases me that you finally decided that I was right."

"We'll see." I took another sip of champagne to hide my smile.

The air in the ballroom thickened.

Except for the tiny muscle in his jaw, Ash's face was a mask of indifference.

The skin on my arms pebbled, and I suddenly wished I was armed. What had changed the mood, shot everyone into DEFCON 1, rip a mf'ers head off level of readiness?

"Get out of my house," Uncle Raul said.

I spun around, and there, two feet away, stood Carlos, with four deputies spread out behind him like a badge-wearing boy band. And to make it worse, one of those deputies was Johnson, who stared at me with malice in his eyes and a broad grin on his evil face.

Chapter 32

"I'M SURPRISED IT TOOK you this long to wind up in a jail cell." The not-so-good Deputy Johnson stood on the other side of the bars with his arms crossed over his wide chest.

An hour earlier, Carlos hadn't wasted time or pleasantries. "Gwendolyn Carter, you're under arrest for the murder of Ilona Hatcher." With great joy, he read me my rights before cuffing me.

Eventually, either Ash, Kyle, or Mr. Z would rescue me from the pokey. Until then, I had to put up with that sneering dipshit and his friends.

I flipped Deputy Johnson off, because really, what was he going to do, lock me up?

Oops, he'd already done that. I walked five steps to the hard bed and sat, leaning back on my hands. "If you weren't wearing that badge, you'd be either in Huntsville Prison or the cell next door."

"This time, your mother's money —" He tapped the heel of his hand against his forehead. "—my bad. Your mommy's dead, right?" The fake frown slipped into something far scarier. Frightening enough that I hoped he never worked a solo shift while I was their guest. His next words pierced my soul like a bullet. "You're probably as responsible for her death as you are for Ilona's."

"Enough." Carlos' voice whipped with enough power to raise the hair on my arms.

"I'm not saying anything that you—"

"Keep it professional." The *if you can* in Carlos' voice remained unsaid but was crystal-damned-clear.

I scooted back on the bunk, leaning against the wall. Twice in one week, I was rocking the jailbird outfit of gray and white striped jumpsuit and black slip-on shoes that they call sneakers, but every Chinatown I'd ever visited called them slippers.

The whole mug shot business? Humiliating. This arrest was the real deal. No drunk tank. No going past go. No two hundred dollars.

"You okay?" Carlos stood at the bars to my cell, his hands dangling over one of the crossbeams.

Despite arresting me for murder, suspecting that I'd used the foulest of magic to kill Duncan, the chick in the grocery store, and now Ilona, Carlos still didn't view me as a threat. Honestly, it was insulting that he didn't recognize the badass-ness contained in my hot middle-aged body.

I exhaled loudly and sagged at the ugly truth. Unless it came down to me and him in a Hoodoo, Texas Battle Royale, I doubted I could harm Carlos.

His buddy, on the other hand...

"Gwendolyn."

"What?" I snapped, annoyed that his buttery smooth voice yanked me out of my blood-lust fantasy. "What do you want to hear? Well, you won't be getting shit without my attorney present. How about that?"

"If you need anything, let me know." He watched me for a few seconds, then sighed and headed for the door.

"Hope you're happy," I said, my voice low enough that hopefully only he heard me.

Carlos stopped. What he didn't do was face me.

Coward.

"You'll finally get your revenge." This time, he did turn around, so I looked him in the face and said what I should have said years ago. "Maybe this is payment of my karmic debt. But at least punish me for something I actually did."

"Like murder Duncan?"

And there it was.

"You want to go there? Okay. Are you saying that the Tribunal was so incompetent that they set a murderer free?" I snapped my fingers. "Oh, I know, or my family bribed them."

"Shut up."

"Why? Hitting too close to home?"

"No." His voice was damned near a growl. This time when Carlos' eyes turned amber, they stayed that way.

I was both annoyed and mesmerized. How dare he stand there acting like the injured party. Especially when, like now, it was me who faced the ultimate penalty for something I hadn't done.

When I opened my mouth to speak, Carlos jabbed a finger in my direction. "Don't fucking sit there lying out of your pretty mouth. I. Know." He gripped the bars of the cell as if he planned to rip them open.

Okay... Now I was scared. But I was too damned proud to back down. Rather than lower my gaze and soften my posture to appear less aggressive, I did the opposite and met Carlos' anger with judgment.

"Carlos—"

Scalding power washed through the room as hatred filled my former friend and lover's eyes. "Why'd you fuck him? Why did you betray me, Gwen?"

"I have no idea wh—"

"For once in your overprivileged life, tell the damn truth." He jammed his fingers through his hair and let out a bitter laugh. "That's what I get. I should have listened when I was warned to stay the hell away from you."

I flinched.

The first emotion that slammed into me was a hurt so ancient, it ached, but it didn't get to settle in and hang out. Because rage slipped in and went off like a rocket. How. Dare. He.

My left hand sizzled. I sprang off the hard cot. Oh, this jackass wanted to fight? Good. He'd better be prepared for the torrent of pent-up rage, hurt, and betrayal. He broke my heart in a way that took years of therapy to accept that Carlos' lack of trust wasn't on me.

Well, you know what they say about plans. I raised my fist—and froze. This time, the light show wasn't contained by my skin. Swirls of Prussian blue and aquamarine hovered over my hand and pools of intense silver rippled around my fingertips. A silent voice whispered and coaxed me to say yes, to finally embrace all of me, the light and the dark, the good as well as the morally gray.

All I had to do was point and push. Simple. Easy. Evil.

Heat gathered in the center of my chest as my vision narrowed, focusing fully on the threat.

"Destroy, escape, evade. Destroy, escape, evade." The words were no longer a whisper, but a war cry. And the voice, wasn't mine—but masculine.

No, no, no, no, and fuck no.

I tucked my glowing arm against my chest and spun around, giving Carlos my back. Like a child frozen in terror because of the big bad scary beast under the bed, I squeezed my eyes closed. But there was no hiding from this monster, for the monster was me.

"Turn around." Carlos' voice was almost back to normal.

Could I say the same about my Thor hand?

Chapter 33

BEFORE I DID ANYTHING, I whispered a prayer to the ancestors, or anyone who'd freaking listen, but a sister needed help. What I didn't reach out and touch was that part of me that coaxed me to destroy.

What in the seven hells was that?

"Don't make me have to repeat myself," Carlos' voice was soft, but I'd seen enough prison movies to know I didn't want to force him to do a cell extraction.

So without opening my eyes, I did as he asked.

"What the fuck is that?" When I neither answered nor opened my eyes, Carlos cursed. "Cletus. Why the hell is she still wearing jewelry?"

My eyes snapped open, and only then did I notice the lack of light show around my hand.

Cletus? Deputy Dickhead's real name was Cletus? No wonder he was perpetually grumpy. He must hate his parents. Or rather, they hated him. Which, after being in his presence a mere few hours, I understood why.

Old Cletus himself lumbered down the hall, pausing outside my cell. "Couldn't get the damn thing off," he said, glaring at me like it was my fault.

Nope, I soooo didn't want to find myself alone and unarmed with that shifter.

"Who cares? It's not like I'm going to hang myself with a bracelet."

"No, you're too damn selfish to just go ahead and die." Cletus clenched his fists and his already big body started to swell.

I sucked in a quick breath and plopped down on the hard bunk. Carlos' anger—I got. Not enough to frame me for murder, but to be pissed? Absolutely. But Deputy Dickhead? I didn't know that man. He wasn't part of the pack when I left. And I had my doubts he was even a wolf.

Before the whole dying thing, I was good at seeing auras and recognizing supernaturals, but something had gone wrong. Or was it that I hadn't bothered to try?

I stared at Cletus, not only with my eyes, but that other part of me. Nothing. It was as if that slice of my gift had been shoved into a safe. One to which I lacked access.

I blocked out Carlos and Deputy Johnson's conversation, closing my eyes and laying my hands on my thighs, palms up and index fingers touching my thumbs. With each inhale, I sought peace.

Just like that, the door cracked. Then, like a mental SWAT team, my will kicked that blockage wide open. All I could do was grin. This was a little thing, but I'd done it on my own. No Loretta, no Rose, and no Ash. No matter how insignificant the weapon, each had a place in the arsenal.

This time when I looked at Cletus, who was staring at me, I knew. I saw his bear. There was something else, but—

"What did you do?" Cletus narrowed his eyes and stepped forward. Only Carlos' hand against his chest stopped that train.

Thank goodness, since those tracks were headed straight for me.

Carlos stood firm against the larger man. "Go home."

"I don't know why you would care after what she —"

"Would you prefer an unpaid vacation? I can make that happen."

Deputy Dickhead was smarter than he looked. He ripped his gaze from me and shook his head. "That won't be necessary."

"Good." Carlos' shoulders dropped, followed by his hand. "See you tomorrow?"

"Yeah." Without sparing me another threatening glance, the not-so-good deputy left.

Carlos sighed and stared off into space. More than likely, he was listening and waiting to see if Johnson followed orders. After a couple minutes of heavy silence, Carlos relaxed. When he looked at me again, it was as if he planned to say something epic before shaking his head and leaving me to my own jailbird devices.

Finally able to breathe, I lay down, interlaced my fingers behind my head, and stared at the graffitied ceiling. Okay. How in the hell was I supposed to fix this? I wasn't sure how long I had, but justice in Hoodoo, Texas was swift and brutal.

I'd like to believe that in this town, the innocent didn't receive undeserving sentences. And I sure as hell didn't want to be the first.

Magic and lies got me into this mess, but nothing short of finding and killing the Adze would keep me on this side of the grave.

"Get comfortable, Gwen; you're going to be here awhile." When I didn't respond, Carlos sighed, then heavy frustrated footsteps moved down the hall.

Chapter 34

TURNED OUT THAT CARLOS was wrong.

I sat parked in front of Aunt Rose's home, freshly showered and spitting mad. For the eight thousandth time, my fingers found their way to the wide metal band circling my neck.

Keeping it real, I thought if I ever rocked a collar, it would be for a kinky sex thing, not the equivalent of a magical town arrest bracelet.

I had not one, but two lawyers clad in expertly tailored black suits bust me out of the Hoodoo jail. And since neither was Ash, that should have made Carlos happy. It did not.

Kyle, Mr. Z., and I, along with Carlos, piled into a conference room rather than the interrogation room from my last visit to his not-so-fine establishment.

Carlos shook his head. When he spoke, his voice had been as flat as his expression. He'd been too controlled, too polite, too everything. Which, unless he'd had a personality transplant in the last twenty-five years, meant he was about to snap. Not good with anyone, especially a werewolf wearing a badge and a gun. "Gwendolyn's been charged with murder. As much as I like her —"

I snorted.

He shifted that hard gaze to me. "The past is just that. What we need to worry about is now. The clock started tonight. You have seven days to prove your innocence."

"Since we're doing the whole heart to heart," Kyle put his interlaced fingers on the large wooden table, "this is a load of crap. We both know Gwendolyn didn't kill anything other than your ego."

Carlos made a sound that was neither a chuckle nor a groan, but that tortuous space in-between. He then looked from Kyle to Mr. Z., who was leaning against the wall looking like a long, lean Asian mob enforcer. Carlos

223

leaned his hands on the table. "Look, I'm not such an asshole that I'd ignore the truth." His gaze shifted down and to the right before returning to mine. "At least not forever."

"That's supposed to mean something to me…why?" I raised my wrists and the chain dangled between my handcuffs. "I've been on the receiving end of your *truth*. It sucks."

"Do you have to make shit so hard?" Carlos stared at me like he was trying to beam information into my skull.

I shrugged. "That's how I roll."

Carlos closed his eyes, and judging by his lips, counted to ten before he spoke again. "Despite you ignoring my advice to roll your sweet ass right back out of town, I—"

"Wait. You think my ass is still sweet?" Okay, maybe this wasn't the time for inappropriate humor, but I was crawling out of my skin. I was scared, like terrified.

There was a reason Hoodoo was so safe. Why, a woman could be drunk as a skunk and walk through the streets like Lady Godiva, yet arrive home unscathed. Because to commit a crime in Hoodoo against one of its citizens was not a mistake one made twice.

Because they wouldn't live that long.

In other words, Hoodoo, Texas, was a sundown town for criminals.

"Gwen," Mr. Z said from his exalted spot holding up the wall. "Focus."

Properly chastised, I sank lower in my seat. "As you were saying, Sheriff."

"There is a way for Gwendolyn to leave your jail to assist in her defense." Mr. Z finally moved from against the wall. "I'm certain no one will like it." He put his briefcase on the table.

Carlos, still looking bored, exhaled an exasperated breath. "Unless you have a judge in there, it's not going to help."

Mr. Z. unsnapped the briefcase and laid his hands on top. "This may change your mind," he said as he unlatched and opened the case.

Everyone gasped as a blast of heat followed by a wave of suffocating malice circled the room before settling around me like a straitjacket.

"Is that…?" Carlos asked, his voice straddling the line between awed and disgusted.

"No." I shook my head so fast, I would need a chiropractor if I lived long enough. "I... I don't want it anywhere near me."

Until that very moment, I considered ancestral trauma nonsense, a fairytale. But that plain iron collar shook me to my core. It made me want to run into the night. Hell, it brought back memories that did not and have never belonged to me. Sprinting through the woods. Dogs and men carrying torches and rifles hunting, taunting, and chasing me.

"I-I'm going to be sick," I whispered past the fear, anger, and bile rising in my throat.

"Breathe." Mr. Z rubbed small circles on my back. "It will pass."

"Phillip." Kyle looked at Mr. Z. "What is that?"

"This collar prevents Gwendolyn from leaving Hoodoo's borders." Phillip looked down at me, sympathy filling his dark eyes.

"How does an ugly necklace keep anyone from escaping?" Kyle, apparently still playing human, asked, looking from Carlos back to Mr. Z.

"Because if Gwendolyn leaves the boundaries of this town, she'll die," Carlos said.

I shook off the memory of the jail and everything else, flipping the mirrored visor down. Sick it might be, but if I had to wear this damned thing, I refused to be ashamed. I'd killed no one. Since, according to Mr. Z., the collar hadn't been seen in decades, few would know of its existence, or the purpose.

And for those who knew, I hoped they realized that if I wasn't dangerous before, I was now completely out of fucks. I hopped out of the van and jogged up the stairs. This house and the beings in it – both living and dead – were my people. They'd had my back even when I didn't want them to.

Hopefully, those bridges hadn't been incinerated.

Chapter 35

MISS ELEANOR AND I walked down the corridor to Aunt Rose's private office with only our steady breaths and padded footsteps denting the silence. The hallway was empty, which of course made sense, as it was late morning. Some rumors regarding vampires were true, but others?

Not so much.

Yes, they were nocturnal creatures, but thanks to UV-blocking glass and automatic light-blocking storm windows, even the youngest of the congregation's vampires, if awake, could walk around the house during the day. Of course, they all didn't live in the main house, but had separate quarters elsewhere on the property. There was also an entire underground system created centuries ago that no one, even human servants, were allowed, without having their memories obliterated.

I stopped at the closed door to Aunt Rose's office, glancing left then right. Since these walls absolutely had ears, I slipped my cellphone from my pocket and typed:

Thanks for the diary. As you know, things have been a little crazy, so I haven't had time to read it. Could you come over for dinner tomorrow tonight to chat?

I turned the screen to Miss Eleanor.

"We didn't have an opportunity to speak last night." Her eyes darted back and forth reading the screen, then nodded. "Despite the circumstances, we're pleased you're home."

I returned the phone to my purse. Now, with both hands free, I first touched my watch, then flashed seven fingers.

Once again, I was rewarded with a nod before Eleanor unlocked and opened Aunt Rose's office.

I'd only moved two feet inside the room before I was rooted in place.

It wasn't because the room, which, like my aunt, hadn't changed. I inhaled and closed my eyes, memories of sitting at the smaller secretary's desk having play meetings or doing my homework or drawing pictures. Wow, I was such a little dork imitating my aunt as she tackled bookkeeping for the ranch, managing and tracking investments, or other congregation business.

The smile tugging at my lips was both wistful and a bit happy. My childhood may have been different than most, but I'd been blessed to be surrounded by powerful, smart, and resourceful women. Whether they were moms or witches, wolves, vampires, or root workers, the women I'd grown up around were all special in their own right.

My gaze travelled around the familiar room, only to have my world thoroughly rocked again.

My MFA thesis painting hung above the fireplace. A canvas I'd filled with love and longing of the place I called home—the Double R Ranch. Rather than paint the house, I recreated one of my favorite moments, Aunt Rose and Uncle Raul bent low over their horses, racing across the back forty.

East Texas had more trees than hills, but my family got lucky with the land grants. The unofficial finish line for most races rested atop a gentle rise. Whomever made it past two giant oaks standing like soldiers held bragging rights until they were dethroned in the next competition.

My heart squeezed, then overflowed. Aunt Rose was the secret benefactor who'd purchased my project for an obscene amount of money. The same woman who'd refused to attend my graduation, despite it being at night, then forbade anyone connected to the vampire congregation to attend. The same woman who'd demanded that I major in something more practical than art if I wished for her to fund my education.

The woman who never, since I'd come into her life, shared neither pride nor praise for my accomplishments. I pressed the side of my fist against my mouth to stifle a sob. That just wasn't done in the Ignacio house. To show emotion was weakness, tears a vulnerability.

No wonder I was so jacked up.

I wasn't sure what it was, a ripple of energy, a subtle whiff of perfume, or the almost imperceptible brush of air, but I turned around.

And there she was. The beautiful and impassive Aunt Rose stood watching me, her face cold and body tight.

We were both a mess. While I still hadn't forgiven her for the lifetime of lies, she'd gifted me something else—a future. Oh, I was still pressed about the omissions regarding my bound powers, but the longer I watched Aunt Rose, the less I gave a shit about anything other than this moment.

Without a doubt, love was equally as overwhelming as the shock, anger, denial, and terror I'd experienced earlier. I was grateful to be both the giver and recipient of such emotion.

And it must have shone through in my expression, because the unnatural stillness eased from Aunt Rose's body before she crossed the room. Had I mentioned how beautiful she was? Seriously, if I didn't love her, it would be so easy to hate a woman who never aged or gained a pound. Life wasn't fair.

Something about a Black woman rocking a yellow dress that just made me...happy. And Auntie was working the wraparound she wore this late morning.

Not to mention the heels.

Which was why I'd worn something other than jeans and cowboy boots for this meeting. Women dressed for ourselves first, other women second, then sexual interests third—be they man, woman, or other.

"Thanks for the magical bail." I tapped the collar keeping me chained to Hoodoo. "Otherwise, I doubt Carlos would have released me."

"Oh, you were going to leave that jail one way or the other." Aunt Rose pursed her full lips.

Okay... I'm not sure I liked the sound of that, but the intent, I was totally down with. Because this bitch wasn't built for jail.

When Aunt Rose reached my side, we gave each other cheek air kisses. But when she tried to pull away, I caught hold of her hands. "I appreciate you. Especially that you and Uncle Raul interrupted your lives to take me in and protect me, and all I gave you was grief."

"No, child. Raising you was a touch of bitter sprinkled in with the sweet, but that is to be expected, considering the circumstances."

"I guess." I squeezed her hands. "But thank you all the same."

Someone knocked at the door.

"Enter," Aunt Rose called out, her voice sharp, as if our tender moment hadn't occurred. The cuff Ash gave me peeked from beneath my thin cashmere sweater. "You and I need to have a discussion about that...man."

"I doubt he'll be an issue." I shrugged nonchalantly. To say I was disappointed with his absence this morning was an understatement. Especially considering all the destiny bullshit.

Asshole.

Aunt Rose's gaze ricocheted from the bracelet to my face before making an odd, strangled sound. "You may wish it so, but that will not be your reality."

Merri, wearing a closed mouth smile and another flowy dress, this time white with small yellow flowers, approached me with an extended hand, which I accepted. "I pray the outcome of this meeting and your trial delivers justice."

"So do I, Merri. So do I." I nodded and smiled while noting the formality of her tone.

Miss Eleanor stepped forward, her gray eyes pinning me to the oriental carpet. "Has Ilona told you anything?"

I looked at the three women, stopping at Aunt Rose, who gave me a tiny nod of encouragement. Time to shit or get off the proverbial pot. Eleanor's question confirmed that Merri hadn't shared about our meeting. While I still didn't trust the witch with my life, she craved power. Freeing me would give her favor not only with the vampires, but the town's root workers. I exhaled and laid it out. "No, but Duncan has."

Eleanor gasped and clapped her palm against her chest.

Merri's wrapped her arms around her waist.

And Aunt Rose? Well, her expression was as impassive as ever, but her gaze wasn't on me, but Merri. Interesting.

May as well rip the bandage off. However, something, be it intuition, a sixth sense or the ancestors, nudged me. Eleanor and Aunt Rose deserved the entire truth; Merri, however, could wait until Miss Eleanor and I had a conversation. "Ilona isn't the only dead witch in Hoodoo, but my guess is that whoever killed Duncan did them in too."

It was impressive witnessing Miss Eleanor build herself back up, pushing aside the newly reopened grief to handle her business. "Did Ilona share this?"

I shook my head, reluctant to add more pain to Miss Eleanor's bitter cup. "No, she didn't. She couldn't. Her mouth had been sewn shut."

Chapter 36

SINCE, APPARENTLY, Merri had kept our prior conversation private, I was forced to replay encounters with the ever-increasing number of dead witches. After describing the women, Eleanor confirmed that not only were they witches from the Hoodoo coven, but they'd left Texas to join their magical sisters elsewhere.

Allegedly.

Armed with that information, Merri was tasked with contacting the covens in question to confirm they'd never arrived, and to suss out if those other groups were losing witches.

And me? All I needed to do was search for the party framing me and remain alive for the next seven days. Oh, and accept the irritating fact that Ash, like most males, human or not, was unreliable.

Which, if I were being honest, stung more than it should have. Because more than my body ached for Ash. Whether it was trauma bonding, loneliness, or as he proclaimed, destiny, I longed for a place to belong. Arms I could fall into for safety and comfort. Arms that belonged only to me.

Eleanor and I paused at the front door. Looking up into her beautiful aged face was a punch in the gut. Damn, I'd missed her laughter, love, and hugs. "You don't...hate me?" I finally asked, probably sounding like an insecure ten-year-old.

She tilted her head and smiled before cupping my cheeks with her soft hands. "Oh, sweetheart, how could I?"

I could name a thousand reasons, but highest on the list was that I'd failed her by upholding Duncan's request for confidentiality. Had I said something, anything, maybe he'd have a family of his own, a chance to leave a legacy, and most importantly a real life.

"But Rita—"

"Isn't the only person two-stepping with guilt. I watched Duncan deal with his envy and powerlessness. And did nothing. Neither my words nor Rita's could return the magic that was absorbed by his sister." She sighed and dropped her hands. "But you, darlin', were always there for him. You'll never know how much I appreciated that."

"Thank you," I whispered.

"Just between you and me, I'd hoped that you and Duncan would eventually find your happiness with each other. If I had to choose a daughter in-law, it would have been you."

I pressed my lips together. It was a beautiful thought, but once puberty came a-knocking, I was all about Carlos. A wave of sadness tangled my stomach into a ball of conflicting emotions. With Duncan's death, I'd lost Carlos' friendship, his love, and most of all, his respect.

"Gwennie," Miss Eleanor said, dragging me from the quicksand of unpleasant memories. "It's okay. I promise."

The swish of shoes against the travertine tile drew my attention to the archway. There stood Merri wearing a tender smile and hopeful brown eyes, watching Miss Eleanor and me.

Turning away from my new ally, and without lowering my voice, I asked Miss Eleanor, "Would you like to speak with your son?"

Miss Eleanor gasped and slapped her hand over her mouth. As her eyes widened, her head swiveled back and forth looking around the sleek entry hall. "He's here?"

I chuckled and shook my head. "No. He can't enter the ranch."

"But you've talked to him? How is he? Does he know—"

"Whoa." I raised a palm in her direction. "Slow down. Tomorrow, when you come by, he can answer your questions."

"How is he?" she whispered.

Uh...dead. Not a great answer. So I said, "Still Duncan. From what I know, he hasn't suffered, and has watched over you and Rita."

"Thank you." Miss Eleanor squeezed my hands, warmth and gratitude shining through from her massive heart. "I know this might be too much to ask, but..."

No, no, no, no, no. Please don't say what I think you are. Against my will, my face scrunched.

"May I bring Rita?"

And... of course.

I loved Miss Eleanor and all, but I couldn't do it. Why in the Sam Hill should I open myself up for abuse? I wasn't Captain Save a Ho... I opened my mouth go let out a resounding no.

But couldn't.

Shit. I wished I was the bitch people believed me to be.

"She'll behave," Miss Eleanor promised.

I rolled my eyes, then dipped my chin to emphasize my point. "Brother or not, I won't be disrespected in my home."

"Deal." Eleanor kissed my cheek, then ushered me out of the massive front doors before I changed my mind. "We'll see you tomorrow night."

I nodded, feeling lighter than the circumstances warranted. Unconsciously, I traced the bespelled collar circling my neck. The massive porch should be at odds with the Spanish Colonial-style home. But like everything else in Hoodoo, it was anachronistic, beautiful, and just flat-out worked.

With one last glance at the pair of high-backed rocking chairs, I jogged down the stairs, blissfully ignoring the reality breathing down my neck. And came to a screeching, heart-denting halt when I reached the ground.

Ash, the star of many a sexual fantasy and dirty thought, stood leaning against Stella's driver's side door. Dressed down in jeans topped with an untucked black shirt with alternating thick and thin vertical blue stripes, he managed to still look like a wet dream.

Well, as of today, Ash could go occupy someone else's every thought.

"If you'll excuse me," I said, now standing in front of him, twirling my key ring around my index finger.

"No, Gwendolyn, I won't."

I gave him the no-the-fuck-you-didn't glare, and opened my mouth to let it rip. I was tired of not just Ash's, but most of the men in this town's shit.

Before a syllable so much as fell from my mouth, he spoke. "That overdue conversation? We'll be having it now."

"Hard pass. I have a life to save—my own." I snapped my fingers, sighed, then gave an exaggerated glance at the sky. "Oh, my bad. You weren't around when I was released. I have seven fucking days to prove my innocence. Or I'm going to die," I said, my voice hovering on hysteria's edge.

Ash, ever so cool, and acting as if my proclamation meant less than nothing, reached a finger toward the disgusting collar.

I retreated. But not fast enough.

He captured my wrist in an inescapable hold that may as well have been another handcuff.

My heart thudded. Not in lust or even confusion, but disquiet. Never had Ash unleashed his speed or strength. Especially with me. "Done playing human, are we?" I asked once my lungs regained partial function. My brain obviously had other ideas, seeing that it allowed my attitude to take center stage.

"Yes. I'm also finished with the rules. Not only did your family allow that beast to remove you from their home, they prevented me from intervening."

"They had no choice."

"I'd destroy the universe to keep you safe."

"Yet, that didn't exactly work last time, did it?"

As Ash pressed his lips tighter, the fingers circling my wrist loosened.

"Wait. What rules?"

Ash's lush lips parted as he looked at the house behind me. Anger... no, that wasn't the correct word; it was more like a mixture of disgust and wrath darkened his already inky eyes. "It is not in my power to say."

My nose stung. Almost as if almost forty years of tears decided to make an appearance.

When I woke in the hospital, even after learning of my mother's death—I didn't cry. I couldn't. It was as if a part of me, that which experienced true sorrow and pure joy, was trapped inside a locked vault to which I lacked the combination. Was that a side effect of binding my powers?

Well, lucky for me, I'd been left with a few emotions—anger being one of them.

Hey, a girl's got to use what she's got. I let those feelings of betrayal and disappointment blend and bubble until I was good and mad. Were my problems Ash's doing? No.

Call me Petty Patty, but I wouldn't let rightness stop me from dumping a load of mess on Ash's head. "Of course not, *Prince*. As we say here in Texas, fuck you and the horse you rode in on."

Ash grinned.

Yes, grinned. If I wasn't pissed before, I was ready to explode. Wind, which started as a breeze brushing my cheek, increased, moving Ash's dark hair from his forehead. Starting at my feet, my skin first tightened, then heated as if my anger was the kindling sparking a wildfire of fury that raged through the rest of my body in an increasing crescendo.

Both Ash and I glanced at my hand, which was now raised between us with Ash's strong fingers still circling my wrists.

I gasped.

Ash groaned as if the arcs of electricity shooting from my hand to his were an aphrodisiac.

"Let go," I said in a voice that wasn't mine. It was as if other versions of myself from times and places both in the far past and distant future conjoined in one furious body.

"Not on your life," Ash said, his voice deepened to a dangerous bass. He hadn't yelled, but the words slipped through the maelstrom like a hot knife through frozen butter.

My vision narrowed. With each fill of my lungs, the wind intensified until Ash and I stood at the eye of our personal tunnel cloud.

The right side of Ash's mouth curved upward. Unconcerned with my wrath and the wind, he spoke. Without yelling or raising his voice in the slightest, his next words eased past my anger, penetrating my skin, and slipped straight into my soul. "The only thing I'll be fucking, Gwendolyn Carter, is you."

Alrighty now.

I may have still been pissed, but those words missed my heart, stimulating my ovaries to release the last two eggs holding on for dear life.

While standing in the funnel cloud that was now a dangerous mixture of lust combined with anger, I lost focus.

Ash, however, didn't. He wrapped his free arm around me and pressed his body against mine before whispering, "This is not the trip I wished to take you on."

And my world went black.

MY WORLD HADN'T GONE black. No. A more suitable description would have been a nebula, a darkness filled with sparks of light and swaths of blues and purples with golden splashes across the middle.

And I wanted to stay there, in the space in between.

Because, baby, anything was preferable to my current unstable reality. Unfortunately, my feet returned to the ground, but I kept my eyes squeezed shut, knowing without seeing that I was no longer at the Double R.

I inhaled. Gone was the humid air that smelled faintly of a newly mown lawn and orange blossoms. Instead, the air was unmoving, almost stale, as if we were in a room that hadn't been opened in a millennium.

My monster wasn't hiding under the bed, but in front of me, against me, trapping me. And luring me. "What have you done?" I whispered as I opened my eyes to unbroken darkness so heavy, I could no longer breathe.

Had he taken me to a tomb?

No, no, no, no, no.

"Calm down." Ash's chest rumbled against mine.

Until that moment, I hadn't realized my arms were around his shoulders, holding on for dear life. I dropped them and focused on my left hand. I could use my little night light right about now.

Setting Ash on fire would be a bonus.

He sighed, but thankfully loosened his arms before I kneed him in his junk. A pulse of power, this one gentler, rippled through me, before dim light illuminated my feet. But it wasn't from me. It was almost like dozens of invisible tealights filled the room with a soft golden glow.

I rolled my shoulders before looking up at Ash to rip him a new one. But for what? Not being human? No. I didn't have the time or energy to lie to myself, because keeping it one hundred, Ash had attempted to share.

But I wasn't ready.

Damn, it sucked being self-aware.

I may have been pissed, and him powerful, but I didn't believe I was in danger. I was just all up in my feelings. The ones I'd finally admitted to, only for him to ghost me.

I raised my chin, ready to give ole boy the "let's be friends" speech. But damn...

Words, breaths, and hell, even my heart may have stopped. Mostly because out of Ash's back protruded a wicked set of wings.

Chapter 37

DID I, GWENDOLYN CARTER, seer of ghosts, niece of vampires, and former girlfriend of a werewolf freaking faint? I filled my lungs with a shaky breath and covered my mouth with my hand.

Dear ancestors, my life was going to—

"Good, you're awake." Ash, minus the wings and his shirt, stood at my bedroom window, legs spread wide and hands behind his back. He looked every bit like a general at parade-rest, waiting to address the unruly troops. At Uncle Raul's party, Ash had been introduced as a prince, but that seemed too unimportant a title for the being standing before me.

If Ash was a mere prince, how much swagger did his king have? You know what? I didn't want to know—at all.

"W-what are you?" I whispered. The man may have looked like an angel, but there was nothing holy about the vibes pouring off him. It wasn't malevolent, per se, but it washed over my skin, caressing and examining as if probing an opening, a weakness, a wound to...

To what? To heal, or worse, to exploit. Well, I wasn't the one, and this sure as shit wasn't the day. I shoved the covers aside and sat up, thankful that my shoes were the only missing clothing.

"Lying was never my intention." Ash's lips tightened. "Had we encountered one another sooner, none of this would have happened."

"None of what? The deceptions? Who else was in on the joke?" I exhaled through pursed lips before sucking in another breath. "If you say some bullshit like you can't share, I'll...I'll. Damn...is there anyone in this family who didn't know what's going on?"

I pressed the heels of my hands against my forehead. Sorry, but this timeline sucked.

"Unfortunately, that number would be relegated to the human portion of your relatives."

My shoulders relaxed a little. Thank goodness for that at least. I stood at another one of those crossroads—run and hide or take the knocks like a woman.

I chose the latter. Curling up in a ball to wish away reality wasn't an option. Not if I wanted to live. Time to put on the big-girl panties. "Fine," I finally said, tone as sharp as my anger. "Why not contact me earlier, seeing that you knew who I was?"

"I was forced to make do with protecting you."

I raised my chin. "How exactly did you do that?" Because I sure as shit would have noticed Ash lurking on the periphery of my life. He wasn't one easily ignored.

Ash's lips quirked as he watched me with a be-careful-what-you-wish-for expression. When I didn't reconsider, he shrugged. "I killed those who meant you harm," he said as easily as if asking me to pass the sugar.

Okaaaay. Who needs flowers when you can leave corpses strewn about? Unable to fully process my feelings, I just sat there and stared at my sexy Jack the Ripper.

"You have particularly bad taste in bed partners. I saw it as my duty to rid you of them."

That asshole.

"You have got to be fucking kidding me." I sprang off the bed. Before I knew it, I was up in his face and poked his chest with my index finger. "I was almost sent to prison because of you!"

"I would have never allowed that to happen." He captured my hand, pressing it flat against his chest. "As for why I didn't tell you in Morocco... I wanted you to experience my world, to accept me as a man. No expectations. No prejudices."

Had I not been watching, I would have missed the flicker of... was that uncertainty?

The emotion was gone before it could settle in. But rather than speak, instead of uttering words like...a freaking apology, he pressed his lips together.

I chuckled; I couldn't help myself. It was either that or scream. And after the week I'd had, I doubted I'd stop until I was medicated. I tugged at my hand, but unsurprisingly, Ash held tight.

"Seriously, dude? Why go through the trouble? You've had a stable of beautiful women on your arm." And in his bed.

"They weren't you."

Those three simple words smashed into me like a bulldozer.

Whether it was the wings or the big dick energy, color me mesmerized. What did it say about me that he'd just casually dropped that he'd been killing folks and I shrugged it off?

I needed to call my therapist—stat.

"So, let's have it." I slapped my free hand against my thigh "What are you?"

Ash's smile grew sad around the edges.

"Baby, I've already seen the show. Besides, where would I go?" I tapped the metal collar with my index finger. "Can't leave town, remember?" That whole exploding head thing gave new meaning to monitored arrest.

I patted his chest with the hand he held captive. "I'm done with the fainting. And FYI, if you tell anyone, I'll deny it." His lips parted, but I placed a finger against them. "No more talk. Show me."

In the space of a heartbeat, wings once again shot from his back. They appeared leathery rather than feathered and towered two feet above him. *And was he taller?*

Ash took an exaggerated breath, which reminded me that air was a good thing.

I sucked in my own bit of oxygen, then shifted my weight. Unlike earlier, there was no fear or shock, just pure, unadulterated wonder, along with a splash of envy. Every nerve in my body lit up like twinkling Christmas lights as I fought to keep from trailing a finger across the inside of the silken black magnificence protruding from Ash's back.

Ash and his wings were... magnificent.

Judging from the distance from the twelve-foot ceiling, I'd say from the pointed tips to where they grazed the floor, Ash's wings were eleven feet long. And the span, about half as much. Whoa. I should have paid more attention in physics. How did they work?

They looked like a bad-ass combination of a raven, a bat, and a butterfly.

When I finally glanced back at Ash's face, it revealed... nothing. I shook my head, then shrugged, then shook it again. "I-I don't know where to start, what to ask."

Or how to feel.

"Talk to me." Ash finally released my hand.

Should I retreat, run for my life, or touch him all over? Despite wanting to do all three, all I was capable of at the moment was standing frozen on the antique rug. "Are you..." I swallowed, looked from his impossibly beautiful face to his glossy black wings then back again. "...an angel?"

Ash laughed. Like he full-on tossed his head back and let it rip. It was sexy. It was honest. It was real. You could tell a lot about a person in what they found humorous. While he didn't appear to be laughing at me, I suspected I wouldn't appreciate the punchline.

And I was right.

"No." Ash shook his head as he captured his lower lip between his teeth. "Try further south—like a lot further."

For the first time in my life, my mind didn't take the express train to the gutter. But standing this close to the expanse of yummy tattooed tan skin, it took a few seconds too long for the synapses to fire.

"Oh." The sound came out somewhere between a squeak and an actual word. My eyes widened as every story from Sunday school, and each sermon with promises of the lake of fire and worse echoed through my mind.

I mean, this wasn't possible, right? The childish part of me, the one who was certain a monster lived under the bed, wanted to run and hide. But the woman needed facts. I rolled my shoulders, stretched my neck from side to side, then ripped the bandage off. "I hate riddles. What are you?"

"A demon."

I nodded. "Okay."

"Okay? That's it?"

I let out a chuff of air. "Hell naw." I wrapped my arms around my waist and paced across the floor.

It all made so much more sense now. No wonder Ash never questioned the exploding head incident. Nor did he question Loretta's burying coffin nails in the yard or sprinkling Florida water on my porch and in my house. I thought Ash was just a cool guy who accepted people with different beliefs.

Not another whole damned species.

My brain whipped from the past, returning to the confusing present. I spun around and faced him. "Wait—is Hell a real place? What about the lake of fire and eternal torment for the wicked and all that business?"

"Yes, and not quite." He scratched the back of his neck. "You're taking this better than I expected."

"Oh, I'm freaking out on the inside." I relaxed my hands, stretching my fingers before drumming them against my thighs. "When were you planning to tell me?"

Ash swiped a hand down his face. "Disaster follows you like a stray puppy. Ideally, we'd have both exposed our secrets last night. All of them. Then I planned a feast, with you as the entrée."

A strangled laugh escaped as I found sudden interest in the vase of irises.

"Since we're embracing truth, hospitality demands you inform your guests before inviting them to sleep with ghosts. Oh, and let's not forget eavesdropping through walls. "So..." Ash extended a hand. "Hello, pot."

"I was right not to trust you." I snapped, hoping he hadn't noticed my blush. I wiggled my index finger, pointing back and forth between us. "Ignoring the wings and all that business, we wouldn't have worked. Because, a: I want to keep my soul, thank you very much. And b: we come from two different worlds."

"Give it a rest. It isn't as if you were raised in a workhouse alongside Oliver Twist."

A chuckle slipped before I could rein it in. "What about the soul thing?"

"Not interested."

"How am I supposed to believe you?" I damned near shouted.

Rather than yell back, Ash didn't respond at all. He just went... still. Like he did before. When he expected rejection.

Had that happened before? Well, I guess when your species had the reputation for stealing souls and leading us into temptation. Which, at this point, I could really get down with. The institutions that convinced me that Ash and his kind were all evil were the same people who burned witches, endorsed the enslavement of people, and wiped out civilizations. Separating folks from their magic was their modus operandi.

So why the fuck should I believe them?

"Shit. That was rude. I am so sorry." I crossed the room until I stood looking up into his striking but stern face. "You guys need better PR."

"I accept your apology." Ash dipped his chin. "There's something else. Would you like to hear it tonight? It can wait."

While I appreciated the choice, it felt like a would you rather see the bullet coming kind of question. "Will I like it?"

He shook his head and gave me the expression I hated most—pity. "Probably not."

I plopped down on one of the armchairs and bent my right leg, tucking it up under my left. If I was about to get another bucketload of bad news, may as well get some information first. My version of sugar making the medicine go down easier. "Did you know about my aunt and uncle when I met you?"

"Yes." Ash watched me for a couple seconds before he spoke again. "We could continue this discussion in the morning."

"It'll suck just as much. Let's just rip that bandage off."

"As you wish, Gwendolyn." He sat in the chair across from me, leaning his forearms and elbows on his knees. "It shouldn't have come to this, because in your case, knowledge truly is power. Power which has been stolen from you."

He knew.

I lowered my gaze, staring at his long interlaced fingers. Yet another sin of omission to lay at Aunt Rose's feet. Oh, I'm sure Uncle Raul was aware, but when it came to me, he usually deferred to his wife's decisions. Occasionally, he refereed when my raging teenage hormones and her inflexible vampire attitudes couldn't find a path to compromise.

Too bad he wasn't here tonight. I had a feeling I could use a shield.

"You and I have something else in common aside from our love of ink. You have a legendary demon in your family tree."

Chapter 38

OKAY, DEALING WITH a hot guy with wings sticking out of his back? No big deal. Living in a haunted house with a ghostly staff and secret passages? Not a problem.

But this...

"Gwendolyn, are you al—"

I shook my head and gave him the shut-the-hell-up hand. "Not right now. I need..." A lobotomy. Or the bright white light to let me know I was dead, or better yet, in a coma. But that couldn't be the case, since it felt like my heart had been trapped in a vise. And that puppy was cranked tighter every second.

A paper bag would've been great right about now. Because a panic attack was in my near future. Maybe this was a sick jest. You know, the kind where you say something horrible first, only to say it was a joke before saying a lesser bad thing?

One glance at Ash's tight lips and concerned eyes and the answer to that one was a big fat fucking dream on.

Ash's voice was low and soothing. "I know it's a lot, but you *will* be okay."

"Okay? Okay?" My voice rose with every syllable. "You have got to be freaking kidding me! I am anything but okay." I hopped off the chair and resumed pacing, stomping from one end of the rug to the other. The soft carpet could have been a bed of nails, and I doubt I'd have felt a thing. Pain would've been an improvement over the incandescent rage slithering beneath my skin.

Luckily, my lightning tank was empty, since I'd probably set my damned house on fire—or worse. Although I wouldn't mind shooting a bolt or two at Ash.

Pressure pulsed against my skull. It was too much—all of it. I jabbed a finger at my neck. "Do you see this?" I screamed loud enough that they probably heard me miles away in The Woodlands. "Nothing is ever going to be okay again."

These odds were not in my favor.

I never understood why people just... surrendered, gave up, and accepted whatever crumbs life tossed at their feet. I was raised to fight; surrender wasn't a part of my vocabulary.

Until tonight. Until I discovered I was the demon spawn that I'd been called so long ago.

Ash watched me, eyes wide, body braced for the wild woman to attack.

I needed answers. Now. I could fry his ass later. *Outside.*

"Yes, I'd noted the odd choice of accessories." When I didn't explode or go on another rampage, he continued, even allowing a sprinkling of levity in his voice. "What is it? And may I suggest a refund?"

I pulled out my television announcer voice. "Well, Ash, I'm glad you asked. It's my punishment. I have seven days to prove that I didn't kill that Ilona."

"Or what?"

"I die." I slapped my palm against my upper chest and leaned back like a proper southern belle. "Oh, hold on to your hell hounds, sugar, it gets better. If I leave the borders of Hoodoo. I die. If I try to remove it—I die. And trust me, it would be a death even a demon would love."

"I won't allow anyone to harm you, whether it's seven days or seven hundred years."

"And how exactly would you do that when I can't leave town? Where would you take me, Hell?"

Ash's face changed slightly, the ridge beneath his eyebrows becoming more prominent, his cheekbones sharper.

Lord, don't let him get extra teeth and a monster face. Not tonight, not now. I was already being held together by adrenaline and attitude. If dude went into full-on demon mode, I'd expire on the spot.

"That could be arranged, as well as an improvement over Texas."

Okay, now I was flat-out pissed off. I know we're our own special kind of crazy, and frequently told Florida to hold our beer, but Texas was home. Sorry, but wings or no wings, he needed to step back with that noise.

"But even that would be a risk. However, you haven't asked the right question. It's not where I would take you, but when."

"Can we not?" I shook my head. "You're sounding like my aunt."

"How does she propose saving you?"

Saying the words aloud doused my anger like a bucket of cold creek water. "By making me a vampire."

Ash stilled, that unnatural movement that reminded me of the raging silence before a storm. "Is that what you want?"

"Fifteen minutes ago, I'd've said no. That I'd rather die. That my soul may be tarnished, and even a little bit wicked—but at least I had one. But that's probably not the case—is it?"

Ash winced. "If you have questions..."

"No." I rubbed my index finger down the bridge of my nose, then shook my head. The lack of a soul hadn't been true six weeks ago when I died. But now...I wasn't so sure. Did Hoodoo heaven have a no-return policy? "I'm afraid I've reached my truth limit for the year."

Ash nodded, a sharp jerky motion. And just like that, the wings were gone. Tucked into his back or wherever the hell they went. And I wasn't sure whether it pleased me or not, but a long-sleeved black t-shirt appeared, covering his delicious chest.

But still, he didn't come closer, which probably was a wise move.

"Get some sleep," he said, or rather, ordered.

I snorted. "Yeah, right. Like that's about to happen."

"I could... stay." His eyes were filled with the kind of heat a woman would sell a less favorite body part to experience.

Did I forgive him for lying? Hell no. Was my jacked-up DNA his fault? Not even.

But did watching the desire waft across Ash's stark face help smooth my jagged edges? Call me shallow, but hell to the yeah.

"Thanks for the offer, but no offense, I've seen enough of you for the night." That was a bitchy thing to say, but as far as I was concerned, his demon ass deserved it.

Slowly, as if giving me time to run and lock myself in the bathroom, Ash approached, gently cupping my cheeks, then placing a tender but quick kiss on my forehead. "Rest well."

Like that was going to happen.

Before I could ask further questions, Ash softly closed the door behind him.

Shit. This was all... A lot. Gee, talk about the understatement of the millennium. I walked back around to the far side of the bed, just standing there, staring out the window and wishing I were anywhere, even on the fat moon above the cemetery.

I was part demon. Wow.

That was... I shivered, then pressed my lips together to keep from screaming. Because, once I started, I probably wouldn't stop until they tranquilized me.

I was part demon.

That explained more about myself than I wanted to examine. I unbuttoned my top as I stumbled to the full-length mirror, turning around to look over my shoulder at the wings tattooed on my back. Talk about irony. I'd always been fascinated with not only birds but butterflies, bats, bees, and anything pulsing with life and the ability to soar through the air.

Was my DNA connected to my ability to see ghosts? What about the whole lightning thing; was that too about being demon born?

Chapter 39

THE COUNTDOWN TO MY conviction and execution moved merrily along. It was now full dark at Azure House, and I was ready to make things right. I'd opted for comfort when it came to my outfit for reconciliation—a pair of loose-fitting boyfriend jeans, a tailored baby blue men's button-down shirt rescued from a yard sale, and a kick-ass turquoise-encrusted belt buckle. And to make it all better, I rocked my well-loved boots.

Hey, it was better than an old blanket or worn stuffed animal. If I had to meet my maker in less than a week, I planned to do it wearing these bad boys.

Ash's bomb along with the one wrapped around my neck was a divider between me and sleep. I did, however, use the time wisely. I read Eleanor's diary, filled with the daily magical and mundane life of the coven covering the short period before, during, and a few months after the accident and I crafted a list of questions.

From her writings, Eleanor wished to train me. But it wasn't from a place of kindness, but rather to create a weapon. For her, I wasn't the wounded orphaned child who'd been snatched from death's greedy jaws, but an asset to the vampires—and the coven.

I'm not going to lie, that shit... cut deep. Eleanor was more Atilla the Hun rather than the Magical Mary Poppins I'd crafted in my youthful mind. Fool me once...

Yesterday, when I opened my eyes to sunny skies and a hopeful future, I had no fucking clue that another false accusation would again send the Jenga tower called my life toppling.

The real kick in the coochie was how horribly I'd treated Aunt Rose. For it was she who declared that I'd have as normal of a childhood as she could create. Aunt Rose, along with the counsel of Uncle Raul, concluded that binding the unstable powers inherited from my sperm donor would prevent him from locating me. For her, I was the child she'd never bear. A gift that her rebellious but beloved niece gifted her.

One that Aunt Rose intended to treasure.

Well, I had no idea how much time I had until the Grim Reaper came calling for my tattered soul, so I had shit to do.

Before I finally drifted off to sleep a little past sunrise, I reached out to Phillip for guidance. Grand gestures weren't my forte, and aside from Uncle Raul, he knew my aunt better than anyone. Once the gloating and lecturing ended, Phillip arranged a private dinner with Miss Eleanor, Aunt Rose and me.

The rest?

Well, that was on me.

I checked the mirror in the foyer and the innocuous silver chopsticks holding my locs up in a messy top bun. Hopefully, I wouldn't need them, but they were convenient for stabbing a motherfucker.

One of the ranch hands returned Stella, so once I reached the van, I would retrieve my 9mm. After grabbing my keys, I jerked the front door open, then jumped back, squeaking like a little boy.

"Whoa, sorry about that." Merri raised her hands in surrender while she stepped back. The witch was a cottage core dream in her flowy white eyelet dress. Were I a less secure woman, Merri with her too perky but slightly wide nose and perfectly coiffed afro would be at the top of my do-not-fuck-with list.

But I didn't roll like that.

Much.

"What's up?" I stepped outside, locking the door behind me.

Merri scrunched her nose, then filled her voice with something that sounded like sympathy. "I'm sure you've had enough surprises lately, but Eleanor invited me to join the three of you tonight."

The stare I aimed at Merri was neutral but suspicious. Who the hell was Eleanor to invite Merri to something so... private? Naw, this was making me feel a certain kind of way, and it wasn't good.

The tiny smile raising the corner of Merri's lips exposed a wicked set of dimples as she nodded in something like respect. "Hey, I get it." She shrugged. "I thought it would be cool to ride together, but I'll understand if you don't want me there. No hard feelings." She walked off the porch with swan-like grace.

But we both knew beneath that pretty face was a ruthlessness that matched any vampire I'd ever met.

"I'm all out of sweet lies, so I'll start with being real." I hiked my tote on my shoulder as I joined Merri at the bottom of the stairs. "The conversation I need to have with them is family business." I felt like the scarred wizard boy, except tattooed and middle-aged.

But I still didn't know the identity of *my* enemy.

"That's cool." Merri dipped her chin, then headed for her Bronco.

At this point in my impending death, I couldn't afford to push away allies. I was all up in my feelings about things that had nothing to do with Merri. "Wait," I called out as I sped up to walk beside her on the curved driveway. "Is that offer for a ride still open?"

Merri's shoulders relaxed.

"Look, once we're done with the family shit, we all need to touch bases."

"Trust me, I understand the legacy of complicated families." She squeezed my shoulder. "That's why I'm here."

In that moment, Merri's dark brown eyes reminded me once again of Aunt Rose's, not only in the long lashes and slightly upturned corners, but they had that I've-seen-some-shit look that survivors of tragedy share.

Would I see that same expression should I look too deeply at myself?

I glanced over my shoulder at the clean and inviting porch, the white paint that gave the perfect background to pots filled with elephant ears, ferns, and caladiums. Azure House looked nothing like the decrepit monstrosity I'd first encountered.

In less than a week, I'd fallen head over heels in love with her.

Even with all her crooks, crannies, and unexplored secrets, Azure House felt more like home than any place I'd lived since I left the Double R. My nose tingled before I sucked in a disbelieving breath. Not only did I not want to lose my life, I didn't want to be separated from my new home.

Not yet, and if I had to be honest, maybe not ever.

Tonight's empty house and unexpected solitude gave me something I had little left of—time.

Time to acknowledge that regardless of how I felt about Ash and his lies... I needed him. So, I had composed a second list of questions. Most importantly, the name of my distant demonic ancestor.

I sighed as I opened the door to Merri's green Bronco.

"Hey, you okay?" she asked as she rounded the hood to the driver's side, her voice so concerned, I regretted my earlier ungenerous thoughts.

Maybe I needed to return to bed and sleep another eighteen hours. "Not really, but I'll survive. I always do." The door closed behind me with a solid thud.

"And I for one am glad."

"Me too." *Most of the time.*

Merri turned on the car, then rolled slowly down the driveway. "Are you enjoying your Azure House? Gotta say, I can't get over the magical makeover. She's... remarkable."

"Thank you." I watched the yellow-tinged lights behind the sheer curtains and smiled. Between Lucille, my ghostly lady's maid and detective, and my killer library, I wouldn't trade them for anything.

Well, except for my life.

Lucille, bless her ghostly heart wanted to continue tailing Carlos, but her first attempt hadn't discovered much, other than they'd found traces of blood and one of Ilona's earrings in Stella. But I preferred she stay close to her beloved Azure House.

I looked over at Merri and smiled. "I've made numerous bad decisions over the years, but moving into the family home wasn't one of them."

"Looks like Azure House agrees." Merri turned on the music, filling the cab with slow and rhythmical reggae. "I hate to do this to you, but I have a confession to make."

Chapter 40

"OH YEAH?" I LEANED my head against the soft leather seat, admiring the play of shadow and the glow of the orange light from the dashboard against Merri's dark brown skin.

"I tried to buy your property from under you. Multiple times." Merri grinned, which took her from pretty to beautiful.

I shrugged and returned her smile, although mine was half-hearted and a bit petty. Whoa... Other than the obvious, what was wrong with me? Maybe I was just hangry. I exhaled and smiled, this one genuine. "All's fair in love and business."

"I'm glad you think so." She slowed then stopped at the stop sign. "No offense, but—"

I raised my palm to stop her. "Why is it when someone starts a sentence with 'no offense,' they're about to say something foul?"

You know that feeling of dread that sat in the bottom of your gut, nudging, poking, and prodding you to be careful, that a disaster was imminent? Well, mine just woke the fuck up.

Her dark fingers flexed as she pressed her palm against the steering wheel, putting her pale pink French manicure on full display.

The skin on my arms pebbled, and I inhaled a solid breath to calm myself. Merri was nice and all, but silence—mostly hers—would be good about now.

Merri snorted, then shook her head. "You're not going to make this easy, are you."

"Nope," I answered, giving the little p an extra little pop. "That's not in my nature."

"I heard." Merri laughed again, the sound musical, light, and joyous. "Why *are* you staying? You've made it clear with your absence that you wanted nothing to do with magic, or the town."

I clenched my teeth, not out of annoyance, but because she was right. All my life, I'd hated that I saw ghosts. I'd been tired of being a freak. Despite loving my family and friends, the younger version of me prayed every night to become blissfully ignorant of the supernatural. To become... normal.

In therapy, I could never be transparent enough to expose my most secret fear—that I too was a monster. Especially when that honesty would be construed as psychosis.

What if the disdain for magic was the very thing placing me in jeopardy? I curled my right hand into a fist and bowed my head.

Aunt Rose knew I wasn't ready to face my truth when I left Hoodoo at eighteen. Hell, I was barely amenable at forty-five. It was past time to learn this life's lesson: to accept myself, flaws, magic, and all.

But as much as I refused to confront the ugly fact, there was a more than a seventy percent chance that I was toast. So what *did* I want to do if these were my final days?

The things that I loved.

I wanted to draw, paint and dance. Run naked in the rain. Go horseback riding at the Double R. And most of all... make love to Ash Modeus. Talk about going out with a bang. That thought almost made a smile burst through the gloom.

If indeed I was gonna die in six days, then I'd be damned if I did it curled up in the fetal position. Screw that. I was Gwendolyn fucking Carter. I'd wouldn't march to death without a fight. Although, it would be cool if I could do it minus about fifteen pounds.

Confidence raised my chin and infused my spine with steel. I absorbed the power and grace of the ancestors. My people didn't survive the Middle Passage and enslavement for me to become a coward on a dark Texas road.

Fuck that noise.

I was my enemy's biggest nightmare—a menopausal woman with a mission. I put all that fire in my grin. Turning to Merri, I raised a single brow. "At least some of the rumors were true." Then I turned to face the road ahead.

We continued down the inky two-lane street, so dark the yellow dividing line appeared to merge with the sky. Surrounded by soft steel drums and comfortable silence, my thoughts drifted to Ash. The man *and* the wings were glorious. Even if Ash's face would have become monstrous, I'm certain he'd still be beautiful—even if it was a horrible one. It was Ash, in whatever form, that held my fascination captive.

"Would you consider selling me Azure House when you leave Hoodoo?" Merri asked, her voice little more than a whisper.

It took me less than a nanosecond to respond. "Had you propositioned me that first night we met at The Ancestors, I wouldn't have hesitated."

Silence swung between us like a pendulum.

"And now?"

"No." I gave her the sorry-not-sorry smile. "I couldn't imagine my life without Azure House." Even if it only meant visiting every so often. I'd lost as much distancing myself from my people and my roots as I had in denying my magic.

No more.

"Can't blame a sister for trying." Merri shrugged.

The music paused, and the name Shannon flashed across the console.

"Excuse me." Merri tapped her earbud to make the call private.

"No worries." I looked out the passenger window to give the illusion of privacy. I squinted and peered out into the trees and scrub bushes. Was that... movement? Probably a herd of wild hogs. Some farmer was going to be pissed when they found their rooted-up fields.

"Sorry about that, Gwen. Slight change of plans. We need to swing by the bookstore to grab Rita." Merri hit the blinker and turned right, the direction of downtown Hoodoo. "Eleanor said it was okay, if not..."

"It's fine." I nodded yes, but the rest of me disagreed.

I continued to stare out the window as Bob Marley became Lenny Kravitz and we reached the edge of town. Hmm... Where were the cars? I glanced at my watch. It was only twenty past eight. Folks shouldn't have locked themselves in the house this early.

Merri cleared her throat. "Speaking of Rita, have you two kissed and made up?"

"Not even. I haven't seen her since she came to the house." I distractedly glanced at the unusually empty streets. Perhaps there was some kind of game on. "But I'll try again. The past is just that. I owe it to the girls we once were to mend our relationship. At least one more time."

"It sucks that you have to deal with Rita on top of everything else."

"They say people are in your life for a reason, a season, or a lifetime." I drummed my short fingernails against the door handle. "I'd hoped for the latter, but c'est la vie."

The fine hairs on my arms rose as everything, butthole and all, clenched. But... why?

I exhaled and closed my eyes, rewinding and replaying the prior thirty seconds. Since we'd been chatting, I wasn't paying attention. It was as if we'd driven through a waterfall. But it wasn't a sheet of water we pushed through, but an aversion spell.

"Did you feel that?" I pressed the side of my fist against my solar plexus. "That was... weird," I whispered into the darkness before glancing at Merri, the shadows dissecting her face making her appear sinister. I slid my right hand up to my waist, and shit.

I wasn't carrying.

Since I was armed with only my bad fashion sense and dull wits, my options were limited. Hopefully, Merri would think my sudden change of mood was related to my lost friendship.

Like I'd done so many times since Ash had given me this bracelet, I rubbed my thumb back and forth across the unpolished gemstones and soft gold.

"That cuff is exquisite. Aren't you afraid to wear that around?"

"Thanks, but like this," I tapped the unadorned steel band around my neck, "it won't come off."

We were both silent for a few moments. The cab was now filled with Reba's country music and my regret. There was so much more I wanted to accomplish, places to visit, people to meet. Instead, I was running around like I was trapped in a Texas version of *Murder, She Wrote*.

"You seem like a decent woman; you don't deserve what's happening. You're going to find the answers—I promise."

"It is what it is. But thanks." I looked away from Merri and the faux sympathetic smile.

Glancing back at the witch, I saw she had the kind of full lips that women pay money for. Something, I'm not sure what, flash of light or a bit of movement, caught my attention.

I glanced at the back seat, and there behind Merri, was Eleanor.

My heart jumped and damned near galloped to my throat before I did the mother of slow blinks. When I opened my eyes again, Eleanor, clear as day and deader than my love for punk rock, shook her head frantically. Terror, sorrow, and fury filled her translucent blue eyes and damned near radiated off her spirit. And unfortunately, just like Ilona the redhead, Miss Eleanor's mouth was sewn shut.

Eleanor might not have been capable of speech, but she raised her arm, pointing at the back of Merri's head.

Oh, fuck.

Like that moment in a horror movie when the hapless heroine looks over her shoulder to see the monster, I had no choice. Only there was no mask-wearing super-sized dude chasing me through the woods.

No, I turned my head, and looked down the barrel of a chrome-plated 9 mm.

Chapter 41

"SO, WAS IT RITA OR Eleanor?"

You know, it really sucked when evil came in pretty packages. And the bitch sitting next to me was good enough that she'd fooled scores of people to last this long.

I opened my mouth and nothing came out. Wow. I wasn't as quick with pithy comebacks as Kyle, but the only thing that went through my mind was *What now*?

I licked my lips and swallowed, thankful that my bladder was holding up. Seriously, that would be the worst bit of humiliation. I mean, walking straight into the lion's den without question was bad enough, but peeing my pants?

Hell to the no.

"Hm. Must be Eleanor; she's the only one strong enough to break through my spell. Ask her what went wrong." Merri laughed, her cackle more hyena than human.

My gaze darted around the interior searching for a pen, a can of pepper spray, or something to get me out of this mess. But I had to give it to the old girl, she didn't seem to have a problem driving while keeping her gun hand steady. She took keeping one eye on the road to a new level.

All I needed was for Merri to look away for a second, one second to take a chance and push the gun up and my fist into her perfect face.

"Whoops." Merri released the steering wheel for a second to quickly tap her fingers against her lips as if she'd made a silly little mistake. "Eleanor can't exactly do that now, can she?" She pulled to the deserted shoulder next to the feed store parking lot and the County Road 312 sign.

I slid my tongue between my upper teeth and lip to keep from saying anything too stupid. "The whole head exploding, bug spell was pretty gruesome."

"Thank you, it's one of my favorites," she said, her eyes brightening as if she'd just won a four-year paid scholarship to Oxford.

This chick was twisted. And I had no plans to add my name to her victim list.

"You're second in command, and it's a good chance Rita wants nothing to do with the coven. So why go through all this trouble? It's not like Miss Eleanor's life and reign was finite. She's human."

"Unlike you." Merri nodded toward the dash. "Open the glove box."

With her finger on the trigger and hand steady, that left me little choice but to obey. "Fine, now what?"

"Killing you here wasn't part of the plan. But I will. If you so much as even breathe wrong — you'll die."

"It's going to happen anyway. Why shouldn't I fight?"

Merri smiled. "It's time for another family reunion of sorts. I overheard that you saw your mother. It would have made things easier had you remained dead. At least for me."

"Sorry, but not sorry." I shrugged and gave her a closed-mouth smirk.

"That's okay, I'm giving you a second one-way ticket to the other side. Tonight, hopefully, you'll meet that demon ancestor. But seeing that I'm not a complete bitch, I'll give you a choice."

"I vote for option three. Letting me go."

"Thank you for not begging and sniveling; that shit gets so old. So, here are your options: slow and painful. Because the deed doesn't have to be done at a specific location. Your corpse—or head and heart—would be sufficient. But she needs to see that I am a witch of my word."

"She who?"

Merri transferred the gun to her right hand and pulled something from the door well. The soft snick told me exactly what it was. A knife.

"Don't concern yourself with the details. You wouldn't know her anyhow."

Was this the moment where experts advise never let them take you to a secondary location? Too bad for me, I'd already failed on that account. But letting this heifer drive me to my death without even a little bit of a fight?

Screw that.

With every bit of concentration I owned, I did a mental deep dive for that spark, that simmering rage that had always hovered in the recesses of my mind. What was wrong with me that I hadn't thought to zap her witchy ass earlier? Spark by spark, I fed the smoldering energy into my left hand.

My fingertips buzzed and my palm sizzled. *Please don't glow.* I wasn't sure if the small amount of juice was enough, but I'd take it. If my hand was a vehicle and energy the gas, my poor tank was half-full.

But a woman had to work with what she had.

Agony radiated from my thigh, shooting first down my left leg before spreading upward to my torso. Unable to breathe, I did an origami imitation, and folded in half.

Still hunched over, I glared at Merri's hand and the knife now coated with my blood. "What the fuck?" I yelled, really wanting her to die right about now.

She pulled out her best Sunday bless-your-heart voice. "Sweetheart, do you really think I'm not aware of the gift from your daddy? At least the deadbeat left you something."

That was from my father? How exactly did she know that? I pressed my lips together to keep from asking. Even if Merri and truth were distant acquaintances, I wouldn't give that bitch the satisfaction.

She nodded to the cupholder separating us. "Put the damn gloves on." She waited and watched, likely hoping I'd make a run for it so she could stab me someplace far more painful.

I slid my hand into a soft driving glove. To look at it, it appeared like nothing more than a well-crafted piece of tan leather. But once my hand was fully seated, my fingers were... dead, for lack of a better word. I'd expected something larger and lead-lined. Then again, why bother with metal when you can use magic?

Merri nodded. "Now the handcuffs. FYI, try something, anything, and I *will* kill you. You've stolen everything else from me. Have the decency to die correctly."

I wanted to say, *Ma'am, this is a Wendy's,* but Miss Looney Toons had the boiling bunny eyes, so she'd probably miss the joke. I did as she asked and put the handcuffs on.

"Thank you." Merri hopped out of the SUV, walking around the front, looking for an excuse to put a bullet between my brows.

As soon as the door opened, I spoke. "I haven't known you long enough to have stolen anything worth killing for. Are you certain you have the right person?"

Rather than answer, she ignored me and motioned with the barrel of the pistol to raise my hands. Then, with the speed and dexterity of a woman roping cattle, she secured my hands to the oh-shit handle above the door.

When she returned to the driver's seat and was all buckled up, sis actually signaled before merging onto the empty road. She may have been a murderous magical bitch, but at least she was a good driver.

So, where were we?" She put the gun in the door well beside her, then snapped her fingers. "Oh yeah, I was asking you whether our visitor was Eleanor or Rita."

I just stared at her, contemplating kicking the side of her head. Hell, if I was going to go, maybe I could take her with me.

"Oh, it's not a trick question. Just curious. I figured since Rita still hates you, I doubted she'd bother with a warning."

I shifted, taking some of the pressure off my wrists, and stared at a distant house and the closer patch of six or so golden flickering lights nearer to the ground. Fireflies—big ones. How long had it been since I'd seen those? I thought pesticides took them all out.

My vision blurred. Eleanor and Rita were... dead.

Knowing that I'd never have the chance to rebuild a better newer friendship with Rita hit a place long buried. I wouldn't cry, fuck that.

I tugged on the handcuffs. The scrape of the metal against the tender flesh of my wrists cleared my mind.

The threat and my abduction might have failed if we'd entered town from the other direction—which would have taken us by The Ancestors. Someone in that parking lot could have spotted us and told Purnell or any of a dozen of my cousins what was up.

But Merri knew that.

That bitch better know something else: I would never roll over and die. And if I had to go, I'd damn sure try to take her ass with me. I turned back to the wicked witch of East Texas without bothering to disguise my disdain. "I thought you liked Eleanor," I asked, my voice as icy as my resolve.

"Oh, I do. I mean, did. She was a lovely woman."

"Yet you killed her anyway. What about Rita?" I added, hoping that she'd missed that I'd excluded her earlier.

"Same, but she was a little self-righteous for my tastes." Merri flicked her hand, as if brushing off the mere inconvenience of death. "It's not personal, it's business."

"Business." Seeing that I was the one bleeding and handcuffed, this shit felt mighty personal to me.

Wait...

Could Merri's greed could work to my advantage? Because if this was about money, I had more than enough—as did my family. Yeah, right. I almost snorted. If this was a movie, Merri would get the cash and kill me anyway. But if I could at least delay... someone would notice my absence.

Hell, at this point, I wouldn't even care if it was Carlos. "Where do I fit in in your deadly puzzle?" I finally asked.

Merri made a tsking sound, as if I was an inattentive schoolgirl who'd failed the pop quiz. "And they told me that you were the smart one. Almost as clever as me."

"I don't think so. See, if I ever kidnap and kill someone, it won't be about money. That shit will be personal as hell." *Like what I'm going to do to you as soon as I get the opportunity.* "So if you'll oblige, I'd like to understand, because you and I read from a different playbook."

"That's where you're wrong, Gwendolyn. You and I are more alike than different."

"I doubt it," I mumbled as I scoured the streets for a rescuer.

Merri stopped at the single light in downtown Hoodoo, and like the other roads on our way into town, the streets were deserted. Perhaps people were tucked away in their homes chilling, eating popcorn, and watching movies. Or sitting around drinking skinny margaritas and chardonnay at a Mary Kay party. All wondering why they reeaally didn't want to leave the house.

"Do you? You didn't remain in Azure House because you miss your family. No, it was something a lot more basic."

"Like you said earlier, you don't know me. So how about missing me with the psychotherapy."

The light finally changed, and we drove down Main Street, past Conjure Ink and Creekside Café.

"If that's what you want." The smile that spread across Merri's beautiful face was almost scarier than the gun now resting on her lap. It was an I'm-about-to-rock-your-world grin. "So, what's up, cuz?"

Chapter 42

SOMETHING WAS SERIOUSLY wrong with this chick. I sure as hell would know if I had another...

No.

No. Fucking. Way.

I frowned. Then stared at her, like truly studied Merri's features. It clicked—all of it. How she looked so much like Aunt Rose. Why, despite being attractive, Merri's flirting felt so... ick. I opened and closed my mouth, looking every bit like a fish stranded on the shore drowning in air.

Greed—of money, of knowledge, of power—sent people into wars, ripped families apart, and motivated the less ethically inclined to lie, steal, and unfortunately for me—kill.

"You already had everything." She slammed the brakes, sending the SUV screeching to a stop in the middle of the deserted street. "Was it necessary to take Azure House from me too?" Merri's buttery-smooth alto was too calm and way too fucking rational.

While I was anything but.

"Too? Lady, I don't know you." My voice was sharper than I'd intended, but what the hell was she going to do, kill me? Oh wait, that was already on tonight's agenda.

"It didn't have to be this way, Gwen. I could have been happy had Rose accepted and turned me. Then, waiting for your little mortal life to end wouldn't have been a problem."

Except, I wasn't so sure about my mortality now.

"It's forbidden..." And for good reason. According to vampire lore, the last witch who became a vampire in the Americas slaughtered her way from South America to Mexico, killing entire villages before she was stopped in Guadalajara.

If it was hard to hide thousands of bodies pre-internet, now, it would be impossible.

"Gwen." Merri snapped her fingers three times in quick succession. "Keep up. You haven't asked the right questions. I want to get to the good part. My family owned yours."

"Then you're as much of a victim—"

"Wrong," she said, sounding almost like the time-out buzzer. "My ancestors were as Black as yours." Her maniacal giggle sent a shiver down my spine, and it wasn't the good kind.

"So how are you my cousin?"

"Don't be naïve. Or as blind as your aunt." Merri's beatific smile clashed with her wild eyes. "Looks like the past has repeated itself."

As we moved down the road, Merri forgot the most important part of the family tale. My ancestor escaped. And somehow, so would I. The only difference was, I'd make damned sure Merri's evil branch of the family tree was pruned.

The movies made it look easy to be strung up by your arms. In fact, it sucked. My shoulders, along with my leg...

Hold up.

I glanced at my thick thigh and the hole in my artfully tattered jeans, noting the absence of not only a river of blood, but pain. It no longer hurt. I'd bet one of Merri's body parts that it wasn't the extra layer of fat healing me.

I peered through my arms wearing a smile that would've made my demon ancestor proud. "I've got bad news for you, *cuz*. You may get the house, the land, and even the money. But you'll never be the blood heir. The secrets in that house are mine. So good luck with that."

If I died, I hoped Lucille and the other ghostly staff I had yet to meet would make the rest of Merri's life, this one and the next, hell. Then again, I had contacts in the bad place. Maybe they could give her the special treatment.

"That may be true, Gwen. But at least you won't have it. I don't know what that bitch of an ancestor of yours did, but generations of wealth, the kind that legacies are created from, was stolen from us." She clenched the steering wheel. "It's been my life's mission to steal it back."

"Not trying to be a smart ass, but how do you know it wasn't poor financial management, or just plain old bad luck?"

"Good question. But I'm a historian with ninja-level research skills. The contacts I made through the coven and the congregation here in Hoodoo filled in the blanks. Your ancestor wanted revenge. She was so petty, she couldn't see the bigger picture, make a sacrifice for the greater good. So, she made a deal with the devil—for one of her future daughters."

Right now, I didn't give a shit what my ancestor promised. Because without her strength, resilience, and ingenuity—I wouldn't be here.

Wait...wait...wait.

When she said devil, did she like mean capital d devil, like Lucifer himself, or a run-of-the-mill demon.

Like Ash.

"I'll give you the abbreviated version. From the time your ancestor Cosette encountered your demon sire, my family lost everything within a week.."

Time to shift away from the family stuff so Miss Batshit doesn't reconsider and kill me now. "So, Miss Eleanor...the other witches... I don't get it."

"I know you may find this hard to believe, but not everything revolves around the talented Gwen Carter."

Okay...not only was the heifer murderous, but jealous.

"What does it have to do with? Once you have the money, then what? Move on to another coven and destroy that one too?"

Merri sighed and shook her head. "Oh, you sweet summer child. I'm not going anywhere. It's time for a management change in Hoodoo. The money is mine, but other interested parties want the house when I'm done. Phase two is ridding the town of the pack."

"Good luck with *that*."

"Thank your former lover for that one. He's made it clear how much he despises you. Any who...once the vampire congregation discovers your body riddled with bite marks on pack land, they'll eliminate each other."

"And you'll sweep in and pick up the pieces?"

Merri shrugged "It's a dirty job and all that."

I really hated this woman.

Merri slowed, then stopped in the middle of the road before shutting off the SUV. The soft clickety-clack of the engine and my increasingly frantic breathing interrupted the quiet.

We'd reached the end of the line. In front of us was the Crossroads, the place where folks came to petition for favors. On the other side of the intersection after a small rise was the railroad tracks. But that wasn't what put the fear of God in me. Not even close.

The problem was that on the other side of the intersection was the beginning of the township Oakridge—and my death.

"Don't get your hopes up for someone riding to your rescue. We've placed barriers—both magical and non—on all the roads." Merri opened the driver's side door as she looked at me. "I truly believe, had our circumstances been different, you and I would have been friends."

"I've seen how you treat your friends, remember?" *Thanks, but no thanks.*

"That's true. But if it makes any difference, I do miss them." Merri shrugged, then hopped out of the van.

I tugged on my wrist, hoping I'd acquired superhuman strength the last few miles. Nope. Once I survived the night, the first thing on the agenda was resuming an exercise regimen.

Merri tugged my door open and looked at me as if I was a bear attempting to gnaw my foot off to escape her trap.

Trust me, if that were an option, I'd be a chewing bitch.

"Don't bother. It's reinforced. You know, I do I appreciate that you haven't begged for your life, like your former friend Rita. It's tiresome and pathetic."

Something about Merri's nonchalant tone as she discussed ending a life broke something. That rage, that incendiary anger, bubbled like a fine champagne. This fury was icy. Rather than sliding down my left arm as it had in the past, this calming burn had a different agenda. It slithered upward from the center my chest, forking like a river at the base of my neck, only to slide down each side of my spine.

"You're welcome." I licked my lips, then shifted my hips so my legs hung over the side of this seat. "Since we're playing a believe-it-or-not-game, I also have a confession."

Merri tilted her head, and even frowning, she was cute. Reason two hundred forty-two why this wench needed to die.

In groups of twos and threes, women—I assumed they were witches—appeared from the darkness, and spread out into the crossroad. All except one. She headed toward us.

I was out of time as well as chances.

Merri opened her mouth, but I was done. With a quickness that would have made my kickboxing instructor proud, I extended my leg, planting my boot square in the middle of her face.

Even if I knew I was about to pay for it, watching the blood decorate the front of Merri's white lace dress was a thing of freaking beauty. Welp, nothing in life is free, and this was one price I was willing to pay.

Chapter 43

THIS TIME STARING DOWN the barrel of Merri's gun, I was a hell of a lot happier. When I shifted my gaze from the weapon to her dark brown eyes, I watched the promise of my death dancing in their depths. With a will that impressed even me, I silently dared Merri to do it, to lose her cool and end it here and now.

Fuck it; hopefully, some of her DNA would be splattered across the passenger seat or door. If by chance Carlos found the SUV, it would make it easier to solve the crime. Not that he'd care. And not that he'd have the time if Merri and her band of evil witches had their way. The pack would be fighting for their land as well as their lives.

A witch, one I'd seen around town a few times, placed her fingers on Merri's arm, gently pushing it down. "No, not like this. We're too close to the finish line to fail."

"No, Isabella. Whether it's here or fifty feet away, doesn't matter."

Isabella sighed, almost as if this was an old argument. What was with these witches? It was like the eviler they were, the prettier. With her bright red hair, Isabella looked more like she should be playing the bagpipes or some shit.

"Fine," Merri snapped.

Isabella nodded at her partner in crime, then damned near glided the few steps, placing herself between Merri and me. I was so busy admiring her glossy hair, I missed the flash of sharp stainless steel until the knife was planted in my side.

I wheezed in pain and tried to jerk away, but that bitch wasn't having it.

"I crave your pain." To emphasize the point, she twisted the knife.

I refused to cry out, to give Isabella the satisfaction. So I bit down on the inside of my cheek until my mouth filled with the thick, salty tang of blood.

Rather than uncuffing me, Isabella, who'd moved into the number one spot on my kill list, unlocked the handcuffs.

As I lowered my arms, I wasn't sure which hurt worse: my shoulders, my gnawed-on cheek, or my side. Hopefully, this wound would heal quicker than the last because I needed a freaking miracle.

Isabella pressed the flat of her sticky blade against my face, sliding it upward toward my eye. "You'll lose this next time."

Terrified of nodding and doing Isabella's dirty work for her, I whispered, "Okay."

"Good, I'm glad we could reach an understanding."

The witch pulled me from the SUV, making sure to dig her talons in my fleshy bicep. You know, as twisted as Merri's reasons were for wanting me dead, at least I understood them—sorta. Isabella just enjoyed inflicting pain.

The other witches had placed themselves in twos and threes at each point of The Crossroads, unintelligible chanting filling the night air and pressing against my skin like a thick fog. Trees rustled in the distance.

I looked over, praying that someone was running to the rescue.

Yeah, right. There was nothing but leaves and my overactive imagination.

Isabella pressed the edge of the knife against my throat as she guided me toward the crossroads, and the invisible boundary between life and death.

I was out of time.

The witches' chanting grew louder, more insistent as they swayed from side to side, as if listening to music only they heard, singing to an evil melody.

"Ograt Bat Mahalat. Ograt Bat Mahalat," they sang out in discordant harmony that made me want to run and hide from the bad thing was lurking beyond the veil.

I wasn't sure how to explain it, but something changed.

The air got so still, I imagined the molecules hovering, afraid to collide. The clear and cloudless skies felt as though the stars watched and waited for the impending doom. Before the universe and I could wonder too much longer, power, unlike anything I'd ever felt, hummed through the earth.

Like an arc of electricity, the force whipped through each point of the intersection—north, south, east, and west. The witches first jerked, then broke out in dance as if they were doing a ring shout or had caught the spirit during Sunday church service.

When the power reached out for me, it enveloped my feet and consumed me limb by limb until I threw my head back and moaned. If this was the power that had seduced these witches, I understood.

Even if... the price was someone else's life.

The energy was seduction incarnate. A promise of power and passion.

Like hot asphalt on a sultry summer day, the air above the center of the crossroads wavered, then a woman appeared. No smoke, no lightning, no nothing. One moment, the space was empty, and the next, it was filled by a beautiful...no, that was the wrong word. The woman standing before me appeared as a handsome woman of indeterminant age, and equally indeterminant ethnic background. Seeing that she appeared out of thin air, and rocked a dainty but wicked pair of red wings, she had probably never been human. But my frail almost human mind needed a label. The being, with her light brown skin, tight curly hair, and regal narrow face and distinctly Black features reminded me of the people of Ethiopia.

Merri, who was off to my right made a noise as if she'd been punched before bowing from the waist, keeping her eyes on the asphalt as she spoke. "We welcome and thank you, Queen Ograt Bat Mahalat, and bring to you an offering."

"Rise." Her voice was deep, musical, and infused with power. "Why did you summon me tonight, witch?"

Hm, she reminded me of someone else. Unfortunately, my brain cells were preoccupied with trying find a way to escape Isabella and the knife pressed against my neck.

"I tire of you, witch." Her face sharpened as she looked around the clearing, skipping right past me. "Where is my sacrifice?"

"I can help you with that." Isabella twisted my right arm behind my back and pressed the steel against my neck hard enough that warm blood trailed down my neck, puddling on the indentation above my collarbone. "My strong and terrible Queen, we pray you accept our offering."

Their queen frowned as if I was a walking sack of rotted meat. I was torn between relieved and offended. Not that I planned to ask the terrible queen what her problem was.

Merri licked her lips. "The sheep's grandsire is your—"

No, that bitch didn't call me a sheep. I swear on all that's holy and unholy that she was gonna learn tonight. That heifer wrote a check her ass won't be able to cash.

A pair of halogen headlights pierced the circle of dense fog, circling but not entering the intersection.

I squinted, deflating at the lack of police bars. Where was the damn cavalry when you needed them?

The driver's side door opened, exposing a massive and familiar male. What a spectacle we must have been, between the witches, me being held at knife point, and the chick with wings. Finally, he walked out of the shadows, stepping in front of the SUV.

I gasped. Never would I have ever believed that Deputy Dickhead would elicit anything from me but disdain. After whispering a small prayer of gratitude, I smiled. From this moment forward, the good deputy would forever be known as...

He walked not toward the threat, but to the passenger side of his vehicle.

Why wasn't he pulling out his oversized gun and yelling *freeze*?

Thanks to the retina-searing headlights, I could barely make out the slender shape, short hair, and pale flowered housedress, the kind popular in the 1970s. The kind that...

My heart thudded to a thick stop as my eyes darted back around the four points of the intersection before landing on Merri's satisfied face.

Chapter 44

WHY? WHY WOULD THEY pull Loretta into my nightmare? Not only was she the kindest and funniest person in Hoodoo, Loretta was one of the most beloved elders. She had nothing to do with the inheritance, Azure House, or even the curse. I had to do something, anything to remove my rock, my heart, my favorite person on the planet from danger.

Deputy Dickhead shoved Loretta, and all I could do was stare in horror as her frail body pitched forward.

"Noooo!" I struggled against Isabella's hold, not giving a shit about the knife. I'd sacrifice my entire head to protect Loretta. A booted foot hit the back of my right knee, sending me sprawling to the ground. The only thing that kept me from kissing the asphalt were the now raw heels of my hands. "Let her go." The plea shredded the last of my dignity.

Well, unless I pulled a miracle out of my ass, both Loretta and I would die tonight.

"The male is acceptable," Queen Ograt sighed and waved her hand in my direction, "as payment for taking this pathetic creature off..."

I looked up into her stunning face to find her staring at my right arm—or rather—the bracelet I'd received from Ash.

"Stand, girl." When I didn't move fast enough, she flicked two fingers, and I was jerked to my feet like a marionette controlled by invisible strings. "How dare you steal from me." It would have been easier had the Queen of Scary yelled. But no... That calm, melodious voice held the promise of pain that would last an eternity.

This night was a complete shit show. I'd been kidnapped, handcuffed, stabbed twice, and watched my beloved cousin abused. A woman can take only so damn much.

I raised my chin and my voice. "Look, lady, I'm tired and about to lose my shit. This was a gift." Judging from the gasps around me, I'd made a faux pas. Well, too bad. I was out of fucks for the evening.

"From whom?" Ograt or whatever the hell her name was, glided closer and grabbed my wrist. "I asked you a question, human."

Damn it. Was Ash a thief as well as a liar? I really had questionable tastes. Since I was already in front of the bus, no need to drag him with me. I smiled and answered Queen Terrible's question. "Merri." I smirked and exhaled. *How you like those apples, bitch.* "She gave it to me."

"You *liar.* Her fuck toy, Ash Modeus, Prince of some desert hovel, gave it to her." Merri lowered her voice. "I could bring him to you, should you wish."

Queen Ograt curled the fingers of her right hand, raising it slowly as her black eyes studied me as if I'd just become interesting. "I need nothing from you, witch."

A desperate choking sound interrupted my stare down with the Queen of Mean. I gaped at the flailing Merri scratching at her neck to remove the invisible claws keeping her airborne. Couldn't have happened to a better person, if you asked me.

"I agree, human." The Queen opened her hand, releasing Merri, then returned her full attention me.

Yikes. Please tell me she didn't pick that out of my head.

"I could," her sultry voice whispered though my mind, *"but that would be an ugly way to begin a friendship."*

I struggled to keep my mind and expression blank, but I sure as shit hoped to never again see this woman.

If I thought her voice was seductive, her soft rolling laughter inside my head was X-rated. *"Thank you. But enough about me. How is it you know my Asmodai?"* When I didn't answer, she added, *"The one you call Ash."*

Her Asmodai. *Her* Ash? I clenched my teeth.

Look, I knew I shouldn't get heated about a male I'd barely kissed, but as much as he'd proclaimed me his, Ash Modeus, or whatever the heck his name was, belonged to me. Everything around us, the witches, the deputy, and even the fog ceased to matter as I stared into the Queen's deep brown eyes, about to share that detail.

But a twinge of something, almost like a gentle breeze, riffled through my mind like a dealer shuffling a deck of cards. Oddly enough, when the motion stopped, she extracted a memory—Ash and I speeding through the Sahara laughing, Ash and I having the Mediterranean picnic on my bedroom floor. And Ash and I sitting in the dark limousine as he snapped the cuff around my wrist.

Those were all fine and dandy.

But standing in the crossroads with the terrible queen, a memory that I'd prefer to remain hidden appeared. The night my mother died. Eight-year-old me in the dark car speeding up Highway 45 at the FM 2920 exit. The love in her eyes when she told me stories about our family, then fear and—

"No!" I shouted, or at least I thought I did, as I imagined forcing the queen out then imagining a smooth steel barrier surrounding my mind.

That night. That pain was private.

I sniffed, then swiped the back of my hand beneath my nose, inwardly grimacing at the smear of red. Why? Why did everything in this freaking town involve in blood?

"Because that is the way of life, especially for us women. It is not a punishment, but a gift," Queen Ograt said, her voice almost kind. "You possess incredible power. Own it. Use it." Before I could respond, she raised a finger that looked more like a talon and touched it to the center of my chest, below my breasts.

Pain so intense it stole my soul along with my breath bent me in half. What in the Sam Houston did she do to me? She may as well have used her hands like the jaws of life prying my chest cavity open. I patted my torso, from my collar bone to my soft stomach, expecting a gaping hole large enough that my intestines peeked out like a pink tongue against my brown skin.

But there was... nothing. No blood, no trauma, just...me, but different. It was like with that single touch, she'd torn me asunder and remade me. If that was the case, it would have been cool had she skipped the agony portion of the program.

That talon was once again beneath my chin, standing me up. Once I was stable on my feet, the Queen of Mean's eyes flickered, as if she wanted to tell me something, before deciding otherwise.

The silence around us fell, and I was once again bombarded by the chanting of witches and the rumble of Deputy Johnson's SUV.

Queen Terrible turned to Merri. "Whatever it is you plan to do, make it quick. I need to go see my child." To me, she said, "Embrace your magic or die—it's up to you."

Loretta, still on her knees, extended a hand toward me. "Run, save yourself. I've had a good life." Her glance flickered down to my cuffed and gloved hands before returning her pissed-off gaze to mine. "You are more than that hand. You are your great-grandmother's child."

I really wished everyone would skip the cryptic—

Holy shit. Or should I say unholy shit? I, Gwendolyn Carter, had demon blood pulsing through my veins.

Queen Ograt watched me with bored interest, as if waiting for me to either hurry up and die, or prove my bad-assness. Or was she in a hurry to get to her Asmodeus or whatever the hell she'd called him. Well, sorry, sister—he's off the market.

"Enough of this bullshit." Deputy Dickhead pressed the barrel of a ridiculously big gun against Loretta's temple. "You took the life of the woman I loved. Figured I'd return the favor."

He jerked Loretta to her feet by her frail arm. "How about a front row seat to her death right before I send you to hell."

Merri yelled, "Johnson, stick to the plan. That's not what we—"

"Fuck your plan. I don't give a shit about you or the coven." Deputy Johnson's dark face was twisted with not only rage, but an indescribable pain.

I shook my head. "No. I didn't kill that woman."

"Olivia!" he screamed, spittle flying out of his mouth. "Say it. Say her fucking name, you lying bitch."

Now that was unnecessary. Well, at least he didn't call me the "c" word. I blew out a breath and lowered my shoulders, ignoring the swaying branches of the oleander bushes on the side of the road. "Olivia didn't deserve to die. But I'm not—"

A loud explosion split the night, followed by Johnson's bald head whipping first back then forward, exposing a perfect hole between his eyes before he crumpled to the ground.

Even without silver bullets, he wouldn't survive losing the back of his skull.

Everyone stared at Merri, but that didn't stop her from pointing her gun at Loretta. "I've had enough." She glared at me. "Walk your ass across the border. Save your cousin's life."

I shook my head. "No." Like give me a freaking break. No way in hell would she allow Loretta to leave the crossroads alive.

"Fine." Merri returned her gaze to Loretta and pulled the trigger.

Chapter 45

YOU KNOW HOW PEOPLE say time stood still? It didn't exactly do that, but it sure as hell slowed down. The bullet spiraled through the air like a perfectly tossed football, spinning as it homed in on its target.

Then I saw something else.

In my mind's eye, I pictured a sword, a flaming purple tool of vengeance as well as a set of glossy black of wings fringed with white. I imagined them bursting from my back, raising me off the ground, then placing my newer, stronger body between Loretta and danger. I felt so free, so whole, so... me.

This was the me I was always supposed to be: unafraid, uncaring, and ab-so-fucking-lutely fierce. No longer hidden was, a creature who didn't give a damn if she torched the world. Later, I could think about it, but right now, this shit was incredible.

Something slammed into my chest, pushing me back until I widened my feet, stabilizing myself. Three soft pings drew my attention to the glittering asphalt and the flattened shiny bullets between my now bare feet. I opened my mouth and it wasn't curses that fell out, but a mighty roar.

If I thought my anger overwhelming before, that was nothing. This...this delicious, glorious wrath begged to be freed. This was menopausal mood swings on steroids. Who the hell was I do deny it?

I grinned and stalked to Merri. She needed to die.

One quick glance over my shoulder and a nod to the grinning Loretta, then I stretched my arm out to the side, rotating my wrist and the sword, watching streaks of purple form a glowing infinity symbol in the air.

Yelling drew my attention back to the crossroads, and one by one, the dead witches that I'd met in Hoodoo appeared, accompanied by a dozen or so additional spirits—men, women, and more than a few children. As one, they turned to the intersection, then headed straight for Merri.

I lumbered forward, ignoring that I was now taller than my original five foot seven. And I definitely didn't want to think about the freaking talons wrapped around my cool-ass sword hilt.

Merri shook her head and retreated. Not from the ghosts, but me. Good. I smiled. Well, it probably was more of a baring of fangs, but hey, I had to work with what I had. And right now, I wasn't tripping about this whole demon getup.

As a matter of fact, I embraced it, relished in it. And was fucking grateful for every bit of my evil DNA. For without it, not only I, but Loretta would be dead.

Merri tossed her gun aside and dropped to her knees. Only she wasn't begging; her shining brown eyes were filled with...awe?

I don't think so, bitch.

Her mouth was moving, but I couldn't hear over the song of revenge singing through my new body. When I reached Merri, I gripped her hair, pulling her to her feet, then a little more.

Movement to my right caught my attention.

I swiveled, aiming my sword at the intruder. They could die right along with Merri. They would all die, and I would bathe in their blood, relish in their pain and all that jazz.

Only, it wasn't a witch, or even the bitchy queen. No, it was Carlos.

He kept yelling something, something I couldn't understand.

Didn't matter, especially if he was dirty as Deputy Dickhead. I glanced at the gun in his hand and the handcuffs at his waist, then opened my mouth and let her rip. The sound that came from my mouth would have done a banshee proud.

Kill. Kill. Kill. The refrain reverberated not only through my mind, but my body. It was as if my heart took in rage and pumped out the need for violence.

Carlos' lips continued to move. He pointed first at Merri, then my sword, and spoke again.

Fuck that and fuck him.

I pointed that sword at his chest.

Instead of aiming that puny gun at me, he placed it on the ground, motioning for the other deputies to stop and do the same.

The pressure in my head eased and Carlos' words broke through.

"Don't do it, Gwendolyn. We know the truth. I know everything. Let me handle it."

I scooted back, dragging the witch with me.

"She's mine," I said. Or at least I thought I said it. It kinda sucked talking around the extra teeth. And after running my tongue across the edges, calling them teeth might have been an understatement.

"Not yet. We need information. We need to know who else she's working with."

"Sh-she killed Eleanor and Rita," I wailed, probably sounding like a demon kindergartener.

"No, Gwennie." Carlos stepped closer, his empty hands raised, palms toward me. "Rita's alive. There's a reason you've only seen Eleanor." He stepped between me and the still dangling and whimpering like a bitch Merri, and reached up to touch my cheek. "She's not worth it."

Carlos might have been many things—unyielding, unforgiving, un-freaking-believably hot, and a jerk—but he wasn't a liar. At least he didn't used to be. I didn't want to let her go. Merri needed to pay for her sins, and I was the judge, jury, and winged executioner.

But my mind, it wasn't rational, wasn't functioning right now.

I looked around the crossroads, the handcuffed witches cowering as they stared at me with a mixture of horror and fear on their traitorous faces. Good, they should be afraid, they should die.

But I didn't have to be the one who did the deed. I didn't want to be a monster. Fine, I wasn't human, I could deal with that, accept it even. A spear of shame sliced through me for the years of silent judgment of the supernaturals I loved.

Or at least I thought I had. But how could I love anyone if I didn't love myself first—magic and all.

I opened my hand, dropping Merri to the ground.

"Thank you, Gwen," Carlos whispered as he motioned for someone to gather the trash. He reached up and fiddled with the death sentence of a collar circling my neck. It opened, and he whispered, "You did the right thing."

"Merri, you're under arrest." A deputy, one I didn't know, gave me plenty of room as he pulled the sobbing woman from the ground.

I rolled my eyes then looked down at Carlos.

Hol' up. I was taller than damned near everyone at the Crossroads. I could get down with that. What I didn't want to deal with was the stares from the shifters looking at me like I was an aberration.

Once upon a time, I would have hung my head in shame. But not tonight, motherfucker.

Carlos crossed his arms and chuckled.

"What?" I snapped.

"The wings, they're kind of bad-ass." He reached up, trailing a finger along the inside of said wings.

I sucked in a little breath. And whoa, talk about an erogenous zone. It was like there was a direct path from my new appendages to my lady bits. I couldn't do this, not here, and not with Carlos.

Been there, done that, got the broken heart to prove it.

The crossroads were quiet, like the inhabitants held their breath, waiting for me to... what? Breathe fire? Rip Carlos' arms off? Or even better, take the witches wicked souls to hell? Of the three options, only one was possible, and that was if Carlos was too drugged to run.

Even then, I doubted I could ever hurt the man who once upon a time filled my teenaged brain—and heart.

"Aren't you afraid of this..." I motioned to my body with my taloned hands. "...new me?" I didn't bother whispering since every non-human in the vicinity would hear anyway.

"Nah." Carlos shook his head. "Unless you're hormonal. Now *that's* frightening." He chuckled as he squeezed my shoulder.

As cool as this new body felt, and looked, all I wanted right now was to be me, Gwen, the middle-aged, soft-bodied, quasi-badass ghost-seeing, tattoo artist.

Whispers whipped around me, and I frowned when it hit me that, now, I was looking up at Carlos.

Who was looking right back—and not at my eyes. And it didn't take special abilities to know he appreciated this body a lot more than the other.

He removed his shirt and handed it to me. "Not that I mind, but you...uh... may want to put this on."

Apparently, after a night of trauma, I wasn't the sharpest tool in the shed. I frowned and looked down at my naked breasts.

Yup, still sagging.

"Shit." I snatched his still warm tan uniform shirt. "Where are my clothes?"

"Destroyed most likely," Carlos said, not bothering to hide the chuckle in his voice.

"My boots." I looked around frantically. They'd been with me through so much, I couldn't bear their loss.

"I wish I could say they went the way of your jeans." Carlos frowned as if something stank. "But I think I saw them over there." He jerked a thumb over his shoulder. "I apologize for..." He exhaled through those kissable lips.

Damn. If he was going to be an asshole, it would be easier if he were an ugly one. But he had work to do. Perhaps eventually Carlos and I could, if not be friends, at least frenemies. The kind who didn't try to kill each other.

One of the deputies manhandled the handcuffed, gagged, and struggling Merri, leading her to one of the squad cars.

I took a step, but Carlos gripped my bicep with his strong fingers. "Don't. Merri will get what's coming to her, I promise."

Queen Ograt whatever the hell the rest of her name was, who I'd forgotten about in all the ruckus, stepped forward. "It won't be coming from you, Sheriff. Those witches' debt just came due."

Chapter 46

THE WITCHES HAD A PRICE to pay, but I didn't want to see it. To tell the truth, I was done with blood and death for the night. Right now, all I wanted was a glass of bourbon and to be surrounded by people. Which was why I was sitting in front of The Ancestors waiting for Ash and Kyle.

Okay, those two weren't exactly people, but when I stopped by the house to get cleaned up, I had a good long talk with myself in the shower. So what Ash wasn't human—neither was I. Humanity, or lack thereof, didn't stop me from loving Carlos back in the day, or half of my family.

Speaking of Carlos, I had a shit ton of unanswered questions, like how he managed to be Johnny-on-the-spot and ride in to the rescue tonight. The other thing was personal: why did he believe I slept with Duncan?

But at this point, did it even matter? We still hadn't discovered the Adze, so the danger still existed. Then there was Aunt Rose...

Blech. Shifting did something to my perimenopausal brain. I was getting soft.

Kyle's rental car pulled into the parking lot, and my jaw eased. My bestie was a freaking god, like...wow. The grin that spread across my face got even bigger when a grumpy-looking Ash left the car—on the passenger side.

Poor baby hated not being in charge.

I tooted my horn, then waved as I turned off Stella's ignition. I loved my sweet little van, but it might be time to buy a truck. Best to be prepared when gully washers came through.

Ash's gaze snapped in my direction before he walked toward me like a fashion model with the lights illuminating him from behind. The man was hot, I had to give him that.

Similar to what happened earlier when the Queen was digging around in my mind, memories appeared like a film reel playing backwards. The most recent years went by in a blur: traveling, meeting people famous and infamous. Going around the country working tattoo shows. My art gallery opening in New York.

Then everything zipped by. The next thing I knew, I was in my teenage years, living on a ranch filled with witches and vampires. Rebellion. Learning to tattoo. Then it went further back, to the most painful night of my life.

What was happening? I didn't want to see this. But like quicksand, the memories trapped me, holding me hostage, was I going insane?

My chest tightened, and it was like breathing through a straw as I recalled my mother and me in her car—and she was terrified, but trying to hide it behind stories of a town called Hoodoo.

"Where are we going?" I'd asked.

"Home."

Okay, that sounded great, except we didn't have a home. My mother was the center of my world, and I hers. But we'd started doing more running than moving, and I needed to know why.

"What are you afraid of, Mommy?"

"It doesn't matter, because we're going to be safe. You remember that number I gave you?" she asked, and only when I recited it back, did she nod. "Good girl. You're finally going to meet your family."

That made me smile. I'd never told my mom, but it sucked watching other kids with two parents, two people to depend on. The only person I had on my team was my mom. And I knew telling her that would make her sad. But since she'd brought it up, I asked. "My father?"

Her face got scary.

I shrank back against the door.

When she looked at me, her face changed again. It wasn't happy exactly, but not pissed off either. "No, and you're never to ask about him again."

"Yes, ma'am."

The car was quiet for a bit, until I reached and touched her cold arm. "I promise. And I'll never try to find him." Mommy insisted that I was always enough—on my own. Everything I needed to survive and succeed lived inside of me.

I guess I needed to start believing her.

"I love you more than life itself. You know that, right? Promise that if anything happens to me, you'll call that number." She gripped the steering wheel so tight, her dark knuckles glowed in the moonlight. "There's so much I should have told you about the world, our family, and oh God... Everything. But I'm going to fix that."

"We have time," I whispered into the darkness. Even to me, the words came out like a prayer.

"I hope so, baby, I sure hope so."

Then my world slowed down and imploded. I watched the shards of my life splatter across the black asphalt. I had just glanced up at the green and white highway sign; we were on Highway 45 just outside of Houston and had passed the exit for FM 2920 when it happened.

It was the middle[1] of the night, and very few cars were on the road, so when my mother screamed and slammed on the brakes, I thought that maybe an 18-wheeler had swerved into our lane. But no, it was a man—with massive black wings.

Why would an angel want to kill us? As much as we went to church, we should be protected. Watching the blood roll down Mommy's face, I knew right then the only thing I could believe in was myself.

Then, in my mind's eye, I looked at the beautiful angel of death again, and suffered my most painful wound of the night.

That angel was no angel at all—but Ash.

THE END

Read a short story about Tammy, the adorable cashier, at https://reggi.club/tammy

Reviews help not only authors, but readers, if you prefer to write, Goodreads, Amazon, or Bookbub would be awesome. If that's not your jam, please share on the social media platform of your choosing.

---

1. https://www.example.com

Ramblings of a messy mind

WHEW, OCCASIONALLY, I doubted this day would ever arrive. But here we are!

This is where I'm supposed to say it was difficult and tumultuous. Well, it was—but not in the way you think.

Why the hell don't we have *real*, sit down, lay all that shit on the table talks about menopause? Because baby... Let's just say it had me in its grips. Forget hot flashes. The brain fog, the mood swings, the inability to concentrate took its toll. What's that joke about men being the cause of most female problems: menstruation and menopause? Well, it's true.

I'm so grateful to the group of authors who made paranormal women's fiction a thing. For too long, especially in the United States, women become invisible after thirty-five. Hell, we're just getting to the good part. We won't even mention the disrespect at forty-five; It's at a whole different level.

So, imagine the joy it brought to create characters who are comfortable in their own skin without being hypercritical about either their ages or bodies. Yes, Gwen mentions her baby Buddha belly, but what woman doesn't? (Personally, I have a pony keg, but we won't talk about that.)

I appreciate you for coming along on this journey, and I hope you hang on for the ride. There's so much more to come. While I didn't promote Return to Hoodoo as a romance, Gwen will find her way to love—eventually.

To keep up to date on new releases and stuff join my newsletter at https://reggi.club/bbb. If you're not about that newsletter life, text BOURBON, to 855-976-9071. Don't worry, I'm too lazy to flood your phone or email with messages.

Be good. And if you can't do that, don't get caught.